Nocturne of Fog

Book One of the Ember King's Inheritance

Martlet di Rotstein

Contents

For the golden dream that has ever lived in my heart, for lighting my path.
For my family, for everything.

Maps

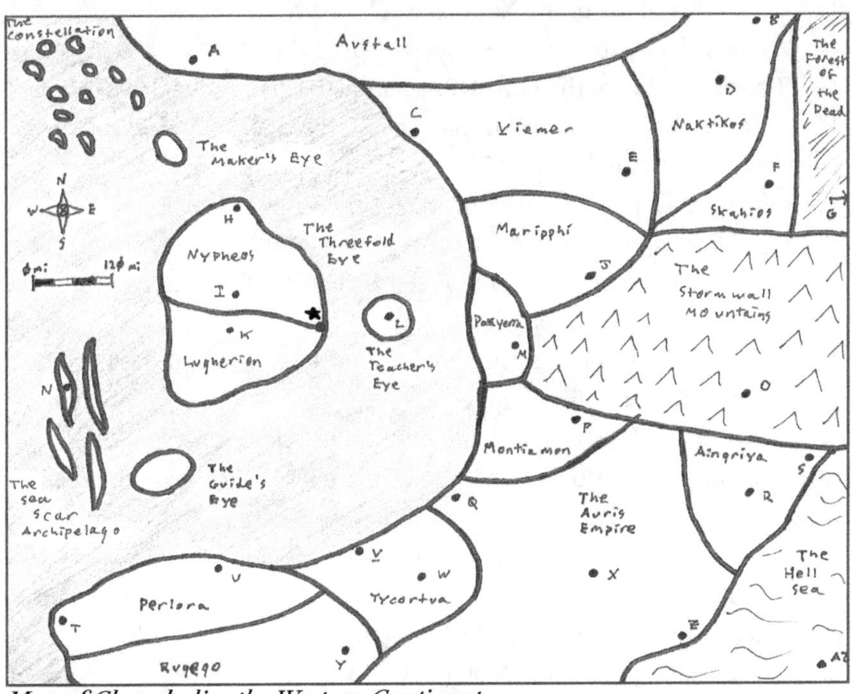

Map of Chevaladin, the Western Continent

Witch of the Lake: *Wow. These maps are garbage.*

The Winter Swallow: *Oi! I'm a mysterious hero, not a cartographer.*

WotL: *... Letting that slide, couldn't you have just had one of your knights do it for you?*

Mage of the Blossoming Wind: *I think you mean—*

WotL: *NO.*

MotBW: *The Rounds of Winter.*

WotL: *I refuse to acknowledge that name.*

Key

A – Leafpond, Capital of the Kritocracy of Austall.

B – Afallach, A historic Naktikan village.

C – Port Squallbreak, The principal port of the Noocracy of Viemer.

D – Dragongate, Capital of the Stratocracy of Naktikos.

E – Windhall, Capital of the Noocracy of Viemer.

F – Wintersedge, Capital of the Noocracy of Skahios.

G – Tírádis, Capital of the Forest-folk nation, insofar as they have a capital.

H – Seras' Aria, The principal port of the Meritocracy of Nypheos.

I – Moonsight, Capital of the Meritocracy of Nypheos.

J – Rainhome, Capital of the Magocracy of Maripphi.

K – Sunsight, Capital of the Monarchy of Lugherion.

L – High Worldheart, Holy See of the Scholastic Faith, the Path of the Teacher.

M – World's Eye, Capital of the Monarchy of Pazyerra, built on the site of the capital of the old Sunfire Empire.

N – Cove Castle, The principal safe port of the Sea Scar Archipelago.

O – Solitude, Capital of the Mountain-folk nation, insofar as they have a capital.

P – Rangeshadow, Capital of the Monarchy of Montiamon.

Q – Port Daystar, The principal port of the Auris Empire. Previously known as Port Dunshore when under the jurisdiction of the Monarchy of Caretony.

R – Greenleaf, Capital of the Monarchy of Aingriya.

S – Sandspires, The principal trade center of the Monarchy of Aingriya. Connects both the Desert-folk to the east and the Mountain-folk to the north with the continent at large.

T – World's End, The principal trade center of the Aristocracy of Perlora.

U – Springstone, Capital of the Aristocracy of Perlora.

V – Port Dicefall, The principal port of the Monarchy of Tycortua.

W – Riverluck, Capital of the Monarchy of Tycortua.

X – Dawnbreak, Capital of the Auris Empire.

Y – Summerfire, Capital of the Aristocracy of Rugego.

Z – Duskguard, A trading post and fortress by which the Desert-folk travel to the Auris Empire and vice versa.

A2 – Heartfire Bastion, Capital of the Desert-folk nation, insofar as they have a capital.

Star – City of the Scales, A fortress city on the border of Nypheos and Lugherion. Home to the Order of the Eagle, it acts as a neutral zone between the two ancient enemy nations and headquarters of the world's defense against calamity.

- ***WotL:*** *What's with the star marking the City of the Scales? Did you forget what you were doing in the middle of making the map?*

- ***TWS:*** *... No. And I didn't lose the geographic feature map either. I promise.*

Note: Chevaladin is not a name used for the continent by those living on it, who have no knowledge of other lands. It's only really a title personally given to the land for convenience's sake. Similarly, not really a continent based on size.

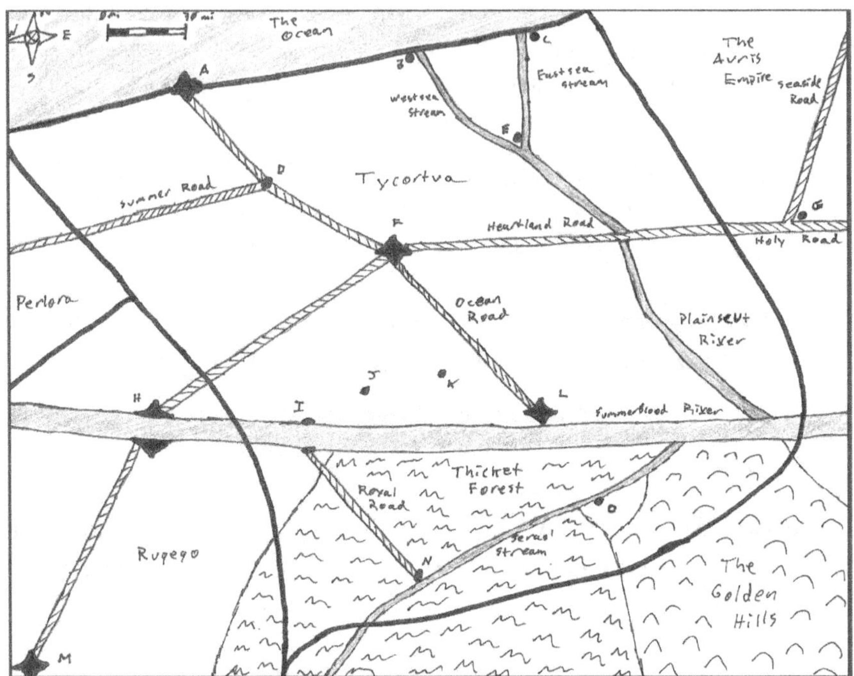

Map of the Monarchy of Tycortua and Nearby Localities

WotL: *So those squiggles are trees and the upside down U's are hills? Amazing. If it weren't for your awful handwriting, this map might almost be legible.*

TWS: *Hey now. It gets the point across.*

MotBW: *If it bothers you so much, why don't you just draw the maps for him next time?*

WotL: *Because unlike you two layabouts I actually have better things to do.*

TWS: *Oh really? And what, pray tell, are you doing right now? Because if I remember correctly—*

WotL: *We agreed the affairs of Morningstar are important.*

MotBW: *Ah yes. I remember overhearing that discussion. I seem to recall it was you, alone, in a room reading a tome about the lost Blessing. Certainly no bias on that subject, hmm?*

WotL: *Quiet you.*

Key

A – Port Dicefall, The principal port of the Monarchy of Tycortua. It's position near the Summer Road and on a highway to Plainsheart puts it at the center of all trade activity in Tycortua.

B – Seras' Watch, A small fishing village. Not especially important save for the lighthouse after which it takes its name. The lighthouse of Seras' Watch was supposedly built by the River Sage for the twin purposes of watching for the Crystal Queen's return from the lost lands to the west and offering up her prayers in the hopes that the Ember King's seal upon the Dusk Tyrant might remain.

C – Sunlit Bay, A small fishing village. Has some ties with the Auris Empire as their preferred port of trade, outside of their own Port Daystar. Virtually all Auran river traffic north from Riverbreak ends up in Sunlit Bay.

D – Wayside Inn, A small town which grew around the inn after which it is named. It's importance largely derives from its at the terminus of the Summer Road and proximity to Port Dicefall. In short, it stands on the path of two of the four major points of entry into Tycortua.

E – Riverbreak, A town that stands at the fork of the Plainscut River. Nearly all river trade that does not pass into Perlora or Rugego passes through River-break, making it a notable trading post.

F – Plainsheart, The economic capital of Tycortua. It stands in the center of the Tycortuan plains, nearly equidistant from Riverluck, the ocean, and all neighboring countries. All overland travel through Tycortua passes through Plainsheart.

G – Crossroads, A small Auran town that stands at, well, the crossroads where the Heartland Road splits into the Holy Road which leads deeper into the Emprie and the Seaside Road which leads up to Montiamon and, eventually, Pazyerra. Important because it's a fortress through which the Empire can restrict western travel north.

H – Fortune's Bridge, A city built on either side of the Summerblood, with a large bridge connecting the two halves. The northern half of Fortune's Bridge and the surrounding areas originally belonged to Perlora, but Rugego conquered the land in the hopes of having their own means of entry into Tycortua and a way east that didn't lead through Auran owned sections of Thicket Forest and the Golden Hills.

I – Woodcutter's Crossing, A small town built on either side of the Sum-merblood, a ferry service connecting the two. Though it serves mostly as a way for the lumbering towns in southern Tycortua to send timber north, it's also notable as Tycortua's most prominent crossing of the great river and route by which the royal family usually travels to their summer palace.

J – Zephyr's Blessing, A small town on the Tycortuan plains. Not especially noteworthy save for the fact that certain travelers visited it on their journey.

K – Chancewind, An ancient town built around a monastery said to have been founded by the River Sage, Seras, herself.

L – Riverluck, Capital of the Monarchy of Tycortua.

M – Summerfire, Capital of the Aristocracy of Rugego.

N – Forest's Favor, A city built deep within Thicket Forest. It grew around the Tycortuan royal family's summer palace. The palace itself was originally meant as Zephyros' hunting lodge, explaining its location within otherwise dangerous lands. In modern times the defenses around Forest's Favor are strong enough that the forest creatures cannot threaten it, supplemented by the fact that it serves as a posting for members of the Tycortuan Regulars to experience active combat against those same monsters.

O – Regina's Bounty, A small village in the notably rural southern Tycortua. Mostly grows wheat and other staple foods for subsistence. The wines and brandies they ship up Seras' Stream to the Summerblood have a minor following among other farming towns, but are not especially famous. Only worth note as the home of Allard Fortunata and Erica Greenmaiden, as well as the local legend that it serves as the site of Seras's grave.

Dramatis Personae

Allard Fortunata: A young man from the small village of Regina's Bounty. Currently working in the palace at Riverluck as squire to the Crownguard.

Erica Greenmaiden: A young woman from the small village of Regina's Bounty. Currently working in the palace at Riverluck as a mage in training and assistant to the heir.

Princess Adelaide Angelica Tycortua: The crown princess of the Monarchy of Tycortua. Erica and Allard were hired to be her retainers.

Levi Olivier Crownguard: The current generation's Crownguard, personal bodyguard to the royal family of Tycortua. Possesses one of the seven suits of Ancient's Armor and the Storm Warlord's blade, Whisperwind.

King Thierry Naimon Tycortua: The king of the Monarchy of Tycortua and Adelaide's father.

Estelle Faucheux: The castellan of the palace of Riverluck. Supervises Allard and Erica.

Viola Bradamante Faucheux: A maid in the palace of Riverluck, training under Estelle. Erica's friend.

Jareth Lapointe: A captain of the palace guard in Riverluck. Acquainted with Allard.

Elroy Rousseau: A member of the Tycortua Regulars. Lina's partner.

Lina Fortier: A member of the Tycortua Regulars. Elroy's partner.

Viscount Kasmy Merlo of the Twelve: A member of the Perloran envoy.

Duke Gerald Vela: A member of the Perloran envoy. Viscount Kasmy's patron.

Viscount Myron Rendón of the Twelve: A member of the Perloran envoy.

Thanasis Rendón: A young mage in training from Perlora. Viscount Myron's son.

Chancellor Lukas Erling: One of the chancellors of the Auris Empire. Head of the Auran envoy.

General Neriah eDubris: One of the generals of the Auris Empire. Possesses one of the seven suits of Ancient's Armor and wields a storied magical blade, Dawnsong.

Praetor Edan eAbila: Head of the guards sent to accompany the Auran envoy and Neriah's subordinate.

Lady Ornella Sativus: A member of the Rugegan envoy.

Lady Severina Tagetes: A member of the Rugegan envoy.

Captain Celio Hirundo: Captain of the Rugegan guard.

Xavier Stormtide: A strange traveler who claims to be from another world.

"Knife": A vampire sent to attack Riverluck.

Prologue

Loamday: 30th of Viviaus, Year 1980 R.S.

Knife walked down the empty night streets of Riverluck accompanied by a billowing fog. Or at least they were empty after they passed. The drunks wandering home shrunk back in fear, many retreating back into the pools of light shed by the open doors of the roaring taverns. The thieves and footpads lurking in the alleyways had enough sense to seek out easier prey. Knife didn't care. So long as such fools didn't get in the way, they were no problem. The Master had told them which manor to go to. Nothing else was important. Knife drew to a stop at the edge of a park, surveying the buildings that rose out of the hill ahead. Their eyes flit back and forth to take a quick count (*forty-seven*), stopping at the palace on the hill's top before circling back to one manor about three quarters of the way up. Destination set, Knife looked back down at the park ahead. Cobbled paths wound their way beneath lilac bushes, flowers just blooming with the coming of a new spring. Carved stone benches stood every so often along the banks of a murmuring stream. Approaching the stream, they shook their head with annoyance.

Thirty minutes and three more parks with streams later, Knife stood beneath the streetlamp before the manor's walls, if they could even be called that. Anyone could climb them and the wrought iron gate had gaps wide enough for a child to slip through. A cursory review showed the manor to be a fine thing, as the homes of Tycortuan nobility tended to be. While the homes and shops of lower Riverluck were constructed of limestone, or whitewashed wood in the poorer areas, the manor was built all from marble. Carvings of flowering vines and birds in flight climbed up its walls, topped with rooftop gardens and terraces. They certainly looked pretty, but Knife could only think of them as easy handholds. The soft yellow glow of sunstone lamps shone through nearly half of the silver framed windows. At regular intervals, bobbing lights showed the passage of guards. Counting the windows ahead (*thirty*), Knife settled on one two floors up to the left. With a glance backwards, they checked the progress of the fog. For a moment, it stood stopped in a line, swirling in patterns that almost formed familiar shapes. Then it inched forward and swirled about Knife's legs, like a cat rubbing up against its master. Once it coiled up around Knife's arm, they thrust a hand forward and the fog surged towards the manor, the streetlamps' sunstones going out with the cracking sound of a magic overload as it passed. After a count of three, Knife dashed towards the gate.

Taking two quick steps, Knife pushed hard off the ground, leaping over the ten foot tall gate with five feet to spare. Just before landing, they tucked into a roll, letting the momentum of their jump bring them back to standing, and came up running. The grounds of the manor went by in a flash (*four seconds*) and Knife scrambled up the side of the tower to the right of the entry way. With a fluid grace, they were quickly (*two seconds)* perched just below the tower's open rooftop. Looking through the fog to the chosen window, Knife could just see the light of a lantern held in place before it. With a curt nod, they pushed off the tower wall and shot towards the window like an arrow from a bow.

The glass shattered upon impact, tearing through Knife's cloak. They didn't feel a thing, save for the pressure of a body against their boot. Knife fell with the guard, landing with their knees upon his chest, looking down into his widening eyes. They wasted no time, bending down and sinking their fangs into his neck. With a simple twisting motion, the guard stopped struggling. The walls of the manor were painted in the lurid red of fresh blood. Standing up, Knife looked down the hall, towards where the master bedroom was supposed to be. A second guard stood with a horrified expression plastered across his face, frozen with fear. The clatter of his lantern upon the marble floor snapped him out of his reverie and he opened his mouth to scream. Knife's hand darted toward their belt, where one of many daggers lay sheathed. As they gripped the dagger's hilt, they spied something out of the corner of their eye. The shattered fragments of the window panes lay on the floor, spread out like a sunburst. Knife tried to keep their hand moving, but already knew what was happening. Frustration welled up within them as they froze and counted the glass shards (*sixty-two*). A second later their hand flew forward and the dagger spun through the air, planting itself into the second guard's back. But it was too late and though the guard's scream cut off with a startled squawk, even that sound echoed through the sleeping manor. Knife let out an irritated sigh as they ran forward, retrieving their dagger from the guard's back as he fell. They reached down to grab another dagger and brought it up to slit the guard's throat as they passed. Already the sounds of alarmed movement rang throughout the manor.

Knife quickly shut the door behind themselves and slouched against it. They reached down and pulled the crossbow bolt from their shoulder. They sighed and shook their head. They had been clumsy this time. The hole from the bolt was nothing compared to the slashes crisscrossing their tunic. Knife waited for a minute, relaxing after they heard the sound of boots stamping against stone. With their pursuers past, they had enough time to complete their mission. They surveyed the room they had ducked into, looking for a good hiding place. The room looked to be a cleaning closet, ill-used judging by the dust covering the shelves. Knife reached into their pouch and pulled out the delicate device within. The synthesized lattice-stone glowed faintly as a dark purple mist swirled slightly around it. The energy radiating from it felt almost comforting against Knife's skin as they held it. A wistful smile broke their face as they placed the device behind a bucket, careful not to disturb any of the dust. Knife's face slipped back into stoicism as they turned back towards the door. With the mission complete, the only thing left to do was cover their tracks. They slipped a dagger into either hand and felt their teeth extending. There was still a lord to kill after all. Though Knife lived for the missions, times like this almost made them happy.

Chapter 1

Seaday: 1st of Hernus, Year 1980 R.S.

T he morning sun had just begun to peek over the horizon as the chatter and bustle of life began to spread through the city of Riverluck. The capital of Tycortua woke piecemeal, starting at the docks on the shores of the Summerblood where workers set about making preparations for boats to arrive from up river and sailors finished up their own work before setting off towards Rugego. Moving up past the limestone houses and shops of the low city, people started to wander the tree-lined streets in small clusters of ones and twos. This early, the parks scattered about the low city stood empty, the sound of birds singing in their bushes and trees a companion to the burbling of streams. Further up Riverluck's hill, the clamor lessened and that noise which remained grew somewhat muted as it entered the noble neighborhoods of the high city. The parks here were filled with carefully pruned shrubs and meticulously tended flower beds, man-made springs replacing the streams of the low city. The streets, unlike those further down the hill, stood empty. The manors of glass and marble lining these streets stood silent sentry over the peaceful heart of Tycortua's capital.

The noise of daily life swept all the way up to the palace topping Riverluck's hill, the clatter of cookware in the royal kitchens a mere prelude to the work of the day with the cooks rising before the other servants to start on breakfast. Looking at the city of Riverluck in full, the palace was like a jewel set in the crest of a crown, constructed of marble and glass like the manor houses around and below it but on a much greater scale. Entire walls of glass lined the rooms and hallways within, illuminating the interior while the exterior sparkled in the morning sun, making the building look almost like an enormous diamond. As the city began to wake up, its noise trickled in through one of the few sets of wooden shutters in the palace's walls, waking the young man sleeping within. Stretching as he rose, Allard shook his head, bemused. *Over three years here and I still wake up at dawn.*

Looking towards the wooden shutters covering the single window in his room, light sneaking through the small gaps between the slats, he sat in bed for a moment remembering the home he had left behind. Regina's Bounty was, quite frankly, just about the least interesting village in Tycortua. Isolated on the southern side of the Summerblood, it stood right between Thicket Forest and the Golden Hills, so it was more trouble than it was worth for most travelers and its only claim to fame lay in local legends with little evidence supporting them. Allard was glad to be in Riverluck, where things were more exciting and he stood a chance to see the world, but even still, just like some of his habits, affection lingered for his home. Shaking his head, he stood up and started about preparing for the day. He grabbed a softly humming device – a disc of clay set with traceries of bronze wiring around a central lattice-stone – from the nightstand next to his bed and considered the glowing red firestone within. *With spring here, I suppose I shouldn't need a heater anymore,* he thought as he flicked the switch at the top, turning off the device.

Allard walked the length of his small room to the wardrobe on the wall opposite his bed. Opening it revealed several shelves of odds and ends stacked above a layer of neatly folded clothes. He set down the heater and rummaged about for a bit before pulling out a device nearly identical to the heater save the light blue icestone set in place of the firestone. Setting this down in the heater's place upon the nightstand, Allard nodded with satisfaction and started towards the door.

Allard wandered the halls of the palace aimlessly after exiting his room. The morning sun streaming in through the windows shone against the polished marble of the walls and floor, almost making it glow and rendering the sunstone lamps hanging at regular intervals superfluous. Navy blue carpets ran down the center of the halls, muffling Allard's footsteps. He couldn't help but shake his head in wonder as he walked along the carpet. A yard's length of these finely made things could probably buy an entire house back in Regina's Bounty, and here they covered the floors. To say nothing of the deep green tapestries adorning the walls, embroidered with scenes from myth and history. Allard smiled as he passed one depicting Chephirah Camdyn's duel with the evil king Sanborn of Montiamon. Though the Forest-folk seemed to think of that incident as an embarrassment and exiled her afterwards, Allard couldn't help but feel inspired by the warden's heroism.

He shifted his feet into a simple duelist's stance: knees bent, feet set perpendicular to each other, and one arm forward as though gripping a sword. Closing his eyes, he imagined himself standing in that great hall, blade pointed at Sanborn, lounging on his throne, and demanding he release Ivalyn. Allard put his imaginary sword through a brief engagement, mirroring the strikes and parries he'd been learning as a squire. Laughing at his own childishness, he shook his head and continued on his way, glad Levi hadn't seen that embarrassment to his training.

With no responsibilities to speak of for at least two more hours, three if a certain someone refused to get up, Allard headed towards the kitchen. He knew the guards from the night watch had just been relieved and would be grabbing a quick meal before heading off for a nap. Even if he was barely more than acquainted with any of them, there were worse things to do with his free time than taking his breakfast with them. And Jareth still owed him five silver moons for betting Allard couldn't shoot an apple off a barrel at forty paces. But he hadn't even made it halfway there before he was interrupted, a figure in the dress of a palace maid dashing out from a side hallway and skidding to a halt before him. Giving a small sigh, Allard pulled to a stop and considered the woman before him. Standing nearly a head shorter than Allard, she looked up at him with blue eyes wide with excitement. Jet black hair cascaded down her back, forming an almost eerie contrast with her pale skin, but Allard knew her well enough to know it was mostly an affectation. For a moment the two of them simply looked at each other, neither willing to make the first move, but eventually Allard decided to simply get it over with. Taking a step to the side, he raised his hand in greeting, a strained smile plastered across his face. "Good morning, Viola. I would love to stay and chat, but I am afraid I am quite busy this morning."

Before he even finished speaking he tried to take a step forward, but immediately found his way blocked once more, Viola shifting along with him. Apparently aware of just how stilted Allard's greeting was, Viola's face twisted with annoyance as she replied, "Would you stop that, Al! It's not like I'm some sort of changeling, ready to transform and eat you the moment you stop to talk with me for more than five seconds."

Still hopeful he could make his escape before things got too bad, Allard looked out the window, refusing to meet her eyes, and carefully considered what he was going to say next. "What are you talking about? I just need to get going, since I am so busy—"

Viola cut him off, expression hurt."Want to try and think of a better excuse than that? Unless Addy decided to start her morning at a record time, you have nothing going on and we both know it."

Standing with arms crossed, Viola glared daggers at Allard, silently willing him to say something different. Allard looked down the hallway past her, hoping someone might come to his rescue, but it was just as empty as it had been before. Accepting whatever fate lay before him, Allard looked back down at Viola, unable to restrain a hint of resignation from entering his voice. "I guess you're right, I can spare some time to catch up."

Mouth widening into a grin, Viola's face lit up with genuine pleasure, though Allard knew better than to be fooled. Turning, she started down the hall in the same direction Allard had been going, chatting back at him as she went and simply assuming he'd follow. "Did you hear about the ambassadors that are supposed to be coming today? Rugego and Perlora aside, there's supposed to be some coming from the Auris Empire. From the Empire! I've always wondered what the nobility is like over there, with all that zealous indignation filling their policy."

She said it with all the excitement her smile implied, but it only made Allard roll his eyes. "Oh, you mean the ambassadors coming for the meeting between the Western Alliance and the Empire? The meeting that everyone in the palace has been setting up for the past month? Somehow it slipped by me."

This earned him a light jab in the shoulder from Viola. "No need to be so rude, Al. It's just a way to start the conversation. I was *going* to use that to tell you about the festival the king's holding for them. A week-long celebration to welcome travelers from other countries and what not. But I guess you know everything so I can just leave it at that."

Viola turned towards Allard with a curious expression on her face, but he was too distracted to notice. Hearing about a festival reminded him of the parties they'd had back home. Since joining the palace staff, he'd been forced to attend all the formal events for each holiday as a member of Adelaide's retinue. Those were interesting, but nothing like the simple fun of a commoner's celebration. Heart soaring at the mere thought of it, he cracked a small smile. "I hadn't heard about that. It sounds like it'll be something to see, and maybe something I'll actually be able to see if it goes on all week. I'll have to make sure to free some time to check it out one morning."

A devious glint entered Viola's eyes, giving Allard a sense of looming dread. "Oh I know, I know. It can be so hard to find free time here, can't it?" Viola giggled. "It makes me glad that I can talk to someone else who knows how hard it is to get some spare time."

Allard combed a hand through his hair and made sure his next step took him a little bit away from Viola. "Y-yeah. That's true. Not everyone around here can really understand—"

"Which is why I need you to deliver this to Estelle right now. Thanks Allard! I won't forget how helpful you've been."

Viola shoved something into his hands and darted back the way they'd come even as she spoke. Before Allard could protest, she was gone. Looking down at the object in his hands, Allard found it to be a package about the size of a large book, wrapped in simple brown paper. Feeling defeated, he shook his head, replying to the empty hall, "Yeah. I'm sure you will remember. You'll remember who you can shove your chores off onto next time."

The door standing at the end of the hallway always looked imposing to Allard and today was no exception. Even though the door was the same as most of the others in the palace, knowing it was Estelle's office made it seem to stretch all the way to the ceiling, covering the rest of the hallway in shadows. Allard looked down at the package in his hands and sighed. A small part of him complained that this wasn't his problem, that he could just leave it be and let Viola get scolded for her own negligence, but he knew he couldn't do that. Even if he hated reporting in to the castellan and each step closer to the door made his legs feel a pound heavier, it was his responsibility, by choice or not. He stopped before the door and raised a hand to knock, but froze on hearing the sound of voices within.

"...And he was found dead in his bedroom."

Though he couldn't recognize the speaker, the muffled voice was unmistakably male and therefore unmistakably not Estelle's. Not entirely sure what to do, Allard stood completely still, stunned into inaction with his knuckles still hanging just above the door's surface. After a moment, he heard Estelle respond, her voice strained in a way Allard had never heard before. "His entire guard? And was his body like the others? Torn apart?"

Recoiling like he'd been struck, Allard took a step back and gripped the package tightly with both hands, simply to give them something to do so they'd stop trembling. The first voice continued. "No. Beyond one puzzling discrepancy and the bite marks, the body was untouched. What's more troubling in this case is the lack of blood."

Well aware that he was listening in on a conversation he really shouldn't be hearing, Allard took a deep breath and knocked on the door before Estelle could inquire further. There was a brief moment of silence before Estelle responded, her tone as crisp and clear as usual. "You may enter."

Allard opened the door and stepped inside. The office within was immaculately kept and gave the distinct impression of order and precision. The sunstone lamp set in the ceiling reinforced this sentiment, filling the room with a steady white light that while bright enough to read by, had none of the warmth of genuine sunlight to encourage comfort. The entire wall opposite the door was dominated by a massive bookshelf, filled with personnel files and monthly reports on the palace's expenses from the past ten years, sorted and labeled by date. A small writing desk rested against the wall to the bookshelf's left, an autoquill resting upon it next to a neat stack of blank paper and a paired letterboard. The rest of the room was kept clean and clear save for another desk that stood in its exact center, down to the inch. Made of a dark wood that gave it an air of indomitable solidity, it stood covered in a clutter uncharacteristic when compared to the rest of the room, a sign that it was the main workstation of the room. The high-backed chair behind it was occupied by a woman in a plain canvas robe belying the authority she sat with, as though she were the queen of her own office and all others could stand in line, while the chair closer to Allard stood recently vacated. The man standing next to it, just as unfamiliar to Allard as his voice, was dressed in the uniform of the city guard and had a face lined by a lack of sleep. Seeing he'd been all but dismissed, he bowed to Estelle. "I will take my leave then. A full report will be sent up to the castle by noon today."

With that, he turned and left the room. In the silence that followed, Estelle glared at Allard with a stony expression he had come to dread. Even with her steely gray hair, she had none of the other signs of age and Allard knew she was easily strong enough to beat him senseless if given a reason, to say nothing of the more probable tongue-lashing he'd get if he made a misstep. After a few seconds, enough to set him on edge and make their roles clear, she spoke, waving towards the unoccupied chair. "Why don't you take a seat Mister Fortunata?" He swallowed once and did as instructed. For a moment, the two simply stared at each other until Estelle broke the silence with a sigh. "Did you have a reason for coming here? Or has interrupting my business become your new hobby?"

Wincing, Allard set his eyes to look at anything except her, blurting out a quick apology as he thrust forward the package. "I'm sorry, ma'am! I have a delivery for you. Viola told me to give this package to you."

Estelle raised an eyebrow as Allard held the package over her desk, delicately removing from his hands and inspecting it. She halted her movements upon seeing the crown and mountain seal of Montiamon upon it, turning her gaze back to Allard with eyes narrowed. "And if my niece had this package in her possession and knew to deliver it to me, why, pray tell, are you here instead of her?"

Allard sighed heavily. Fundamentally, he knew there was no good way out of this situation. Lying to Estelle was simply not an option. But throwing Viola under the cart would only serve to bite him in the back later. Lightly massaging his forehead, he resigned himself to his fate. "Begging your pardon, but you know what Viola's like. She pushed this off on me without giving me a chance to refuse so she could go down to the city and slack off."

Rolling her eyes, Estelle set the package onto her desk with a loud thud. Though the sudden noise sounded for all the world like a judge's gavel falling to Allard, her reply was more frustrated than angry, and little of it directed at him. "Honestly! What am I going to do with that girl? I suppose if she can afford to be so carefree, that means I haven't given her enough to do. And you need to stop being such a pushover. If that is all, you may go, Mister Fortunata." Allard rose and turned towards the door, but Estelle shot one last remark his way before he could escape. "Oh, one other thing. Since you are going to tell Miss Greenmaiden anyways, please inform Mister Crownguard of what you overheard come breakfast."

Allard winced once more, ashamed that she had all but read his mind, and exited the office. With much of the morning gone after his detour through the palace depths, he steeled himself for the day's work and set off.

Stopping before the finely carved doorway, Allard regarded it with a kind of dry humor. His first few month's here, he'd stopped to examine each of the spiraling knot shapes along its length every morning. But now, after seeing it almost every day for three years, he hardly even noticed. Shaking his head, he started to reach for the brass handle, but paused on hearing the sounds of an argument from within. The voices were muffled and unintelligible, but the scene beyond the door still played out in Allard's head as he stood there, a common enough occurrence in his daily life. With a small laugh, he lightly knocked on the door and stepped back to wait. The commotion within didn't stop, merely changing its direction towards Allard as a young woman's voice shouted at him through the heavy teak door. "Oh, what is it now?! It's only ten and Levi's already being a nuisance, so unless you're here—"

Her tirade was cut off by a rather tired sounding voice, the speaker's tone insistent and close to begging. "*Please* come in."

Allard laughed again as he opened the door, permission little more than a formality in this case. The room beyond was hardly changed from the last time he had been there. That had only been a day ago, but all the same, it hardly ever changed, giving it an almost timeless feel. The dark wood of the walls and floor somehow managed to give off an almost homey feel despite their expense, like he'd stepped into a log cabin in the mountains instead of a royal study. Together with the cluster of plush chairs by the fireplace and their errant companion behind the cluttered desk, it seemed to Allard as though he'd just stepped into the reading room of an ancient library or the salon of an eccentric mage's workshop. Only one of those chairs was currently occupied however, as the other two occupants of the room stood facing each other over a small tea table, complete with three empty cups and a fourth filled with what must have been cold tea at this point. The person further from the doorway, a man in his mid-twenties, had an altogether beleaguered look. The patient look on his face and impeccably ironed coat gave the impression of a temperate person, but in this instance his patience seemed to have worn through and the only thing left to keep his irritation in check was a strong will. Allard had little need to guess, but the likely source of this irritation was the young woman currently yelling at him. With her extravagant silk dress and sparkling silver necklace set with several sapphires, even the most casual of observers would be able to tell that she was of a high bred family. Thirty seconds in the same room with her would cement that claim.

Somehow still unaware of Allard's presence, the young woman glared at her companion, growling at him through clenched teeth. "And I've told you a thousand times not to cut me—"

The man raised a hand in greeting once Allard entered, hastily putting on a sly smile as he ignored her and addressed him. "Good morning to you, Sir Allard. Odd of you to be so late. Did something untoward keep you?"

The young woman whirled towards the door with a murderous glare in her eyes. On seeing Allard, her face softened, but in a way that somehow preserved the glare. Storming towards him, she flung her hands to the side in exasperation. "And where exactly have you been, Al? We've been waiting for you for half an hour! The tea is gone, but I have already had three cups anyways so I cannot stomach any more. And I am hungry besides! You know we cannot go to breakfast without you."

Amused that she claimed to simultaneously be hungry and full, Allard's face twisted into a wry smile as he responded, "You know that isn't true, right? You don't need me to do anything."

This was met with an immediate rejection, the young woman slashing her arm through the air fast enough to rattle the tea set next to her, as if she could cut the very idea in two. "That is neither here nor there. You know my intention and if you truly wish to claim that my station allows me to act with no consideration for you, then you are subject to a standing order to attend to me at breakfast, so there. And stop trying to avoid the question. Do not bother trying to say you overslept since you never do. It is downright inhuman, you farm people and your unnatural ability to wake up at the crack of dawn."

Taking an involuntary step back, Allard raised his hands defensively. "I wasn't trying to avoid the question, Adelaide, it's just not that important. Viola bullied me into delivering some package to Estelle. I swear, she just wanted to slack off and shove her work onto me." The beginnings of a growl started to form in Adelaide's throat so Allard smiled in what he hoped was a placating manner, deciding to shift the blame. "But like I said, it isn't important. What were you guys discussing?"

The man gaped at him with a look that seemed to say *why would you bring that up again?* The hostility drained from Adelaide's face, replaced by annoyance as she spoke until her tone shifted into a kind of false bravado as if she'd convinced herself out her irritation. "I was simply explaining to Levi how due to the coming of spring, I, as an honorable and just member of Tycortua's royal family, ought to go out into the kingdom to survey the lands and ensure the prosperity of our people for the coming—"

The final occupant of the room, a woman just older than Allard who'd been content to lounge in her chair and observe up till this point, rolled her eyes and laughed as she chimed in. "Addy's bored, Al. She wants to go on a vacation."

Adelaide turned towards her, this time with less hostility and more the air of someone pouting. "That isn't true, Erica. I'm only thinking of the good of the people here."

Hearing such a bold-faced lie, Levi sighed and rested the palm of his hand against his forehead. "Even if I were to ignore the safety issues inherent in letting Tycortua's heir prance about the countryside with only a single knight and two half-trained servants for protection, and I know you would not let us take anyone else, so do not try to pull the wool over my eyes, that is not the issue here. You are only trying to avoid your responsibilities. The meeting between the Western Alliance and the Auris Empire is not some inconsequential thing that can be merely discarded with a passing fancy all because you cannot be bothered to study current affairs."

Walking back towards the tea table, Adelaide let out an irritated breath, idly picking up the last full cup and swirling its contents in time with a shake of her head. "You say that, but anyone who knows anything about the Empire already knows how it will turn out. The war between the Auris Empire and Montiamon shows no signs of dying down, so the Empire will ask us for support to break their deadlock. We will continue to take a neutral stance since my father has no interest in getting involved in a war he has no stake in. Furthermore, giving an inch to the Empire would be just as good as letting them take the entire country as one of their 'Protectorate States'. It starts with one embassy and then after a generation of concessions, we have nothing more than a seat in their senate.

As for the rest of the Alliance, they will follow our lead since we stand between them and conquest. I rather would say it is 'some inconsequential thing.'"

Levi frowned, unwilling to disagree with anything she'd said, but held his ground, raising one finger and replying in a stern tone, the very image of a lecturing teacher. "Be that as it may, the political machinations or lack thereof are not the issue in this case. Your presence is required as a matter of honor and good will, to show that His Majesty takes the talks seriously and that you are invested in maintaining the Western Alliance once you take the throne. And to that point, there are still the discussions amongst the members of the Western Alliance to consider. Envoys from Perlora arrived last night and the delegation from Rugego should be here any day now, so you must be prepared to greet them as equals."

Taking a sip of the tea, Adelaide frowned in dissatisfaction, presumably in equal parts at Levi's words and discovering the tea to be cold. Making a disgusted noise, she set the tea cup down and ran behind Allard, putting her hands on his shoulders as if she could use him as a shield. "Al help! Levi's trying to waste my talents." She paused for a moment after her complaint, spinning back around to face Allard from the front with a sly smiling on her face as she continued. "But it's good that you're here now. You go hunting with some of the other servants every once and a while, right? I'm sure you could think of somewhere good for us to go? Right?"

Looking down at Adelaide's smiling face, Allard couldn't ignore the unalloyed trust in her eyes. But when he glanced over at Levi, he could plainly see that while the man maintained his calm demeanor, his gaze was cold enough to freeze ice. Trying to keep them both happy, Allard looked back down at her with a forced laugh. "Y-yeah. I'm sure I could think of something. But can we discuss that another time? Breakfast is still waiting after all."

Crossing her arms, Adelaide frowned, clearly unconvinced by such a non-committal answer. "Fine. But don't think I'm going to forget this. I'm taking it as a promise. And you still haven't explained to me why you were hanging around with some maid instead of your dear friends who were waiting patiently for you to *keep your word* and show up to breakfast like you'd *promised*."

On that heavily unsubtle note, she turned and walked out of the study, expecting the rest of them to follow. Allard winced, seeing that his attempts to play the negotiator had failed miserably. Levi set out to follow before Adelaide could get too far, patting Allard's shoulder as he passed. "I would say that you have my sympathy, but all things considered, I am honestly glad she is annoyed at you now. Consider it a lesson in covering for your comrades under heavy fire, Sir Allard."

With the two of them gone, Allard stood and waited as Erica got up from her chair. In contrast to the well-tailored clothing worn by Adelaide and Levi, she wore a simple dress made of a sturdy tan cloth. Almost a perfect match to Allard's clothing. In that same way, she looked close enough to Allard to be his sister, with the same sandy brown hair and hazel eyes, but he'd also noticed her sardonic smile and curious eyes had grown more to resemble Levi's and Adelaide's, respectively, the longer they'd been in Riverluck. The former cropped up again, as she came to Allard's side. "So what was in the package Vi had you deliver, Al? Anything important?"

Shrugging, Allard walked back to the tea table, placing empty cups on the tray. It wasn't really his job, but he always felt bad leaving things for someone else to clean up when it took so little effort for him to do the same. "Figures you'd be the one to ask the important questions. But I couldn't tell much about it without opening it. Just a simple package. Standard rectangular shape, wrapped in brown paper. The only interesting thing I saw was the seal. It looks like Adelaide's father received a message from the king of Montiamon."

Erica raised her eyebrows. Proximity to the meeting with their enemy aside, any sort of diplomatic overtures from Montiamon was strange, their reputation somewhat dubious since the reign of King Sanborn. "Really? What do you think it means?"

Allard shot a glare back at her, tea tray in hand. "You think I know? Levi doesn't teach me about current events, just hitting people with a sword. It's definitely worth keeping an eye on, but Montiamon aside, something else caught my attention this morning."

Seeing he was done cleaning up, Erica started towards the door assuming Allard would follow, a mischievous smile slipping onto her face as she went. "Oh? You mean besides the glittering charm of our dear Viola?"

Allard rolled his eyes as he followed. "Oh shut up. You're as bad as Paula and Viola's as bad as Mal. I'm serious, this is actually important. When I was delivering that package to Estelle's office, I overheard her talking to someone else. It was a messenger from one of the noble houses. Apparently the lord of the house was murdered. Along with his entire guard."

Erica's face paled, the humor draining from her in an instant, and she missed a step. Catching herself on the door frame, she recomposed herself, eyes narrowing. "Seriously? The entire house guard? But there was no advanced warning, so it must have been a small group. Somebody would have noticed a group of foreign soldiers, right? And since it was one of the lords. Do you think..."

Her words trailed off and she furrowed her brow in thought, her conclusion obvious enough. Allard shrugged, drawing up next to her in the doorway. "Assassination? Hard to say. Especially since I don't know which house. If it's a Summer or Autumn house, I could see it. Trying to hamstring our military or economy would make sense. But Spring or Winter? Either way, it did remind me of something. Do you remember when we met Adelaide? Exactly why she was passing through Regina's Bounty?"

The question was more or less rhetorical, Allard knowing full well she did remember, but Erica answered nonetheless. "Because the war between Montiamon and Auris had just started, right? And Addy's dad was worried that one of them might attack Riverluck in order to drag us into it so he had Levi sneak her to the summer palace in Forest's Favor using back roads."

Allard nodded as he responded, waving her on. "Yeah. And what started the war?"

Thinking for a moment, Erica's brow furrowed again, this time in confusion. "What started it? I don't know. I thought the Empire was just trying to claim more land, using one of their overblown excuses about how 'Montiamon was corrupted by the great darkness of evil and must be cleansed in the light of the Endless Flame'?"

Unamused by her impression, Allard gave her a level look, tired of dancing around the subject. "Yeah. And for evidence, they claimed that several of their high ranking generals had been assassinated by a demon sent from the North. 'A demon that could tear through entire companies of soldiers and left its targets completely drained of blood.' Guess what the report I overheard said about the lord's body."

Just as familiar with the old campfire monster stories as Allard, Erica's eyes widened as far as they would go. Stories about things like goblins and other fae lurking in the woods were common enough that it was common knowledge to know how to avoid them. What Allard was implying, on the other hand, was the kind of thing you heard about in heroic tales. Letting out a wooden laugh,

Erica stared at him askance. "Oh come on, a vampire loose in Riverluck? If we were up north near the Forest of the Dead, maybe, but those things don't just spring up around populated cities. And why would a vampire be assassinating people? What would it have to gain from it?"

The two stopped before a pair of doors carved with images of trees, branches heavy with fruit. The smell of cooking meat and fresh bread drifted out from within. "Uh huh. Can't necromancers control undead creatures? Certainly gives more potential motives. And it's not like there haven't been stories of vampire lords trying to conquer a region. But in any case, as inane as her intention is, Adelaide's idea of sneaking out of the city for a few days might not be such a bad idea if there are more attacks. If we get her out without most people knowing, then she'd be safe until things die down."

Erica shook her head, at a loss. "Look, I don't study necromancy. It's not especially relevant to my field of magic. So I don't know just how hard it is to control an intelligent undead. As for the other, I don't have any complaints, but you can pitch that to Levi. Now unless there's anything else, we should head in for breakfast." She paused for a moment, mischievous smile returning. "I'd hate for you to get yelled at more than you need to."

Without waiting for Allard to respond, she opened the doors and disappeared within. Allard stood there for a moment longer, taking the time to look down the hallway in either direction. An empty gesture, but talking about monsters had turned his mind thoughts to paranoia, the skin on the back of his neck crawling as though someone were staring at him. *I don't even want to think about what it'd look like if that thing came here.* As if trying to shake off his sudden gloom, he shook his head and entered the dining room.

Chapter 2

Seaday: 1st of Hernus, Year 1980 R.S.

Breakfast passed uneventfully to Erica's eyes, despite the morning's excitement. Or if not excitement, then deviation from the routine. Either way, any disruption quickly faded as they settled back into normalcy – Allard, Adelaide, and Erica chatting casually over their meal while Levi kept to the fringes, only occasionally offering a quip. And so at the end of a mere half hour, they went their separate ways as they often did; Levi and Allard going off to do whatever it was they did as the Crownguard and his squire while Erica and Adelaide studied magic. Or more to the point, Erica studied magic while Adelaide fiddled around with lattice-stones. The distinction between the two fields was an academic one, to an extent, since lattice-stones were themselves crystallized elemental energy and the effects they produced therefore innately magical, but both magi and engineers would agree that the former was more of an art and the latter a science. With this in mind, Erica's duties rarely had anything to do with actually helping Adelaide in her studies, their afternoons often consisting of Adelaide tinkering on her own while Erica supervised and read her books when not needed. Today was little different, proving the return to routine, with Erica going over the theory of physical resonance of the spirit as presented by *Arcana of the White Angel*, an excessively dry tome on healing magic, as Adelaide looked over the same minute device she'd been working on for the past three months.

The device was no larger than the size of a clenched fist and consisted of a single forcestone, softly glowing in the teal-ish blue of its kind, carefully ensconced within four metal claws, basic bronze instead of a more valuable meal or magically induced alloy, these claws tapering for a way past the end of the crystal until they thinned into wires that could be bent. A simple enough design that could be activated by connecting the wires, though the lack of a true activation key like a switch or a button proved it to be a theoretical model with no real use. That and the bars of heavy defianium keeping it pinned to the work table, necessary when working with a propulsion system. On the other side of the table, Adelaide set down the book she'd been consulting with a heavy sigh. "I just don't get it. It makes no sense that forcestones can only be activated at minimum or maximum output, no matter the regulating inscriptions applied. None of the other basic lattice-stones work that way."

A complaint so common from her that Erica hardly even knew what she was expected to say at this point. For the past several months, Adelaide had been studying Teufel's propulsion problem, one of the seven Millennium Problems that had stymied lattice engineers for all of recorded history. As far as Erica knew, it referred to forcestones' inability to cast energy in a steady flow, accelerating objects they were configured to at either the speed of an old donkey or twice the speed of a galecaster bolt with no in-between, a problem that merchants in particular wanted solved in the name of faster transport. Setting aside *Arcana of the White Angel*, Erica crossed the room to inspect the diagrams Adelaide had been consulting – several slightly different patterns written in a subscript of Mystic that was far blockier and, for lack of a better term, efficient than the flowing language Erica was used to. She couldn't actually understand what any of them did, but had enough of an understanding to at least form a comparative example in her own area of expertise. "Maybe it's just impossible on a matter of Inception. These designs are meant to impose the engineer's spell upon the crystal's flow, right? So maybe the crystal's natural Inception contradicts the engineer's too strongly for them to function properly."

Among the three pillars of magic – Inception, Conviction, and Conception – Inception governed the manner in which one's personal understanding shaped how magic worked for them; the source of the wildly different schools of magic born in the many nations of the world. A law that was particularly relevant in this case since it was another distinction between the art of magic and lattice engineering. For magi, the Inception of the caster shaped how they cast. For engineers, the Inception of the engineer, not the user of the device, shaped how it worked. To wit, a Tycortuan citizen could use a Montian device and a Skahian device just the same. Theory Adelaide knew well enough, a frown splitting her face as she considered Erica's hypothesis. "That's absurd. Lattice-stones can't have a natural Inception, or there'd be no need for regulating inscriptions. And inscriptions are closer to Conception than Inception anyways. As long as you know the logic of a school of engineering, you can write in it, no matter what you were first trained in."

The conversation firmly steered into a discussion on her terms, speaking in broad magical theory instead of cold science, Erica nodded and walked back to her chair. Rummaging around through her bag, she pulled out a thin volume, printed more recently than many of her other tomes. Erica made sure to always keep a copy of *Johannes' Fundamentals of Magic* close at hand, the book a good basic resource no matter what she was studying. And most importantly, it served her well when she needed a reference for the fundamental pillars of magic. Spurred by Adelaide's words, she flipped to the chapter on Conception – how one's understanding of a spell shaped its casting. Satisfied that the book confirmed her suspicions, she nodded thoughtfully, spinning back to address Adelaide. "But the way Conception works, any two casters, or in this case engineers, can perform the exact same spell and achieve different results, so long as the results meet the base premise of the spell. With these inscriptions, they can be written one hundred times by one hundred different engineers and reach the same conclusion each time, right?"

Adelaide's frown deepened. Plucking the forcestone from its setting, she placed it on the table. Opening a drawer on her side of the desk, she slowly pulled out similar lattice-stones one by one, lining them up in a neat line. "But if lattice-stones had a unifying Inception, wouldn't that mean they would work differently depending on where they were harvested? I can tell you for a fact that all of these work the same. I've tested them. And they were supplied from caches as far apart as the Constellation Archipelago and the Mountain-folk mines at Solitude."

It was certainly a reasonable argument, and one that if Erica hadn't exactly expected, she was prepared to respond to. Even without knowing much about the intricacies of lattice engineering, she knew enough about the basics to recognize that they would play right into her argument. Making her way around the table, she opened a drawer and pulled out a heavy, leather coat with a deep red firestone sewn into the collar, a smith's heat resistant coat that Adelaide used from time to time. "And what about these? Weapons and armor socketed with lattice-stones in the... 'base configuration' is it? They still experience magical effects without any sort of inscription. Doesn't that indicate there's some kind of rule directing their flows in the absence of human intervention?"

Letting out an indignant scoff, Adelaide snatched the coat away and stuffed it back into its drawer. But Erica could tell most of her attitude was bluster. Even her response was filled with a kind of false scorn, only barely masking the fact that it was a thinly veiled statement of concession. "That's one thing and this is another. Base configuration hardly counts as engineering. The magical effects you were talking about are closer to enchantments cast by a mage, extending the field of elemental alignment generated by the lattice-stone over the object."

Chuckling, Erica bumped Adelaide's shoulder, replying with a lightly chiding tone. "Oh yeah? So it's just an extension of the natural order of their elemental flows?" Eyes sparkling, she held out a hand and whispered a few words of Mystic. After a moment, a small orb of pulsing energy, the same color as the stones, appeared in her hand and she continued. "And if I applied this energy to an object, enchanting it according to my Inception in the Tycortuan school of sorcery as I was the one who cast the spell, wouldn't that be the same kind of extension of the flows of magic? One that would continue to work the same for whoever used the object, even if they were someone with a vastly different Inception like a Nyphean hero-mage?"

Growing increasingly frustrated, Adelaide shook her head with a tremendous force. As the younger girl's face colored, Erica could tell that she'd succeeded in getting under her skin more than anything else. Her point stood, but by now Adelaide was too wound up to offer any real discussion. "I said that's one thing and this is another, so that's that! It's not the same at all. Lattice-stones are *naturally* crystallized elemental energy, formed around a *natural* locus of that element. They're a part of the world and only work in devices because we say they should! Trying to give them an Inception of their own would be like giving trees an Inception to grow fruit or cows an Inception to produce milk."

Erica didn't have much to respond to that, especially since it wasn't much of an argument in the first place, more an annoyed outburst. Even so, she felt it was too good an opportunity to pass up. Closing her hand around the spell to extinguish it, she let a sly smile slide over her face, shooting Adelaide a sidelong glance as she continued. "Oh yeah? But–"

There was little need for her to think of an argument, contrived or otherwise. Adelaide cut her off before she could get more than a few words in. "No! I'm not going to sit here and listen to you explain how cows are magi because they fill some sacred duty in the natural order by producing milk *like they're supposed to simply by living!*" Letting out an irritated breath, she shook her head and walked over to her chair so she could slump down into it with arms crossed. "Honestly. You just don't appreciate the intricacies of engineering. If we could make up for our ignorance with grit and good feelings like magi, then there wouldn't be so much competition over regulating inscription quality and output. It's almost like you're fine with letting Montian engineers and Skahian glyphmasters corner the market."

Such flippant dismissal of the sheer amount of study required to properly learn spells according to one's Conception, especially when the original spell was sourced in another Inception's school, as 'grit and good feelings' irritated Erica. All the more since she'd spent the last month translating an Austallan mirror-mage's exorcism ritual into proper Tycortuan sorcery and Adelaide knew just how hard she'd been working on it. But mention of the Montian engineers reminded her of something else and she decided to let it go for the moment, swearing that she'd remember to bring that quip up next time Adelaide decided to interrupt her studies. Making her way back to her own chair, she tried to keep her tone casual and force down her annoyance as she flipped *Johannes' Fundamentals of Magic* open again, holding the book out to Adelaide as she replied, "Well I don't know about the engineering practices of other nations, only magical theory. Here Archmage Johannes argues that a mage's Inception is the language with which they speak to magic and Conception the individual words spoken. With engineers, since your inscriptions are literal written language, doesn't this apply all the more? And if you're speaking to magic, presumably it has language with which to speak back."

Much to Erica's surprise, rather than respond immediately with her prior indignation, Adelaide took the lecture silently, face softening to a thoughtful frown as she read the indicated passage. The silence started to drag on long enough that Erica started to worry she'd actually managed to offend the princess, but eventually Adelaide stirred, nodding to herself as she rummaged through her own belongings. Pulling out a lattice-stone device she'd made when she was first starting out – a simple detector of magical energy in the form of a bracelet, a clear magestone set in a leather band and surrounded by a thin tracery of bronze wiring – she held it up to Erica, the irritation in her voice replaced with curiosity as she replied, "So if magic has an Inception, its own language that it speaks in, would you say that there's a 'word' for each element? That maybe a device like this could be tuned to track that particular word?"

While the shift in topic was somewhat sudden, Erica felt more panicked than confused since the topic was not one she felt confident in discussing. For as long as she'd been studying magic, elementalism had managed to escape her grasp, spells classified in the holy domains like wards, healings, and cleansings more her specialty. She'd been reading through *Alistair's Elemental Invocations* on and off since coming to the palace in the hopes of picking something up, but a minor hastening spell was the best she'd been able to manage. Hoping to gloss over her ignorance and return to something she could talk about she shrugged. "I don't know. You're the engineer, so you tell me. Don't you just need the right inscription?"

Adelaide shook her head, eyes glimmering with a barely contained enthusiasm as she leaned forward to continue. "No, no, no. I don't mean specifically in terms of lattice engineering, but magic in general. Could you isolate... How do you put it? A single color from the flows?"

While hardly the best metaphor, Erica understood what Adelaide was trying to say. Fundamentally, magic was something that didn't register to the core human senses. For mages who could sense it, the only way to truly describe what magic was like was to phrase it in terms of other senses. For instance, describing elemental flows as 'colors', associations built up by the mage's Inception such as red for fire, blue for water, or gold for light. This also had the added benefit of making their interactions in spells easier to describe, like differently colored threads weaving together to form a patterned tapestry. Erica still wasn't sure how this related to the previous conversation, but was happy it was at least a question she could answer, putting aside her confusion with a shrug. "I guess that depends on the situation. Theoretically, you could probably align a spell or inscription with a particular element and cause it to react in the presence of that element, but it would likely be hard to do in practice. There's a lot of each element in the world, so it'd be difficult to filter out background flows while still having a meaningful reaction."

Adelaide nodded thoughtfully before replying. "Alright, but what if you were looking for a particular locus of energy? An element contained within something that alters the way the magic interacts with the world. Like maybe a person. Could you track someone by their elemental attachments?"

All of the sudden, the pieces fell into place and Erica understood why Adelaide was so interested in this topic. Not even bothering to hide her annoyance, she fixed Adelaide with a level stare, replying in a deliberate, stern monotone she hoped would gently steer the conversation back on course. "Environmental magic would still react more strongly, since it's purer in composition. And that's not how personal elemental affinity works anyways."

Much to Erica's chagrin, Adelaide continued to try and feign ignorance, though her sheepish smile proved just how well she knew she wasn't getting away with anything. Waving off the comment on elemental affinity, something Erica had hoped would grab her attention for how little most people seemed to understand it, she continued, unphased. "I don't mean people like humans, but something like a person tied to an element on a fundamental level. Something like forest sidhe or the Skahian Snow-folk."

Sighing, Erica leaned over and rapped Adelaide lightly on the head. "Leave it, Addy. Those kinds of things are for Levi and the palace guard to take care of. And stop eavesdropping on Al and I. It's rude."

Adelaide slipped out of her chair, putting it between her and Erica as if it could protect her. She frowned at Erica, her reply more of a sulk than anything else. "Well I wouldn't have to eavesdrop if you let me join your conversations. Honestly, it's not like–" Erica glowered at her, showing just how poor of an excuse she found Adelaide's argument and cutting her off before she could pick up steam. Yet Adelaide continued unabated, apparently ignoring Erica's irritation. "And why should I leave it be? It's not like I'm saying I'll go out and fight this vampire myself, just that I'd help find it. It is my responsibility to help protect the people of my country, is it not? In this way I would simply be performing my duty as given by my rank."

Thinking back to the conversation that morning, Erica found herself growing more confused than angry. Still worried, since involving Adelaide in vampire hunting sounded like a recipe for disaster, but that was a distant, abstract possibility when compared to the readily present contradiction. "Responsibility, huh? But don't you have other, less dangerous, responsibilities to take care of? Why are you so fixated on this when you could be helping just as much with the diplomatic meeting with the Empire? And I thought you liked helping your dad with his work."

Just like that, Adelaide's entire mood shifted. Straightening up, she scoffed, shaking her head scornfully. Erica had expected her to try some thin excuse, hiding her own irresponsible desires behind a facade of high-sounding meaningless blather, but instead she spoke plainly, her intentions clear. "Well it is just that, Erica. I want to help in meaningful ways. As I already said, this meeting is pointless, the conclusion foregone. Even if we assume this monster to be an anomaly, struck once and done, it stands as more a threat than the Aurans. They dare not attack with no cause. Not if it will unite the south against them."

Now that they'd started talking about politics over simpler topics like magical theory, Erica was lost for words. She knew Levi would have the right thing to say in this situation, coolly pointing out the flaws she knew were present in Adelaide's argument, but she simply didn't know enough to counter. For instance, despite her friend's confidence that the Empire wouldn't invade unprovoked, she'd grown up hearing other friends tell stories about how the Aurans were just over the Golden Hills, no more than two days travel from Regina's Bounty. She'd never truly thought it would happen, but some part of her always believed she'd wake one morning to find crimson-clad legionnaires camped in the town square. More than that, she still couldn't figure out what to say to a friend as inconsistent as Adelaide, committed to duty one second and ready to run haring off into the wilderness the next. Shaking her head, she replied weakly, well aware she'd silently conceded at least part of the argument. "Well I don't know much about that either, but you might as well give up on monster hunting. Tracking this vampire, if that's what it is, would be as meaningless as you claim the meetings are. You probably wouldn't be able to distinguish between sources of necromantic energy like the vampire and a minor bonewalker, for example. And either way, you'd probably just end up with a compass pointing towards the Forest of the Dead."

Clicking her tongue, Adelaide retreated back to her desk, shaking her head as she bent over her diagrams again. "Fine then. If that is how it must be, I shall simply content myself with running over the size to output calculations of forcestones once more. At least studying an impossible to solve problem is more meaningful than staying abreast of current affairs."

The conversation quite clearly over, Erica decided to return to her own studies, pulling out *Arcana of the White Angel* once more. But no matter how much she tried to get into the book, admittedly a task even on the best days, her mood had been firmly soured. On the one hand, she felt dissatisfied with her last word, feeling that she'd let Adelaide down by not knowing the right things to say. And on the other hand, now that Adelaide had expressed interest in it, the news about the dead lord's manor and the vampire hung over her like a cloud that simply refused to go away. It was probably nothing, a struck and done anomaly like Adelaide had said, and Levi would probably be able to handle it regardless, like she'd said, but it felt too personal now. Shaking her head, she stood and headed towards the door, only pausing briefly at the threshold to offer a brief word of explanation as she left, though Adelaide barely reacted, not even looking up from her desk.

From there, she set a steady pace through the halls of the palace, walking a path she'd taken many times before. In the middle of the day the halls were bustling with palace staff going about their business and guards on patrol, but none of them offered her any trouble and she was able to quickly cross to the opposite wing. The first time she'd gone this way, it had taken well over an hour, both from getting lost and from stopping every so often to look at the tapestries and paintings she passed, but now she could do it in less than ten minutes. Before long, she found herself before the relatively unassuming door to the palace chapel. While most of the nobility in Riverluck tended to attend Sunday services at Saint Cornelius' Cathedral, built right on the boundary between the upper and lower districts, and the royal family were no exception, it was also common fashion for those who could manage it to build a chapel in their homes. For most, this meant little more than a prayer room where they could hold a mass if a priest was willing to come to them. The palace chapel, on the other hand, was large enough that it was all but a full on Teacher's hall, Father Arthur permanently assigned there.

As for the chapel itself, it managed to keep up the relative austerity that propriety demanded of holy grounds, but that was only when considering the finery of the palace around it. Chapel or not, being built for the royal family of Tycortua meant it was nicer than any similar structures by far. For instance, while the door was relatively unassuming, this was only insofar as it had been made from simple oak stained to a deep brown as opposed to the exotic, imported woods most of the other doors in the palace were made from. And that was ignoring the stained glass set in the fanlight above the door and sidelights flanking it. Going even further, walking into the chapel proved the door to be rather an anomaly in its simplicity. The chapel had been built to jut out from the palace's east wing, the stained glass windows lining its walls catching the morning light and painting the interior with colored light that made a striking contrast with the white marble of the walls and floors.

Nobody was present as Erica entered, Father Arthur presumably out for lunch, but that suited her just as well. She didn't especially want to stay long. Stopping at the font, she eyed the statue of Seras set in its basin, acting as a fountain for the font with holy water pouring down from between her cupped hands. Strictly speaking, official church doctrine did not support the veneration of the River Sage and she wasn't even considered a saint, but many priests were willing to let it slide since she'd helped save the world. And such veneration was far more common in Riverluck than it was back in Regina's Bounty, making it something Erica was still getting used to in some ways. Much the same, she still didn't know how to feel about the statue on general principle. Growing up, the Champions of the Four Corners had been far off figures, even the likes of Seras' supposed grave in the forest outside of Regina's Bounty mysterious enough to make them little more than stories. But seeing the statue here in front of her, all she could think was that the River Sage looked far too human. Just a woman in long, flowing clerical robes, no crown of stars or staff made from Maripphi thousand-year willow. Not even the Ancient's Armor the Storm Warlord and Ember King were said to have or the diamond sword the Crystal Queen wielded. For all her fame and fabled holy power, the thing that stood out most to Erica were the eyes. It might have only been a quirk of the artist's design, but she always felt that her eyes looked, for lack of a better term, empty, like they were nothing more than mirror-smooth ponds.

Shaking her head, she snapped herself out of her reverie and started back towards her destination, dipping her hand in the basin to bless herself as she passed, quickly touching forehead, heart, and stomach in the sign of the Three. She briefly considered taking a bottle of holy water, just for a bit of extra security since blessed objects were supposed to disrupt the unholy magic that formed and animated undead like vampires, but decided that was a little bit too disrespectful. Her destination lay at the other end of the chapel, one of the twin bookshelves flanking the altar. Since the Path of the Teacher had a strong dedication to education, the Teacher's name alone proving just how strong, every Teacher's hall from the smallest chapel to the largest cathedral was required to have a section devoted to educational supplies, especially texts and tomes. Erica had heard the Grand Cathedral at High Worldheart had an entire library attached, one of the most extensive in the world, but the palace chapel only had the two token shelves, most of Riverluck's knowledge stored in the city university's library. Even still, there were enough to serve Erica's purposes well. Scanning the shelves briefly, she found the volume she was looking for, a thin prayer book she'd read a few times before, and slipped it into her pocket. Only a simple prayer book for most, but also a brief summary of a handful of defensive spells for those trained in holy magic. Nodding in satisfaction, she patted the book as she headed back towards the door. But she was unable to put either the book or the second silent concession she'd made to Adelaide in taking it, all but admitting she was planning on encountering the vampire, from her thoughts. *It's just to refresh my memory. Just in case.*

But before she'd crossed even half of the chapel's length, she heard the door opening. Even though she knew there was no reason for her to do so, she acted on instinct and ducked into one of the pews, hiding under it and pressing herself up against the kneelers. She cursed herself as she heard footsteps on the marble, knowing she'd probably end up having an awkward conversation with Father Arthur when she got caught and had to explain just why she was sneaking around the chapel, but her irritation was wiped away by uncertainty when she heard Levi's voice break the silence. "Are you really sure we need to be so worried about all of this, Your Majesty?"

Erica's blood froze as she realized that this certainly wasn't a conversation she was supposed to be hearing and while she would have been fine passing them normally, coming out of hiding now would be an even more awkward conversation than the one she would have had with the priest.

King Thierry replied shortly after, a wry humor in his voice, "It's just a prayer, Levi. That seems an appropriate response to a paranoid suspicion."

"Well yes, but... it is just that we have already gone for a third of the year without anything... Well, anything. Is it not more likely that what happened is unrelated? Even if it is a vampire, can we really say that it came from... there?"

The king sighed. "Quit dancing around the subject, Levi. You not saying it won't make it any less real. And you heard what Archmage Dwyer said. It's been two thousand years since the Dusk Tyrant fell. Exactly two thousand. And magic likes round numbers."

Erica's eyes widened and she was barely able to keep herself quiet, clamping a hand over her mouth to avoid gasping. The Dusk Tyrant. A name anyone would recognize. The man, assuming he was human, that had threatened to take over the world two thousand years ago until the Champions of the Four Corners defeated him. And as a mage herself, at least a mage in training, Erica recognized the truth to the king's words. Magic did like round numbers. More to the point, it liked things that were significant, being a force of mystery, of meaning and intention, at its core. If anything were going to happen surrounding the Dusk Tyrant, now would be the time. At least this was the best time for the next five hundred or so years. And the proof of it could be found in the events of the last millennial anniversary of the Dusk Tyrant's defeat, when he was supposedly resurrected and shattered the continent-spanning Sunfire Empire.

But for Levi's part, he didn't sound especially sold on the idea. "Maybe, but it seems entirely too convenient to blame our problems on an ancient evil. Would it not make more sense for the Dusk Tyrant's first target to be Pazyerra in either case? To strike at the last remnant of his killer's legacy?"

Erica could almost imagine the king's shrug simply from his blasé tone. "Perhaps. But that still doesn't change my initial point. It's only a prayer made in response to a minor suspicion. No more, no less." No response came for a time. Eventually, King Thierry said, "Then if you would let me get to it? King or not, Estelle will still have my head if I shirk my duties for too long."

Erica's mind spun as she considered what she'd heard, desperately wishing she had someone to talk to about it all. Eventually, she heard their footsteps once more, the king presumably done praying, and then the sound of the door opening and closing once more. Slowly emerging from her hiding place, she scanned the room to make sure the coast was clear. Once she was satisfied, she quickly got up and headed towards the door, returning to Adelaide's study.

She worried that she was rushing on her way back, that her haste would raise suspicion in the guards, but nobody seemed to notice or care and she was able to get back without incident. Adelaide was gone on her own errand when she got back, returning a short time later with another textbook in hand and in a much happier mood then she'd been in when Erica left, but that did little to ease Erica's uncertainty. One problem had been solved, through the simple matter of giving her friend a bit of time and space, but another, much more complicated problem had risen in its place. Even though she'd taken a break to calm her mind, she still couldn't bring herself to focus, worrying over the same thoughts again and again as she wondered just what it would mean if Allard's vampire was related to the Dusk Tyrant.

Chapter 3

Seaday: 1st of Hernus, Year 1980 R.S.

Blinking sweat out of his eyes, Allard continued to carefully circle Levi, watching for an opening. For as much as he'd been glad to see the sun and clear skies this morning, he was starting to begrudge the noon heat. Even on a good day, training was a pain, but the heat made it worse, sweat blinding him and loosening his grip on the sword.

Well I guess it does make sense if we're preparing for battle in all—

His thoughts were cut off suddenly as Levi lunged forward, taking advantage of his distraction to slam the wooden practice blade into his stomach, knocking the wind out of him. With a heavy "oof" Allard's knees buckled and he let go of his sword, falling to the ground in a rather undignified heap. Looking up, he found Levi's sword pointed squarely at his head, a wry frown that needed no explanation on his face. Once the point was made, Levi flicked his sword back and returned to the other side of the practice ring, setting himself in a ready position. "Again."

Taking a moment to catch his breath, Allard slowly got to his feet and picked up his sword. He put himself in a stance, mirroring Levi's, and the two started to circle each other again.

After a few rotations, Allard advanced with a few quick steps, swinging more to test Levi's defense than anything else. The blow was easily parried and Allard immediately knew that he was in a bad spot as Levi began to riposte. He found himself pushed back again and again, just barely keeping Levi's strikes from landing, until he felt his foot touch the outer boundary of the practice ring. He glanced back briefly, but that was enough. Levi lunged forward and hooked Allard's leg with his own. Unbalanced, Allard fell flat on his back, the breath knocked out of him. When he looked up, Levi's sword stood poised for the kill once more, this time pointed at his chest.

The knight returned to his position once again, but this time he nodded his head towards Allard, an appraising look in his eyes. "Distracted today, are we, Sir Allard?"

Letting out a humorless chuckle, Allard picked himself up again with a shake of his head. "Right. Because I usually fare so much better against you."

Shrugging, Levi replied, "You do always lose, but usually with mediocrity, not truly poor skill."

The brutal honesty stung, but Allard could hardly claim otherwise. He'd been learning to use a sword every since he came to Riverluck, but the best anyone could say about his skill was that he knew how to wield a sword. Three years of effort was hardly enough for him to be called 'good' and he knew that in a fight against anyone that actually knew how to use a sword, he'd hardly last a minute. Letting it go for the moment, he just shook his head and set himself at the ready. "Again."

Levi shrugged, starting into the tedious circling. Intent on actually landing a blow this time, Allard wasted no time in lunging towards Levi, assailing him with his own flurry of slashes in the hopes of keeping him too busy to attack. But instead of letting himself get pushed back as Allard had, Levi maintained control, continuing to circle as he retreated, calmly parrying. Eventually Allard realized his plan had thoroughly failed as his arm started to get tired. He struck again, but this time slightly slower than before. Free hand darting forward, Levi caught Allard's wrist and yanked him off balance, rapping him on the shoulder with the hilt of his practice blade. Allard reflexively dropped his sword, swiftly finding the smooth wood of Levi's blade at his throat. Levi fixed him with a stern glare, voice almost scolding when he spoke, "Allard. *What* is the matter?"

Releasing him, Levi nodded towards one of the benches lining the training grounds where they'd left an everfull pitcher. Following him, Allard stretched himself out with a groan, shaking his head. "Oh, just the usual. I don't really see the point in all of this."

Levi picked up the pitcher and tapped the waterstone on its inside rim. After waiting for a few seconds as it filled, he poured both himself and Allard a cup before turning it off once more. Waiting until Allard had taken several gulps of water, he nodded thoughtfully, gesturing to the training grounds. "One would think it is only natural that you should learn how to use the sword if you are to be my squire."

Allard rolled his eyes, letting out another humorless chuckle. "But that's just it. What's the point in being your squire when Crownguard is a hereditary position? Seras's Stars, just going by surname I'll never be a Crownguard unless someone in your family adopts me."

Nodding, Levi conceded the point. When Adelaide had forcibly requested Allard join her staff, and by extension Erica who'd volunteered to accompany as his friend, it had been easy enough to find a position for Erica since mages were always in demand. But Allard presented a rather complicated problem, since he wasn't especially qualified for any job at the palace, particularly one where they could justify his spending time with the heir. And seeing as they had, once you sifted through the excuses, been hired to be Adelaide's friends, that was a rather important consideration. So they came up with a new position that was more or less a joke to anyone who bothered to look: Crownguard in training. On paper, training a secondary personal knight to the heir made sense. When that position was defined by an exceedingly rare set of armor and a one of a kind sword that was passed down in a family who was so tied to the job that it and their name were interchangeable, it became something of a moot point. Both Allard and Levi knew this, as did most of the palace. Yet despite conceding the point, Levi refused to let up. "Even still, it cannot hurt for you to know how to defend yourself. Even if you will never wear my armor or wield Whisperwind, you can still protect Adelaide if I am not there. I cannot be everywhere at once."

That seemed a fairly thin excuse to Allard, but he decided he was better off picking his battles. Arguing himself out of a job probably wasn't the wisest choice. "Alright, but why a sword? I already know how to use a bow, can't I just train with that?"

Levi smiled, a tone of sarcasm in his reply, "You would make a fine addition to the Ranger Corp if you joined the army, I am sure. But most of the things you would find yourself guarding against will not politely face you from twenty paces. How do you intend to defend yourself with a bow, much less Adelaide, when they stand at arm's length?"

Sighing, Allard sat back on the bench, setting his cup and practice sword aside. "Well yeah, maybe. But I'm still not going to ever be as good as anyone who's been training for their entire life. And I certainly won't ever be better than you."

No response came for a time, long enough that Allard began to worry that he'd said something wrong. Looking back to Levi showed that a strange melancholy had overtaken the knight, his expression distant as he nodded. "Yes. You never will be able to match a lifetime's worth of effort, will you?" Then, as if he suddenly remembered he was speaking aloud, he shook his head and continued as normal. "But that does not mean your imperfect effort is in vain, yes?"

For a brief moment, Allard weighed his options, trying to decide whether or not he should try and push further into whatever that had been about. Finally, he decided that it wasn't worth the effort and that if Levi wanted to talk about it, he would. And in either case, he felt like this conversation had gone on for too long in a direction that ill-suited his mood, namely one that proved he had little leg to stand on. Shrugging, he decided it was best to just try and divert discussion away from himself. "I guess. But either way, your Ancient's Armor makes effort a moot point, right?"

Clenching a fist, Levi summoned one of his armor's gauntlets, the glossy blue metal coalescing out of a thin mist as he drew it back from Void-Space. Stretching the armored hand forward, he grasped the air and seemed to tear it aside, Whisperwind forming in his hand with a crackle of lightning. Giving the sword a few casual swings he spun it back to point at Allard, like a teacher calling on a student. "But can magic replace the skill of the one who wields it? Tell me, just how do these make me any better than another knight?"

The entire question seemed preposterous to Allard. He understood the point Levi was trying to make, but when the wearers of Ancient's Armor were regarded as almost like an army unto themselves, it felt as though Levi's entire argument was flawed. Allard had grown up hearing stories about old Crownguards breaking an invading force's lines to say nothing of the famous tales like the Gray Knight of Viemer storming World's Eye to uncrown the mad King Wilvan or the Black Knight of Naktikos single-handedly defending Northern holds against flocks of dragons. Sure, those were heroic tales of once in a generation figures, but that didn't mean their armor didn't help make things easier. But that wasn't the answer Levi was looking for and Allard knew it. Frowning, he waved his hand through the air, as though he could grab hold of some invisible blade. "Well putting aside increased speed and maximized strength, since the Crownguard plate was forged with the power of wind, I'd say the fact that it summons a windstorm to protect you." He paused, taking a look at the sword. "And as for Whisperwind. It's a nice sword? I've never been exactly sure what made it so special if I'm being honest."

Scoffing, Levi swung the blade again, sparks of electricity crackling in its wake. "'A nice sword' is putting it lightly, but comparatively you are right. For this argument, the point lies with the armor. Yes, all seven sets of Ancient's Armor make you as strong as the strongest of mundane humans and the particular enchantments upon my own make me far swifter than all but the wardens of the Forest-folk, but what are strength and speed if used poorly? I would wager most would move too fast and fall on their face if they tried to fight in this. And as for a windstorm? Yes it can scatter swarms of enemies, but what about in close spaces? Or among your allies? Against a single enemy, it may do more harm than good if they know it is coming. Ancient's Armor makes a formidable fighter all the more formidable. It does not turn a greenhorn into a great knight."

"And I suppose you're going to say the same goes for all warded armor and honed weapons? That I'll only be able to use the enchantments on them well if I know how to use unenchanted equipment well?"

Levi smiled, dismissing his armaments once more. "Quite so. Now you are beginning to understand. So, once you have finished catching your breath, let us get back to it." He paused, eyes narrowing. "Though perhaps... Yes. Ignore that and follow me."

Levi spun and began walking purposefully towards the training ground's exit. Startled by the sudden change of pace, Allard rushed to his feet, running after Levi. Looking at the knight, Allard found he had a thoughtful expression on his face that seemed at odds with his current focus. Furrowing his brow, Allard said, "What's going on Levi? Is there something I should be worried about?"

They entered the palace guard's barracks and Levi turned to head up the stairs. The knight shrugged. "I should think not, but our discussion did remind me of a way in which I have perhaps been lax in your training."

Levi continued upwards, the stairs around them already losing much of their luster, the carefully cleaned and ordered stone giving way to walls that, while no less solid than their companions, were less finished, the bricks unpainted and the seams between them visible. More than that, a thin layer of dust covered stairs, railing, and walls. Giving it all a wary look, Allard said, "Lax? If you ask me, I think you've done just about as well as could be expected given my own inexperience. And what in our conversation reminded you of the attic?"

They finally reached the end of the stairs on the sixth story, coming out on a landing that was in much the same condition as the rest of the upper floors. Looking out over the edge showed the exposed joists of the fifth floor's ceiling. But at the end of the landing stood a door that looked out of place, made from a rough-textured, gray stone Allard didn't recognize with a fist sized magestone set in the center of a circle of carved runes. Levi touched the stone and the runes began to glow, seams splitting the door into a dozen segments that then alternated between rising into the ceiling and sinking into the floor. He turned back to Allard, gesturing him inside. "I realized that our conversation on your skill was based entirely on the assumption you would be fighting enemies on a human scale. Recent events have reminded me that this is not the case. So without further ado, welcome to my office."

The room beyond was massive, running the entire length of the barracks, not a small building in itself, and it was filled wall to wall with more assorted combat paraphernalia than Allard would have thought even the entire palace guard below would have needed, much less Levi alone. One wall was lined with weapon racks, each of them carefully ordered with a particular type of weapon that started with standard arming swords near the door before turning to far more exotic tools Allard hardly recognized in the distance. The other wall was stacked with bookshelves, perhaps twice as many dusty tomes filling them as there were weapons on the other side. And off in the distance, Allard thought he could see large shapes through the gloom of the unlit room, things like immense, monstrous skulls and what he thought was an over-sized ballista. Taking it all in, he couldn't keep the awe from his voice as he almost unconsciously spoke. "Your office? What is all of this stuff? This has been here the whole time?"

Laughing, Levi left Allard to wander as he headed towards a desk nestled in between two of the bookshelves, rifling through some of the books there. "Indeed. This is what could be called the Crownguard collection. Not my family's wealth or treasures you understand, but the accumulated knowledge and equipment of two thousand years' worth of monster hunters and knights. I realized I should let you start studying some of the things I have kept here since I *should* be training you as a monster hunter, not merely a swordsman." He stopped searching for a moment, looking up at the wall before him with an annoyed expression. "And I must admit I have been rather lazy about such skills myself, if I am to be perfectly honest."

Putting two and two together, Allard whirled back around to face Levi, ignoring the artifacts that had held his interest up till now. "Wait. If you only just thought about it, does that mean this has something to do with the vampire that attacked the lord's manor?"

Levi fixed him with a curious expression and Allard realized that he wasn't exactly supposed to know about that and only Erica had known he had. Wincing, he prepared himself for a scolding, but Levi just sighed, massaging his forehead as he did. "So you know about Lord Reinhardt, hmm? I suppose that means Miss Greenmaiden knows as well? That could be helpful, but I am not looking forward to keeping Adelaide from taking interest."

Relieved, Allard gestured reassuringly. "Don't worry, I only told Erica. So I was right? This is about the vampire?"

Turning back to his desk, Levi found what he was looking for, pulling a thin volume from a stack of newer looking books. Proffering it to Allard, he shook his head as he replied. "Yes. And I am quite sure there is no way whatsoever Her Highness will overhear you two talking about it. You have always been excellent at keeping secrets."

Glowering, Allard snatched the book from his hands. "Hey! We have secrets." This earned him an expectant stare in response as Levi dared him to prove it and Allard decided it wasn't worth going there, well aware of how obviously he was trying to change the topic as he continued. "Are you going to actually start explaining this monster hunting stuff, or do I just get a book?"

Levi shook his head, returning to peruse the shelves with a well practiced air. "To the first point, we do not know our killer is a vampire yet, we merely suspect as much. As for the second, I believe it is related, but what spurred me to this may be something else entirely." He looked back at Allard, eyes more serious than he'd ever seen on him before. "Last night, I was attacked returning from here to the palace. My assailant looked human, albeit missing an arm, but clearly was not. Their speed and strength were enough to press me even in Ancient's Armor."

Eyes wide, Allard drew in a sharp breath, scarcely able to believe that something like that could happen in the palace grounds. "But you won, right?"

Even if he didn't realize how inane of a response that was, Levi's sardonic glance back was enough of an answer. "Yes. And no. I was able to drive them off, but unable to land a significant blow." His eyes and mouth both narrowed. "It hardly felt a fight at all. I think they were merely testing my defenses. I have already warned the guard to stay alert, because I doubt this is the last I have seen of whoever it was."

The doubt in Levi's voice was enough to send a shiver down Allard's spine. He'd known from hearing about the state of Lord Reinhardt's house guard that the attacker was no one to be trifled with. But hearing Levi say that they seemed like a match for him hammered home just how much of a threat they was. Or at least could be, if it was the same person. Even after knowing Levi for three years, Allard still couldn't help but think of him as almost invincible, more the shining image of a knight who rode into a common village than a man whenever he wore the armor. Allard looked down at the book, sobered by the thought. "So what's this then? A beginner's guide to monster hunting?"

Though the question had been meant as a joke of sorts, Levi nodded. "To a point. Tell me what you know of monster hunters in general. And I mean the specific profession, not the simple descriptor of anyone who goes out and kills magical beasts."

Allard shrugged. "Honestly, I didn't really think there was that much of a difference. I thought one was just more focused than the other."

If Levi was disappointed by the response, he didn't show it, merely pulling another book from the shelf and opening it to read himself. Based on the almost absent response he gave to Allard, it was unrelated, Levi researching something for himself even as he instructed Allard. "That is a sufficient understanding for any common purpose, but the distinction is a bit more nuanced than that. To call someone a true monster hunter means they must possess a certain knowledge about what they hunt. That one can gain through time and study." With this, he gestured towards the shelves stretching off into the gloom. "The other, far more prevalent, factor is possessing the skills and tools necessary to take them down. As we are both human, there is a limit to what we can do going up against monsters stronger and faster than us or fiends possessing mystical abilities. To become a true monster hunter, one must learn to overcome that gap."

Flipping through the thin book in his hands, Allard saw it was something like a spellbook. The first few pages were a breakdown of the three fundamental laws of magic, which Allard skipped, but from there it had several basic spells and details on fighting styles supplemented by magic that would have looked more at home in a combat manual than a spellbook. "You want me to learn magic now too? Even though I'm still working on getting my swordsmanship down?"

Levi nodded as he tapped a section in his book before snapping the tome shut, replacing it on the shelf. "No. Not precisely. Certainly not to the extent that Miss Greenmaiden is learning magic. I merely wish for you to start considering a fighting style. Some way for you to push yourself beyond human limitations so you can fight things that are not human. Remember, even the Tycortua Regulars usually have some kind of trick up their sleeves. You need not even limit yourself to magic, should you find the mystic arts beyond your grasp." He frowned, face set with irritation as he continued. "I, for instance, use my equipment to overcome the gap."

The fact that Levi's justification for himself seemed to run contrary to his earlier point was not lost on Allard, but he had a good idea that Levi was already well aware of the fact. Closing his book, he nodded, but couldn't keep the uncertainty from his voice as he responded, "Right. But what if my Conviction's just not up to it? What if I just can't no matter how hard I try?"

Levi patted him on the shoulder, giving him a reassuring nod. "Just consider it. Overthinking whether or not you can does little to help when it comes to Conviction. It is far easier to *believe* you can do something, and I mean to believe truly within your heart, when you think that you can." He started towards the door, waving over his shoulder as he went. "Now I need to go ask Miss Greenmaiden for a favor. Take the rest of the day to study. The door will close after you on your way out."

With that, he was gone, leaving Allard alone in the attic. Looking around, Allard began meandering through the room, taking in the sheer breadth of how much had been stored up there. Perusing the weapon racks, after passing beyond the standard issue weapons for a Tycortuan soldier, he found himself looking at the likes of Austallan batons made entirely of wood, the large zwei-handers Rugegan Landsknechts wielded, and even Desert-folk daggers made from fangs, claws, and carapace, all coming from animals he had no hope of identifying. And once he drew close enough to the looming shapes at the far end, he found that his initial assessment was correct, a massive ballista taking up easily half of the far wall, though closer inspection proved it to be more similar to a galecaster, a synthesized windstone the size of his head resting at the bottom of a long barrel that had been heavily carved with magic symbols and reinforcement spells. He paused long enough to wonder how they got it up there and how they would get it down if they needed to use it before moving on to the skeletons. Those were a different story altogether. They stood neatly assembled within rope partitions, like some kind of a morbid display. He recognized some of the beasts, like the distinct shape of a griffon and the common enough silhouette of a fae wolf. But the vast majority of them were completely foreign to him, some of them so large that only skulls were displayed.

But through all of it, Allard knew he was just stalling. The book Levi had given him felt like a lead weight in his pocket, impossible for him to ignore. It was the same kind of thing that always gave him pause. He'd left Regina's Bounty, among other reasons, so he could get to see more of the world. And here he was training to be a genuine monster hunter, learning how to use a sword and magic just like the heroes in the stories he'd always read and heard. But somehow it just didn't feel right to him. He'd gone to Riverluck, but that's as far as he'd gone. He was learning how to use a sword, but he hadn't ever even been in a real fight. He was going to start looking into magic, but couldn't help but feel that he couldn't do it, that he wasn't worthy of being able to do it. *By Seras' Stars, I saw more monsters while hunting back home than I have in three years here.*

All in all, it simply didn't feel right, like he was doing things out of order. On some level, he wondered if he was more afraid that he'd succeed than that he'd fail, that being able to do those kinds of things without following the proper steps and having the right adventures meant his old dream was worth nothing. Taking a deep breath, he shook his head, putting all of that out of mind. "I only said I'd consider it."

Speaking only to break the silence, hearing his voice helped reassure him nonetheless. Done putting things off, he started towards the door, taking the book from his pocket as he left. Opening it up, he started reading as he walked, already expecting he had a long day ahead of him.

Chapter 4

Seaday: 1st of Hernus, Year 1980 R.S.

Erica looked about the manor's entrance hall with a disinterest forged by years surrounded by opulence. She'd been surprised when Levi asked her to accompany him to Lord Reinhardt's manor after lunch to investigate what had happened. More than that, she wasn't exactly sure why he'd asked her for help, but hadn't seen much reason to refuse. Thus, after a brief walk through the Nobles' District, she found herself standing in a murdered man's house, regarding his wealth with apathy. Though she knew the furnishings were exceedingly fine and the paintings along the walls worth more than a small house, they still stood as nothing when compared to the wealth that abounded within the palace. Even more than that, the finery's glimmer was dulled by the pervading disquiet that filled the manor. The fact that the normal day's affairs were being taken care of with the same efficiency as always only served to bring more attention to the horror of last night, as though the staff were pointedly ignoring an uninvited guest. She shook her head and looked back towards where Levi was speaking with the manor's butler. The man's face was lined with weariness and his movements seemed halfhearted as he responded to Levi's queries. *And what's the point of any of this stuff anyways? It has no meaning and it can't help anyone.*

After a few minutes, he bowed and exited the entrance hall. Levi stood still for a moment, staring after him, before shaking his head and returning to where Erica waited. She snapped herself from her musings as he approached, straightening as she addressed him as if coming to attention. "What's the verdict, Levi?"

He shrugged, his tone as disinterested as his reaction, "The butler was unable to add anything beyond what was written in the report. If we are to find something, it must be through our own efforts." He turned and started towards the door the butler had exited through, motioning for Erica to follow as he continued. "I believe we had best start by tracing the vampire's path through the manor. According to the butler, it entered through a window on the third floor."

With nothing to add, Erica nodded and followed silently. But as soon as she crossed the threshold Erica felt a chill run down her spine, a slight crawling sensation that refused to vanish and only intensified the further the two walked through the halls. The timing of it all seemed far too convenient to be coincidental, such a feeling of dread overtaking her the moment she entered the scene of a tragedy. It was entirely possible she was only being paranoid, the knowledge that the manor had seen death making her expect to be unsettled, but even still, she couldn't help but feel something was off. Spurred by this dread, she closed her eyes and pushed out with her senses, as though attempting to see with eyes and hear with ears that were not there. Then, as though a curtain had been lifted, her 'vision' was filled with the usual flow of magic that surrounded her, the omnipresent dull glow of its energy that filled the atmosphere of the world. Immediately around her, she could feel it swirling up her body, like an upside down tornado centered on her chest. Looking ahead towards Levi, she could see it crackling towards him, streamers of energy trailing through the air like bolts of lightning, striking him and dissipating in puffs of silvery mist. A reaction she'd always found odd, but time had shown her that was simply how Levi was. Focusing on the manor's walls, however, showed unexpected results. Most buildings showed only the ambient energy of their construction, the faint greenish gray that filled stone, dulled after being worked by human hands. Here, she could see streaks of deep purple running through them, like a mineral vein through a cliff side.

Before she could consider the matter further, Levi shook her shoulder, drawing her attention back into the physical world. "It would seem we have arrived, Miss Greenmaiden." The two of them stood before an empty window frame, the wind whistling eerily through it. Erica peered around the corridor looking for any other signs of conflict, but could find none. The walls and floors were even remarkably clean, looking as though the stone had been freshly cut and polished. Noticing her inspection, Levi nodded. "The staff took it upon themselves to clean the stains that were left behind. From what I understand, two of the house guards were caught here when the vampire entered."

Nodding absently, Erica knelt down and ran her eyes over the windowsill. "And the broken glass I see. Though I'm sure that was more for safety concerns than for..." She paused as she tried to think of the words to say, but her mind rebelled against the thought of that kind of violence. "Other reasons."

Running a hand along the wall opposite the window, feeling for any imperfections or marks unseen, Levi shook his head. "Just as you have said. I am not sure what more we can find here. If anything helpful remained after the attack, it was cleaned away. If you will follow me, it seems it went this way next."

With that, he turned and began walking back the way they had come, though he did slacken his pace to let Erica catch up. As Erica stood up and followed him, she turned her thoughts back to what she'd seen before. "One other thing, Levi. I was looking for anything out of the ordinary magically, since something's been bothering me since we entered the house. There is something off, though I'm not entirely sure what. It looked almost like a hint of dark magic worked its way into the building."

Levi rubbed his chin in thought. "What precisely do you mean by 'a slight bit of dark magic'? I wager by the manner of your phrasing it is not something so simple as an enchantment or curse cast over the house?"

"Probably not. It didn't look like anything concrete or a specific spell that had been wrought. With things like that, you'll get a much more specific pattern. This looked almost like something that was naturally occurring."

Levi thought for a moment, humming slightly as he did so. Turning to face Erica, he responded with a skeptical look on his face, "Could it be that the negative emotions of the dead have returned to form a supernatural phenomenon? Something like how the residual anger of the unjustly murdered forms ire-wraiths?"

Erica rolled her eyes. "If it were something that simple, then I wouldn't have brought it up. Minor hauntings like that happen all the time and are easily cleared up. They show up more like a slight darkening of the magic in the air. This was more solid than that – an individual stream of energy running through everything else." She snapped her fingers and pointed at Levi. "Maybe if you think of dye being poured into water. It's like that first moment when there are two distinct and separate liquids occupying the area. You can tell what's water and what's dye."

Eyes narrowing, a serious expression stole over Levi's face. "Do you mean to tell me this dark magic will eventually spread throughout the entire manor? Can we then be certain it will content itself to stop there?"

It was a good question, and one Erica was embarrassed to admit she didn't have a good answer for. While it seemed similar to the kind of things she trained to stop, she had no idea what the dark magic's purpose actually was. Looking to the side to hide her unease, she idly traced the patterns painted on the wall with her hand as she walked. "I don't know. I would have to check back again in a few days to find out if it's spreading. And I wouldn't know where it would stop until it actually did stop. This kind of thing is beyond my scope."

The two of them walked in silence afterwards, letting the weight of the conversation hang over them both. After a few minutes, Levi drew to a stop in the middle of an intersection between two hallways. "It would seem this is the next place of note upon the vampire's trail. Though it had encounters with a few guards caught on their own before here, this was the first point of major resistance it faced."

Looking more closely, the signs of combat here were obvious, damage not even a thorough scrubbing could remove. A few scores ran along the walls, where swords had been turned aside or missed their mark. One wall had small holes punched through it, though the offending crossbow bolts had been removed, and the faint smell of smoke lingered in the air, the floor sooty and singed in places. Awed by the first scene of true battle she'd ever seen, Erica shook her head. "How many people did the vampire fight?"

Levi paused from his inspection of a cracked floor stone and looked up at her. "The reports I was given stated that six guardsmen attempted to hold it off with their swords while two with galecasters hung back and harried it with bolts. Their strategy, I imagine, was for the last member of their contingent, their mage, to bring it down with the most powerful spell he could manage."

At the mention of galecasters, Erica's eyes widened. Though she wasn't as well versed in lattice engineering as Adelaide, even she'd heard of the magically constructed crossbows. As they were powered by a lattice-stone synthesized from a windstone and a forcestone set at the base of the stock, they could fire bolts with twice the force of a regular crossbow and required no time to reload. That made them a terror to face on the battlefield, especially in the hands of a skilled marksman. But it also made them expensive enough that only the truly wealthy could afford one, much less two. "Even with that they couldn't stop it? I can't imagine it escaped unscathed with bolts coming at it that fast. Do you know what kind of mage they had? I'd think pyromancer from the residue, but..."

"Quite so. Though I understand many mages have more than one trick up their sleeves, so to speak. And I find that to be most troubling, knowing from my own studies just how good a job fire does at exterminating monsters." Shaking his head, he reached to his side and brought up a dagger, holding it out towards Erica. "As another note, the staff found this while they were cleaning. Since it is most assuredly not standard issue, they assumed that it belonged to the vampire. Can you tell if there is anything special about it?"

Taking it from Levi, Erica raised an eyebrow as she looked over the dagger, made from a dull, gray metal that was immediately recognizable to her. "You mean besides the fact that it's made of iron? I would imagine that something like this isn't standard issue." Turning it over in her hands, she looked for any notable markings or inscriptions, but found none. "What exactly do you expect me to find on this?"

Cracking a wry smile, Levi shrugged. "I do not know. That *is* why I asked you. You are the mage after all. I know that iron cannot be enchanted, but dark magic can work many kinds of sorcery beyond the purview of regular magic. Is there some way a curse could take hold where an enchantment could not?"

Returning the dagger to Levi, Erica shook her head. "It doesn't work like that. Magic is magic after all. The reason that iron can't be enchanted is because it's utterly physical by its spiritual nature. It's the spiritual representation of absolute physicality, like how gold is the spiritual representation of absolute wealth or silver the spiritual representation of absolute purity. Its very nature rejects magic of any kind."

Somewhat disappointed, Levi put the dagger away. "So there is absolutely nothing that can be done to distinguish this dagger from any other?"

"I'm afraid not. Though this dagger does tell us something about the vampire. If it's using daggers that can't hold or channel magic, then it's a safe bet that it can't use magic whatsoever. Most implements held by magi are used in one of two ways. The first is to act as a kind of focus, allowing them to more easily cast their spells. The second is to act as a physical anchor for their spells, something more commonly seen in warrior-mages who cast spells on their weapons."

"I see. So it would be to its disadvantage to use a dagger that could perform neither of those roles if it could use magic." Pausing as something occurred to him, he looked up sharply and met Erica's gaze with questioning eyes. "But can we really be sure this means it cannot use any magic at all? What if its magic is merely the type that would not be used as a weapon or does not require a focus? After all, I can recall stories of vampires hypnotizing people who look into their eyes."

Erica chuckled lightly. "That is a logical response, but there's more to it than that. It goes back to Conception. If you act with the intention of using absolute physicality, you can't also act with the intention of using something supernatural. No matter how you try to conceive of a spell, it can't can't get around the fact that you're trying to incorporate something completely nonmagical. Actively holding something made of iron, like one of those daggers, makes it act like a lightning rod for any magic you might use. It would draw any magical energy you attempted to muster towards it and prevent you from putting together a spell. And you couldn't even try shutting down another mage with it because they aren't the one with the intention to use it."

Levi nodded. "Very well. Though I am not willing to say for certain this vampire cannot use magic and intend to assume it can when planning counter-measures, I am convinced and it is valuable information to possess." He paused and took a sweeping look about the intersection. "Is there anything else you can think of here?"

"I don't think so. There doesn't seem to be much here besides the signs of combat. All it really tells us is that this vampire is just as capable as we heard."

"Unfortunately so. Well then, shall we be off? There is one more location to visit."

He turned and continued straight through the intersection, deeper into the manor. Erica followed as they ascended up to the fourth floor, finally stopping at the beginning of a long hall. From what she could see, the staff had not managed to do anything beyond a cursory cleaning here, only removing the bodies. Shattered furniture lay scattered about the hallway, giving testament to failed fortifications that had been set up to protect the doorway at its end. Here, the walls were stained with dried blood, a rusty brown color that contrasted the stark white of the marble. Closer to the doors, the walls were covered in slash marks, like a wild animal had used them to sharpen its claws. The grand double doors themselves lay ruined, one side hanging loosely on its hinges while the other had fallen to the ground in two pieces. Erica suppressed a shudder as she stepped over the threshold into a bedroom far too clean when compared to the carnage outside. Levi immediately walked to the room's corner and bent down, as if to pick something up. "Lord Reinhardt's body was found here. The staff have, obviously, removed it, but little else has been touched."

Surveying the room, Erica furrowed her brow. She'd noticed the contrast to the hallway as soon as she entered the room, but even with a closer inspection there was virtually nothing to indicate anything had gone wrong beyond the broken doors. The bed was still perfectly made, the nightstand undisturbed, and the dresser closed and intact. And not a single stain could be found on any of the surfaces. "Well I guess it makes sense that if the vampire drained him dry, there wouldn't be any bloodstains, but did the lord do nothing to resist? I can't see any signs of struggle."

Letting out a sigh, Levi stood up and dusted off his hands. "Ah, but that is just the thing. It seems that when the body was found, an arm obviously not belonging to Lord Reinhardt was found in this room, indicating he had fought back. And I can assure you, while he was certainly no master swordsman, he knew enough of the blade to hold his own." He paused and crouched down once more to peer under the bed, voice muffled as he continued. "I suppose if the vampire does not bleed, then it is reasonable to assume it would also leave no bloodstains behind. However, The truly strange part of this is that Lord Reinhardt was also missing an arm and it could not be found."

"Are you saying the vampire took his arm? But why would it do that? As some sort of revenge for the wound inflicted on it?"

"That is the question. My knowledge of vampires, though I will admit it consists only of ghost stories and a cursory perusal of an encyclopedia of the undead, gives no reason as to why it would take a limb." Levi paused and peeked his head over the edge of the bed. "Would inspection of the severed arm aid your efforts any? If we are quick, we can recover it before it is sent to the nearest Teacher's hall for purification and incineration."

At the thought of touching lifeless and rotting flesh, further warped from mere death by the unholy magics that previously animated it, Erica felt sick. "I can't think of anything I'd do with it. No spells I know can trace a monster from its parts and..." She shook her head, nausea rising again. "No. I don't want to see it."

Levi nodded as he crawled to the other side of the bed, lifting its skirt once more before giving up with a resigned look on his face, finding nothing. "Understandable. And thus I feel I have reached the end of my investigative powers, with nary a clue to be found. If you would, Miss Greenmaiden?"

Erica took a length of chalk from her pocket and knelt at the foot of the bed where she began drawing a circle of runes on the floor, spelling out words in

Mystic script. "I don't think I'll be able to do anything, but I'll give it a try." She looked back up at Levi with a level gaze. "You do realize that my specialties are in protective, cleansing, and growth magic, right?"

Levi merely shrugged. "As I have said, you are the mage, not me. And I was under the impression that magic was virtually limitless. Is that not so?"

Erica rolled her eyes as she continued with her circle, now working on a stylized flame in an attempt to draw the Counselor's Torch. "There are limitations on magic, but primarily it works how you believe it should work. That's how Inception and Conviction come into play, the former setting the limits and rules of the school of magic you ascribe to and the latter determining if you believe you can use those limits and rules. That's why most magi need their incantations and why I'm drawing this circle now instead of just waving a hand and getting what I want. Shouldn't you know this?"

Clicking his tongue, a flash of uncharacteristic anger flashed over Levi's face. But just as quickly as it came, it was gone, and he replied in a distracted and almost idle tone. "Hmm. But I had always thought the rules were what was key, not the belief. That if you knew the right methods, you could do anything, but if you didn't you could do nothing. If it's based off of what you believe, then shouldn't it be easy to do what you want? Can't you just tell yourself that you can do it?"

There seemed to be something the knight left unsaid, but Erica paid it no mind, looking down at her finished drawing with satisfaction. After replacing the chalk in her pocket, she responded with a note of hesitance in her voice, well aware she wasn't lecturing Adelaide this time. "Well there are more to rules than that. The rules about incantations and foci and magic circles that mages follow exist because that's how we believe they should. That's why there are so many variants upon the process, schools of Inception for each nation and culture. It's all about what magic really is: the power of that which cannot be explained. Pure mystery given meaning through intention. Humans can't use magic in its natural form because it's fundamentally impossible to understand so what we call magic, the spells we cast and the rules that we follow, are our way to try and make the unexplainable understood. To apply our sense of meaning onto this force of mystery and direct it according to our intention. Not explain it or know it, but make the world's mysteries into our own mysteries and shape the world as we desire." She sighed and closed her eyes, her voice growing remorseful as she continued. "And as for the second point, it isn't that easy to change what you believe. Even if you say one thing, a person's heart is harder to convince."

Levi chuckled. "That is true enough." He took a step back and folded his arms behind his back. "Well then, I suppose I should leave you to it."

Erica nodded and closed her eyes, once more focusing her senses on the magic around her. *I'll try the Ghost Vision spell first. If we can see what happened with our own eyes, that should clear things up.* Removing a small glass lens from another pocket, she placed it in the center of the magic circle and began speaking in Mystic Script. Magic energy rose from somewhere in her chest, running down her arms to gather in her palms in a lazily swirling spiral. After over a minute of chanting the passage, making sure to keep her voice clear and even, she raised both hands above the lens, speaking the last line of Empire Common in a commanding tone. "Let me see the ghosts of the past, phantoms of days gone by."

The energy rushed from her hands and the magic circle flashed with a golden light, leaving behind only the Counselor's Torch, which had been burned into the floor. Erica gently picked up the lens and held it before one eye, looking towards the doorway. Through it, she could see a translucent copy of the doors superimposed over their current wreckage, the image fully intact. She raised her free hand next to the lens and twisted it as though turning a knob. The phantom doors shifted rapidly through a flurry of movements as they opened and closed again, brief flashes of human figures appearing between them. Eventually, they burst forward in a shower of splinters. At this, Erica stopped turning her hand and lowered the lens. Muttering in Mystic, she tapped its front. "Let your light shine forward, so that all may see."

A faint silvery blue light shone from the lens, as though it were a bullseye lantern. Within that light, the translucent copies Erica had seen sprung into view, the broken doors hanging in the air like they had been trapped in amber. Levi nodded approvingly. "So this will let us see what happened then?"

Erica shrugged, causing the image before her to shudder slightly. "To an extent. It isn't as good with people and fine images, but it should give us the gist of things."

She began to twist her hand once more, this time more slowly. As she did, the door began to fall at a leisurely pace. Shortly thereafter, a figure appeared in the doorway, little more than wisps of smoke in the shape of a person with blazing red eyes and a swirling core of inky black darkness. Erica stepped to the side and followed the figure's movement with the lens, watching as it entered the room. There, another person-shaped wisp appeared; this one less distinct, lacking eyes, and with a small sphere of light at its core. The light wisp swung its arm at the first, as though wielding a sword. The dark one flowed to the side, moving out of the way of the swing. In the slowed perception of the lens, the two wisps danced back and forth in this manner over several more passes. Finally, the light wisp lunged forward, its arm swinging down towards the dark wisp. A line of smoke tumbled to the floor, coalescing into the form of a severed arm with clawed fingers, wrapped in tattered and worn black cloth. But the dark wisp continued forward, not caring about its wound. It barreled into the light wisp, taking it to the floor where it faded into the form of an unnaturally pale man. The dark wisp paused for a moment, bringing its free arm down to sever one of the corpse's arms. Picking it up, it turned towards the door and left, at a leisurely pace made into a crawl through the lens' slowed time.

Levi shook his head and sighed. "Not to complain, but that told us little, only confirming what we already knew."

Just as disappointed as Levi, Erica whispered a word of Mystic and snapped her fingers in front of the lens, dispelling its magic and causing the silvery blue light to fade away. "I still have another idea or two to try. Don't give up just yet."

Reaching into her pocket, she pulled out a set of seven dice, each with a different number of faces. She placed all of them in the palm of her hand, holding them before her. Muttering another passage of Mystic, she tossed the dice into the air where, instead of falling, they swiftly arranged themselves into a circle, floating before her. Erica clapped her hands together and finished the spell once again in that same clear and commanding tone. "Divine spirit of guidance, show us the path forward. Reveal that which has been hidden."

In response, a Counselor's Torch appeared in the middle of the circle, made from a soft golden light. Erica let out a breath and focused inward for a moment. *Two major spells in this short a time... I'm already at less than half capacity. I won't be of much use for anything else today.*

She shook her head and watched the Torch floating in front of her, flickering slightly in an unseen wind. Levi coughed lightly and inspected the circle of floating dice, tilting his head first one way, then the other. "As fascinating as all of this is, Miss Greenmaiden, how precisely does it help?"

Erica raised and hand drew it lightly through the air, as though directing the dice. The circle hovered following her movements, performing a circuit of the room. On seeing no change in the Torch she lowered her hand and scowled. "It's a type of augury spell. Meant to show us the proper path to take. I'd hoped that it might uncover something we'd missed, but it isn't reacting to anything."

Though it rarely came up in daily conversation, Levi was just as devout as the rest of the palace and as he put two and two together, he leaned forward with sudden interest. "Augury? You mean the Counselor is actually speaking to us through that spell?"

Hesitant to disappoint him, and even more hesitant to say something close to blasphemous, Erica shrugged, trying to stay casual as she replied. "Well, it's hard to say. This kind of thing's been a topic of great debate among magi for generations, especially since people of different faiths can cast the same spell and get the same results." Resting her face on one hand, she sighed. "And it looks like this is a case of the Three helping those who help themselves. We can still ask one question of the spell and get an accurate answer, albeit one open to interpretation. Do you have any ideas?"

Levi furrowed his brow. "Can we not ask them to simply show us the vampire's purpose here?"

Holding out her hands to either side, Erica prepared to complete the spell as she replied. "Well I suppose that's as good a question as any." She paused, closing her eyes and continuing in a low tone. "Divine spirit of guidance. Show us our enemy's intentions. Make clear their goal."

As she clapped her hands together, the dice fell to the floor in a clatter. The Counselor's Torch hovered in place for a moment longer, before blazing up. When the golden flames cleared, an arrow of light remained in the Torch's place, pointing back out the doors to the room and down through the floor. After a few seconds, the arrow dissipated, fading in a shower of golden sparks. Levi ran a hand through his hair as he looked in the arrow's direction. "Not to disparage, but that answer was more than a little vague."

Erica flung her arms up in frustration, again, more at the situation than Levi's reaction. "Well that's the best we're going to get. I did say the answer we got would be open to interpretation. At least it told us the vampire's purpose here wasn't to kill Lord Reinhardt. And that its purpose was still something in the house."

Levi frowned, muttering more to himself than in reply. "So it's purpose was grave enough that assassinating a member of the nobility was either distraction or inconvenience. But as deep in the manor as these chambers are, it must be the former..." He trailed off, then jerked back to attention, as though only then remembering Erica was present. "Is there anything else you have to do?"

Thinking back to her earlier discovery, Erica said, "Kind of. We can do it on the way out though. I want to see if I can trace the source of the dark magic I had mentioned earlier."

Levi nodded and gestured towards the doorway. "Very well. Lead on then."

As before, Erica closed her eyes and focused inward, opening her magical senses and swiftly catching sight of the veins of purple energy running through the manor's walls. Following the energy's flow, she walked blindly alongside it. She started slightly at feeling a hand on her shoulder, but calmed down after realizing Levi had placed it there to guide her while her eyes were closed. She slowly made her way through the manor's halls, going down two flights of stairs before stopping. Casting her senses around, the energy flow seemed to split in two directions midway down this hall. Opening her eyes, she was greeted with the sight of a servant's corridor, lined with unadorned doorways. She turned to face Levi with confusion written across her face. "As far as I can tell, the origin is somewhere around her."

He furrowed his brow and stepped up to a door, opening it. Within was a simple room, unfurnished save for a bed and a wardrobe. "I do not see anything here, and there is not much space to hide. Shall we check the other doors then?"

Erica nodded and moved to the doorway opposite his. They worked their way down the hall in that manner checking a total of eight doorways. Five were sleeping quarters much like the first. The other two were storage closets, filled with cleaning supplies and an assortment of lattice-stone devices; heaters, coolers, and the like. Erica shook her head after checking the last doorway. "I saw nothing out of the ordinary. It looks like we found nothing after all."

Levi sighed and started back the way they had come, motioning for Erica to follow. "I am afraid I must agree, Miss Greenmaiden. With any luck, the city guard will find something in their patrols, making all of this easier on us." He looked up at the ceiling as they walked, rubbing his chin in thought. "With that done, let us return to the palace. I still have work to attend to and I would ask that you report to Estelle, informing her of our discoveries here, scant though they were. Thank you again for granting me this favor, Miss Greenmaiden. If neither Estelle nor Adelaide have other tasks for you, you may take the rest of the afternoon off on my authority."

The idea of free time was appealing to Erica; a new book of philosophy by Austall's Saint of Swords waited on her nightstand and Viola would surely be willing to chat if she didn't feel like reading, but relaxation felt beyond her. Even though the vampire shouldn't be her problem, and Levi and the city guard would likely take care of it, seeing the results of its destruction made the whole situation feel oddly personal to Erica. "I'm glad to help. But as much as I would like to slack off, it feels too irresponsible given the situation. Maybe I should spend my time studying up on vampires and effective countermeasures instead."

Though she'd meant it more as a joke, Levi shook his head with grim severity and let out a mirthless chuckle. "Too true, Miss Greenmaiden. Too true."

Chapter 5

Magiaday: 2nd of Hernus, Year 1980 R.S.

T he sun had already risen a bit more than Allard had hoped by the time he slipped out the servant's entrance and into the gardens with this week's letters in hand. He knew he still had a few more hours until Adelaide would wake up, but yesterday morning left him somewhat on edge. As he made his way towards one of the palace ground's side gates, he half expected to see Viola pop up from out of nowhere, finding a way to shove more work onto him before he even knew what had happened. But he was able to make it to his destination without incident, only passing a patrol of guards who didn't offer anything more than a nod of acknowledgment.

On getting to the gate, he found Erica already waiting for him, stretching with a yawn as he approached. She leapt to her feet with a smirk, eyes twinkling with smug laughter. "Sleeping in today, hmm Al?"

He rolled his eyes at this. Even back home she'd made fun of him for getting up later than her, even when it was only a difference of a few minutes. "Yeah, yeah. Let's get going already before someone forces me to deliver something again."

The two of them headed through the gate and began making their way towards the lower city where they were more accustomed to spending their free time. This early in the morning, the streets were virtually empty, the day in the Nobles' District not truly starting until mid-morning. But that suited Allard just as well. They weren't planning to spend any time in the carefully curated parks that had been so well tended they gained a kind of unnatural unapproachability despite their beauty, nor window shopping among the vastly over priced boutiques and eateries the wealthy favored. And in a different way, the lack of passersby served their purposes. While they certainly their errand to run at the post office and wanted to check on the festival preparations after, those were only convenient additions to the morning's trip, he and Erica having agreed to meet in a more private setting so they could discuss things without fear of prying ears. One set of ears in particular.

Once they were a few streets from the palace, Allard paused to make sure nobody else was nearby. After satisfying himself that at the very least nobody was near enough to overhear them, he turned back to Erica expectantly. "Well? What's the story?"

She shot him a sullen look, waving an arm at a nearby fountain shaped like the flowering trees surrounding it, water spilling over its stone leaves and into the small channel that bisected the street they were walking down. "Really? Already? Can't I enjoy the scenery a little bit? Soak in the peace and quiet?"

He met her glare with an equally flat stare. "Ah yes. The same statue we pass every week. How dare I keep you from noticing it?"

She let out a grumble of irritation. "There isn't much to say anyways. There's some kind of dark magic filling Lord Reinhardt's house, but that's about all I found. I couldn't even confirm if the attacker was a vampire or some other type of human monster, though Levi seems content to take exsanguination as enough proof." She shrugged. "And whoever it was, they did steal one of Lord Reinhardt's arms after losing one of their own."

"Huh. Levi said he got attacked by a one armed guy that same night. Think it's the same person?" Erica didn't even bother replying, just staring at him flatly until he got her point. "Yeah, yeah. Too coincidental for there to be two one-armed madmen who can match Ancient's Armor running around the city. But why steal the arm?"

"That's what I'm trying to figure out. I'll admit that I'm hardly an expert on how monsters work, even if we're assuming undead and vampires, but nothing I know of explains it."

Thinking back on the stories that he'd heard, the kind of campfire tales he and his friends would tell on their hunting trips, Allard found himself inclined to agree. Most of the common tales of monsters would only lead to the conclusion that it stole the arm to eat it, but that wouldn't match up to the apparent state of the rest of the victims, nor the odd coincidence of losing its own arm. And there were the kinds of stories about monsters stealing eyes or tongues, the kinds of body parts that held a particular significance, but not individual arms. Allard did remember a particular story about a necromancer that stitched corpses back together to animate them, but felt it a stretch. He shrugged. "Can vampires replace lost limbs?'

Erica shook her head. "Don't think so. I'll have to look into it, but I don't think vampires should be able to do that kind of thing. Anyway, anything exciting happen for you yesterday? I know you and Levi at least talked about all the murder stuff, but did you find out anything else?"

Allard thought about his discussion with Levi and the book he'd been given, currently set lying open and half read on his nightstand. Nothing in the text had stood out to him. Despite what Levi claimed, it still felt too similar to magic, the supposed tricks and techniques perhaps smaller in scale than a true mage's spells, but no less dramatic. And even though he knew he wasn't supposed to overthink it, he couldn't help but feel like none of it was right for him. Allard could think about himself using magic all he wanted, but it still just didn't feel like something that should be possible for him. "Oh, not much," he eventually said. "Levi just wants me to start learning magic so I can become a true monster hunter."

"Ah. Gotcha. Shouldn't be too much of a problem though, huh? You've been hunting in Thicket Forest for years, so now you're just taking it to the next step, right?"

For as much as they were friends, times like that made Allard hate talking to Erica for how transparent it made him feel. Even though he was clearly worried about something and she was only trying to reassure him, the simple fact that she assumed she knew him so well that she didn't need to ask what was wrong irked him. Smoothing out that annoyance, he opted for one of Levi's half nod, half shrugs. "Maybe. But there's a pretty big difference between deer and monsters. And I just don't know that I'll ever be able to do any sort of magic."

Erica had always had that knack for magic, so trouble with Conviction was something she just couldn't relate to or help with. "Well if you want any help, just let me know. I can at least explain some of the basics to you."

Allard nodded. "Thanks. I might take you up on that once these talks with the Auris Empire are over and we're not as busy."

At this point, they had reached the boundary to the lower district. Simply crossing over the street Riverluck residents called the Main Line brought one from calm and quiet neighborhoods, or rather neighborhoods that were specifically kept calm and quiet for the satisfaction of their residents, into roads bustling with business and chatter and the simple liveliness of daily life. Even though the streets were far wider here beyond the Main Line, they felt narrower because of the crowds filling them, making it impossible to get anywhere without passing within a hairsbreadth of someone else every few steps. Even little more than an hour after dawn, most of the lower district residents had already taken to the streets, starting their business early in the day.

Today, however, things were a little bit different. The streets were certainly still busy, but oftentimes more with the business of setting up stalls and stages for the coming festival. And even as carpenters and enterprising business owners went about putting up their own, filling the air with the sounds of hammering and sawing, just as many were already open. The usual scent of fresh bread from nearby bakeries had been overpowered by the sweet scent of frying dough and hot sugar and the usual cries from hawkers were drowned out by the sounds of fiddles and flutes, musicians playing popular folk songs at the edges of the half-constructed stages. Glad for the change of pace, Allard took a look around himself with a smile. "City people really don't wait around to celebrate, do they?"

Erica laughed, shaking her head with wonder. "I guess not. Though I don't know why you're surprised. This is all we've had for the past three years."

Reminded of the politics behind the celebration, Allard realized there wouldn't be a similar festival held in Regina's Bounty. "Maybe, but I still miss holidays with my family and the gang. I wish they could be here for it."

More than anything else, the biggest difference between their life in River-luck and Regina's Bounty was the fact that he and Erica didn't have a group of friends like their gang back home. Sure, he spent his free time socializing with palace guardsmen, she had her own friends like Viola, and both of them were close with Levi and Adelaide, but it wasn't the same. They'd spent over a decade with Mallory, Nalren, Lalia, Kalan, and Paula, enough time for the roles they'd fall into to feel more natural than anything else. With Erica as the oldest, a full year older than any of the rest of them, back when the naming motif was still 'E' and 'R' instead of 'A' and 'L', she'd fallen into place as the sensible one, along with the more reserved Kalan. That'd made it easy for Allard to take things less seriously, all the more when Nalren and Lalia were there to chide Mallory for his immaturity. Here, with Adelaide as the driving force behind most of their misadventures in the palace, it felt more like when he was looking after Carlin while his parents were away and he had to be more responsible or the house would burn down.

But all of his nostalgic musings were lost on Erica who shot him another pointed stare, suffused with clear disbelief. "Do you really want them here?

Have you forgotten what Mal got us into at the last Midsummer Feast? Or the Hallowed Night the year before? I'm good, thank you very much."

Even remembering how much trouble they'd gotten in, not just on those two occasions either, Allard couldn't help but laugh. Out of all of their friends, Mallory had a strong tendency for scheming. To put it another way, once he got an idea in his head, he set himself to it and dragged the rest of them in with him. Yet despite knowing the consequences, they'd always found it easier to just go along with his ideas instead of arguing, even when it did end in, for instance, the seven of them spending an entire night sleeping in the old oak tree in the town square or washing all the town's dishes for the next month as punishment. Allard flashed Erica a grin as he replied, "Oh come on. Even with Nalren and Lalia on your side, you still got outvoted fair and square. And it was fun, wasn't it?"

The disbelief soured into withering derision. "I still remember how my hands got after all that scrubbing. And of course we got outvoted. You always side with Mal, Kal always sides with you, and Paula won't argue with her brother. And look!" She pointed alternately to the crowds, a nearby park filled with delicate beds of pale blue crocuses, and a wide fountain carved to resemble a griffon, two fiddlers sitting on the edge of its basin as they played. "There's far too many things and too many people for Mal to not get a bad idea. And this time it would probably result in property damage."

Allard could see her point. There was plenty of fuel for the fire, so to speak, and Mal simply wasn't the type to not follow an impulse. But he wasn't going to tell her she was right. Shrugging, he turned his thoughts back to those old holidays back home. For as much as the ones in the city were more extravagant and, quite frankly, interesting, they couldn't match up to the simple nostalgia of what he'd grown up with. "I stand by what I said. I think I'd rather have another dance in the town square with people I know than push my way through a crowd for fancy pastries and silly knickknacks."

A mischievous glimmer entered her eyes and she nudged his shoulder. "Well you only enjoyed those dances because you had an excellent partner."

Allard rolled his eyest. "Yeah, yeah. Lalia is pretty good at dancing, but I think Kal's already got her booked." This earned him a light punch, but Erica laughed nonetheless. Pausing for a moment, he continued somewhat solemnly as he pulled the pair of letters out of his pocket. "Do you know how all of them are?

These have only been for my parents and Carlin, so I mostly only hear about general news back."

Taking her own letters out, Erica flipped through them, showing that while there were a few more than Allard's two, it was still only enough to cover her parents and siblings. "Nope. Last I heard from Paula, Mal had taken it into his head to 'follow in our footsteps' and 'prove to that arrogant knight he chose the wrong guy'. So who knows what's happened since."

All of which sounded about right to Allard. Making a mental note to ask Carlin about them in next week's letter, he nodded. "I hope they're doing well."

Erica's own expression was somewhat withdrawn and wistful when she replied, "Yeah, me too. Maybe we can get some time to go home for a holiday later this year. Like Midsummer Feast or..." Her eyes became distant as she fixed her gaze on a nearby fountain. "Or Enkindling Week."

Enkindling Week was held yearly in late summer, just before Inferns turned to Ventans, in celebration of the victory of the Ember King and the rest of the Champions of the Four Corners over the Dusk Tyrant at the Battle of Ash-star Tomb. As such, the holiday was one of the most important and universally celebrated across the continent aside from the solstice and equinox feasts. But the fact that Erica seemed so hesitant to mention it sparked a flicker of worry in Allard. Brow furrowing, he looked at her askance. "I'm sure we could make it home for Enkindling Week and I bet Adelaide would beg to come with us. What's got you so on edge about it?"

Heading towards the fountain which was carved in the image of the Champions of the Four Corners, she looked up at the statue of the Ember King and frowned. "So you know how this year's the second millennial anniversary of the Battle of Ash-star Tomb?" Allard nodded. "Well, I happened to overhear the king talking to Levi about that. It sounded like the king thinks something's going to happen this year and that the whole vampire thing might be a part of it."

Allard listened as she explained what she heard in the palace chapel. He knew what happened a thousand years ago, when the Dusk Tyrant was revived and shattered the Sunfire Empire, only failing to destroy the world because of the great hero known as the Scalebound. But even knowing that, it felt too convenient to believe that something would happen again on the anniversary. Following Erica's gaze, he looked up at the statue of the Ember King himself, the knight standing stalwart with the holy blade from which his empire took its name raised. "Magic likes round numbers? Is that actually something that makes sense to you, because it sounds like garbage to me."

"I guess you're getting a little lesson on magic after all. Simply put, yes and no. What it comes down to is that magic is fundamentally a force of mystery, of the things that cannot be properly explained by the natural laws of humankind. It's all about meaning and intention."

"But if it's a force of mystery, wouldn't that mean it would happen any other year except the most obvious one?"

"Not exactly. Think of it this way: in the stories that we read and hear, things always happen on significant dates. They always happen after ten or twenty five or a hundred years and so on. And it's because that kind of thing makes more sense to us, speaks more to our spirits or something. So it means far more to us if things happen on those dates because those dates mean more to us. And for something like the two thousandth anniversary of one of the most important events in history, there's an astronomical amount of meaning attached."

Allard sighed. "So you're telling me that something will probably happen this year because the whole world believes that something should happen this year?"

Erica smiled. "You shouldn't be that surprised that belief is so important to magic. Conviction is one of the three pillars of magic after all. But it is another yes and no. Magic is still a force of mystery and works like you'd expect and believe right up until it doesn't. It's less that something will happen this year and more that if something were going to happen in the past thousand years, it would happen this year."

Allard threw his hands up in the air. "So what are we supposed to do? Just wait around until something does happen and a group of heroes saves us? Or should we go find those heroes and prepare in advance? Because that might be a little bit hard since Regina was supposed to have 'traveled to this world from a lost city of crystal' and Zephyros was, if I remember correctly, 'a demonic warrior of the sun who fell from the heavens above to aid in the fight against his mortal enemy'. And even Ignatius and Seras, the two relatively normal ones, were a prince and a veritable saint respectively. Not exactly the easiest things to find."

It felt far easier to think of them as the Crystal Queen and Storm Warlord, the Ember King and River Sage, than as real people who had actually done those things. Historical or not, the heroic quality of their tales made them seem just as inhuman as the statues above them. Erica ran her eyes along each of them in turn. "I assume that by 'we', you mean humanity as a whole and not the two of us? And it's a 'warrior of the morning star', not the sun. Zephyros wasn't a Battlecrow. And I don't know. What do you think we should do? On the scale of humanity, either the people in charge of this kind of thing will do something or they won't. And the Order of the Eagle is supposed to take care of catastrophes like this. And if it's just the two of us, what *can* we do? We're not exactly the most powerful of people. I'm not even entirely sure why we're looking into this vampire thing, Dusk Tyrant or not."

Allard agreed. They weren't the kind of people who could do anything about something like that. Levi and Adelaide maybe, but not the two of them. And they didn't really have a good reason for trying to figure out what was behind the attack on Lord Reinhardt's manor. They'd just fallen into it after Allard heard about it. *You know why you're interested. It's because you want to be the one to fix it. To save the day. To be--*

"If we look into it like this," he said, "we might find something the actual investigators missed and we can send it along to Levi so he can catch the bad guy. As for the other... You're better at magic. *Is* there any sort of preparation the two of us could do, something to help Adelaide's dad and Levi if things do go south?"

Erica reached out, putting her hand on the statue of Seras. "I wonder. I'm not about to recommend that we drop everything to try and become legendary heroes, but like you said with the vampire, if we keep our eyes open and stay on guard, maybe we can spot things before they get too bad. Let Levi know. Send a message to the watchers in the Order."

Allard glanced up at the statue of the Ember King, thinking about what it would be like to wield the holy sword Sunfire. Gesturing with the letters, he stood. "Well we should get these to post, huh?"

Erica slipped her letters back into her pocket. "Yeah. We've wasted enough time as it is."

The two of them started back towards the docks and the Riverluck post office. But before they'd taken more than three steps, Allard frowned as something occurring to him. "Hey, Erica? You know that crystal tree a little ways from Regina's Bounty in Thicket Forest? The one the village myths say is Seras' grave?"

"Yeah?"

Allard closed his eyes, picturing the tree. He didn't know what it was actually made of, but it grew just like any other tree, with water springing up into a pool from beneath its roots and dripping from its branches to form a small brook that joined Seras's Stream nearby. At night, it visibly glowed, the droplets of water catching the starlight so they looked like tiny bits of diamond falling into the pool. The tales told of the kind of magic Seras's grave had and the strange things that would happen if you visited on such and such day or at a specific time of night. "Well, what if it really is Seras's grave? What kind of meaning would that have, two kids from around where the River Sage died working for the descendant of the Storm Warlord and the current wielder of his blade right when the Dusk Tyrant was supposed to come again?"

Erica didn't respond.

Chapter 6

Magiaday: 2nd of Hernus, Year 1980 R.S.

Erica looked over the incantation once more and sighed. The flowing Mystic script seemed to run together, forming a sinuous line of incomprehensible ink, and for as useful as a spell to 'smite thine enemies with fire' seemed, she couldn't get in the mood today. What Allard said that morning kept echoing through her head, ruining her concentration the instant she focused on a word. Erica snapped the tome closed and looked across the study at Adelaide, who was sitting behind her desk, oblivious to the world around her as she stared back and forth between a textbook in her lap and a construction of bronze wire and a clear lattice-stone standing amidst a pile of discarded notes. *Oh how I envy you,* Erica thought. *Able to spend the morning reading in Empire Common.*

Erica rose from her chair and walked to the room's bookshelf. *I think that's quite enough of* Alistair's Elemental Evocations *for today,* she thought as she placed the tome in the first empty space she saw. Drawing her finger along the spines of the books, she stopped at a familiar volume – *Rites of Land and Sky* – and withdrew it. Thumbing through the first few pages, she ambled over towards Adelaide's desk, peering over her shoulder into the softly glowing lattice-stone's depths. "How are things on this front, Addy?"

Adelaide let out a startled yelp and slammed her book shut, dropping it in the process. Erica caught a glimpse of a cover illustrated with the image of a knight fighting a snarling beast before Adelaide pushed it beneath her desk with a foot. Stuttering slightly Adelaide turned to Erica, her face bright red. "D-don't sneak up on me like that, Erica. You'll stop my heart one of these days if you keep doing that." Taking a breath to compose herself, she continued in an even voice. "And things are going as expected. Horribly tedious. Teufel's propulsion problem is just as frustratingly unsolvable today as it was yesterday. It may shock you to know that running comparative benchmark tests of the output of various types of lattice-stones is far from interesting."

Erica nodded with a wry smile on her face. "Uh-huh. That sounds dreadful." Muttering a brief line of Mystic script, she pulled her hand towards herself gently. The book Adelaide shoved away gently glided out from its hiding place beneath the desk and floated before Erica. Adelaide yelped once more and attempted to leap towards the book, tripping over her chair in the process. Erica plucked it from the air and walked around to the front of the desk, looking over its title. "Ah, yes. *An Adventurer's Guide to Monsters for the Scholarly Noble.* I do recall seeing that on the required reading list for both lattice engineers and upcoming princesses. Perfectly in line with your studies, hmm Addy?"

Stumbling to her feet, Adelaide dashed after Erica. She reached for the book, but Erica held it above her head and beyond Adelaide's reach. "Aaah! Give that back Erica!"

Erica looked at the cover once more, eyes narrowing. "Now Adelaide. This new research topic of yours has nothing to do with the vampire, right? Because I know I told you to leave it to Levi and the guard."

Adelaide flinched back as though struck, eyes wide with sheepish guilt thinly veiled as innocence. "N-no. Of course it–"

Not fooled for a second, Erica frowned, leaning down to put her eyes on level with Adelaide's. "Because if Allard and I are going to take you out to the countryside, we'll be going somewhere nice and peaceful with no monsters about. So forget about it."

Just like that, Adelaide's eyes brightened and she broke out into a smile. "You mean you'll do it? You'll find some place for us to go?"

Erica sighed. "Of course. The land around Regina's Bounty isn't very exciting, but Allard and I grew up there. We can find a good campsite." Adelaide laughed and clapped her hands. Erica smirked and set the book down on Adelaide's head, laughing as she fumbled to catch it. "After you finish your work for the meetings."

Gasping in exaggerated betrayal, Adelaide looked up at Erica with a face like that of a wounded dog. "How could you Erica? I thought we were friends. Levi's turned you against me."

Erica chuckled and started back towards her seat, looking down at *Rites of the Land and Sky* once more. "Ah, you see, it's because we're friends that I really must insist. If I disobey you, you'll pout and complain. If I disobey Levi, he'll get all red in the face and start yelling, hands flying all about. Plus I'm really only thinking of his health. Last time he got angry at us, it looked like his head was going to burst."

Adelaide giggled as she walked back towards her desk, but stopped when a knock sounded on the door. Before either of them could respond, it opened slightly to reveal Viola standing in the hallway, looking harried and out of breath. Sparing a moment to wave at Erica, she curtsied to Adelaide and spoke in an uncharacteristically formal voice. "Your Highness, the envoys from the Auris Empire have arrived. Your presence is required in the audience hall."

Without waiting for a response, she darted off. While Erica was glad for the interruption, if only because it meant Adelaide couldn't press the issue of the trip any further, she was suddenly struck with a wave of overwhelming panic, realizing just how unnerving the thought of Auran soldiers in the palace was to her. On the other hand, there was the matter of preparation. Turning to give Adelaide's casual working clothes a once over, she shook her head. "And it looks like I'm saved by duty. Let's go get you presentable."

Nearly an hour later, Erica and Adelaide rushed through the palace halls, at a pace just slow enough to be dignified. Adelaide was dressed in the lightest formal gown she owned, hair still slightly damp from the baths in testament to their haste. And on the other hand, Erica walked next to her in the simple white robes of a mage's apprentice, carrying a handful of notes. "Now let's review one more time. The ambassadors that came in from Perlora last night are...?"

Adelaide let out an irritated breath. "This is the fourth time Erica. Viscount Kasmy of the Twelve and his patron Duke Gerald. Viscount Myron of the Twelve and his son Thanasis."

Erica glanced down at her paper briefly before nodding. "And the envoys from the Auris Empire?"

"General Neriah and Praetor Edan escorting Chancellor Lukas."

The two reached the top of the stairs leading down to the main floor. Before Adelaide could start down them, Erica moved in front of her and looked her straight in the eyes. "I know you haven't been studying current affairs like you should've to prepare for this. So please just let your father handle things today. I'll make sure to put you to work tomorrow so you can handle yourself when the Rugegan envoy arrives."

Adelaide rolled her eyes and let out an irritated huff. "Fine. I still think it's pointless, but if it'll make you happy I'll start studying."

Shooting her an unimpressed stare, Erica responded with a quick rap on her friend's shoulder before turning to walk down the stairs. At their bottom, none of the rushed frenzy seen in the servants upstairs could be found. Those that did travel the main halls moved at the unobtrusive speed of a brisk walk with looks of passive indifference upon their faces. Neither of the two spoke as they walked a familiar path to the audience chamber. The halls were bedecked with the same decorations used a few days ago when the Perloran embassy arrived, but they had been subtly placed in more prominent positions than before. The simple, blue wall hangings embroidered with Tycortua's insignia of three swirled lines, to represent a gust of wind, did little to attract the eye, but provided an omnipresent reminder as to precisely whose palace this was. Erica briefly turned upon passing the door to a parlor, through which an irritated voice could be heard speaking at just below a yell, but continued forward without giving it a second thought. The two stopped before the doors to the audience chamber, waiting for the seneschal to announce Adelaide. The doors themselves were immense things, made of light, white oak imported from the Stormwall foothills in Maripphi and carved with scenes of ancient victories and festive hunts around the edges. But even though these pieces had been done with a master's hand and given countless years to age, they were like an apprentice's first attempt at whittling when compared to the two figures that covered the doors' faces. An image of the Ember King locked in combat with Zephyros, Tycortua's founder, during their famed duel on the Champion's Bridge before the latter swore friendship to the former. It served as both a proud remembrance that Tycortua had once supported the greatest hero of this world and a reminder that they stood equal to that hero and his empire.

As the doors swung open Erica swiftly surveyed the room before her. Though the audience chamber was quite impressive, twin rows of marble pillars flanking the way to the dais upon which two silver thrones sat, Erica paid no attention to it. No matter how marvelous the sight was, she had seen it before. Her focus was upon the room's occupants. King Thierry sat in one of the thrones while the other stood empty, as it had for nearly ten years.

Levi stood to the side of the empty throne, dressed in the full armor of the Crownguard family. He stood with a sort of forced casualness, one hand resting on Whisperwind's hilt, but the nod he gave upon meeting Erica's eyes seemed curt, even for him. To the right of the throne, three men stood in a cluster, two in front whispering to each other while the last stood back, almost looming over the two. The two to the front were dressed in nearly identical robes made from a pale green silk and embroidered with Perlora's flower crest upon the left breast. Erica guessed they were the two Councilors of the Twelve, though she had no way to distinguish between the two of them. The third man, presumably Duke Gerald, turned to look when the doors opened and kept his gaze fixed upon Adelaide as she walked the room's length. He bore himself with a shrewd manner, a look of appraisal in his eyes, and the coat and pants he wore, sturdy despite their obvious luxury, reaffirmed the impression of a man who prized practicality. As for the rest of the occupants, Riverluck's assembled nobility, they were as unimportant to Erica's eyes as the decorations, virtually a permanent fixture in their chairs along the left side of the hall.

Erica stopped upon reaching the dais, bowing once to King Thierry before walking off to the right side of the dais where Allard stood waiting next to another young man. Allard was dressed in his formal uniform as Levi's squire and looked as uncomfortable with the clothes as he was with the sword sheathed at his side. The other man, presumably Myron's son Thanasis, stood with a relaxed and almost arrogant posture. The carmine robes he wore, cut in a style much like Erica's, marked him as a mage of some capability. Noticing Erica's inspection, a roguish smirk split his face. Seeing the apprentice's robes she wore, both eyebrows shot up as an intrigued expression took over. To his side, Erica could see Allard rolling his eyes. Erica took up position next to Allard and lightly jabbed his side with her elbow, meeting his baleful glare with a smug smile.

Following Adelaide's entrance, the room was quiet, save for the low murmur of conversation and the occasional shifting of armor from one of the guards. After a few minutes, the seneschal entered the audience chamber and struck his staff of office against the floor three times. In the ensuing silence, he shouted, "From the Auris Empire: The Honored Chancellor Lukas, escorted by the General Neriah."

Immediately after he was done speaking, the doors swung open with a speed astonishing for their size. A man clad in gold-colored plate mail strode through with brash arrogance, as if he were walking into his own home. His eye quickly took in those present, starting with the guards and working their way up to King Thierry, before settling upon Levi with a look of disdain. On the man's heels another armored figure walked at a measured pace, hand never leaving their sword's hilt. The bronze mask worn over their face made it impossible to discern their expression, but from their armaments Erica guessed the soldier was Praetor Edan. A few seconds later, the Chancellor entered the room at a leisurely stroll. His robes of office, though extravagantly made from crimson silk threaded with gold, seemed to be designed more for comfort than to impress. He carried himself with a casual air, almost slouched over and carrying a small wooden box at his side with all the regard one would give to an umbrella on a sunny day. The three of them stopped in the center of the room, roughly five paces from the king's throne, and Neriah glanced towards Chancellor Lukas. After receiving a nod of acquiescence, he stepped forward and addressed the court, "And so I see the rumors are true, Levi Crownguard. You also wear Ancient's Armor. I have always wanted to fight another with its strength and consider myself blessed to have such an opportunity thrust before me." Neriah paused for a moment, looking towards the impassive faces of those upon the dais. "But that is for another day. We are here to discuss peace after all. King Thierry of Tycortua, I present to you Lukas Erling, the esteemed chancellor of our glorious empire. Second only to the emperor, may the Endless Flame bless his reign, himself."

At this, Lukas stepped forward with a laugh. "Winter winds, Neriah. You have no tact about you, do you? Honestly, it's awfully rude to not address the king first." He bowed toward the dais before continuing. "I beg your forgiveness, Thierry, for my general's poor manners. He gets awfully excited about the smallest of things you see."

Levi's eyes narrowed at Lukas' familiar tone, but relaxed upon a small gesture from the King. Thierry waved a hand before him, as though clearing cobwebs. "There is no cause for worry, Chancellor. I understand that all are here with similar goals in mind, and that none of yours would do anything to jeopardize the negotiations. In any case, it might not be such a bad idea to hold a friendly duel of sorts between the two. A bit of sport to help raise the commoners' spirits." On hearing this, Levi's stoic front briefly broke into his usual beleaguered frown, before he forced himself back into composure. Below, Neriah grinned like a child at the Midwinter Festival. "And in any case, it is we who must apologize to you. We were ill prepared for your arrival this morning and you were forced to wait longer than is proper for a guest of your stature."

Lukas shrugged and gestured vaguely with the box. "Oh, it's hardly a problem. It's not as though this will slow anything down really. Our friends from Rugego seem to be running late, so we couldn't have started today anyways. And as for the matter of preparation, we planned on arriving last night in a bit more of a grand fashion, to make things easier and proper, but we ran into a bit of trouble on the road."

Before Thierry could respond, Levi stepped forward. "Trouble? What kind of trouble was it? Our patrols should keep the roads safe this close to the capital."

A wry smile split Neriah's face as he replied, but none of its humor reached his eyes. "Well it would seem that your patrols were not quite extensive enough. Two nights ago, we were set upon by a group of undead fiends, corpses raised by the darkest of magics. It was hardly more than a nuisance for those of us blessed by the holy light of justice, but it was enough to slow us down a day. And enough to prove the dark forces of evil seek to end the righteous cooperation we seek."

Lukas laughed heartily, patting the knight on his shoulder. "Neriah, you sound preposterous, speaking about justice and evil like that with a straight face. It is as he says though, Thierry. A small enough band of zombies to harry us and do little more. It seemed more like happenstance than anything else, so I don't think we need to worry about an assault in force, but it would probably be a good idea for you to step up your patrols. If more bands like this are roaming about, it will cause trouble for the common folk."

The room was silent as Thierry leaned back in his throne to consider what was said, Levi pulling back alongside him to consult. In the pause given, Erica turned to Allard, whispering in a low voice, "Do you think that has anything to do with the other thing?"

"You don't have to be so vague about it," Allard whispered back. "I can't imagine our friend here knows less of the city's happenings than us. And in any case, it's too hard to tell. Two incidents is hardly enough to form anything more than a coincidence. And we shouldn't worry too much about what's going on outside the city walls anyway. We have more than enough on our hands here."

Erica opened her mouth to respond, but stopped upon seeing the king straighten in his throne. "We appreciate your concern, Chancellor, and we will take your news under advisement. But we will also rule our kingdom as we see fit and would ask you to refrain from speaking so nearly to a command to us again." At Lukas' side, the praetor's grip tightened upon her sword's hilt, but she said nothing. "If there is nothing else then we would have you shown to your quarters. After you have settled in, we can continue to exchange pleasantries over lunch."

Lukas nodded. "A good idea. It's been quite the trek from Dawnbreak." Looking at the box in his hand as though just remembering it then, he held it up towards the king. "Though I suppose it would be rather silly of me to bring this the whole way here without giving it to you. A gift from our emperor, may his reign continue to provide my pay, to show our sincerity. Nothing more than a trinket, but formalities must be followed, yes?" Lukas handed the box over to the praetor who approached the dais. Once she reached the bottom step, Levi walked forward to receive it, stepping back once it was in hand. "With that, we'll be off then."

The chancellor started towards the door with something of a spring in his step, completely ignoring the Perlorans and lesser Riverluck nobility. For Neriah's part, the general merely raised a hand in salute to Levi before turning and following, Edan close on his heels. After the doors swung shut with a thunderous boom, Thierry turned to address the Perloran councilors. "Shall we confer until lunch then, my lords? While little of consequence happened, it would be best to begin forming the Western Alliance's position. The chancellor seems the type of man to cut to the core of matters without warning before slipping back into frivolity."

The councilors exchanged glances, a moment of irritation passing between them before they nodded their assent and started towards the door at a pace slow enough for the king and Adelaide to catch up. Levi walked over to where Allard and Erica were standing, greeting both of them in turn. "Sir Allard, Miss Greenmaiden. The two of you are dismissed for the afternoon. Lady Adelaide and I will be too busy to provide tasks for you in any case." Looking at Allard with a sly smile, he held out the Auris Empire's gift. "Though perhaps you would be able to deliver this to Estelle's Office for me? I heard you rather enjoy the trip."

Allard took the package with a sigh. "I wish you wouldn't make fun of me like that. It's hard to retort to someone who's in charge of you."

The two of them started towards the door, chattering amicably. Erica moved to follow them, but stopped when Thanasis placed a hand on her sleeve. He bowed his head in apology before speaking, his tone astonishingly polite despite his earlier bravado. "If you would excuse me, miss? I notice you also wear the robes of a mage. Though I must attend to my father presently, I would be interested in discussing the art with you, if you find that acceptable. I know the Tycortuan and Perloran schools of sorcery both descend from the philosophy of scholarly magic established in the universities at High Worldheart, but I am curious as to the differences."

Erica nodded back with a smile. "My name is Erica. Erica Greenmaiden after the position I seek. And I don't see why not. There's hardly anyone to talk to about magic here anyway. None of my friends know the practice and the guild mages in the city tend to stay away from the palace."

Thanasis laughed. "You'll find guild mages are like that anywhere you go. A little bit of power and they feel like they deserve to run the world." He bowed once before starting towards the door. "In that case, I shall speak with you to set a date tomorrow, Miss Erica."

Watching him go, Erica frowned, feeling uncertain. Even the exciting thought of conversing with a peer about magic could do little to shake the sudden doubt that had taken her. Put simply, the Aurans had been nothing like what she'd expected. Or rather, Lukas had been nothing like what she'd expected. Neriah carried himself with all the self-righteous arrogance the Auris Empire was known for, but the chancellor's casual apathy was more disconcerting. There was something about him that just felt wrong, a strangely sharp cast to his eyes she'd noticed as he passed. *I thought the Aurans would be up to something, but not like this. They're supposed to be straightforward, not schemers.*

Realizing she'd get herself nowhere spinning her thoughts in circles, Erica shook her head and set her doubts aside for later, hopefully when she could discuss with Levi or Adelaide. Looking back at the throne, she let one more thought echo in her head before setting off after her friends. *And in any case, we've done nothing to antagonize them. Why would they be scheming against us in the first place?*

Chapter 7

Magiaday: 2nd of Hernus, Year 1980 R.S.

"**S**o? What do you think about the Aurans? Say what you will about their arrogance, at least their armor is stylish."

Allard lowered his combat manual and fixed Viola with a level stare. Since Adelaide and Levi left for lunch, he and Erica had tried to find a quiet place to weather the afternoon. But even with the dignitaries and nobles safely out of sight, the palace halls and rooms surged with activity as Estelle directed the staff to prepare things for the king's guests. So with no other alternative, they fled to the safety of Adelaide's study, aware she'd ordered the cleaning staff to leave her wing of the palace alone whenever possible. And yet despite this command, and a second order specific to the person in question, Viola followed the two of them and plopped into Levi's chair the moment she entered the room. For the past hour, she'd made no pretense of working, merely chatting with Erica while Allard tried to wrap his head around spell-sword techniques. Tried and failed, largely. "Does it matter if their armor's stylish? I think most soldiers care more about coverage."

Both heads turned his way, fixing him with a pair of inscrutable gazes. Viola smiled as she replied, "But that's the best part! The way the brass plates shine with bronze mail cascading between them... Armor's only good for looks anyway. Like Phlox says, 'More heroes and knights die to a dagger in their bedroom than on the field of battle.'"

While Allard tried to place the name of the unfamiliar maid, Erica shot her friend a sidelong glance, deliberately shutting her book of choice and stowing it in her bag. "Calm down, Vi. If Neriah heard you talking like that, he might think you were threatening him."

"Ugh. Don't remind me. Impenetrable and ubiquitous; that armor's not stylish at all. At least Levi has the grace to keep his set of Ancient's Armor in line with the chivalric romances. Shining and blue in his kingdom's colors, not a gaudy, golden spectacle."

The old tales of Ancient's Armor sprang to Allard's head, most notably their number. Of the seven suits, two were lost to history, two were lost when the Sunfire Empire fell, two were always a mystery, and the last was the Crownguard plate. Which begged the question, "Where did the Auris Empire get Neriah's armor anyway?"

Erica rolled her eyes. "Of all the times for Addy to not be here. Do you really not know, Al? I thought that kind of story was up your alley."

Allard met this with a scoff. "I'm talking about history, Erica, not myth and legend. I can tell you about how the Flame-speaker and the Knight of Gold-fire first took the throne, but not how she spoke with the Endless Flame or where he got his armor."

Viola rose from her seat and started rummaging through Adelaide's desk, eventually removing a box of tea leaves from behind a spool of bronze wiring. "That's great, but why do we care about either? Their religion's as shaky as the historical justification they give for their conquest."

When she saw the maid blatantly stealing from Adelaide, Erica shot her a level stare. But Viola only took out another tea cup, setting it on the desk with a deliberate clack. Shaking her head, Erica continued, "But it is about their conquests, isn't it? The plate of light is one of the reasons their army is as indomitable as it is. We're the only country that can match its power."

Allard shrugged. "Well, yeah. But we still have the advantage over them thanks to the Royal Griffon Corp. They don't have anything to rival our flight."

Spinning away from her tea preparations with eyes glimmering, Viola replied, "Do you think that's what this is all about? A ploy to get a clutch of eggs from one of the aeries?"

Erica frowned. "What? The talks or the assassin?"

"Either. Both. They haven't been able to make any headway against the Ain-griyans thanks to the Pegasean Hussars, right? And the only other aerial soldiers are the Lugheri Dragoons, but they're as likely to give up a dracoswallow as we are a griffon."

As she finished speaking, Viola picked up the tea cups and handed one to Erica. She locked eyes with Allard as she sat and took a sip with a smug grin, but he was too distracted to notice the slight. Hearing the maid mention the Pegasean Hussars reminded him of something that bothered him, but he'd never had occasion to think about. The war between the Auris Empire and Montiamon had lasted as long as it did because of Aingriya's support. Neither country alone could match the empire's might, and even together they couldn't manage an offensive, but their defense was impenetrable. With two fronts, the Aurans were forced to split their forces and suffer a delay in communication. The Pegasean Hussars circumvented such delay, flying between the two nations over any blockade the Aurans could manage. And that was without mentioning the guerilla tactics the Aingriyans used to harry any invasion into their mountainous lands. But even with all the tactical advantage behind the alliance, that didn't answer one question. "Why did the Aingriyans ally with Montimaon anyway? They don't have any stake in a war against the empire, do they?"

The two allied countries were separated by a stretch of Auran land. They had no shared trade routes, no common heritage, no prior grudge against the empire. In point of fact, their last attempt at an alliance ended in disaster, with Montiamon ostracized by the rest of the continent's nations. And yet for all of these thoughts running through Allard's head, Erica simply shrugged as if it were the most obvious thing in the world. "Probably because they thought war was inevitable. People have been trying to conquer Aingriya since the fall of the Sunfire Empire." She shook her head. "It's not even the first time the Auris Empire tried."

"No, that's not what I mean," Allard replied. Then he nodded in concession. "Well, it is a good point, but I was talking about the fact that they're friendly at all. I would've thought they'd hate each other after what happened with Sanborn and Ivalyn."

Viola leaned forward in her seat, spilling tea as she shouted a reply. "No, no, no! That's part of what makes the story so great! Even after everything Chephirah Camdyn did for her friend, Ivalyn had to stay in Rangeshadow. Since it was a political marriage, it would've meant war for her to return home." She smiled dreamily and continued, "It's tragic, but the dedication she bore for the protection of her country is inspiring."

Erica sighed. "I think we've lost track of the conversation "

"But Sanborn and Ivalyn *is* about the Aurans, isn't it?" Unconvinced, Erica shot Viola a flat stare. Yet the maid was undaunted by her friend's skepticism and laughed as she continued, "Well it is! But if that's not good enough for you, then we can go back to what Allard said, or at least implied, when he brought up the Griffon Corps: what do we have that the Aurans want? It's not people, since their army is larger than ours. It isn't the Crownguard plate since they have Neriah's armor. It can't even be port access since they conquered Port Daystar years ago."

Though she was ostensibly on his side, Allard still felt put off by Viola's support. It felt less like support and more like sacrifice. Shrugging off his unease, he replied, "Sure. Right. Which brings me back to my initial question: where did they get Neriah's plate?" He paused, gesturing to Viola. "Did they steal it from someone like she suggested with the griffon eggs?"

Viola let out a triumphant laugh. "It just makes sense! They conquer and steal all in the name of holy orders. It's not like they could've just made a set of Ancients' Armor and they don't grow on trees."

Erica shot her a wry smile. "Oh yeah? But don't those 'holy orders' matter? Justified or not, that is why they declared war on Montiamon."

Viola started to reply, mostly bluster going by her expression, but Allard cut her off, brow furrowed in thought. "That reminds me: the Aurans claim General Cyrus was righteous and virtuous and that's why the supposed demon assassin killed him, but can we trust their opinion? If the other general we've met is any indication, I don't know that I believe them."

Erica nodded. "I think I agree. I certainly wouldn't say any of them deserve to die, but I didn't like any of the Auran envoys. Neriah seems like a self-righteous zealot, Edan all but his shadow, and Chancellor Lukas..."

Remembering the oddly sharp cast to the chancellor's eyes, his irises a brown that almost looked madder red beneath his auburn hair and the pupils narrow like a marksman's, Allard shuddered. "Yeah. There's something strange about him. I can't put my finger on it, but... What does he even do as a chancellor anyway? I thought the *Empire* was ruled by an emperor."

Letting out an irritated breath, Viola replied as if by rote. "The chancellors are supposed to act as intermediaries between regional governors and the emperor, or empress as the case may be. Just like how the generals ostensibly enforce his command among the army. These days they do seem to rule though, since nobody's heard from the current emperor since he was crowned." She let out a wry laugh. "Seras's Stars, nobody even knows who he is."

Exchanging a glance with Allard, Erica frowned. "Why do you know so much about the structure of the Auran government?"

Viola's mood soured further and she took a deep gulp of tea, replying over the lip of the tea cup when she was finished. "Olivia went to Pazyerra, Phlox went to Perlora, and Marisol went to Viemer. Estelle's been holding me in reserve in case we get an embassy in Dawnbreak. I learned about the current notable figures."

Though aware Viola's training under Estelle extended far beyond her duties as a maid, Allard hadn't realized it included higher education. Neither had he known just how many maids like her Estelle had trained. Disturbed at the idea of four Viola's, he pushed the thought out of mind. "So what did you learn about Chancellor Lukas then? Is there anything suspicious about him?"

Viola let out a harsh laugh. "Ha! Everything about him's suspicious. From what Tycortua's been able to learn, he appeared out of nowhere some three years ago. He barely leaves his estate and keeps secretive company. Quite frankly, we aren't even sure he's Auran."

Allard's eyes widened. "Three years ago? And nobody brought that up earlier? Seras's Stars, there's no way it's coincidence that he appeared right around when General Cyrus was killed."

Viola shook her head. "It's been noted. By the Auran Inquisition themselves. Yet he still has not only the Emperor's trust, but General Neriah's."

Allard furrowed his brow in thought. "Then is he here as a representative because the Emperor trusts him? Or because of his diplomatic skill?"

Erica chimed in at this, gesturing to Viola with her tea cup. "Or because the Emperor *doesn't* trust him as much as we thought? If the chancellors have as much influence as Vi says, I'd think you would want to keep the ones you can count on in the capital. To consolidate power."

Allard started to respond, but a knock at the door interrupted him. He exchanged a glance with Erica, and watched as Viola ducked behind Adelaide's desk, before answering. One of the palace footmen stood on the other side, offering a small bow when he saw Allard. "Mister Fortunata. If you would come with me, Sir Crownguard has another task for you." Erica stood, ready to follow, but the footman raised a hand to forestall her. "You may stay, Miss Greenmaiden. Her Highness shall return shortly."

With a brief wave to Erica, Allard slipped out of the study and followed the footman. As they made their way through the palace halls, he regarded the servant with a wary eye. Viola's mention of her peers set his nerves on edge, Estelle training footmen as well as maids. He had no way of knowing if his guide was one of the castellan's students, and no reason to fear even if he was, but it was a disconcerting thought nonetheless. *I'd guess* those *servants will have more on their plate with the Aurans here. I just hope they don't have to actually do anything.* As he thought about it, Allard found his mind drifting to another eerie conclusion. *But other countries have 'maids' and 'footmen' as well. So far I've assumed this vampire is either an independent monster or some necromancer's servant, but what if it is from Montiamon like the Aurans say? Or another country?*

For as much as stories liked to make a big deal about assassins, they were rarely used in practice, at least on a national level. Quite simply, they were viewed as a distasteful means that no ruler would ever admit to using or even possessing. But at the same time, every nation assumed the others had them, simply as a matter of safety. Which left nothing more than rumors and ghost stories, like the tales that a rash of illnesses and hunting accidents among the more extreme southern nobility from around twenty years ago were all connected by a single, elusive figure – one whose identity changed with every telling. So the better question than whether or not a nation would condone the presence of a vampire was the question of whether or not they would willingly resort to murder to achieve their goals. Allard frowned. *I don't want to say anything that might imply the Aurans are right, but would Montiamon use assassins, vampiric or human?*

He found himself wishing he could discuss that question with Adelaide, or at least Erica. Loath as he was to admit it, he knew very little of Montiamon's history beyond the story of Sanborn and Ivalyn and a handful of older chivalric romances. There seemed to be little else he needed to know, with their monarchy still languishing under the shadow of an evil king. Allard knew nothing of the current king – King Lambert, a rather young ruler only a few years older than Levi – but if he was of Evil King Sanborn's bloodline, that seemed to be all he needed to know. He might not be bad enough for a hero like Chephirah Camdyn to take notice, but if he were truly a just man, Allard figured he would've heard something. *And even decent rulers can be tempted to the practical solution when their country is on the line.*

Before he could consider the matter further, the footman tapped his shoulder with a soft cough. Snapped from his reverse, Allard realized he could hear conversation from around the corner ahead of him. A few steps later, he found himself facing a familiar collection of dignitaries. Levi and Adelaide stood on one side of the hall across from Viscount Myron and Thanasis, both duos accompanied by a scattering of Riverluck nobles. And Neriah and Edan stood between the two groups, the general glancing back and forth between them with a scowl on his face. The footman bowed to Levi as he approached. "Sir. Your squire, as requested."

"Thank you, Mister Lécuyer. You may go." The knight turned to Allard, gesturing to the Aurans as he continued. "General Neriah has expressed his interest in inspecting the barracks, to ensure the soldiers of the chancellor's honor guard received proper accommodations. If you would escort him and the praetor, Sir Allard?"

Neriah let out a harsh laugh. "Ha! 'Proper accommodations'. There can be no consideration of propriety when you look at us like thieves in the night. If you visited us at Dawnbreak, we would teach you the meaning of hospitality with all the magnanimity of the Endless Flame."

Levi nodded, eyes widened slightly as if to say 'just so'. Allard bowed, suppressing a frown of discomfort. "Of course, sir. It would be my pleasure."

He started down the hallway, but Adelaide stopped him before he reached the Aurans. "Come back to the study when you're down, Al. I have something to talk about with you and Erica."

With that, Levi took her by the shoulder and gently guided her in the other direction. The rest of the nobles filtered out after them, though only Thanasis bothered to acknowledge Allard. In short time, he was left alone with the Aurans, both soldiers staring impassively at him. After a few seconds Allard steeled himself, slipping past them. "Right. If you would come this way."

The three continued silently until they exited into the gardens. As soon as they were outside, Edan cast a glance back at the palace. "Your princess is awfully glib, is she not?"

Allard let out a snort of laughter. "Yeah, she..." Then he remembered who he was talking to and swallowed his words, coughing once before continuing. "Begging your pardon, madam. I mean to say she is known for her carefree attitude."

Neriah frowned at the praetor. "Silence, Edan. It is not our place to judge the prudence of Zephyros' heirs. And you saw as well as I: she comported herself with dignity in the meeting." He turned to Allard, nodding in concession. "Forgive my subordinate, squire. She little understands the relationship between retainer and liege. Particularly a liege so young. Such friendship is understandable."

The general's familiarity set Allard on edge. After witnessing his bloodthirsty arrogance upon greeting Levi, any courtesy felt forced and artificial. "Ah. Right. Are you friends with the chancellor then?"

"Hmm. Not so. I ill-like that stranger, but I trust his skill and intellect. Even if he refuses to explain the reason behind his actions, like sending one of my fellow generals on a diplomatic mission to Naktikos, I know his intentions are directed towards the protection of the emperor, may the Endless Flame bless his reign." His frown deepened, eyes growing distant as he continued. "I suppose I meant to say I admire your princess' exuberance insofar as I wish the same for my own emperor, may the Endless Flame bless his reign. I know of the burdens placed upon him and all he has sacrificed."

Edan clicked her tongue. "Pah. Lukas is an insufferable man, if you will excuse my temerity, General. So intoxicated with his own wiles he refuses to lift a finger to work himself. Taking your example, the order he gave to General Verena was nothing more than an excuse to remove one of his greatest critics from the country."

"Perhaps." Neriah shot her a sidelong glance before turning to Allard. "And what of you, squire to Crownguard? I imagine I see a kindred spirit in you, but that may be nothing more than words of wistful nostalgia."

Allard's unease grew further still. "A kindred spirit? What do you mean? I'm no battle leader or even a real soldier. I can barely hold my own with a sword."

"But your princess commands your absolute loyalty, does she not? I sense there is little you would not do for her."

Allard let out a harsh laugh. "Ha. I don't know about absolute loyalty. I'd really rather she just stayed safe without my help."

Neriah nodded in understanding, a flash of something similar to Levi's usual expression running across his face. "Let us say that much is true for now. Then why do you serve her? When I asked Crownguard of you, curious about his retinue, he told me you were a mere villager a scant few years ago. Why then do you serve?"

"Well I do like Adelaide – I mean Her Highness." Allard paused, finding it hard to actually speak his next thoughts aloud. "But I guess it's because I always liked the old stories of knights. This seemed like my chance to be something like them."

"And what is it you admire about those knights?"

Their devotion to their oaths and righteousness. Allard couldn't bring himself to say it, knowing what Neriah would say. Knowing he would claim little distinction between his absolute loyalty and that devotion. Instead, he let out a harsh laugh and changed the subject. "Doesn't matter. I don't think I could be a knight like that anyway. I already told you I'm not a swordsman and a bow is hardly a knightly weapon."

"Perhaps you're no swordsman now, but I sense you have the potential. You already move well and have keen eyes." He gestured at Allard's feet and the squire realized he'd been unconsciously walking in a hunter's stalk the whole time. "Your greatest failing is that Crownguard is your blademaster. With a proper teacher, you could be that kind of swordsman."

Allard glared at him. "Ha. And I suppose you're that teacher?"

Neriah shook his head. "Hardly. I'm no more a teacher than Crownguard. And my style would suit you worse than his. I'm a soldier and he a monster hunter. If you truly admire the knights of chivalric romances, you need a champion."

"A champion? Do you mean one of the winners of the Nyphean Tournaments of the Council? Or the grand duelist of the Maripphi circuit?"

At this, Neriah let out a sigh, fixing Allard with a put upon gaze. "Come now, squire, there's no need to play coy. I'm talking about those knights you admire so much. A champion who can shine like an ember of the Endless Flame's light."

Loath as he was to admit it, Allard did understand what Neriah meant. Not necessarily a hero like the Ember King, though he certainly fit both definitions, but a swordsman who approached their duty with devotion. The likes of the Saint of Swords or the Spell-blade of Maripphi, who took their peoples' burdens as their own and fought for them, not for themselves. As Neriah admitted, he was a soldier, someone who fought for his nation and emperor. And as much as Allard liked Levi, he couldn't deny that the knight fought for the sake of a single person's safety, no more or less. *Absolute loyalty, huh?* Allard shook his head, irritated that he found himself agreeing with the Auran. *I guess it's still loyalty no matter if it's a person, an oath, or an ideal you're loyal to.*

Apparently content that he'd given Allard something to think about, Neriah remained silent and left him to his contemplation for the rest of the trip. When they did arrive at the barracks, Allard found himself with little to do but follow behind the general as he conversed with his troops, asking about their accommodations and any issues that had come up. The Auran honor guard did draw Allard's attention, however. It was no large contingent, each nation's envoy allowed twenty troops within the palace grounds with the rest of their escort kept camped outside the northern walls of Riverluck, but a few of their number stood out. While the majority of the honor guard consisted of legionnaires with arms and armor similar to Edan's, only lacking the praetorian mask, four wore distinct clerical robes, dyed crimson save for a strip of black around the hems, and carried a brass censer over their shoulders in lieu of a lance. Though he'd never seen one in person, Allard had heard enough stories to know what an Auran inquisitor was supposed to look like.

The thought of heretic-hunters prowling around Tycortua disturbed Allard. Not only were they infamous for their zeal, even among the Aurans, but they weren't exactly numerous enough that every army could field one. The presence of four at once was all but unprecedented. They didn't look particularly threatening as he passed them, not too different from Tycortua's own battle clerics, but the way their eyes lingered on him kept the stories of their talents at the front of his mind. They were not infamous for their martial ability, after all, but their mystical might. *Are they here because the Aurans are* that *worried about this vampire,? Or is it some kind of plot?* He found his thoughts turning back to Viola's talk of schemes and griffon eggs. *But the inquisitors aren't spies, are they?*

When they reached the end of the hall, Neriah nodded in satisfaction. "This will do for the moment, squire, though it cannot match the standard of our own barracks. You may inform Crownguard of as much." Allard bowed and turned to leave, but Neriah stopped him with a hand on his shoulder. "And there is one other thing I would have you tell Crownguard. Though no one in Tycortua seems to think much of the Montian demon's attack on your Lord Reinhardt, it rarely leaves my mind. I mean to see that fiend dead for its murder of my fellow general, with or without Crownguard's help."

Allard frowned. "Is that what you wanted me to tell him?"

"Far from it." A wolfish grin crossed Neriah's face. "Even if he does not take this threat seriously, I would ask that you give him a warning: the fiend comes with the fog. He would do well to remember that."

With that, the general released Allard and stepped aside to speak with one of the inquisitors. Neriah's parting words disturbed him, but Allard was simply relieved to be dismissed. The moment he stepped out into the afternoon sunlight, and away from the inquisitors' prying eyes, it was almost like a weight lifted from his back. Unable to help himself, he ran back for Adelaide's study, eager to share the news and get a more knowledgeable perspective on the heretic hunters' presence. But as he stepped into the palace, one lingering thought tickled at the back of his mind and he turned to survey the Nobles' District below. *I wonder: was there fog on the night of Lord Reinhardt's death?*

Chapter 8

Magiaday: 2nd of Hernus, Year 1980 R.S.

"Alright, Erica. Come help me find something."

Erica barely had time to register Adelaide's presence before the princess swept past her and started rummaging through the books on her shelf. Setting aside the tea set she was in the process of cleaning, Viola having conveniently disappeared when she heard Adelaide was returning, Erica followed with a frown. "What's wrong? Is it something that Perlorans said?"

Adelaide scoffed. "Hardly. Didn't I already tell you? These talks are nothing but a sham. They spent the whole meeting explaining how their naval forces are tied up fighting pirates in the Sea Scar, even after the Riptide Captain's personal crusade, and too much of their trade income is spent on infrastructural and agricultural reforms to provide any supplies should the Aurans declare war on the Western Alliance. All excuses so they can leave the difficult work in our hands."

"And what about the Rugegans? Their borders are secure, so they should be able to offer military support if necessary, right?"

Waving off Erica's words, Adelaide turned back to the bookshelf and replied offhand as she tossed aside unwanted texts. "Sure, if military support mattered. I said the Perlorans were giving excuses, right? When the Rugegans show up, I'm sure they'll have their own story to spin too."

"Then what's so important?" Erica asked as she straightened up the discarded books. Then, seeing a cover illustrated with the Champions of the Four Corners among the stack, she shot Adelaide a sidelong stare and continued. "And why are you looking at children's stories?"

Suspicious of the timing of the princess' sudden interest in ancient lore, Erica tried to turn her gaze stern. But Adelaide remained undaunted, snatching the volume back from Erica. "Because it *is* important, thank you very much. This morning I was in my father's office looking..." She trailed off, breaking eye contact before continuing. "Never mind why I was in my father's office. But I found a letter from the Order of the Eagle to my father asking him to keep an eye out for any activity that calls to mind the Dusk Tyrant. And beneath it was a missive to Estelle, ordering her to consult with Levi on new security measures."

The latter came as no surprise to Erica after what she overheard in the chapel, even less of a surprise than Adelaide stumbling upon that information herself, but the former flooded her. She'd heard of the famed order of course, its free-knights and free-mages called the Watchers at Midnight for their sworn duty to ensure no calamity like that brought by the Dusk Tyrant could come again, but she never imagined them as anything other than a distant power. Until that moment, she'd always felt they were more like a modern version of the heroes from the chivalric romances Allard and Viola liked; knights and mages no more real than a dream who traveled strange other-worlds and fought monsters that didn't exist outside of nightmares. She gaped, discarded tomes forgotten. "The Order of the Eagle? Do you know if they're sending someone here? Or did they only want to open communications?"

Adelaide smiled triumphantly, knowing she'd managed to hook Erica. "The letter didn't mention any delegation, but who knows. It was signed by Grand-master Fionn himself." She stood, posing with one hand on her chest as she continued. "So there you have it. It's my responsibility to study the Order's mission so I can prepare for further contact."

The sheer temerity of the claim snapped Erica back to reality. "Oh yeah? Responsibility, huh? And just how does the talks with the Aurans relate to the Order?"

At this, Adelaide withdrew *An Adventurer's Guide to Monsters for the Scholarly Noble* from her dress pocket and thrust it open towards Erica. "Vampires of course! I pay attention, I'll have you know. If undead are involved, it's no stretch to think the Dusk Tyrant is too, right? He was raised as a death knight when he destroyed the Sunfire Empire, after all."

Erica accepted the book with a raised eyebrow and scanned the page it was open to, the entry on vampires. Much to her surprise, it did a better job of explaining the creatures than she expected from the overwrought title, even the illustration a detailed sketch instead of a dramatized painting. As she flipped through the next few pages, she found similar entries on the likes of liches, reapers, and death knights, as clear a sign as any what put the idea in the princess's head. Snapping the book shut, Erica let out a heavy sigh. "Yes, that's true, but that's all he was. He took his vengeance but had little other motivation or intelligence and certainly not enough necromantic ability to control a vampire. Even if he's revived again, I doubt it will be as more than a shadow of what he once was. Wherever this vampire comes from, it isn't the Dusk Tyrant."

Adelaide scowled. "But what about the numerological theory of magic? A third time should matter far more for something like resurrection. Both relate to the domain of the soul."

"That's not how magic works. Try to force meaning and you'll lose it." Realizing she stood no chance arguing on her own terms, Erica picked up the story on the Champions. "And if you're talking about monsters and the Dusk Tyrant, how do you explain the Dusk Reaver? Whatever it was, it certainly wasn't undead."

Erica flipped to the illustration of the Ember King's first true opponent as Adelaide grumbled and wracked her brain for a reply. The picture was more stylized than those drawn by the so-called Desert Lion who wrote Adelaide's book, but it depicted a gangly, shadowy figure, only vaguely humanoid in outline. Nowhere close enough to any living thing Erica had heard of to represent one necromantically raised in body or spirit. Taking the book and staring at it with a furrowed brow, Adelaide replied. "Well, that's an entirely different—"

A quick knock at the door interrupted her. Before either girl could respond, it opened and Allard slipped inside. "Erica, did you know there are inquisitors—"

Adelaide ran to his side and forced a book into his hand. "Al! Quick! What do vampires have in common with the Dusk Reaver?"

Allard looked back and forth between his two friends in confusion. "Is this some kind of riddle or a genuine question?"

Erica glared at the princess. "Genuine. Addy's taken it to head that whoever murdered Lord Reinhardt has something to do with the Dusk Tyrant."

"Well if it's not pressing then, about the Auran Inquisitors..."

As he trailed off, Adelaide grabbed his hand and dragged him towards the room's chairs, rolling her eyes as she responded. "Let them do as they will. They're part of the honor guard, so until they try anything we have to tolerate their presence. And my father's hospitable, not naive. He has eyes on them, so he'll know the second they do try anything and put a stop to it. Now, will you answer my question?"

Despite Adelaide's confidence, Erica found herself less than reassured. The Auran inquisitors did not, as a general rule, travel outside the borders of the empire. Their purpose lay in rooting out corruption, at least by the standards of the Auran faith, within their citizenry. Moreover, she'd read about the particular style of magic they practiced when studying the schools of Inception native to Tycortua. While Tycortua had the Truthspeakers, law mages who could make one's word binding, the Auran Inquisitors were more truth finders. Their magic did not so much ensure one's faithfulness as drag the truth out by force. *If they really mean to try something, I'd be willing to bet they'll start by proving we're spying on them.*

Yet Allard seemed convinced, taking a seat across from Adelaide with a shrug. "I'm afraid I can't really tell you much about the Dusk Reaver. For as important as it was in setting the Ember King on his journey, that's all it really did. I mean, its most famous accomplishment is dying, so... But it's usually called some kind of monster of darkness, so I doubt it was undead. Maybe demonic, but that's just a guess at best."

With little support from Allard, Adelaide sank into her chair. "But necromancy and death knights..."

Shaking her head, Erica started putting books away. "Exactly, Addy. Necromancy. If the Dusk Tyrant does return, it will be because someone brought him back. Someone around today. So stop looking for ghosts in the past."

Allard nodded. "Yeah. And from what the stories say about the Dusk Tyrant, he wasn't the kind of person to use assassins. He challenged enemies directly, whether in a duel or with his army."

Withering further, Adelaide said, "Fine. I'll concede the point that maybe the Dusk Tyrant isn't behind this vampire." She paused and leaned forward with a bright smile as she continued. "But that doesn't mean I shouldn't study the stories. Everything you just told me says there is still someone who's a threat, just whoever's trying to revive the Dusk Tyrant. That's who the Order of the Eagle wants my father to find."

"The Order of the Eagle? You didn't tell me the Watchers were involved, Erica."

Erica stifled a sigh. She knew that she lost Allard with that. Just as well as Adelaide knew what she was doing when she mentioned the Order. But another knock sounded as she tried to think up a reply and Levi leaned in through the doorway. "May I speak with you for a moment, Miss Greenmaiden?"

Erica shot a questioning glance back at Allard who simply shrugged. Following Levi out into the hall, she said, "I was wondering where you went off to. I thought you'd come back with Addy."

The knight waved off her question and ambled back the way he'd come with a noncommittal noise. "Mm. There were some small matters I was required to attend to. One such being the matter I wished to speak with you about." Erica started to protest, but Levi raised a hand to forestall her. "And I will not hear you speak of a lack of suitability. You are directly involved already. You will recall our investigation of the late Lord Reinhardt's manor, yes? It would seem Chancellor Lukas also took an interest."

Though she disliked the idea of meeting the chancellor again, Erica understood and nodded. "Oh. I can see how I might be helpful then. Do you need me to explain what we found again?"

"Not quite. He requested leave to allow his experts to examine the manor themselves, in case they might discover something we missed."

Allard's question, unfortunately drowned out by Adelaide's half-baked theories, rang in Erica's head. "The inquisitors, huh?"

This earned her a sidelong glance. "Hm. Sir Allard told you, I suppose? But just so. And with that in mind, I wished to make certain we found nothing that would best be left undiscovered."

Erica ran through the previous day's work in her head again and again, trying to find anything suspicious in what she'd found. Nothing stood out to her of course, but with everything she'd heard of the Inquisitors she couldn't be certain. By all accounts, they still hadn't explained why they blamed Montiamon for the vampire's last assumed attack beyond vague accusations of corruption and darkness. An overt curse seemed like a far more substantial excuse. "Would the Aurans use something from that kind of investigation to frame us? I thought they claimed it was the same thing that killed their General Cyrus. And they already blamed that on Montiamon."

"Perhaps. Perhaps not. I do not find myself in a trusting mood when inquisitors are involved, however." His expression cleared and he continued in a lighter tone. "So? Is there anything I should know? Or that they should not, rather?"

Less than certain, Erica shook her head. "I don't think so. Though I'll admit I have no idea what might set the inquisitors off."

"Hmm. Understood. I will relay that on to His Majesty," Levi said with a nod. They walked in silence for a few seconds until Levi glanced back over his shoulder. "And as for Lady Adelaide? Is she causing any trouble?"

Erica let out a harsh laugh. "Ha. How recently do you mean?" Levi shot her a level stare. "Yeah, yeah. She's still been pestering me about that camping trip, but otherwise nothing more than usual."

By that point they reached the intersection leading into the central wing of the palace and Levi drew to a stop. He turned and started saying a quick farewell, but Erica wasn't listening. Catching sight of one of the banners emblazoned with Tycortua's crest, the crest of the Storm Warlord, she reconsidered Adelaide's recent outburst and just who she was talking to. *Levi did keep a level head when talking to Addy's dad about the same thing.* Though the knight was still speaking, Erica had no intention of letting him go and interjected, "Actually, now that I think about it, there is something new that's come up. Apparently her newest scheme to avoid work is to blame Lord Reinhardt's murder on the Dusk Tyrant."

Levi frowned, grumbling with dissatisfaction. "So she found out then. I suppose it cannot be helped. I imagine you will have a difficult time keeping her on task in the coming days." He paused and glanced at Erica, then held up a hand to reassure her as he continued. "But there should be little for you to concern yourself with. To explain, His Majesty expressed something of a similar concern recently; I understand the Watchers at Midnight spoke with him. I imagine such fears are unfounded, however."

Realizing that he said as much because he didn't know she'd eavesdropping, Erica let out a nervous chuckle, trying to act natural as she responded. "Oh. Oh yeah? Something Addy and Al said did stick with me though. When they were talking about the Dusk Tyrant, Al said assassinations weren't his style and Addy brought up the possibility of someone trying to revive him like the Witch of the New Moon did. For argument's sake, if there is a necromancer like that, what would motivate them? If they're different enough from the Dusk Tyrant to use different means, are they after the same goal as him?"

Raising a hand to his chin, Levi took a moment to think, pacing until eventually he stood facing the same banner that caught Erica's attention. He tapped the hilt of Whisperwind, the sword kept sheathed at his side instead of hidden in Void-space while the Aurans roamed the halls, eventually shaking his head. "I cannot say for certain, of course, but I find such a conversation largely irrelevant. From what the stories tell us, the Dusk Tyrant only wished to conquer and rule in life. It is unlikely one in the modern era would wish to restore such a man to power. More likely than not, he would usurp their ambitions and they would find themselves betrayed by the power they wished to wield. And as for a personal devotion, the stories do not paint him as an inspiring figure, merely an imposing one. In point of fact, I would wager it more likely a cult with such persistence to last millennia would form around the Ember King."

"Has anyone ever tried to resurrect him? Or one of the three other Champions?"

Levi waved the question aside. "If such a blasphemous ritual has taken place, no one ever heard of it."

Erica nodded in concession. Even putting aside how noteworthy such an attempt would be, nobody was entirely certain where any of the Champions died or were buried, information important in establishing a connection to the dead. Not like with the Dusk Tyrant and Ash-star Tomb. "Right. Anyway, if the Dusk Tyrant would be so hard to control, why would anyone want him back?"

"As I said, the Dusk Tyrant himself is largely irrelevant. In this conversation, he is nothing more than power. A power that someone could claim for their own or point at their enemies and set loose."

"Why would anyone be willing to go so far for power? If you allied yourself with the Dusk Tyrant, you'd be making the whole continent your enemy."

At a loss, Levi through his arms up. "And that is just it. I cannot claim any understanding, the idea of it is as foreign to me as it is to you, but when I say the Dusk Tyrant's power would be claimed, I mean that in more than one sense. Making yourself the continent's enemy... It would be taking up the mantle of the Dusk Tyrant, making yourself into the same thing he was in his time. I can think of no goal worth making myself a villain, but there are surely those desperate or resolved enough to pursue any means, any power, to get what they want."

The mention of mantles and roles stood out to Erica. More than anything else, it reminded her of magic, the ideals of meaning and intention. She'd always thought of the Dusk Tyrant as a singular entity, the very definition of destruction in the form of a man, but it seemed to her Levi was implying something far more different. "'The mantle of the Dusk Tyrant'? Then was he just someone as 'desperate or resolved' as you say taking the place of someone before him? Like the calamity that caused the diaspora of the Folk. Was another Dusk Tyrant behind that?"

Levi shook his head. "Impossible to say. I have never spoken with one of the Folk myself, but my understanding is they are peoples older than the Dusk Tyrant. And I think it would be arrogant to assume our problems, even so broad as to include this entire continent, could extend so far back. Such a saying would only serve to prop ourselves up for defeating something beyond their means or put aside our own responsibility in their perpetuation. The Dusk Tyrant was no more than a man; from where Viemer now lies if the tales are correct. And a dead man now, his ambitions for an empire dead with him. If we wish to prevent the rise of another Dusk Tyrant, we should look to our fellow humans and solve our human problems."

Though the idea of living during an era of new myth, when another great villain might rise for another great hero to face, was absurd and silly to even consider, Erica was surprised to find it felt easier to believe than the opposite. If every trouble facing the world was nothing more than a 'human problem' as Levi put it, then that meant the source of every trouble was in human shortcomings. And to her, it seemed easier to strike down an evil mage or monstrous fiend than to change the hearts of an entire people; the latter a more impossible task than anything magic could resolve. The thought of it left her uncomfortable. For as similar as it was to the story-book chivalry she was used to hearing about from Allard, it felt more like an admission of weakness than an ideal to admire. "But what if it isn't a human problem? What if someone tries to force it to become a matter of myth and magic?"

Levi scoffed, turning away from the banner. "Then they are a fool. I believe you as a mage should know that magic mislikes bowing to the whims of another."

Despite the conviction with which Levi spoke, Erica remained unsure. "I suppose. Is there anything else then?"

"No. Thank you for your aid, but that will be all." He started to leave, but then turned around with a sigh. "I may as well accompany you though. I should report to His Majesty and check on the palace guard, but I doubt any orders will come in this late and it would be best to disabuse Lady Adelaide of any outlandish ideas before too long."

With that, he started back for Adelaide's study. As she followed, Erica found her mind turning back to the Ember King. The thought of resurrecting him was virtually blasphemy, but to her mind, it was precisely the kind of justification the Auris Empire might use for their crusades. *For that matter, their crusade might be a misguided attempt to remake the Sunfire Empire.*

The natural assumption was that the Dusk Tyrant might return on the anniversary of his death. That was the way things worked in stories, the kind of repetition magic liked. But it would be just as significant, possess the same kind of grim duality, if the world's hero returned corrupted instead in the place of his old enemy. All the more so with Levi's talk of mantles. If the presence of an evil was more important than the evil itself, there was no reason the Ember King's shade could not fill the void. And the two empires, Sunfire and Auris, also shared that kind of duality. Two ostensibly holy empires who idealized light and fire with armies led by a knight in Ancient's Armor. It was just an idle, paranoid thought, but the coincidence was uncanny. *And I can certainly think of a mastermind behind it all.* The eerie suspicion she felt looking at Chancellor Lukas crept into the back of her mind. *If he's not from the Empire, where* did *he come from?*

She tried to shake the thoughts from her head, aware of how silly it all was. Vampire or not, the assassin was a problem facing them. The war between the Auris Empire and Montiamon was a problem facing them. And both of them were more important than any new Dusk Tyrant or evil mastermind. Belaboring the point would do nothing but feed paranoia. *By Seras's stars, just this morning Al and I were talking about how skeptical we were of all this myth and legend.*

As Levi swept into the study with a snide remark in response to something Adelaide said, Erica paused on the threshold. Looking back and forth between Allard and Adelaide, she wondered whether she should mention the conversation to either of them. Any part of it. The princess stood on her chair in a vain effort to loom over Levi and explain herself to him while Allard notably didn't tell her to get down. And this was just with the slightest hint of the Dusk Tyrant she'd dug up herself. *Those two feed into each other. If Addy catches the scent of an adventure, she'll pass over her camping trip idea for it. And Al will complain, but he won't stop her.*

Even though she knew she'd already made her decision, Erica found herself dissatisfied. It felt disingenuous and she hated leaving the problem unsolved, but she couldn't think of a better way to keep either of her friends from doing something ill-conceived than to simply distract them. Deliberately furrowing her brow, she swept into the room and asked, "Hey, Al. Do you remember if Vi said anything about the inquisitors when she was here?"

Adelaide's head whirled towards the tea set and she leapt from her chair with a screech. "That self-entitled tea thief! That was darjeeling! Why would you let her in here? Go find her, Al!"

Shooting Erica a pained look, Allard threw up his hands and trudged for the door. Pausing as he passed, he leaned in to whisper, "What was that for? You know those two will pass me back and forth until the situation reaches Estelle and I'm the one that gets in trouble."

Though she wasn't certain why, Erica was well aware Viola and Adelaide held a long-standing grudge. And that the grudge was a good way to keep both of their attentions away from things she'd rather they not think about. Keeping Allard busy was just an added bonus. Patting him on the shoulder, and already thinking of how she'd tell him about Levi's perspective on the Dusk Tyrant when she was ready, Erica replied, "The inquisitors are snooping. I'll explain later, but we should keep an eye on them."

That seemed to satisfy Allard and he nodded back confidently, face only melting into a grimace when he thought she couldn't see. Taking her seat, she watched Adelaide search the room for any other signs of Viola's presence, Levi following behind the princess with a bemused smile. Erica frowned, thinking about vampires, inquisitors, and ancient evils. *What am I going to do when I finally can't keep them out of trouble?*

Chapter 9

Sunday: 3rd of Hernus, Year 1980 R.S.

Allard stood on an endless plain. The dusty, gray ground spread out in every direction under a uniform sky the color of dirty snow. Everything was lit by a sort of dim half-light. Looking about, Allard realized he was alone. He began to walk forward, if only for the lack of anything better to do. With each step, the dust covering the ground clung to his boots, yet looking behind him revealed no footprints. Turning forward once more, Allard was greeted with the sight of an enormous void, like a gaping maw that filled the horizon. Dots of light, like stars, appeared scattered throughout it, giving the impression that a piece of the night sky had been torn down. Allard started to take another step forward, hardly even realizing himself what he was doing, but stopped suddenly when a woman appeared in front of him. She looked as though she were made of blue light and wore extravagant robes, ones that might be seen on an archmage or high priestess. Her mouth moved yet no words came. Allard opened his mouth to ask what was going on or where he was or anything to help him understand the situation, but before he could get a word out, the world shook and then seemed to blur like it had been immersed in water.

Allard fell to the floor with a great thump. Picking himself up, he saw that he was in his room in Riverluck Palace, on the floor next to his bed. A moment later, he saw that Adelaide stood before him, arms crossed. "Are you awake now? I've been practically shouting at you for the past minute." She spared a look towards his still shuttered window as she continued. "We should really get going before it gets too late."

Allard paused to rub the sleep out of his eyes and sighed. "What are you doing in my room at this time of night?" He rose, pulling open the shutters to check the time. Outside, the moon hung low on the horizon, casting a ghostly glow over a fog-shrouded Riverluck. "It can't be more than an hour past midnight."

Adelaide gave a triumphant grin in reply. "What do you mean this time of night? This is the perfect time for us to be sneaking about. After all, you did say that you would take me somewhere to get away from the meetings, right?" She pointed towards two bags piled against the doorway. "And I've already packed and everything."

As much as Allard wanted to complain about her selfishness, her guileless tone made it clear there was no conceit behind her actions, just sheer irresponsible insouciance. He contented himself with a roll of his eyes and walked over to the bags, channeling his annoyance through them with his retort. "Why are you going through my stuff too?" Upon opening the second bag, Allard stopped and looked back over his shoulder. "Are these Erica's clothes?"

Adelaide spun, flaring what Allard could now see was a plain wool dress about her legs. "Well of course they are. We need to blend in, right? I wouldn't be able to do that in my normal clothes, would I?"

When she stood still once more, hands proudly on her hips, the difference was only further pronounced – Erica's four years and couple of inches leaving Adelaide all but swimming in her clothes. Allard placed a hand upon his forehead and stood up, deciding to address more important issues than clothing. "You seriously have no sense of personal space, do you? And on that subject, why are we not taking Levi and Erica with us?"

That was enough to sour her mood. "You know as well as I do that Levi wouldn't let us go. And it's the same with Erica. She did promise me she'd help you find a place for us to go, but that didn't fool me. She was clearly just saying what I wanted to hear. And either way, it doesn't matter. We're here now and we're going."

Allard fixed her with a level stare. "And you think that's going to convince me this is a good idea? Somehow I think it'll end poorly for me if I run away with the crown princess in the middle of the night. The only way that's a good idea is if you want me to get arrested for treason and kidnapping."

Scoffing, Adelaide waved off his concerns. "Oh don't be ridiculous. Who'd arrest you if I tell them not to? I'll just get Levi to say this was a practical test of your training as his squire or something."

Unconvinced, Allard continued to stare her down. Already reasonably sure he couldn't convince her with a common sense based approach, her decided to switch tactics. "Fine. Whatever. But putting that aside, now that the Aurans are here, isn't it just about the worst time possible for you to leave? The talks will start any day and if you leave, they'll see it as conspiracy or something, right?"

He knew he'd misstepped immediately, Adelaide grinning triumphantly once more. From the way her eyes glittered, he could tell she'd been expecting him to try such a lazy argument about politics he didn't fully understand. Reaching down to the floor, she picked up his bag and pushed it into his hands. As he stumbled back, more out of surprise than from force, she hoisted her own bag over her shoulder and started towards the window. "But that is exactly why it is the best possible time to leave. There *is* precedent, you see. When the Auris Empire first declared war on Montiamon it was because a vampire attacked, or so I assume based on the descriptions of General Cyrus' assassination, and my father responded by sending me to Forest's Favor. So now it would only make sense if, when the Aurans arrived for diplomatic talks and a vampire attacked, such actions were repeated. We would only be maintaining internal consistency."

Allard still didn't fully understand the politics of the situation, but had a good enough idea to know that kind of logic, if you were generous enough to call it logic, was optimistic at best. Technically true, sure, but only in a way that served Adelaide's interest. He sighed, setting his bag back on his bed as he followed after her. "But that still doesn't address the more important question of why we need to leave in the first place. You were sent away for protection last time, in case the capital got drawn into war. This time, there's not much threat of war, just assassination, and the odds of that happening are far worse away from a well defended palace and Levi."

"Does it not? The way I see it, it comes back to the magical theory Erica always talks about. Meaning and intention, yes? Events have happened once and now they're setting up to happen that same way again, so I would say chances are good they *will* happen that same way again. This vampire and the Aurans are already here and the latter have inquisitors lurking about. Can you honestly tell me you do not think one or both of them will act soon? Again in the case of the vampire."

As much as he wanted to disagree, Allard couldn't say she was wrong. Even putting aside magical theory, it did seem like too much of a coincidence that both involved parties were at the same place at the same time. And it did sound like the kind of thing that might happen in a story, an assassin taking a second shot at their enemy when peace is within reach while their enemy used themselves as bait to provide a second chance for revenge. More than that, it seemed like the kind of selfish sacrifice the Aurans might undertake, trying to let their apparent vulnerability in a foreign country draw General Cyrus' assassin out in the open. "Alright, fine. Maybe it is a good idea to get you out of the crossfire for a few days at least, but I still think we should have Levi and Erica come with us in that case. They're way more suited to protecting you than me."

Much to Allard's surprise, Adelaide smiled at him with the utmost confidence. "Experientially, no. One dead wolf says you're wrong." The reference to their first meeting caught him off guard and Adelaide continued before he could recompose himself. "And in any case, they can't come. It's all part of my father's plan you see, in the orders he drafted and sent tonight. Levi was told to take me to Forest's Favor, but that missive's only a smokescreen for the true plan. Estelle's received a secret message to order you to take me somewhere safe. So while everyone's focused on Levi, we can get away without any attention on us."

Well aware that he should replace 'father's' with 'my', 'he' with 'I', and 'drafted' with 'forged', Allard felt a sense of impending doom. He shook his head. "There's no way this is going to end well. But I'm not getting out of this, am I?" He sighed, straightening up and retrieving his bag. "Fine. Then just wait by the window and get ready to follow my lead. I need to get a few things ready."

Resigned to his fate, Allard began running over a list of what to pack. His brief inspection of his bag showed Adelaide had thought of most of the essentials, but he knew there were some things she simply wouldn't have thought of with her inexperience in camping. Noting his nightstand was clear of everything save for the icestone cooler, sunstone lamp, and Levi's manual on magic, he frowned and opened his wardrobe. Most of the clothes were packed already, but they weren't what he was looking for. Rummaging about through the drawers, he pulled out a length of rope and, a few heads of garlic he'd picked up in the kitchens earlier that day, when thoughts of vampire tales came to him in his free time. But even still, he couldn't find what he sought.

Adelaide let out an impatient breath. "If you're looking for that stupid old medallion of yours, I already put it in your bag."

He opened his bag, finding the old bronze disc and slipping it into his pocket. A silly lucky charm, but he felt he could use a bit of luck with what he'd gotten dragged into. After shutting the wardrobe, he grabbed the unstrung bow and quiver leaning against its side. Still feeling mostly unprepared, he placed all of his gear together and sat on his bed, putting on his dust-covered boots and tying the laces tight. As he stood, he glanced at his nightstand one more time and tucked Levi's magic manual into his pocket. With everything ready, he approached the window with rope in hand. "Alright. Let's get going."

Escaping from the palace turned out to be much less of an issue than Allard had anticipated. Sure, the guards patrolled the grounds thoroughly and the gates into the city proper were well watched, but after climbing down the rope he'd lowered from his window, Allard found the night's fog did much to cover their tracks. Even the guards' high powered sunstone lanterns only served to give away their positions instead of piercing the misty gloom. But despite the ease of their flight, Allard couldn't help feeling on edge. The well-tended gardens of the grounds, filled with row upon row of flower beds and neatly trimmed trees interspersed with winding streams and small ponds, were like one of the storied other-worlds in the fog. Between the darkness of night and the dull, muted quality the fog gave to sight and sound, an eerie cast fell upon what should have been beautiful sights. And more than anything, it reminded him of Neriah's warning and he couldn't help but feel like they were making a terrible mistake wandering out into the fog-filled night. All told, he was grateful when Adelaide broke the silent tension, huddling nearer to him with a shiver that spoke of her own nerves as they made their way down a lane lined with silverbells."So what's the plan then?"

Looking around for any roving lights, Allard shivered. Something simply felt off, a sensation of crawling suspicion that refused to leave. Even the trees seemed to be in on the trick, leaves rattling in a light wind like the beating of thousands of unearthly wings. Shrugging off his apprehensions, he imagined how Levi would act and whispered, "I was thinking we should head up to Plainsheart and figure things out from there. It'll take us away from the Auris border and where people think you're supposed to be, so that'll make it easier to lie low."

Adelaide nodded. "And getting past the palace guard?"

Allard grimaced. He'd been planning on taking the side gate again, both because it would be the least heavily guarded and the one he most commonly used, but that didn't give him a good excuse to leave at this time of night, much less with Adelaide in tow. "We'll probably have to pretend you're Erica, so when we get to the gate try to look a bit taller and maybe put on the cloak you packed."

But when they reached the gates, nobody blocked their path. The heavy, bronze-banded doors with wards carved in Mystic script along their planks stood firmly barred, but the gatehouse was dark and empty. Allard exchanged a glance with Adelaide, pulling out his bow and kneeling down to string it. "I'm sure it's nothing, but stick close just in case."

It was a weak attempt at confidence, but Adelaide seemed comforted nonetheless, much of her fear vanishing as the two of them drew closer to the gate. And much to Allard's surprise, he turned out to be right, at least as far as he could tell. There were no signs of combat, no bodies, and no bloodstains. In fact, it looked for all the world like the guard had simply left their post unoccupied. Allard still couldn't imagine what could possibly possess them to do so, but he decided it was beyond his concern and went about unbarring the door. In less than a minute, they were through the gates and out on the city, Allard grimacing as he pulled the gate shut. Someone was sure to get in trouble for leaving it unbarred, and he knew it may well be him on their return, but much like the empty gatehouse, it was beyond his concern for the moment. The two of them stood still for a moment, considering the open streets before them, until Allard shook himself from his reverie, nudging Adelaide and starting down the hill. "Come on. Let's head to the west gate. It should be the easiest to slip through at this hour."

With that, they were off, making their way through unusually empty streets. As they descended through the Nobles' District, neither of the two saw anyone else. It was possible it was nothing more than a trick of the fog, any passersby too far away to see in the gloom, but to Allard's eyes the whole city seemed to be empty. Empty stalls and stages for the festival standing half built rose out of the darkness like the bones of a decaying ghost town. Adelaide gave a start each time one of the city's many statues appeared suddenly from the mist and even though Allard calmly reassured her it was nothing every time, he could only do so after breathing a small sigh of relief himself.

More than the empty streets or parks made ghastly by their stony inhabitants, the fog itself set Allard's nerves. It swirled and spun almost like it was alive. He could swear he saw it forming shapes just at the corner of his vision – snarling beasts and screaming faces – but these phantasms melted back into mist as soon as he looked straight at them. Likewise, the fog was unnaturally cold and clammy, clinging to their skin in an unshakable embrace. By the time they were halfway to the west gate, Allard was overcome with the overwhelming desire to turn back. But that same dread told him he had to keep going, that if they did turn back, it would be admitting their fear to the night and some horror would leap out at them.

After only a few more minutes, the paranoia was too much to bear and Allard forced himself to take a break, pulling Adelaide aside into one of the city's plazas with the excuse of getting his bearings straight. The broad expanse was open enough to at least give him the hope that if something did come after them, he would at least see it coming. As he looked up at the sky, stars only just shining through the fog, he heard Adelaide shuffle nervously, putting her back to his as she surveyed the plaza. Tapping his shoulder, she let out a barely audible whisper, muted by fog and fear both. "Hey Al, doesn't it kind of feel like someone's watching us?"

Allard turned to respond, the movement just in time to avoid the dagger that went whipping by the front of his chest, close enough that he could feel the wind of its passage. Over Adelaide's shoulder, Allard could barely make out a figure in a tattered cloak. A figure with glowing red eyes. He grabbed Adelaide's hand and began running, dragging her along with him. She hardly needed the encouragement, but he couldn't help shouting, more to keep himself from panicking than anything else. "Run! Now!"

The two of them dashed into the night, but the cloaked figure seemed untroubled by this, crouching down as if to draw in strength before leaping to the roof of the adjacent building. The fog seemed to curl about its legs as it soared through the air, like a cat nuzzling up against its owner. Once on the roof, the figure took off after them, hopping from rooftop to rooftop with an unnatural grace and speed, its path straight and clear. Keeping one hand firmly grasped around Adelaide's, Allard rummaged through his pockets with the other. *Come on, where are the crows-begotten things?*

All of the sudden, he heard the flutter of cloth above him and quickly turned down the nearest alley. A glance over his shoulder showed their hunter crouched on the ground and a blade planted into a cracked paving stone. He froze for a moment, realizing the knife would have been planted in either his or Adelaide's back if they'd kept going straight. Then the figure began to rise and Allard realized just what his moment had cost them. Panic started to set in, but Adelaide snapped him out of it, giving a wordless shout as she tossed a handful of pebbles towards the hunter. He suddenly found their roles reversed, Adelaide dragging him along, as she turned back to him with a smile. "Come on. That won't keep him long."

Allard allowed himself a brief smile of his own when his hand clasped around the papery skin of the object he sought, but then his face melted into confusion. "What are you talking about? Why'd that stop him?"

"Well that was the vampire you and Erica were talking about earlier, right? They were just regular stones, but it'll have to count them."

A brief glance backwards showed the figure crouched over as its hooded face moved back and forth frantically, searching the ground. Allard nearly stumbled with shock, missing a step but catching himself. "He'll have to count them? What do you mean? And where are we going?"

The two of them reached the end of the alley and Adelaide turned back onto the street, glancing back at him. "Oh don't worry about that, I have a plan."

Only a few seconds behind them, the vampire emerged onto the street, burning red eyes visible through the fog. Allard pulled his hand from his pocket, clutched around one of the heads of garlic he'd packed and considered the distance between them and the vampire. Letting go of Adelaide's hand, he tore a clove free, shouting after her as he did. "You mentioned a plan, Adelaide? Now would be a great time for one."

"Oh, I'm sure there's one around here somewhere. I thought they were supposed to be all over the place in the Commoners' District."

Allard let out a breath of irritation and turned to face the vampire, barely beyond arm's reach at this point. Hoping Mal's ghost stories were true, he threw the garlic at the vampire's face. The vampire hissed in response and leapt to the side, crashing into a storefront in the process. As the vampire picked itself up, Allard tore another clove free and held it ready to throw, then almost dropped it in surprise when Adelaide let out a triumphant yell. She turned down another alley, trusting him to follow. "This way, Al. We'll be able to buy some time."

Before he could ask what she meant, he heard the sound of trickling water. The stone pavement gave way to grass and soon after, one of the streams that cut through the many gardens of Riverluck rose up out of the fog, only just giving Allard enough warning to leap across it. But even though she'd seemingly known it was coming, Adelaide's leap was less graceful and she collapsed on the other bank, tripping up Allard when he landed. As he struggled to his feet, Allard saw the vampire stalk out of the fog, a casual air to its stride. But then the vampire stopped, hissing in frustration as it ran its eyes over the stream. It reached into its cloak and drew forth another dagger. Allard scrambled back, dragging a flailing Adelaide by her collar as he went. The vampire raised its hand to throw and Allard pushed Adelaide behind a bench, diving after once she landed. A piercing whistle cut through the silence and Allard looked back, finding the dagger quivering in the earth where he'd been standing moments before. Back at the stream, he saw the vampire pacing along the bank, like a caged animal. Brow furrowing in confusion, albeit relieved confusion, he turned to Adelaide. "Not that I'm complaining, but why doesn't it come after us?"

Rubbing her side, Adelaide looked up at him with an angry glare. "You could have been a bit gentler you know. And it can't come after us. Vampires can't cross running water."

Allard watched as the vampire settled in, crouching down in the grass. It flinched on seeing him, one hand darting beneath its cloak, but otherwise contented itself to wait. "I see. And why is that?"

Gently pushing Allard off of her, Adelaide rose up to her knees and dusted herself off with a shrug. "I don't know, that's just how vampires work. The books I read weren't exactly scholarly dissertations. The point is that it can't reach us for now, so we can lose it in the city."

Checking on the vampire again and finding it still an easy target, Allard shrugged his bow off his shoulder and nocked an arrow. "Well, why don't I just deal with it here then?"

Adelaide sighed, shaking her head. "You shouldn't bother. It won't work." She paused, pulling Allard back by his coat just before another dagger bounced off the bench, the ring of metal on stone sharp in the otherwise quiet night. "And be more careful. Just because it can't cross doesn't mean it can't hit you with a throwing knife."

Ignoring her, Allard took aim and let fly, hitting the vampire squarely in the stomach. It hardly seemed to notice, pulling the arrow out and flinging it to the ground with an idle contempt. Allard quietly returned his bow to his shoulder and returned to cover. "I'm beginning to see your point. So where do we go from here?"

Adelaide pointed towards the garden's edge. "We'll go that way, towards the west gate like you said. If we stick to the gardens, we'll be able to keep the vampire from following us using streams."

"And then what? Let it cut us down outside the city walls? And if you keep talking like that, it'll know where we're going, streams or not."

"Oh hush. I know what I'm doing. Have a little faith. Now follow me."

With that, she sprinted towards the nearest edge of the garden, returning to the streets once more. Taking a moment to set himself, Allard burst from cover and ran after her. Once he'd caught up, Adelaide turned down the street in the same direction the stream had been flowing. Allard missed a step, nearly choking in disbelief. "I'm not sure if you noticed, Adelaide, but this way isn't even remotely west. If we keep going this way, we'll end up trapped against the Summerblood."

"Oh good. I was right then. I thought the stream would flow towards the river, but I wasn't sure." On seeing Allard's confused face, she gave him a companionable rap on the shoulder. "Come on, did you really think I'd be clueless enough to tell the vampire where we were going? No. We're going to the river."

Struck by a sudden wave of empathy for Levi, Allard pinched the bridge of his nose. "Thank you for sharing that with me earlier. But my point still stands. If we hit the river, we'll be trapped against it."

"Well, if vampires can't cross running water, the middle of a river seems like the best place to be, at least until daylight. So we'll be safe once we're on the water. As for managing that... We'll just have to borrow a boat."

Allard glared at her, unimpressed. "You want us to steal a boat?"

Adelaide chuckled nervously. "Borrow! And I'll make sure the owner is properly compensated when we return. Besides, if you really think about it, I technically own the entire city."

Desperately hoping she was just trying to justify their actions and not wildly misunderstanding the role of the monarchy, Allard sighed. "You're unbelievable. But I don't have a better plan, so we'll just deal with it when we get there."

As they approached the next intersection, Allard drew to a stop and placed his arm before Adelaide, halting her. Slowly creeping to the edge of the street, he sidled his way along its length, motioning for Adelaide to follow him. At the street corner, he crouched down and pressed himself against the adjacent building, peering first one way and then the other. Nothing more than the roiling fog filling the city met his gaze. Carefully, he slipped across to the other side of the intersection, taking up watch while Adelaide followed. An odd urge to laugh suddenly rose within him. *In any other circumstances, this would look silly. Someone watching might think we're two children playing a game of hide and seek.* After a moment, he brought his bow to hand again and nocked another arrow. *It might not do anything, but at least it feels like I have something to protect me.*

Once Adelaide joined him, he continued forward, eyes scanning the road before them while they made their way to the next intersection. Over the course of an hour that felt like an eternity, they crept through the city in this way, stopping at every crossroads to check for signs of pursuit. Even the slightest sound made Allard flinch, but each time he found himself facing empty road. Every movement he spied from the corner of his eyes set him off, but whenever there was an obvious source, it was only the small animals common to the city – birds flitting from rooftop to rooftop or vermin scurrying about in the gutters. This normalcy of the wildlife only served to make the night seem more unreal. It was easier to believe he could be stalked by a vampire in an empty other-world built to look like Riverluck. The animals reminded him they were not alone, the world was not empty, and therefore, they were unequivocally still in the real world.

Finally, the neat cobblestone streets of the main city center gave way to the packed dirt paths of the riverside neighborhood. The buildings lining the street were no longer sturdy stone houses, looming over Allard like silent giants, but simple wooden cottages that made up for the durability they lacked with a homey warmth. Even the shipping warehouses that rose out of the night in the distance looked more like the barns Allard had grown up knowing than the vast, blocky structures he'd heard of in the likes of Perlora and Lugherion, storage spaces large enough to fit entire neighborhoods. As they trekked further among the tenements of dockworkers and fishermen, the fishy, vegetal scent of the river rose through the fog and the sound of water lapping against its banks grew louder and louder. Hearing it, Adelaide let out a heavy breath and ran a few steps ahead of Allard, the tension all but flowing from her in waves, but Allard couldn't bring himself to share her relief. Well aware they were far from free of danger, he shook his head but said nothing, merely walking after her with a white-knuckled grip on his bow.

Following the soft thunking sound of wood against wood, they found themselves standing atop a pier, lines of boats tied along it. "I would've thought
there'd be a guard or something," Adelaide said. "Anyone could just walk up
here and take a boat and nobody would know."

Trying not to think about why the guards were missing, Allard shrugged.
"This is hardly a normal night. I think most people decided they'd rather stay
inside, even if it meant neglecting their duty." He walked along the pier's length
for a bit, stopping at a small rowboat with two fishing rods stacked next to its
oars. "Here, hop in. This one seems like it'd be the right size for the two of us
to handle. Especially since 'the two of us' means just me."

"Now that's just rude. I can handle an oar." She jumped into the boat with a
spring in her step, but nearly losing her balance on landing, mostly disproving
the point she was trying to make. Looking down at the stern, she continued
in an appreciative tone. "But you did choose a good one. Look, it's got a
forcestone engine to help fight currents. You'll hardly even notice I'm not
rowing with its help."

As she began fiddling around with the engine, Allard followed her down
into the boat, careful of the way it rocked under his weight. "You really aren't
doing much to convince me I'm wrong." Gently nudging her aside, he set about
untying the thick knot mooring the boat as he continued. "And leave that alone
for now. I'll have this free in a minute and then you can mess around with the
engine all you want."

After the final bit of rope slipped free, Allard bent down to pick up the oars
and set them in their locks, but froze as the distinct thud of boots on wood
echoed over the noise of the river. When he turned to face the city, he was
greeted by the unwelcome sight of a familiar figure in a ragged cloak drifting
out of the fog. Not about to give their hunter any time to catch up, Allard set
the boat floating downstream with a frantic push. As they lazily drifted further
away and into the river's current, the vampire lifted its arm, dagger in hand.
Allard quickly dove behind the gunwales, throwing himself over Adelaide. He
was rewarded with the dull thunk of metal hitting wood. In the silence that
followed, Adelaide stared up at him with an exasperated look. "Would you
please stop doing that? I can duck just fine on my own and I won't have to
worry about vampires killing me if you batter me to death."

Allard ignored her and raised his head from cover for one last glance at the
vampire. It stood with an eerie stillness, staring after the boat that now lay

beyond its reach with eyes blazing. Nothing in its pose gave him any indication of emotion, its eyes too alien to discern anything. *Is it even thinking?* He thought, trying to put himself in its shoes. *I imagine it would be annoyed, but it just looks... empty.*

Suppressing a shudder, he put those thoughts out of mind and sat down on the rowing bench, ready for a long night of work. Finally acknowledging his companion, he nodded back towards the stern. "Could you get that forcestone running, Adelaide? I'd like to get as far from here as possible while we can."

Adelaide let out a grumble of annoyance, scowling at him as she crawled past, but did as requested and was happily adjusting the dials on the back of the engine in a matter of seconds. Shortly after, the night air was filled with the soft humming of magic at work and the boat began to glide forward at a slow but steady pace, even without Allard's rowing. Allard took a moment to consider the city they'd just left, hoping for one last glimpse of the palace still safe and sound. But from a distance, he could only see the night fog that hung about Riverluck like curtains drawn around a grand bed. And most disconcertingly of all, it ended in a clean line, almost like it had been sliced away by a knife, mere feet beyond the walls. This time, Allard was unable to suppress the shudder that rose from within. Whatever belief he'd managed to maintain that the fog was natural was wiped away in an instant.

Chapter 10

Sunday: 3rd of Hernus, Year 1980 R.S.

Erica flipped over in her bed one more time and stared out the window. The sky beyond was obscured by a thick fog that seemed simply wrong to her. Riverluck rarely got this kind of weather and, when it did, the mists tended to hang around the Summerblood's banks before burning away at dawn. With a resigned sigh, she sat up and shook off her sheets. She fumbled around on her nightstand for a moment in search of her sunstone lamp. When she couldn't find it, she muttered in irritation and held one hand before her, palm up, punctuating the gesture with a single word in Mystic script. A globe of pale white light appeared, like a glowing pearl hovering in the air before her. With the room lit, she swung her legs down to the floor and stepped into the slippers lying next to her bed. After taking a moment to consider what to do about her sleeplessness, she padded towards her room's door, orb of light following. The hallway outside was empty, as expected given the hour, but without the benefit of the moonlight that usually filtered through the many windows, it seemed darker and more foreboding than most nights, her magical light only serving to deepen the shadows. Shrugging, she pushed a little more magic into her light and headed deeper through the palace in the direction of the kitchens.

Much to her surprise, the door to the kitchen hung ajar, a warm light shining through the slight crack between door and frame. She couldn't imagine why anyone else would be up at this hour. Knocking twice, Erica opened the door and strode through. "Hello? Who's there?"

Inside, she found Levi leaning over a counter, lost in thought. He whirled around in surprise at Erica's greeting, but relaxed on seeing it was her. Raking a hand through his hair, he shook his head with a nervous chuckle. "I would ask what brings you here at this hour, Miss Greenmaiden, but I hardly have a leg to stand upon." He paused to grab a mug off the counter and take a sip to compose himself. "So sleep evades you as well then?"

Shrugging, Erica pulled the door closed behind her. "For whatever reason, yes." Yawning, she crossed the room and stood beside Levi. "The Teacher knows I'm tired enough to sleep, but it's like there's something in the air tonight. Maybe it's just nerves from the envoys' arrival."

Levi shook his head and took another sip from his mug. "Perhaps, but I understand what you mean and find myself in agreement. It feels as though some kind of sorcery courses through me, keeping me awake. As though my muscles have tightened against my will and refuse to relax. Lacking any other recourse, I thought I would come to the kitchen for a cup of warm milk. Would you care to join me?"

"I think I'll take you up on that." She reached up to the cupboards above and drew forth a cup. "So while we're here, I guess we should talk about what's going on, huh? Now that the Auris Empire envoys are here, do you think the vampire's going to attack again? Because if it does have something to do with the war, now seems like it would be the time."

Levi dipped a ladle into a nearby pan and poured milk into Erica's cup. "Perhaps, perhaps not. I still do not know if I fully believe the assailant was a vampire, though it is as good an explanation as any. If I am to be perfectly honest, things are always like this. If there are no vampires in the city, chimeras take to roaming the countryside or Herne's Folk grow bold and goblins begin abducting villagers near Thicket Forest. Always one thing or another. Perhaps this vampire is an assassin sent to disrupt negotiations. Perhaps this is all a convoluted scheme by the Aurans to drag us into war. Or perhaps this year is simply worse than others. Perhaps this year..."

Erica waited for Levi to finish his sentence. He said nothing, however, merely staring into his mug before drinking its remnants in a single gulp. "Is that it then? Do you really not care more about what's happening?"

"You speak as if I do not care, but that is far from the case. It is more a matter of inevitability. No matter what may come, I *will* deal with it. That is my duty and my responsibility, and so it can only be thus. If King Thierry tells me to slay a rampaging dragon with nothing more than my bare hands, then so it will be. Even if it is a true dragon, immune to magic and with scales of steel, and not one of those mongrels the Naktikan slayer-knights fight. It matters not that no one has slain one in living memory, I will find a way." Levi set down his mug with a sharp clack. "And as for you? You hardly have any responsibility to care. If you wished to return to your home, whether out of desire to preserve your safety or a sense of longing, it would be within your rights. Lady Adelaide would be sad to see you go, but she would abide by your decision without a second thought."

Swirling the milk about in her cup, Erica tried to figure out how to put what she was thinking. "It's not about me being here. It's about Allard and Adelaide being here. I've known Al my whole life and no matter what he says, he never would have been content living in Regina's Bounty *his* whole life. A small farm town in the middle of nowhere held nothing for him. He'll never leave Riverluck just like that and I can't leave him alone. There's always been some kind of emptiness in him, something I don't think even he knows about, so I need to be there for him when it finally... breaks." Erica paused for a drink and looked away from Levi, towards the door. "And it's the same with Addy. Do you know why I agreed to work for her when we first met three years ago? You said I didn't have to come along even if she said I did, but it wasn't that. It's because I saw someone who was, despite having everything she could ever want, entirely alone. She made a big fuss about how she needed Al and me to be her replacement servants, but I could tell she just wanted people to talk to. And I couldn't leave that alone either."

Erica set down her cup, milk unfinished but her appetite for it gone. When she looked back towards Levi, she found him staring back at her with a furrowed brow. His eyes were filled with something between sorrow and fear and, after a moment, he looked away, as though he couldn't meet her gaze. "I must confess there is much truth to what you have said. I cannot speak in regards to Sir Allard, but in regards to Lady Adelaide, you are correct in saying she had been alone for a long time. I was always the closest to her and even then, despite having known her since birth much as you have known Sir Allard for his entire life, there stands an insurmountable distance between us. Formality, duty, and respect certainly make up a part of this distance, but all else considered equal, a decade's difference in age does much to harm the friendships of youth. And in testament to my own weakness, Lady Adelaide was never given a chance to make the acquaintance of peers. In any case, I imagine that is quite enough of that sort of talk. It seems to have soured the mood and that is a far cry from what either of us came here for. Shall we retire to the study? Some time with a warm hearth and a good book might do both of us some good."

"Sounds like a good idea. After we clean up here, let's head that way."

After placing the dirty dishes in a nearby sink, Erica returned to the hall and stood waiting for Levi to finish returning the milk jug to cold storage. Walking over to one of the windows, she stared out into the fog beyond, wondering just why it bothered her so much. As she watched, she could almost make out faces swirling in the mist – one moment a nearly human face, mouth twisted in a cruel sneer, and then the next a monstrous beast's face, maw agape in what would be a bloodcurdling roar. She shook her head and turned to face Levi on hearing the door click closed. "I must be more tired than I feel. I keep seeing things out there."

Levi followed her gaze. "An understandable sentiment. The greatest threat a nightwatchman faces is too active an imagination. Nights like these only make matters worse."

Then, with a sharp intake of breath, he shoved Erica to the side scant seconds before the sound of breaking glass echoed through the halls. In the moment Erica lay stunned on the ground, she heard Levi utter a single word of Mystic script – a summoning command – followed by a monstrous snarl and a metallic ring. Looking up, she saw him being pushed slowly back by another figure, its jaws clamped around his now gauntleted arm. The figure looked like a woman, likely a common worker from the lower districts of the city by the cut of her clothes, but those same clothes were ragged and torn and her skin was paler than seemed possible for anything save a corpse. Her eyes burned a hateful red and her fingers ended in a set of wicked claws. Erica caught a glimpse of pointed fangs sliding along the gauntlet's length as they attempted to find purchase in its slick metal.

The sound of another window breaking echoed through the hall and Erica turned to see a similar figure, this one a man, crouched on the floor like an animal poised to strike. Reflexively, Erica brought her arm before her and chanted a line in Mystic script. The spell was only a sentence long, but even then, it was barely quick enough; the figure was mere feet away when she finished with a shout, "Light of the morning, be my shield!"

A thin wall of golden light sprang into existence between Erica and the vampire, the latter barreling into it with a furious hiss. For a moment, the vampire met Erica's gaze from across the glowing shield before it hissed, drawing its arm back and slamming a fist against the shield. The light pulsed once in response then faded slightly, leaving Erica feeling drained. Grimly aware the shield was only a temporary solution, Erica raised one hand before her in the sign of benediction, placed the other over her heart and began chanting once more. She flinched each time the vampire struck the shield, forcing herself to remain calm and keep speaking in a steady voice even as small cracks began to spiderweb their way across the barrier. As her spell drew to a close, the vampire realized it couldn't stop her and turned to flee with a howl of rage. But it couldn't manage more than two steps before Erica thrust out her hand with another shout. "Grant this soul rest and may its evil be purified. Cleanse!"

A circle of runes written in Mystic Script appeared around the vampire, shining with a holy silver light. They burned for only a moment before they were replaced by a pillar of light erupting from the floor. Erica could see the vampire's silhouette within, back arched and arms flung to the side as it cried out in pain. When the spell faded, the vampire knelt on the floor, skin smoking. It looked up at Erica with a peaceful expression, eyes now a light brown, before disintegrating into a pile of dust. A moment later, its remains were swept away by the wind leaking in through the broken window, leaving behind only the faint scent of roses.

Erica turned to check on Levi. In the time that had passed, no more than thirty seconds, he had managed to shove the vampire off of his arm and the two now stood eyeing each other warily, the vampire searching for an opening and Levi hesitant to strike, unsure how to fight something already dead. He spared a glance back towards Erica, only looking long enough to register her safety before turning back. "What's the verdict Miss Greenmaiden? Are weapons of any use here?"

She forced the panic welling up inside her back down for a little longer before replying, "Definitely vampires. I would recommend you take its head. That'll be the fastest way to finish it for now."

The vampire lunged forward while she was still talking, trying to take advantage of Levi's distraction, but the knight saw it coming. He dodged out of the way with a single, almost contemptuous, step backwards. While the vampire was still off balance, he sent a jab forward, planting a gauntleted fist in the vampire's gut and thrust his other hand out to the side. As the vampire stumbled back a few feet, reeling from the strike, Levi spoke the summoning command again. "Whisperwind! Come!"

Lightning crackled and the air filled with the smell of ozone as Levi closed his hand around an unseen object, tearing an ornate sword out of a rift to Void-Space. Tightening his grip, he allowed momentum to carry his arm forward, scoring a deep cut along the vampire's stomach. The vampire attempted to counterattack, raking its claws towards his sword arm, but he simply spoke the summoning command a third time and they claws slid off the glossy, blue metal in a shower of sparks. Not giving his enemy a chance to recover, Levi swept a leg forward and hooked it behind one of the vampires, knocking its feet from under it. As it fell, he swept his sword down on the backhand, neatly severing the vampire's head. Its corpse flailed about for a few moments before slumping over against the wall. The head bounced and rolled to a stop, teeth gnashing in the seconds after its body grew still until the red glow in its eyes faded.

Pausing only to flick his sword clean, Levi muttered a full line of Mystic script under his breath and after the ensuing flash of blue light, stood fully clad in his set of Ancients' Armor. He turned back to face Erica. "Come. We must see to Lady Adelaide's safety. How many spells can you still cast?"

Erica closed her eyes and focused. "I can only do one, maybe two, more of the cleansing rituals. It would be best if you took care of the fighting and I sat back in support." Levi nodded and tensed, ready to run down the corridor towards Adelaide's chambers, but Erica raised a hand to stop him. "Wait. One more thing."

She placed one hand over his forehead and the other over her own. After muttering a few lines of Mystic script, a glowing whirlwind surrounded each of them, spiraling down their bodies before coalescing into the pairs of wings sprouting from their heels. Erica felt her body lighten, as if she weighed only half as much as she had before. "A hastening spell will help us get their faster."

Levi nodded his thanks, then sprinted down the hall faster than she could hope to keep up with, the wind howling from his armor and carrying him forward. In comparison, Erica's spell only let her run about as fast a trained sprinter, albeit without the need to pace herself. As they ran through the hallways, Erica could hear the faint sounds of combat and the occasional scream in the distance, proving their own encounter had not been an isolated incident. Worry grew to fear as she thought about what might have happened to Adelaide and Allard and it felt as though the corridors started to stretch and twist, making their path longer than it should have been.

When she reached Adelaide's chambers, their twin doors looked as peaceful and pretty as ever, inlaid with colored glass in a pattern of vibrant flower petals swept across the sky, but Levi stood just before them with his helmet off and a look of fear in his eyes. Seeing him standing there, back pressed against closed doors, Erica could only think the worst. "Is she…"

Levi shook his head. "Thankfully, nothing of the sort. I found no signs of struggle or combat, but unfortunately neither did I find any signs of her. In fact, her bed was still made from this morning. It would seem she did not retire to sleep at the end of the day."

A wave of relief washed over Erica, replaced by confusion as she considered the implications of Adelaide's absence. "But if she didn't go to sleep tonight, then where– Crows! Why would she be so stupid? I thought I'd talked her out of sneaking away to the countryside, but that must've just convinced her to not take me with her. I'll bet you Al's missing too."

"Well we need to handle things one at a time. For now, it is clear more than two of those creatures slipped into the palace, so my duty requires me to come to His Majesty's aid. I ask that you check after Sir Allard and in doing so investigate Lady Adelaide's whereabouts. If one or both of them are still absent come morning, we can discuss the matter with King Thierry."

Erica thought about walking through the halls alone with terror. If Levi hadn't been there earlier, she'd have been dead before she knew what hit her. "Levi, wait! I know you have to protect the king and I want to help Addy and Al, but is it a good idea for us to split up? I don't know…"

Levi turned and fixed her with a steady gaze. "You and I can defend ourselves, Miss Greenmaiden. They cannot. The answer is clear."

Before she could protest, the low rumble of an explosion shook the hallway, closer than any of the other sounds of combat. Moments later a second detonation sounded and Thanasis turned the corner ahead of them, sleeping robes torn and eyes wide with panic. He failed to notice the two of them at first, his attention firmly fixed on the hallway behind him as he thrust his arm back the way he'd come, casting another spell with a shouted word of Mystic Script. "Burn and fall!"

An arc of flaming darts warped into existence before him, appearing first as a heat distortion and then coalescing into form when the air combusted. They hung still for a moment, then raced down the hallway, following the line of his outstretched arm. There was a series of dull thumps and, shortly after, another vampire turned the corner, clothes singed in several spots and reeking of burnt flesh, but unconcerned and unhindered. Thanasis cursed, looking in either direction for an avenue of retreat. On seeing Erica and Levi, he started running towards them, vampire close on his heels. "Help! Nothing I do slows them down!"

Levi planted his feet into the ground, his sabatons digging into the tile. His whole body tensed, like a snake coiling to strike, before he leapt forward with a sharp crack as the stone beneath him shattered. In the blink of an eye, he closed the space between him and the vampire and planted his fist in its gut before it could react, sending the vampire rocketing back into the wall behind it. Levi pressed his charge and drove Whisperwind through its chest, pinning it to the wall. The vampire writhed as it attempted to push itself free, futilely clawing at Levi. Walking over to a nearby side table, upon which a vase of roses rested, he turned to face Erica. "These die to a stake through the heart, correct?"

Erica nodded and he removed the vase from the table, gently setting it on the ground. Gripping one of the table's legs, he pulled it free with a sharp snap and walked back towards the wall on which the vampire was stuck. Inspecting the length of wood, he nodded in satisfaction and rammed it through the vampire's chest with all the strength the Ancients' Armor gave him. The vampire let out a shrill cry of pain before slumping over. Pulling Whisperwind free, he inspected its length and noted the lack of blood before flicking it to the side and returning it to its sheath.

Thanasis looked back at the dead vampire with a frown "So these are the kind of monster that killed the Empire's general? What are they?"

Erica noticed spots of blood on Thanasis' robes and, holding a hand out over his wounds, muttered a spell. A soft light shone from her hand, tracing its way along the cuts and scratches as they healed. "Vampires, best we can figure. I'd only heard folk tales about them before this, so I don't know that much, but they die to stakes and decapitation. I also have a cleansing ritual that does the trick, but that's all I've got."

As the magical light died down, Thanasis looked over his arms and nodded. "Thank you for that. It's too much to hope that was the last of them, hmm? If you don't mind, could I stay with the two of you?"

"Your assistance would be greatly appreciated," Levi said, striding over, "but I have a few questions for you first. I assume by your presence here that the guest corridors were attacked?"

The Perloran nodded. "Yes. I saw Duke Gerald's guards trying to keep them from the ambassadorial suite he, my father, and Viscount Kasmy were staying in and tried to help. But, well, you can see where that got me."

"But it was only more like these?" Levi asked, gesturing back at the corpse of the vampire. "You saw nothing of a commander or champion among the ones attacking your people?"

Hearing that, Erica understood Levi's uncertainty. She hadn't thought about it when fighting for her life, any monster equivalent in her mind, but these vampires had died too easily. At least when compared to the presumed assassin they were hunting. Three of them had died by their hands alone, while the other had taken out dozens of trained soldiers. There was simply no way the assassin was as weak as these creatures. *For that matter, if even I could stop one of these vampires, the house guard would have been able to at least put up a fight.*

Thanasis shrugged apathetically. "Not that I could see. They all looked as wild and rabid as that one there."

Levi started pacing, muttering to himself as he walked. "...Confidence or arrogance? I need to..."

The end of his sentence was drowned out by an inhuman shriek of pain, followed by the sound of boots on stone. Levi turned to face the sound, placing himself in a guard position between it and the two mages. For Thanasis' part, having Levi to protect him seemed to have restored his confidence and he began repeating the a line of Mystic Script over and over again, cupping his hand around a magically summoned flame as he held a spell at the ready. Figuring they had the situation under control, Erica decided they didn't need what petty help she could offer and turned to keep watch on the other end of the corridor while they fought.

A battered group of five vampires stumbled around the corner, looking far worse for wear in testament to the palace guard's efforts. Three of them had crossbow bolts embedded in their arms and chest. One had even lost its hand, arm ending in a too neat stump that refused to bleed. As soon as they caught sight of Levi standing alone, their eyes widened in a maddened glee, but this turned to shock when they took in Thanasis behind him, arm raised as though preparing to throw something. Those in the front scrambled to get out of the way, tripping over those in the back, but it was too late. Casting his hand forward, Thanasis completed his spell and the flame arced through the air, landing among the vampires and blossoming into a cloud of fire. When the smoke cleared, the vampires were strewn about the hallway, dazed but still intact. Levi took advantage of their stupor and dashed into their midst, cutting two of them down with a swift pair of slashes before the others could regain their feet. By this time, the remaining three had recovered their senses and the two nearest to Levi threw themselves at him. It was a desperate attempt, one clinging to his legs in the hopes of pinning him in place while the other clambered onto his chest, seeking an opening in his armor for its fangs to find purchase, but it did a good job of keeping him occupied. As he stumbled under their weight, the third slipped around Levi, ignoring him and charging the unarmored Erica and Thanasis.

Panicked and unprepared, Erica started chanting the cleansing ritual again, silently praying that she had enough time to finish before the vampire reached her. But despite her fear, she finished the spell with plenty of room to spare, the vampire several feet from her or Thanasis. It was too beaten to even react to the spell, ignoring the glowing runes that surrounded it. It simply continued its charge and in the span of a single step it was done, its raised foot collapsing into dust on contact with the floor and the rest of its body following.

Thanasis nodded his approval, as though fighting monsters was a daily occurrence. Blithely ignoring how much trouble he'd had with one vampire, he sauntered towards the two occupying Levi, chanting a spell as he went. When they turned to mark his passage, he swept his arm forward in a grand motion, shouting, "Scatter and fall!"

A tempestuous wind filled the hallway, dislodging the struggling vampire from its perch on Levi's chest. Arms freed, Levi brought Whisperwind down and dispatched the vampire clinging to his feet. Its companion clambered back to its feet and ran its eyes over the hallway, let out a frustrated wail, and barreled out of a window, the tinkling of broken glass following it.

Levi rushed to the window, Thanasis and Erica close on his heels. Below, the vampire lay splayed out on the ground, its body broken and limbs twisted like a crushed spider's. It futilely attempted to drag itself across the grass, doing little beyond digging furrows in the soft loam. In testament to the palace guard's efficiency, the grounds surrounding the palace were already filled with the warm golden light of sunstone lamps, several bobbing through the fog towards the fallen vampire as they closed in on the sound of a broken window. In only a few seconds, a group of guards stepped out of the mist in an arc, carefully advancing with spears raised. One – epaulets on his shoulders identifying him as an officer – gestured to the others around him and shouted a muffled order. His subordinates took turns setting down their lanterns and hefted their spears, before slowly edging towards the fallen vampire. It clawed and hissed at them, but as soon as they entered spear-range, the officer shouted another order and the guards struck in unison, each pinning one of the vampire's limbs to the ground. The officer then drew his sword and walked up to the helpless vampire, stuck like an insect on a board. It looked up at him and gave one last hate-filled howl before his blade severed its neck. The guard knelt down wiping his sword on the grass before looking up to examine the window from which his prey had leapt. Seeing Levi, he hastily rose to his feet and raised an arm in salute. Levi nodded back and stepped away from the window, content with the guards' work.

Levi muttered a word of Mystic and his armor disappeared in a faint flash. Looking at Thanasis and Erica in turn, he said, "I cannot hear any more signs of struggle within the palace, so the two of you should be safe to return to your chambers. Though I would ask you to continue guarding Lady Adelaide for the moment, Miss Greenmaiden. I must attend to the king and receive the battle reports, but will return to relieve you shortly."

Erica looked back at the door with confusion, but then realized their present company and said nothing, merely nodding.

"Thank you, Sir Crownguard," Thanasis said. "I owe my life to the two of you and assure you my father and I will look into this attack. I don't know what trickery the Aurans are planning, but if they insist on playing with dark forces such as these, they'll slip up eventually and I'll be ready to decry their hypocrisy when they do." He turned to face Erica. "And I must apologize, Miss Erica, but I must ask to delay our appointment a day. I anticipate I will be rather occupied tomorrow."

Disturbed by his accusations towards the Empire, Erica nodded her assent, hoping to speed him off so she could discuss with Levi in private. "That's hardly too much to ask. I would have suggested the same thing."

Thanasis walked away with his head held high, as if neither Levi nor Erica had seen him distressed minutes before. Once he was gone, Erica turned to Levi. "What was that about the Auris Empire? Does he really think they would do something like this. Do we?"

"I cannot say. My instincts tell me they would not stoop to such a distasteful means to accomplish their goals, but that may be exactly why they act so zealously. Few would ever suspect them of using the very monsters they claim to hate. I would ask that you meet with King Thierry and I come morning.

We shall have much to discuss." He looked towards the doors to Adelaide's chambers with a frown. "And could you check on Allard's room? There may be more to trouble us yet."

Too distracted to feel overwhelmed at the thought of attending to the king, Erica mumbled her assent. Levi barely waited for her response, turning as she spoke and muttering a word of thanks as he went. This, combined with the tension with which he carried himself, told her he was much less calm than he let on and his even pace was carefully controlled. It was troubling to see such a seemingly invincible figure fallible; the thought that he could be afraid just like Erica only serving to make her own fears worse. Now that the moment had faded, she felt the rush of energy brought on by panic and action melt away, leaving her feeling drained and tired. In the same way, her magical energy flowed through her body in a mere sluggish current. In the void left by exhaustion, everything began to catch up with her. It felt foolish to panic after the fact, but she couldn't help it as she remembered the first vampire just barely missing its chance to kill her or the second one clawing mere inches away from her face, only separated by a thin barrier. If Levi had been a bit slower, or she a bit less powerful, she'd probably be lying with her throat torn out now.

Trying to shove it from her mind, she hurried back to her room, unconsciously touching a hand to her neck as she did. It was only when she reached the last hallway, seeing her door still hanging slightly ajar from when she'd left earlier, that she remembered Levi's request. Turning to face the doorway across from hers, she took a deep breath and quickly opened the door before her mind could conjure up any worst case scenarios. Peering into the dark room beyond, she was relieved to find it empty, the bed a mess and the window open, but no signs of distress present. Then that relief turned to a different kind of worry as she took in the rope tied to the bed's headboard, dangling over the windowsill. Swallowing, she pulled it back up, shut the window, and latched it closed again. Unwilling to dwell on the possibilities of what might have happened, she shuffled towards her room, whispering under her breath as she went, "I hope you two are alright."

Interlude A

Sunday: 3rd of Hernus, Year 1980 R.S

Knife watched the fog long enough for the patrol to pass out of sight behind a corner of the palace (*two hundred and two seconds*). The heiress was cleverer than they had expected, a minor miscalculation. All told, it would have only taken four movements and fifteen seconds to kill both her and the other if it hadn't been for those pebbles (*seventeen of them*). And even then, they shouldn't have had enough time to escape like that, to use her wiles and exploit Knife's weaknesses. It was the first throw. That's where everything went wrong. The dagger shouldn't have missed. *Couldn't* have missed. But the other had moved at just the right time. Not out of magic or skill, but coincidence. And that bothered them. Coincidences didn't happen. Not when one planned, not when one strategized, not when one was sure of every last thing. *So there must have been something else Knife didn't calculate.*

With nothing else to be done and one target gone, Knife started in the way they should have been going all along, up to the palace. It hardly mattered and they knew it, then and now. Too much time had passed (*one thousand, four hundred and thirty six seconds*) and the lesser ones (*sixty six*) were all gone. To be expected. They were not like Knife. They were little more than nails, and Knife the hammer. Knife was not one to hope, that was a thing for those who had not the appropriate skill or power to complete their missions, but they had wanted the Master's associate to wait for them. Let them lead the charge. With the likes of the Crownguard and the Auran fool, the lesser ones would fall in short time. The Master's associate was a fool. But that didn't change their orders, so they still went to report back and receive further instructions.

The Master's associate, naturally, had done as all fools do and commanded Knife down the same course as before. A failed course. A course proven false. The definition of insanity. And yet there was nothing to be done. The Master's orders were absolute, and therefore his associate's orders were absolute as it was into his hand Knife had been placed. And it was not a knife's place to question where it was thrust. There would be no issue, of course, with completing the mission – a simple matter of four movements and fifteen seconds – but it was frustrating nonetheless. If it were a simple matter, it would be better to complete more complicated matters first. And the Master cared more about recovering the Regalia than eliminating opposition in either case. But again, *It is not Knife's place to question where it is thrust.*

By now, it was rapidly approaching the time where Knife's patience could be described as sulking (*three hundred seconds*), an unacceptable result. So they crouched against the parapet, prepared to leap back into their fog and hare off into the night. But before they could move (*one second*), a familiar sound reached their ears, rising above the clamor of the palace guard and the frightened staff. *Crunch, crunch. Hiss, hiss.* Metal slid upon metal and gravel shifted underneath armored feet. And all in an unmistakable tempo, at least to Knife. They had heard those footsteps once before and that night was unforgettable, seared into their memory as another temporary failure. A failure that wouldn't disappear until it was corrected. Knife did not make excuses, it was unbecoming of a blade to blame its dull edge on its steel, but that night had cost them an arm already and the dead lord's replacement medium hadn't yet conformed to their spiritual patterning. Not a problem tonight. Knife cocked their head to the side, hardly enough for a human to perceive (*one point two degrees*). They *had* been told where to go, but their orders said nothing of the route they were to take.

Course set, Knife leapt from the parapet, but straight down instead of out. They came out of the fog with a minute whistling of air, daggers bared, and plunged upon the stalking Crownguard. But as before, he'd heard. Or sensed. Knife considered this as a bracer caught both blades and flung them back several feet (*eleven*). The noise of passage was too quiet for a normal human's ears, at least too quiet to hear and react like that. So there was something else. *Instinct, training, or something else? How has this sword honed its edge?*

Then they were off again, dashing low before the Crownguard could bring Whisperwind up to bear. The treasured blade, a channel wasted without a reservoir behind it, *was* a problem, but Knife found it unlikely the Crownguard would discover why or how. Not misusing it as he did. Now, they knew to fear only that the blade's lightning might throw their limbs at an inappropriate angle and foul an otherwise well executed throw. That, or burn an otherwise good medium like the dead lord's final spell had. Knife tossed a dagger ahead and kicked off the ground at the last second, diving from above instead of below as the Crownguard should expect, especially after flinching away from the projectile, but again, he exceeded their expectations. The first dagger was batted away by the back of a gauntlet without fear or hesitation. And the second met only soft dirt, the Crownguard stepping aside and letting Knife fall to the ground unhindered. All the better to bring his blade down like an executioner's doom, severing neck and splitting a perfectly good medium. If Knife were like the lesser ones.

They skittered away, escaping Whisperwind with nary a hairsbreadth to spare (*uncountable*). As they turned and set themselves once more, they found the Crownguard staring at them, head tilted and sword pointed. As before, he said nothing. As was natural. It was not a knife's place to converse, so neither was it a sword's. Unwilling to give him a chance to attack, Knife leapt again, but to the side this time. Dashing up the palace wall, in open defiance of that petty thing humans concerned themselves with called gravity, Knife tossed dagger after dagger (*ten over five seconds*). They were all deflected in a magnificent, blue arc, spinning from one to the next with only sparks of electricity to mark the defending blade's passage. *As is natural.*

At the apex of their sprint, Knife spun, hanging upside down in the air for a moment, the only moment in which they could appreciate the perfection of this fight. A fight against an equal tool, a rare specimen of another blade as sharp and devoted as them. And then they fell with all strength, the strength to rend steel and shatter bone. Their daggers were poised to take the Crownguard along the back, to peel apart his prized armor like little more than a peanut's shell. But again, Whisperwind was there. Faster than Knife thought possible, at least by human standards, the Crownguard twisted and all but cut them out of the air, only their daggers keeping the treasured blade from their chest. And even then, their hands burned with crackling electricity and all their hair struggled to rise from beneath their hood with the cloud of static.

They were ready to go another round, but then froze, hearing shouts carry through the fog. Out of the corner of their eyes, they saw dim pinpricks of golden light bobbing closer and closer. Sure enough signs that time was up and the palace guard was there to spoil the fun, if fun were such a thing a knife could feel. And it had only been fourteen seconds. Favoring the Crownguard with one last glance, Knife sped off into the darkness, weaving through trees and bushes faster than eyes unadjusted to the dark could trace.

As they continued on their way, a thread of dissatisfaction wove into their heart. This kind of fight wouldn't happen again. There were few who could match the quality of the Crownguard, in spirit of duty if not skill, and all would be over before they got a chance to face him again. And certainly they wanted to test his mettle again, to discover why a sword like him could best a knife like them. Already they were thinking of ways past that armor (*twelve*), confident they would have found victory if they'd been uninterrupted. But that was not enough for dissatisfaction. There was something else that echoed in Knife's head as they made their way through the streets of Riverluck. *Why couldn't Knife find its mark? If sword and knife are equal, what has Knife failed to calculate?*

Chapter 11

Sunday: 3rd of Hernus, Year 1980 R.S.

Allard groaned as the morning sun shone through his eyelids, forcing him awake. He sat up with a wince, shoulders sore from rowing and back aching from sleeping on the boat's hard boards. Looking about, he was greeted by entirely unfamiliar scenery, the river's south bank shaded by the trees and brambles of Thicket Forest and its north bank filled with nothing but the expansive plains that stretched throughout Tycortua from the Summerblood to the ocean. The water of the river below was remarkably clear, schools of fish swimming alongside their boat and caches of sparkling waterstones visible on the riverbed, their magic speeding the current along. He shook his head and raised his arms to stretch, listening to the sounds of the morning around him. The gentle birdsong and steady rushing of water reminded him of days spent camping next to Seras's Stream back home, but the out of place hum of the boat's magical engine reeled him back from his reminiscence. At the other end of the boat, Adelaide rolled and mumbled, fighting for every minute of sleep. Allard smiled and shook his head, looking about for something to do while he waited for her to wake up. The dagger the vampire had thrown, now stuck in the boat's side, caught his eye. Pulling it out with the slight creak of wood, he turned it over in his hands. He wasn't quite sure what to make of it. The design was simple enough, with a straight blade extending about half a foot from a cruciform hilt. That the blade was obviously not balanced for throwing spoke testament to either the vampire's skill or strength. What gave Allard pause, however, was the metal of the blade itself. Instead of the bronze commonly used for weapons and tools, it was a dull gray with a faint metallic sheen. A plain gray that proved it was not made of a magically forged alloy such as starsteel or windsilver.

He puzzled over the blade for it for several minutes, but stopped on hearing a grumble from Adelaide's side of the boat. "It's too early. Why doesn't the sun go back down for another hour? No civilized person should wake up until at least two hours after dawn." Adelaide blearily rubbed the sleep out of her eyes as she looked about her. Setting her eyes on the dagger in Allard's hands, she tilted her head, a quizzical expression on her face. "Is that one of the vampire's knives?"

Allard nodded and carefully pinched its blade between two fingers, holding the hilt towards Adelaide. "Yeah. Though I can't tell if it's just a normal dagger or not. It looks like it's made from something weird."

Plucking the dagger from his grasp, Adelaide stared at it intently for a few moments. Eventually, she looked back up at Allard with a confused expression. "You're right. This *is* weird. I have no idea why anyone would ever decide to make a weapon out of pig metal."

Allard raised an eyebrow. "I beg your pardon?"

"Pig metal. You know, iron? It has practically no use for anything beyond decoration or construction. While it is a relatively strong metal, since it's magically inert, anything that it can do, enchanted bronze can do better, to say nothing of the likes of defianium. It's sometimes used for things like building supports and fences or stuff like nails and pots, but you'd never see it for a weapon. By Zephyros' Banner, it's a pain to even forge or cast since you can't heat it with magical fire."

Looking out at the trees that slowly glided by, Allard took a moment to think, trying to reconcile this with what he knew of magic. "Well if it's magically inert, doesn't that mean that you could use it to cut through enchantments and spells? Wouldn't that make it a really good way to take down mages?"

Shaking her head, Adelaide set the dagger down. "In theory, yes. But once a spell has produced a physical effect, iron can't do much about it. It can cut through magical energy, but not, say, a lance of lightning or a wall of compressed air. Which means most mages can figure out a way around it as long as they aren't caught off guard." She started rummaging around at the bags piled in the back of the boat. "Well, I think that's a mystery for another day. I'm getting hungry."

Allard nodded. "That's a good idea. We should start thinking about our next move anyways." After a minute, he raised a hand to massage his forehead and turned to face Adelaide. "Adelaide, I know that you tend to lack common sense when it comes to anything outside of your studies, but you did remember to pack food, right?"

Adelaide stared off into the distance, as though just remembering something. "Oh. I suppose that's right, isn't it?" She laughed nervously. "Well I guess I just kind of assumed that you would take care of the food. I've never had to worry about what I'd eat before." Then her unease melted away and she flashed a reassuring smile. "But don't worry. I did remember to bring three tins of tea. Let me know what you'd like in the morning; citrus black, green with ginger, or a mint tisane."

Groaning, Allard lightly rapped her on the head. "Oh good, you had started to sound so knowledgeable, talking about all of that magical theory. I was worried you were actually someone else. I'd hate to think you were a changeling all along" With a sigh he picked up one of the fishing rods lying in the bottom of the boat. "I guess we're lucky this boat had these in it. And you'd better hope that fish like garlic, since I think that's about all I have on me that can be used as bait."

Adelaide snatched up the other rod with a sullen growl, setting it down in her lap and glaring at it with a rare kind of anger. In no small part annoyed himself, Allard speared a clove of garlic on the rod's hook and cast out into the river behind the boat. Not trusting himself to say anything productive, he waited quietly and watched the wake left by his line as it was dragged downstream. Eventually Adelaide broke the silence, her irritation faded. "Either way, we should talk about where we're going. If anything, my mistake just means we need to find a town or something faster. I know that you said we were going to head to Plainsheart, but is that still a good idea? If we land on the south bank, we could cut through Thicket Forest and make our way towards Forest's Favor, just like we did three years ago. I know I was trying to avoid going to the summer palace again, but this would put the river between us and the vampire and we know it can't cross it."

Allard shook his head. "That might sound like a good idea, since the biggest threat we face would be neutralized, but it would end up causing more problems than it solved. Two people traveling through the forest alone and relatively unarmed is just asking for trouble. If we didn't get attacked by wild animals, then the forest spirits or Herne's Folk would likely snatch us up. And I don't fancy leaving their clutches and finding that a century has passed. As a best case scenario."

The boat rocked slightly as Adelaide fumbled around with the other fishing rod and attempted to work the reel's catch. The action almost covered her shudder, but she tripped over her own hands and only managed to unspool the line into a loose tangle at her feet. "We didn't have that kind of trouble last time though. If the forest is so dangerous, why did we go through it then?"

Thinking back to their trip with the palace guard, Allard chuckled. "We got through safely last time because we had a dozen soldiers and a Levi. No beast smaller than a house would dare bother that many people and frankly Levi could handle almost anything you'd be able to find in there. And the wild spirits know better than to mess with a group that large. Believe me, the forest is dangerous. Why do you think so many of the darker fairy tales have it as their setting? Where do you think the tales of goblins snatching up children and sidhe folk leading men astray come from? When my friends and I went hunting in the forest, we hardly ever left sight of the forest's edge. The deepest we ever went was to the Weeping Tree roughly a mile in and our parents went with us."

"Don't *you* tell *me* about the sidhe," Adelaide whispered under her breath, idly crossing one arm across her chest and tapping a rhythm against her shoulder. Then she sighed and set about untangling fishing line as she continued, louder this time. "Well then what do you recommend? If we aren't going into the forest, then our options seem to be either put into shore on the north bank or wait until the forest clears. At that point we might as well just go all the way to Fortune's Crossing. And don't try to tell me we should go back to Riverluck. If the vampire *is* following us, that sounds like a good way to run right into it."

Allard looked up into the pale blue sky, following the movement of a small cloud. The weather was clear today and would likely stay that way for a few days now that spring had come, meaning shelter wasn't too much of a concern. Likewise, if they had good luck fishing, food wouldn't be any trouble and the everfull bottles Adelaide had packed would keep them supplied with fresh water. Realistically, the vampire did remain the biggest problem they faced. "That's a good question. Waiting until we get to Fortune's Bridge seems like the safest thing to do since we'd be in the middle of the river the whole time and the vampire couldn't get us. But it would take a while to get there and we'd be crossing into Rugego. And that might be what the vampire would expect us to do, so we might find him waiting for us. How smart are these things supposed to be?"

At this, Adelaide fixed him with a quizzical stare. "'Him'? Did you see the vampire's face?"

Only then realizing what he'd done, Allard flinched. Somehow, thinking back to that last sight of the vampire on the pier, he was struck by its posture. The way it stood like a hunter. A stance Allard himself had stood in many times. "Ah, no. It's just..." He shook his head, unsure himself why he felt the way he did. "I guess it somehow doesn't feel right to act like he's just some thing. Monster or not, he's still a person, isn't he?"

Pricking her finger on the rod's hook, Adelaide let out a startled yelp and threw it aside. Shaking her head, she turned back to Allard and pointedly ignored her failed attempt to help, instead replying in the studious tone he'd only seen her use around Erica, "Hmm. Arguably the personhood of a vampire is defined by the demon which animates them, but I suppose I can understand your meaning. And as for your initial question, that depends on how old the vampire is. A new vampire will be more or less ruled by its impulses. But if it is more than a few months old, then it will be as intelligent as it was in life. If I had to guess, I would say that ours was probably on the older side. He did not seem particularly reckless."

"Then it really is a gamble as to whether you think he'd figure the same thing as us. My gut instinct says that it's a better idea to land sometime soon and try to find a village nearby, though that might just be because I don't want to wait here for however long it takes us to travel downriver. And that way, we'd act against the obvious expectation of finding shelter and a stable source of food sooner."

"I feel as though you glossed over a few critical details there about food and shelter, but I suppose I shall defer to your judgment. You do know the countryside better than I do. If we wait to land until after you have caught a few fish and we have gotten something to eat, we should have most of the day ahead of us still to cut inland."

With nothing else to say on the topic, Allard nodded and focused once more on his line.

"Allard, truly I must apologize," Adelaide said after a few moments. "I have brought naught but sorrow upon you." He turned to chide her for being foolish, but stopped on seeing her face. Her expression was graver than he had ever seen. "You have only been drawn into these events because I acted as a selfish child. I had no right to take you from your village. I had no reason to take you with me to Riverluck after. You should be safely ensconced at home with your family, not fleeing under the threat of death from an undead monster."

Allard wasn't sure how to respond, her formality throwing him off as much as her words. He sighed, deciding to just say what was on his mind, placing a hand on her shoulder as he spoke. "Look, I appreciate the concern, but it's not necessary. I stayed with you and agreed to work in Riverluck because I wanted to. I spent my entire childhood dreaming of adventure and wishing I could go and be like the heroes in the stories we hear. And maybe this isn't like those stories and I don't get to be a hero, but the past three years I've lived in the palace have been like nothing I ever imagined. I thought that I'd spend my whole life on a farm, never having a real impact in the world. But now the entire world is open to me. So don't be so down about this. It really doesn't fit you at all. When I do go back to Regina's Bounty someday, this will be a great story to tell."

The relief was obvious in Adelaide's eyes. She shrugged Allard's hand off her shoulder and turned to face the forest, as she replied, "Hmph. And why should I take orders from you? If I tell you to accept my apology, then you should insist upon reparations immediately. I practically commanded you to after all." Turning back towards Allard she now bore a mischievous grin with a familiar sparkle in her eyes. "Though it is a shame the Summerblood flows west. I'd like to visit Regina's Bounty again sometime. Last time we didn't stay for more than a night and I didn't know you or Erica yet. I had no idea then how much I was missing out."

Turning back to his fishing rod again, Allard sighed with annoyance, but smiled as he replied, "Yeah, yeah. I'm sure that you would just love to visit Erica's and my childhood homes. Spin everyone in a tizzy by ordering them to cook a feast beyond their measure and constructing a new palace so that you could come by on the weekends. It's probably just as well. In the last letter I got from home, Carlin said that Franz, the blacksmith, had seen the Witch of the New Moon one night. Some of the farmers from just outside of town agreed with him, saying they heard her singing at the edge of Thicket Forest. It looks like even poor little Regina's Bounty isn't escaping from the strange occurrences this spring."

Adelaide looked up at Allard with a confused expression on her face. "Carlin?"

Allard rolled his eyes and glanced back at her in disbelief. "Seriously? That's what you take out of that? Not the ancient mage stalking my home town? He's my younger brother. I know I've told you about him before. You never actually listen when I tell you things about my home, do you?"

Adelaide made a dismissive gesture. "Oh of course, I remember now. Your younger brother. He's about my age, right?" She smiled and leaned forward to poke Allard in the back. "Maybe I should go and recruit him to be my guide next time. He'd probably be much more fun and willing to go along with my plans to mess around with you."

Remembering how gullible his brother had always been, Allard shuddered at the thought of what Adelaide might convince him to do. But before he could quip back, he felt a tug on his fishing rod. He started reeling in, nodding towards the far end of the boat as he replied. "Oh quiet you. Now get one of those buckets ready. I think I've got something here."

The sun had just passed its peak when Allard sat down on the river bank, tying the boat to a nearby tree. All told, he'd managed to catch five decently sized fish that morning. After a disappointingly meager breakfast, they were left with enough to last them through the day. Content that the knot was tight enough, Allard stood up and dusted his hands off. Looking down at the boat, he felt a kind of defeated humor overcome him. *It's not like it matters if it ends up drifting away. It's not like we're coming back for it.*

Casting aside such thoughts, he turned to survey the plains before him. The grass, swaying gently in the breeze and verdant from snow-melt and spring sunlight, had an almost hypnotic effect. Combined with the day's warmth and a small herd of wild sheep grazing in the distance, it gave the impression of a peaceful countryside where he and Adelaide were the only people in the world. Positively idyllic. It took all of his effort to not lay down beneath the tree he'd tied the boat to for a nap, letting the sound of the river lull him to sleep. Forcing himself to remember there was a relentless hunter somewhere in that charming landscape, he walked back down to the boat and rummaged about in his bag. Taking out the small bronze medallion Adelaide had made sure to pack, calling it a 'silly lucky charm', he rubbed off a smudge on its surface and considered its design. It was a simple enough pattern, a sunburst whose lines had worn down over the years, and he'd seen it countless times before, but it never failed to amaze him, the age of the medallion itself making him imagine that it must have been an important crest at one point. He held the medallion close to his mouth, whispering under his breath in something halfway between prayer and hope. "I know my family's always been pretty lucky. Our crops never blight and our dairy cows never get sick. My dad said it's because you were our family's lucky charm when he gave you to me before I left, like his father gave it to him when he got married. Well, if you really are a lucky charm, then I could use all the luck you've got right now."

Adelaide walked up behind him, bag in hand, and snorted with laughter. "I see you're talking to it now. The superstitions of the common folk never cease to amaze me." Despite her sarcastic words, her smile undercut any malice in them. "Now can we get going already? We're burning daylight."

Pocketing the medallion, Allard frowned and hefted his bag over his shoulder, pausing long enough to flick Adelaide in the forehead before replying. "Yeah, yeah. Just because one of us is properly worried about the situation is no reason to make fun of him. Get walking. I'm right behind you."

The two of them set out walking north, chatting amicably beneath a mostly clear sky, but the further along they went and the more Allard had to think about which way to go, the more a gloom cast itself over him as he considered just how out of his depth he was. After no more than ten minutes of silence, at least on his part, Allard turned to face Adelaide, cutting her off as she started saying something about the difference in magical ecology between the wetland meadows and mixed forests of Tycortua. "Come to think of it, what all did you read in your book about vampires? What are we dealing with here?"

Skipping over a fallen branch, Adelaide spun to face Allard and fixed him with a brief glare, annoyed at being interrupted. But then just as quickly as it came it was gone and she started walking backwards as she talked, finger raised as though lecturing him. "Well, starting with the obvious, vampires are undead creatures that drink human blood. Similarly, they can make more vampires by biting other people and completely draining their blood. Their true origin is unknown, since presumably there had to be a preexisting vampire to make more, but it's generally agreed upon that a demonic spirit is what brings them back to life."

Allard nodded. "That does sound familiar, but I was more thinking about weaknesses and abilities. Last night's events proved running water, garlic, and that counting thing, but what else is there? The stories I've heard also say that they don't like holy objects, can't enter a house uninvited, and die when exposed to sunlight. Are any of those true?"

Adelaide shrugged and stumbled, nearly tripping over a rock she hadn't seen. Turning to face forward again, she furrowed her brow with thought. "The 'counting thing' is called arithmomania. And it's hard to say. The book I read was hardly a scholarly thesis. But if the murder you and Erica were talking about was done by this vampire, it's safe to say they can enter homes uninvited. I hardly think anyone in the household would have just let a stranger in at that time of the night."

"Alright. So all we can really count on is what we already knew. Not really a reassuring thought. What about the other side of the story? What can vampires do? The one chasing us seemed to be fast and tough."

"As far as I can tell, vampires are essentially better than humans in every physical regard. They're stronger, faster, tougher, and heal at an accelerated rate. They have a few other magical talents relating to hypnosis and transformation, but neither of those will be a problem for us. Just don't look it in the eyes."

Allard chuckled. "I hadn't planned on doing that anyway. If I'm close enough to see his eyes, I'll have bigger things to worry about."

This earned him a punch in the shoulder, Adelaide unamused by his morbid humor. Neither had more to add to the discussion at this point and the conversation devolved back into light chatter. The day continued on in this way, their trek uninterrupted and Allard learning more than he'd ever wanted to about why mischievous fairies like the plains and malicious fae prefer the forest. The good weather continued to last as Allard had predicted, the sun setting in a sky as clear as the morning's. Allard scanned the horizon as they set up camp for the night, searching for trails of smoke in the sky in the hopes of finding some other sign of civilization, but found himself disappointed. Neither of the two had seen traces of other travelers during the day and this trend continued as night fell. He sat down next to Adelaide with a heavy sigh, wishing for at least a little more direction than 'go north'. Though the small campfire he'd managed to light gave off a cheery glow, he couldn't help but feel a growing sense of unease, fear that they might wander lost until they starved to death. Ignorant of his discontent, Adelaide lightly nudged him with her shoulder. "You know, despite it all, I can't help but be excited. Vampire aside, this is pretty much exactly what I'd hoped for when I asked for you to take me out to the country. I wish Levi and Erica were with us, and it were under better circumstances, but I still feel like everything will be alright."

A branch in the fire collapsed, sending a shower of sparks up into the sky. Allard followed their movement, watching them fade into the stars scattered about like diamonds spilling from a jeweler's bag. "I know what you mean. Being away from the city, away from everyone else, it's like the world has left us behind. It's like our problems don't exist and last night was just a bad dream. I almost don't want to find a town. It seems like once we do everything will start again. That the vampire can't find us out here."

Adelaide giggled and fell backwards to lie on her back. She lifted an arm, tracing shapes among the stars. "Well that's tomorrow's problem. What can you tell me about the sky above us? Without the city lights, I can see so many more stars. Where's the divine bear constellation?"

Allard lay next to her, turning his own eyes to the sky. The rest of the night passed in a hazy bliss, as he pointed out familiar constellations, directing Adelaide's arm. Eventually, she grew quiet and the campfire starting dying down to embers. A few minutes later, the princess' questions were replaced with the soft, steady breathing of sleep. Feeling his eyelids grow heavy, Allard stifled a yawn and moved to the other side of the fire, setting down his bag for a pillow. *It may be tomorrow's problem, but it's still a problem nonetheless.*

As he considered his bag, he remembered the combat manual he'd packed. Thinking about how ineffective his arrows had been against the vampire, he pulled it out and flipped through a few chapters in the campfire's fading light, looking for anything that might help. Coming across a minor spell that was supposed to enchant a weapon with fire, he decided to give it a try. Picking up his bow, he nocked an arrow and aimed out into the night. Feeling like a fool, he spoke the spell and tried to imagine the arrow bursting into flame. Nothing happened. Remembering how Erica described using magic, he tried again several times; focusing on the color red for fire, looking for some kind of pressure or heat within his body to push into the arrow, imagining a magestone trigger going off and a glass heart shattering, and a few other increasingly obtuse methods of imagining magic. But the arrow remained stubbornly unlit and he eventually gave up, unstringing his bow and returning the book to his pack.

Laying down on the ground, he sighed and settled in for a night of uneasy sleep on the hard ground, disappointed in his utter failure, but unsurprised.

Chapter 12

Sunday: 3rd of Hernus, Year 1980 R.S.

Muttering under her breath, Erica ran her hands over her robes once more. As this was the second day in a row she had to attend to the king, there had been no opportunity for her to wash her formal clothes and wrinkles plagued the rumpled white cloth. Giving the robes a critical glare, she wondered if it might be better to wear one of her plain dresses after all. With a defeated sigh, she headed down to the kitchens, tracing last night's path. She considered the day's schedule as she went, but that only served to make her feel all the more daunted and lacking time. As it stood, she only had enough time to grab one of the fresh rolls sitting in a basket near the ovens on arriving at the kitchen, moving on to the king's chambers with little more than a murmured word of thanks to the cook. She paused at the bottom of the stairs leading up to the royal office, sparing a moment to brush the crumbs from her front and calm her nerves. For as much time as she'd spent around Adelaide, she'd only spoken with the king in passing and found herself terrified to be included in his circle of advisors under these circumstances. *For that matter, all the time I spend around Addy makes it easier to forget that she* is *the heir to throne.*

Resigning herself to it, she trudged up the carpeted steps, shaking her head as she went. Levi stood waiting at the top, just outside the double doors set at the end of the hall. The doors were carved from a dark wood in stylized designs of wind and storm, gilded around the edges. Their color and height, combined with the length of the hallway, cast an imposing air, as though visitors approached a judge's chamber instead of mere offices. Levi nodded a greeting to Erica as she approached, the dark circles under his eyes and his unkempt hair speaking to the sleepless night he spent guarding the king. Likewise, when he spoke, his voice lacked the crisp tone he usually maintained, exhaustion replacing it with a curt manner that made every word sound irritated. "I thank you for coming, Miss Greenmaiden. I must apologize for calling upon you at such an hour after a considerably late and stressful night, but the current circumstances supersede all other considerations."

"Oh no, not at all. I understand completely and quite frankly, I'm worried about Addy too. If you hadn't asked me to help, I don't know what I would have done with myself this morning. At least now it feels like I can actually help."

Turning to rap on the door, Levi nodded back at her. "I confess I feel quite the same. I find it constricting to be held cooped up here when the one I am sworn to protect is out who knows where. You speak as though you are powerless in such affairs, but as my skills only pertain to the swinging of a blade, I consider myself the weaker of us by far." He paused on hearing a voice call from within the office in response to his knock. Placing a hand upon the door knob, he turned back to Erica. "Shall we then?"

Erica hardly had time to nod in reply before he opened the door and entered into the room. On seeing the king's chambers for the first time, Erica was struck by a sense of disconnect. While the chambers were certainly a grand affair, the office itself only the first of a series of smaller rooms, and the furnishings lavish, they were far from extravagant and gave more of an impression of a cozy study in a family's residence. For example, though the sturdy desk opposite the door was made of ebony imported from the northern country of Austall and carved with images from an old royal hunt along its front, these carvings in turn embossed with silver-leaf, the desk's surface was just as cluttered with assorted documents, half-read books, and meaningless trinkets as any other Erica had ever seen. The chair behind it, an antique from Pazyerra upholstered in scarlet velvet, stood empty, its owner instead sitting in one of the plush, stuffed armchairs set in an arc around the fireplace, a firestone glowing softly in the hearth. King Thierry sat furthest from the door, almost slumped over as he picked at a platter of pastries that had been set on the tea table before him, but raised his head on hearing the door open. Dropping the pastry he held, he dusted off his hands and straightened his back, addressing the newcomers. "Ah, Sir Crownguard. Miss Greenmaiden. I am glad you could join us. And now that all concerned parties are present, we can begin."

Of the remaining chairs, only two remained vacant for Erica and Levi, Estelle having already claimed the one opposite the king. She sat with a sheaf of notes in one hand and a letterboard resting in her lap, its autoquill resting on the table before her. Likewise, Viola stood at her shoulder holding several additional sets of notes, each separated by a colored ribbon. Levi bowed in response to the king's greeting, moving to take the chair next to him. With only one chair left, Erica curtsied to the king and took the one next to Estelle, resisting the urge to slouch under what she felt was a withering glare. The castellan ignored her, however, instead clearing her throat and typing introductory notes on her letterboard, the room filling with the scratch-scratch of the autoquill as it matched each glyph touched. "If you find it acceptable, Your Majesty, I would recommend we start at the beginning. We can best formulate our reaction to last night's occurrences if we first straighten out the facts."

At a gesture from Estelle, Viola made a circuit of the room, handing a packet of notes to each participant. Glancing down at the papers briefly, Thierry nodded once before looking at each of the room's occupants in turn. Clearing his throat, an air of resolution swept away the sorrow hiding in his eyes. "A sound decision. As we are all aware, the palace was attacked last night by a swarm of undead monstrosities. Intelligence gathered suggests they were vampires and, judging by their relative weakness and lack of any real strategy, very young vampires. We place their numbers at somewhere around a troubling sixty. Thankfully, the casualties reported are low as the palace guard managed to muster in time to prevent the from doing too much harm."

Levi raised a hand. "Your Majesty noted their lack of strategy, but has their true aim been determined as yet?"

Rifling through her papers, Estelle pulled one out and placed it on top of the others. "If you turn to page eleven of the report I provided, you will find the movements of the undead documented in full." Erica flipped to the indicated page and ran her eyes over its contents. Neat rows filled the page listing each vampire by an assigned number, its point of entry, and its point of death and a table at the bottom of the page listed points of frequent traffic throughout the attack. "The swarm of sixty split themselves into roughly five groups. One to assault His Majesty's chambers, one to assault the Perloran envoys, one to assault the Aurans, and one, strangely enough for such creatures, to attempt to break into the royal vault."

Erica looked up with a puzzled expression. "You had said there were five groups, but that was only four. What about the last one?"

Setting down his copy of the notes, Levi picked a cruller off the platter with a shrug. "I would imagine the ultimate group consisted of unassociated vampires spread throughout the castle to cause chaos. Given the kitchens are some distance from any of the indicated targets, the first two we encountered would fit neatly into such a cohort."

Estelle nodded. "Just so, Mister Crownguard."

Rising from his seat, Thierry walked to the fireplace, staring into the depths of its firestone. The stone's steady glow painted the interior of the hearth in a harsh red light, reminiscent of the vampires' eyes. "Yes. And as our fine castellan mentioned, I fail to see the relevance of breaking into the vault. Material wealth hardly seems as though it would concern a vampire and most of the other contents are merely antiques in any case."

Erica shrugged and reached for an apple streusel. "Well who knows what precisely is in the vault? For all we know, you have the crown jewels of the old Sunfire Empire in there."

"That is neither here nor there," Estelle said. "If we were to consider every possible object the vampires *could* have been after that *might* have been in the vault, then we would be here all day. The more pressing issue, and the one more easily addressed, is that they were targeting the participants in the negotiations."

Hearing this, Levi stood and walked to the king's desk, rifling through the papers there as he replied over his shoulder, "That being the case, one must consider the attack on Lord Reinhardt's manor. If these newly formed vampires represent the same mastermind, their tactics make little sense. Though he was a Summer noble, Lord Reinhardt held no military rank, so his death would do nothing to hinder our defensive ability. So why then would they skip from murdering a relatively unimportant noble to assaulting the palace itself? And more troubling, why did they neglect to send their most powerful member, Lord Reinhardt's assassin, in the initial assault? Even when it did come after the fact, the assassin only managing a half-hearted attack on *my* person rather than a more important figure before retreating."

Giving a weary sigh, Thierry turned from the hearth. "In any case, that is my greatest concern, Sir Crownguard. As you have noted, the greatest of their number, let us call it the high vampire for simplicity's sake, contributed little to the attack. If this high vampire had been present, things may have ended quite differently, a fact which seems to indicate it had a different goal in mind. Which brings me to the other conspicuously absent personage in these affairs. Where precisely is my daughter?"

Erica caught Estelle and Levi exchanging a glance as she stood. Bowing once, she spoke in a clear and precise voice. "Your Majesty, as far as I can tell, there is no reason to believe anything conclusive as to Princess Adelaide's condition. This past week she has been discussing her desires to travel the countryside in place of participating in the negotiations. After the invaders were routed last night, I checked Mr. Fortunata's room and discovered a rope leading from his window, presumably his and your daughter's means of egress."

Nodding, Thierry's face softened but the last traces of worry refused to vanish. "That is good to hear. While it simply means we are pushing the problem to a later time, there is still hope that nothing untoward has happened. And if she has your friend with her, at least she isn't alone. And there is no need for you to be so formal, Miss Greenmaiden. I know you are my daughter's friend. You may refer to her and Mister Fortunata as you would normally."

"Actually, Your Majesty, there is one other thing we've discovered," Estelle said. "Mister Crownguard and I discovered a pair of missives in our offices this morning, commanding us to take the princess to two separate locations away from the palace, my own order given precedence over Mister Crownguard's presumably false one. The convoluted nature of such a scheme and its untimely nature both give us little doubt you were not, in fact, the one who sent such orders."

The king let out a heavy sigh, resting his face in one hand. "I can't really say I'm surprised. Something like this was going to happen eventually and I have only myself to blame. I thought having you and Mister Fortunata around might help keep Adelaide busy, Miss Greenmaiden, but it seems it was inevitable. No matter my intentions, keeping her cloistered away for so long only led her to want to leave all the more."

Levi slammed a hand against the desk, the suddenness of the action startling Erica. When he replied, his eyes were filled with a zeal Erica had never seen before. "No! You cannot blame yourself, Your Majesty. The fault lies squarely with my own weakness. If I—"

Thierry cut Levi off with a gesture. "Peace, Levi. You have always done all that you could and I have never had cause to complain about your service. Let's focus on the present, not borrow problems from another time."

The room was silent for several seconds, Levi clearly wanting to say something more, but unwilling to contradict the king. Finally, he returned to his search of the desk and, finding what he was searching for, returned to his seat, holding the paper close to his chest. "Very well. Blame aside, we must ascertain Lady Adelaide's whereabouts. As much faith as I place in Sir Allard, I doubt he could repel the high vampire, should the worst come to pass. My recommendation is that we muster the city garrison in two parts. For the first, allocate the Guard Corp to patrol the streets of Riverluck, performing the twin tasks of searching for clues as to Lady Adelaide's whereabouts and ensuring the safety of the common folk from any further attacks by the undead. As for the second, send contingents of Regulars along the major roads to search farther afield. Likewise, in that way we can be seen listening to the Auran's concerns as to safe travel. A useful bargaining chip perhaps."

Estelle looked up from her letterboard. "A reasonable start, but limited in scope. You've failed to consider transport by river. In addition to sending groups along the roads, we should send out two boats, one up river and one down. Furthermore, you have failed to consider magical means of investigation. It would be wise to speak with Archmage Dwyer and the court mages to see if they can discern the princess' location."

Straightening the mess Levi had made of his desktop, or at least returning it to whatever order had been present among the existing chaos, Thierry chuckled. "Truth be told, I don't know how I'd run this country without you, Estelle. Rational suggestions all around. I will draft a message to the good Archmage to request the spell." Shaking his head, he opened a drawer and placed a pile of unsorted papers into it. He paused for a moment to stare at them before closing the drawer once more and gesturing towards Levi. "And what is it that caught your interest there, Sir Crownguard?"

Setting the paper on the table, Levi shrugged. "The report Estelle drew up in regards to the assault on Lord Reinhardt's household. While it does not pertain to the search for Lady Adelaide, I was curious to see if there was anything reported as missing. Miss Greenmaiden and I did already investigate the manor and noticed nothing out of place, but perhaps comparisons can be drawn to the palace's own inventory. And as for the high vampire..." He trailed off, silent for several seconds before continuing with a shake of his head. "It is nothing. I simply thought I might be able to uncover a hint as to its intentions."

The king nodded slowly, tapping a finger against his mouth in thought as he walked back to the group. "I see. I know Estelle already dismissed the idea of uncovering what our enemies might have wanted to steal, but taking inventory might still be useful. If we find something that stands out, a powerful magic item or object of significance to... unholy means, we could at least hazard a guess as to what they are after. *Or*, if we find something that previously belonged to, say, the Auris Empire, we could goes who might have motive. After we finish with this meeting, I ask that you and Miss Greenmaiden investigate the vault, Sir Crownguard." He glanced at Viola. "Oh, and maybe take Estelle's protégé with you as well, assuming the castellan can spare her."

Estelle started to reply, fixing Viola with a beleaguered glare, but Erica cut her off before she could get a word out. "Wait, why would I go with Levi? Shouldn't the vault be kept secret? Only people involved with this should go in, right?"

"You are hardly an uninvolved party Miss Greenmaiden," Thierry said, smiling. "You are a friend to both my daughter and Sir Crownguard, and that is reason enough for us to trust in your intentions. Even if we are to discount your abilities in the arcane arts, a subject you are more thoroughly studied in than either myself or Sir Crownguard, I am sure Levi would rather a friendly face aid him than a subordinate. And while I must confess to ignorance as to your exact capabilities when it comes to magic, I am confident you shall be of use in this situation."

A knock sounded on the doors to the chambers. The occupants started in surprise, looking at each other in turn. "Did you invite anyone else?" Thierry asked Estelle.

"I did not. Sir Crownguard?" Levi shook his head. Estelle gestured towards the door. "Viola, if you would?"

Nodding, Viola rushed to the door and opened it slightly, speaking through the crack. "May I ask who is calling on King Thierry's chambers?"

There was no response given, the person on the other side instead forcing the door fully open as soon as it was unlatched and Viola barely stepping out of the way in time with a shriek of surprise. With the way clear, General Neriah strode into the room. "King Thierry, I would speak with you. The events of last night have left myself and the other members of the esteemed Chancellor Lukas' entourage most disturbed. By the Flame's light, it was all I could do to keep my dear subordinate, Edan, from charging up here last night and giving you a piece of her mind."

In the silence that followed, Erica noticed Estelle subtly raise her hand. Glancing toward Viola, she saw a brief glint of metal as Viola swiftly slipped her hand in the opposite sleeve, depositing something there. Unaware of the exchange, Levi quickly walked across the room, standing between Neriah and Thierry with anger written upon his face, but before he could say anything, Thierry set a hand on his shoulder. "Peace, Sir Crownguard. I am sure the good general means no harm to anyone in this room. It is hardly in the manner of a soldier to announce his intentions to attack without giving opportunity to make amends." Turning to address Neriah, he stood with a regality that had been absent all morning. "Now, General Neriah, how may we be of service to you and yours? The undead incursion is distressing to our affairs as well so it seems our interests align in this matter."

"Your king's words ring true, Crownguard," Neriah said with a wolfish grin. "I have little interest in fighting you on anything less than an equal footing." Dropping to one knee, he looked up at Thierry. "And as you have said, Your Majesty, our interests align in this matter. A man of less honor might be inclined to believe you had set a trap for us, but the Auris Empire knows you are not that kind of dastard. So this is surely a plot by the same forces that murdered my dear friend, General Cyrus, to sow the dread seeds of discord among the just. The forces that sent their demon to the house of your noble two nights ago, as the inquisitors have discovered."

Unamused, Levi shrugged Thierry's hand off of his shoulder and withdrew a step. "What is your point, Neriah? Nothing you have said thus far is new information. What would you have us do?"

Retaking his feet, Neriah met Levi's eyes with a steely gaze. "My point is that the cooperation between our two nations might see this evil brought down. They sent a full twenty of those foul pit spawn after me last night, so as not to underestimate my abilities. I proved their judgment both wise and lacking. With my blade at your side and the inquisitors at your disposal, we could hunt down the enemy's chief demon and cleanse this world of its vile darkness. And without their pet monster at their side, the forces of Montiamon would swiftly fall beneath the righteous might of the Auris Empire and they would know the glory of the Endless Flame."

Estelle stood and tore a sheet of paper from its place beneath her autoquill. Calmly approaching Neriah, she held it out to him. "I have made you and Mister Erling an appointment with His Majesty, King Thierry, at one hour past tomorrow's lunch. My lord would be happy to hear your concerns at that time and come to an equitable arrangement between our forces. Now, if you would excuse us, His Majesty is in the midst of assessing last night's damages and cannot speak further. A maid will escort you back to your apartments."

Neriah's eyes narrowed. "Is this true, King Thierry? Do you let your subjects decide all matters of state, or only when you lack the backbone to act yourself?"

Levi's hand flew to Whisperwind's hilt. He had drawn it several inches before Thierry's hand closed upon his own, gently pushing it back down. The king placed himself between the two knights, fixing Levi with a stern gaze before turning back to Neriah. "We are willing to ignore your insult this time, General. But bear in mind that if you continue to act in such a way, we will be forced to ask the contingent from the Auris Empire to return home. Moreover, we will be forced to cut off the trade routes between our two nations, lest other countries claim that we are afraid to stand up for our kingdom and use that opportunity to attack." Turning to face Estelle, he smiled. "And as for my castellan, she is a trusted advisor. Those in her position have long assisted the crown of Tycortua with running the palace affairs. While we would ask that she not act without our approval in the future, she has done as we would have wished. So return to your chambers. This matter will not be forgotten, and we will appreciate what help your forces can give in apprehending those responsible for assaulting our very home."

Neriah snatched the paper from Estelle's hand, but he managed to keep his tone civil as he replied, "I will do as you say for the moment. It is, after all, perfectly reasonable for you, as the host, to dictate the circumstances of our meeting. However, know that should you delay the matter further, I will grow restless. If you refuse to address the problem at hand, then I will be forced to act on my own initiative. While I respect you, your authority is as nothing before that of the Endless Flame and the holy mission it has bestowed upon me." He turned towards the door, raising a hand of dismissal as Viola approached. "I managed to find my way here, I can return on my own just as well."

With that, he stalked from the room, slamming the doors shut behind him. Eventually, Estelle returned to her seat, shaking her head. "Honestly, what an insufferable man. I look forward to the day when I can put him in his place."

"There's no need for that kind of talk, Estelle," Thierry said. "I'm sure he means well."

Neither Estelle nor Levi seemed especially convinced by the king's words, the former giving him a level stare while the latter scoffed, saying, "You say as much, Your Majesty, but I would not trust an Auran with my back and Neriah even less. His words have only served to further convince me of the folly of his blind zeal. If it is our desire to uncover the culprit behind these attacks, we should look to Chancellor Lukas first."

Erica frowned. "But I thought it wouldn't make sense for the Auris Empire to be responsible. Putting aside the fact that the high vampire presumably killed one of their generals, they'd never use an 'unholy fiend' like him as their agents, right?"

Levi merely burst out laughing, shaking his head.

Despite his knight's mirth, the king fixed Erica with a quizzical stare, humming softly to himself. Eventually, shaking his head, the king replied, "Well that is just the thing about uncompromising loyalty, Miss Greenmaiden. It often lends itself to using any means necessary to achieve a goal. I am quite certain the Aurans do find these vampires as objectionable as they claim. But I would not be surprised if they did not think twice about using one if it meant serving the ultimate good they believe their Endless Flame has dictated. It is a terrible shame, but too often codes of justice are compromised in the name of that same justice they serve. You can never let yourself grow complacent with your own righteousness."

Erica caught Estelle shooting a glance at the king as he spoke, eyes betraying a hint of sorrow. More than anything else, Erica was surprised to see even that much emotion, more than she'd seen from Estelle previously.

"Either way, we had best be on our way, Miss Greenmaiden," Levi said, helping Erica to her feet. "We have not the time to lose, no matter who is responsible. By your leave, Your Majesty."

"Yes, yes. Search the treasury and let me know what you find. You have my full authority to do whatever needs to be done to verify the properties of any item within. So long as it is moral." The king held out something to Estelle as he continued. "Now Estelle, if you would convey them to the vault with all haste. We have orders to draft and messages to send, so I need you back here as soon as possible."

Erica stood and watched as Estelle hurriedly set about gathering her things from the tea table. Viola attempted to slip from the room unnoticed, but Estelle caught her by the collar before she could take more than two steps, shoving her towards Levi and Erica and following close on her heels. Erica shook her head as she started towards the door, astonished that she felt more exhaustion than wonder at the prospect of seeing the royal vault. *I have a feeling that today is going to be a long day.*

Chapter 13

Sunday: 3rd of Hernus, Year 1980 R.S.

The doors to the palace vault stood imposing before the group, glowing lines of magic running across them from wall to wall, a testament to their security. The rune carved along their length not only kept the doors locked, but sealed off an other points of entry. Reading the various magical locks, Erica understood it was a preposterous idea that vampires would have tried to break in.

Estelle strode forward with key in hand. The key itself was of a notably strange design, having two tines more like the prongs of a tuning fork than the teeth of a key and a glass orb set in the back with a pinprick of red running through it. As the key was held against the door, this red streak began to glow and pulse, the lines on the doors pulsing in time with it as the tines vibrated. Then the doors opened, steadily and soundlessly sliding apart to reveal an impenetrable gloom beyond. Estelle stepped back and pocketed the key and, as she did, Erica noticed that the glass orb was now empty.

"To verify, this is the *only* key that can be used to access the vault?" Levi asked.

Estelle nodded. "Quite so. As the lock is not physical, it requires the proper magical signature to open, that signature being found in royal blood. The current ruling monarch or their heir could open the vault whenever they so pleased, merely at the touch of a hand, so this key is only meant to grant a trusted subject a single time of admittance."

"So does that mean whoever's behind this was going to try to break this enchantment and hope they could do it before we ran into them?" Erica asked. "Or were they planning on..."

"Search the vault first," Erica said, ignoring her question. "If you find something our miscreant might have wanted, then we'll consider how they planned on getting it. I have business to attend to. The vault opens from within, so close the doors behind you when you leave."

With that, she left. The three of them stood there in silence for a moment, looking into the yawning gloom within. Eventually, Levi shrugged, looking to the other two. "Shall we?"

Erica followed after Levi, closing her eyes as she passed through the amorphous darkness covering the threshold. She assumed it marked passage into some kind of other-world, the palace ancient enough for such advanced magics, but when she opened her eyes, she was surprised by what she found. She'd expected to find a room packed with gold and jewels, covering the floor from wall to wall after having been thrown in and piled up with reckless abandon. The room she saw was perhaps as far from that as possible – a long room only twice as wide as the hall they'd just left with shelves, chests, and cabinets lining its walls. Turning around, she could still see the veil of darkness hanging before the threshold, but from this side it was semi-transparent, granting her a view of the hall beyond as Viola followed her through, the enchantment merely obscuring sight of the vault.

"Let us be about our business then," Levi said. "We do not have a moment to lose if we are to inspect the full catalog before the day's end."

Looking at the room once more, Erica took in just how many assorted containers there were. Her eyes widened. "All of it? We're going to look at all of this stuff?"

"Well I doubt we have to check every last coin, unless you think our aspiring necromancer wants base money. But you said yourself that anything in here could be something someone might be after."

As Levi made his way towards the first set of shelves, Erica started counting containers. She stopped after a hundred. "Is there at least a list of what's in all of these?"

Tapping a paper attached to the shelves, Levi nodded without looking back. "Indeed. Each container should have a manifest attached. They shall inform us of what is held within, if not what purpose the contents serve. Some of these treasures are centuries old, after all, stored away and forgotten. Each container..." He paused, trailing off as he picked up a small box. "Save for this one."

Erica was about to ask what made it so special when she recognized the box as the one Lukas had so casually carried in when the Aurans arrived. "Why wasn't it cataloged? Is it somehow dangerous? Do you think that's what they're after"

"No such thing. We merely had no opportunity to sort it as yet. In fact, we do not even know what our fine friends from the Empire gave us yet." He paused on saying this, carefully removing the lid and setting it on the shelf. After looking at the contents, his brow furrowed. "Huh. Could you give this a look, Miss Greenmaiden?"

Figuring it was some sort of enchanted object, Erica opened her senses to the flows of magic as she took the box. Much to her surprise, however, she could hardly even see the box through the lens of her magical senses, only a slight glimmer of something like several threads tied together into a single point. Taking a second look with her eyes, she found the gift from the Auris Empire to be a relatively large gem, about the size of a closed fist. Noting the deep purple color of it, Erica realized it hardly seemed to be of the Aurans' usual aesthetic, such a shade more generally associated with elemental darkness than fire or light. Tracing her finger along it, she noticed there was some sort of inscription on the gem's surface, but not in any language she recognized. "Huh. What... Do you have any idea what this is supposed to be?"

Viola peeked over Erica's shoulder. "Is it some kind of lattice-stone?"

"Maybe, but I have no idea what type. There's no magic coming off of it, so it'd either have to be a passive stone with nothing stored in it or a very strange magestone."

"So there is nothing magical about it that you could perceive, yes?" Levi said, closing the lid and placing the box back on the shelf. "By all accounts it is merely a strange jewel?" Erica nodded. "Then let us put it out of mind for now. I still have questions as to why the Auris Empire would give us something like this, but we should focus on the task at hand. The two of you take that side."

After several hours of sifting through a truly astonishing assortment of odds and ends, Erica sat on the ground with a frown. They were still only close to halfway done. She opened the small wooden box in her hands and looked at the object within. It was labeled as a 'Golden Lady's Key', but the manifest provided no other insight. The object was roughly the length of the palm of her hand with six teeth jutting out from the middle before ending in a point. It was made of a transparent crystal with a shining, golden light threaded down the middle and illuminating the point and possessed a deep resonance of magic within it, but nothing about its flows told Erica what it was supposed to do. Replacing it with a sigh, she shook her head.

That was what set her on edge with their task. They were supposed to be looking for something that an intruder might want, anything powerful or interesting hidden away in the vault, but most of these so-called treasures had no discernible purpose. Any enchantments were too vague or ancient for her to understand and the descriptions were often less than helpful. For instance, even though the thin, crystal slab labeled as a 'Letterslate' was described as 'a personal communication device bound to the user, made with Quatrainian magics', a clear enough description, she couldn't get it to do anything any other rock could do. And that was to say nothing of the items that had no description beyond their labels, like the 'Lanturian Lathe' and 'Galatine Sword'. The former was a marble rod and the latter a finely made sword that glowed slightly as if it were a sunstone, but that still didn't tell her what in the Teacher's name the Lanturians used a lathe for or what a Galatine was.

Turning to her companion, she found Viola inspecting a wooden figure of a horse, painted with black and white stripes. "Have you found anything useful, Vi?"

"Nothing at all. I was hoping I could find something fun to sneak out, but it's all weird bits and bobs. Even that dagger I found back there that makes copies of itself doesn't do anything useful since they aren't honed."

"You were going to steal from the royal treasury?"

Viola shrugged. "I'd hardly call it stealing. More borrowing without asking. They could take it back when I die." She paused to look around the room, picking up a pair of well-worn traveler's boots. "And it's not like anyone would miss these 'Sylphid Sprinters'."

Erica had to admit that Viola was right. None of the things in the vault seemed especially important, as evidenced by the fact that they were stored away instead of in use. Were it not for the preservation enchantments on the room, she had a good idea that everything would have been covered in a layer of dust so thick that you could press your entire hand into it. "What about looking at it from another perspective. Have you found anything that seems historically significant? Like the king said, maybe they aren't looking for something that does anything, just something that's important to them."

"You honestly think whoever's behind the attacks might be willing to risk war all for some trinket with sentimental value?"

"It wouldn't be the first time it's happened."

Viola fixed her with a flat stare. "Sure. Keep telling yourself that." She took a moment to regard the boots once more before continuing. "But either way, no. I can't claim to be an expert in history, but nothing I've seen has stood out."

Letting out an irritated breath, Erica stood and dusted herself. "Thanks anyway. I'll go find another section to start on then."

Before she could leave, Viola grabbed the edge of her skirt and stopped her. "Wait a second. I have a question for you too." Erica gingerly removed Viola's hand from her and gestured for the maid to continue. "Why'd you say the high vampire was a guy? Nobody said anything, but I know the king noticed too."

Erica frowned, only then realizing that she had. There was no reason for her to assume the high vampire was a man – she'd never even seen the monster in person – but as she considered the matter, the vampire she defeated with her cleansing ritual came to mind. Or more to the point, the expression on his face as the spell banished the vampiric demon and he crumbled to dust. *Because monster or not, they were people once.* Finding herself unable to say as much, Erica shook her head. "Hmm. It's nothing. I guess I misspoke."

This earned her a level stare, but Viola simply shrugged and returned to work. For Erica's part, she was more than happy to leave the conversation behind. But she'd hardly taken a step before she pulled to a stop again. *If it is something of purely historical value these vampires were after, then perhaps it relates to Zephyros,* she thought. *He is one bit of history unique to Tycortua, after all. And if I were going to organize a vault, I'd put the oldest things at the back.*

After a few minutes of walking, she found herself in an area that stood at odds with the rest of the vault. The back of the vault was partitioned off from the rest with a curtain and the space on the other side was furnished like personal chambers with an incredibly old and decrepit bedroom set. And in the middle of it all, Levi stood next to a nightstand, holding an ancient, untitled book. He looked up as she approached, flinching in alarm before addressing her. "What brings you this far in, Miss Greenmaiden? Is there something to report? Or did I lose track of time?"

Given the surroundings, if her hypothesis were true, then they were looking at what had been Zephyros' personal belongings. And if that were true, it came as little surprise that Levi might be more interested in the Storm Warlord than normal, given the conversation she'd overheard a few days prior. "No," she said. "We're still only about halfway done and have found the usual. I figure I came back here for the same reasons you did."

"So you also think it has to do with the Dusk Tyrant and hope to find answers within the records of one who stood against him? I suppose I should have guessed a mage would draw such conclusions."

"Maybe. It's just that the only thing I know Tycortua has that nobody else does is one of the Champions of the Four Corners as our founder. And it makes some sense that someone following in the Dusk Tyrant's footsteps would start by attacking his enemies' legacies, but even still..." She shook her head as she trailed off, struggling to put her feelings to words. "I guess it just feels like too neat a conclusion."

"Indeed. The king has expressed some concern with the second millennial anniversary this year, but I find myself disbelieving as well, even knowing how magic works. It simply feels too contrived. But even so, I find there is something else to it, looking at these old things." He rested a hand on the nightstand, the gesture strangely affectionate. "Like a sense of nostalgia towards something I never knew. I fear I might be hoping the Dusk Tyrant will return, though everything within me screams against such an idea. Like how an architect might dream of building a king's sepulcher while yet hoping his monarch's death never comes to pass."

Unsure what to make of that, the sentiment of his words alien to the Levi she knew, Erica turned her focus to the coats in the hopes of putting the thought out of mind. When the silence started to drag, she cleared her throat, deliberately changing the subject. "So? Is there anything interesting back here, or is it just his bed-set?"

Levi gave an almost imperceptible shake of his head, steadying himself and focus returning to his eyes. He picked up the book again, waving it as he replied.

Jarred from his own musings, Levi took a moment to recompose himself before replying, "Unfortunately, it seems our good founder did little conquering, despite the aggression his title indicates. None of the objects here are loot from the Dusk Tyrant's army or his fellow Champions' belongings. I would wager the most interesting items he left behind I already possess in my arms and armor." He gestured at the book he held. "Those and this journal."

The book's cover was black leather, cracked in many places, and the pages within were yellowed with age. She reached for it, but Levi jerked it back, almost unconsciously. "What's wrong? Is there something in there I shouldn't see?"

Levi blinked in surprise. Face flushing, he shook his head. "No, no, no. Er... well, maybe. You see, it's a fascinating account, though mostly in a merely historical sense, not, I'd wager, in any regard a thief might want it. But all the same..." He trailed off, running his free hand through his hair as he tried to marshal his thoughts. "I don't know if it should be made public knowledge, out of respect for the dignity of our founder and the royal line."

His reaction only served to whet her curiosity. "Oh yeah? And what's so undignified about it? I can't imagine history could have painted over our first king being a bloodthirsty tyrant, Champion or no, so that only leaves me to wonder... Is it so bawdy a tale that you're afraid it'll reach Addy's ears if I see it?"

Coughing once to compose himself, Levi firmly took a step backwards and tucked the book into his coat pocket. He fixed her with a stern glare. "Nothing of the sort. Merely things that go beyond the worry of the common folk. Now, I believe you have been working hard enough to deserve a break, Miss Greenmaiden, so please avail yourself of this opportunity for lunch." He paused, then realizing the implications of what he'd suggested. "Crows. That leaves me alone with Miss Faucheux. I suppose I shall be searching this whole place myself."

Well aware he only offered a break to forestall any further questions, Erica fixed him with a level stare. But Levi remained undaunted, returning her gaze with silence. Finally, she shook her head, letting out an irritated breath as she replied, "Fine. I'll go. But I'll only knock once when I get back, so you'd better let me in or you *will* be doing this on your own."

With that settled, she turned on her heel and walked away, too annoyed by Levi's thin attempts to deceive her to give him the satisfaction of having the last word. And yet thin excuse or not, she was hungry. She headed for the kitchens, but drew to a halt when she heard a conversation around the corner ahead of her in the distinct accent of Perlora, a man with an excessively wheedling voice speaking as she approached.

"Of course, sir. I will inform my household to look into matters and see if there are any others that harbor such sentiments."

A deeper and steadier voice replied, "Good. Make it so. I fear that blind patriotism will end up causing more harm than good in the long run. Things are already tenuous enough as it is with Rugego near reliant on us for trade. One wrong push..."

Erica knew too little about the politics of the Western Alliance to know what they were talking about, but knew it was something important if their relationship with a supposed ally was described as 'tenuous'. Though she knew she really shouldn't eavesdrop and it would cause less problems if she made her presence known and continued through, her curiosity got the better of her. Pressing herself up against the wall, she listened as the first voice said, "And as for Myron? He's already spitting fire about his son's close call in the attacks. Should I tell him about this?"

There was a pause before the second responded, "No. There's no need to rile him up further. And with inquisitors lurking about, we can't give them reason to question any of our retinue. I'll keep an eye on him and if things become... problematic, I'll let you know."

With that, footsteps sounded through the halls, one set approaching Erica. She pushed herself off the wall and back a few steps, starting forward as if she'd been walking the whole time. She turned the corner just as one of the Perlorans did, finding it to be Duke Gerald. The man stopped on seeing her, eyes narrowing in a shrewd gaze. He nodded in greeting. "Ah. The princess's assistant. I recall seeing you at the assembly. I understand you helped out young Thanasis the other night."

Erica hastily bowed, trying to look as inconsequential as possible. "Oh no, it was Sir Crownguard who did most of the work. I only helped provide a bit of support."

His eyes told her he believed she was hardly saying everything, but wouldn't press the issue. "In any case, I understand that you are to meet with him for lunch soon, to discuss the magical arts. Might I ask you a favor?"

"Sir?"

"When you talk to him, could you try to put in a good word for unity? There are some in my country that have grown tired of Perlora's dependence on others to defend ourselves. People that would advocate seeking our own fortune through our own strength. I fear that Viscount Myron, and by extension his son, may be such people and I believe that division would be more fatal than any knife in the dark right now."

"Very well. If I can find a way to slip it into the conversation, I will."

Nodding his thanks, the Duke started on his way again. But as he passed, he shot Erica a wry smile and said, "And maybe when you tell your king about the tension I fear, ask him to slip that message along to the Rugegans when they show up."

Erica bowed again, feeling her face flush. Though he'd known she'd been listening in, he seemed content to let things lay as they were. That, combined with everything else surely meant... something. The political implications of such a gesture were beyond her and a part of her feared that she was being manipulated. But that fear was drowned out by the one thought that dominated her mind as she continued forward. *Unity. And what better way is there to unify than to provide a common enemy?*

Chapter 14

Moonday: 4th of Hernus, Year 1980 R.S.

Allard woke with a groan and sat up, back stiff from sleeping on the ground. He muttered to himself as he stood and surveyed the campsite, irritated by his pain. *I used to go camping all the time back home and stuff like this never bothered me.* His gaze settled on the prone form of Adelaide, squirming about and grumbling something about "one more hour." *I suppose life in the palace has put me out of practice.*

He set about rifling through his pack, withdrawing a small pot and a metal bottle with a sky blue icestone set in the cap. Opening the everfull bottle, he nodded in satisfaction on seeing it nearly full with water. After emptying the bottle into the pot, he picked up a small pebble and tossed it at Adelaide, chuckling at the ensuing squawk of surprise. "I'm going to see if I can find something to hunt for breakfast. I remember seeing some wild sheep on our way here and with any luck, there are more around."

Adelaide blindly searched until she found a rock of her own and returned fire in reply, but missed by several feet. "Too early!"

"I should be back in about an hour, two at most," Allard said, stringing his bow. "If I can't find anything within that time, I'll give up. Try to get that pot boiling before I get back."

He set off through the tall grass, the blades slowly waving back and forth in a gentle breeze. Looking back once, he smiled to himself on seeing a thin stream of smoke rising into the air. As he crept forward, not a sound could be heard save for the soft shush, shush of grass against grass. The near silence was disconcerting and Allard couldn't help but shiver slightly, reminded of the same disquiet of two nights ago. While Tycortuan springs were still chilly, and snow could be expected until the month of Sophius, easily lasting through Aquans, the birds should have returned by this time. Not a peep of birdsong rang through the plains, however. Their absence was enough that Allard paused to nock an arrow, more to make himself feel better than anything else. As he continued on his way, it felt as though he were the only person in the world and yet the whole world had its eyes on him.

After roughly a quarter of an hour, he found signs of passage by a medium sized group of animals. The grass had been pressed down in a loose circle, twenty feet at its widest. Picking up a stalk of grass with the end chewed up, Allard twirled it in his fingers and smiled. *It seems to me one of the herds spent the night here. It's not long after dawn, so they can't have gotten too far.* He searched for distinct prints among the crushed grass. After settling on a direction, he jogged off, the prospect of success invigorating him.

Another third of an hour later, Allard crested the top of a knoll and looked down at a herd of wild sheep. Their behavior unnerved him. The entire herd seemed to be acting skittish, nearly every member tensed to run and the few soft bleats they let out subdued. Leveling his bow, he crouched down and started to descend the slope, approaching the herd at a steady pace. Once he felt confident in the distance, he set his sights on a ram near the edge of the herd. He pulled the bow's string back to his ear and slowly breathed in and out thrice. On his fourth breath out, he let fly. He was rewarded with the thunking sound of an arrow hitting flesh as it took the ram in the shoulder. It let out a high bleat of terror, echoed hardly a second later by the whole herd. Allard swiftly nocked and fired another arrow before running forward, this one taking it in the side and knocking it to the ground. By the time Allard reached the sheep, struggling to take its feet, the rest of the herd had run off in the opposite direction. He looked down at the ram, seeing the fear in its eyes. Feeling a hint of remorse, he pulled free the knife sheathed on his belt, whispering softly to the ram as he cut its throat, "I'm sorry."

Despite having hunted since he could aim a bow, Allard still never left behind that sympathy. There was a difference between striking an animal from several feet away and watching its life bleed away by your own hand. *I guess it just feels unchivalrous. Dishonorable.*

After unstringing his bow, Allard tied the bowstave across the ram's belly using the bowstring and hoisted it over his shoulders. Letting out a grunt of exertion, he stumbled a step forward under its weight. Shaking his head, he started back towards the camp. "Teacher above, how am I going to get this all the way back to camp?"

The sun had risen almost halfway to its peak by the time Allard stumbled back into camp. He let the ram fall to the ground with a heavy thud and fell first to his knees, then his face, exhausted. Mumbling through the dirt, he said, "I'm back, in under two hours as promised."

Turning away from the pot, Adelaide shook her head as she looked down at him. Pulling out a pair of small, bronze cups, she set about making tea. "Hmph. *Hardly* under two hours. I was starting to get worried. Honestly, what did you expect me to do if you didn't come back? Go out and find you? Then we'd both be lost."

Pushing himself up onto his elbows, Allard met her scowl with a frown. "Well, that didn't happen, now did it? I suppose I should have considered that before leaving, but I have more confidence in my abilities to navigate the countryside than that."

Sighing, Adelaide placed a cup on the ground before Allard. "Fine. I think you're missing my point, but it's still too early for arguing." Gesturing towards the ram, a look of exasperation crept over her face. "And what exactly do you plan on doing with that? We'll be here all day."

Following her gaze, Allard sat up and considered her complaint. Admittedly, there was too much to butcher in a reasonable amount of time, but it wasn't as if they had a good supply of food either. "Well, we might have to leave some behind, but I should be able to carve off a good portion. What we get from this should last us for a few days, ideally until we reach a town."

Adelaide turned away from the carcass, face paling. "Fine again. But I won't help you. There's no way that I'm touching that thing. Watching you fillet fish was bad enough."

Unsure what exactly she'd expected from a hunting trip, Allard rolled his eyes and turned to the ram. The general silence of the morning persisted through the process. Adelaide proved unwilling to spark any conversation as long as Allard was butchering and he only paused every once in a while, to rinse the blood from his arms and stack cuts of mutton on a spare shirt. Once he had cut, by his measure, enough to sustain both him and Adelaide through at least another three days, he shoved the remnants of the carcass off to the side and rinsed off his hands. Turning towards Adelaide, he picked up the meat and said, "Alright. Let's cook these. Then we'll be good to go."

Adelaide started collecting branches and grass from the surrounding area to build up the fire. While she did this, Allard picked up the pot and dumped out the remaining water contained within. Hanging the pot back over the fire, he placed a single steak in the bottom of the pot and set it sizzling. Soon, the aroma of cooking meat filled the campsite and both occupants' stomachs started to growl. After cooking the first steak to completion, Allard handed half to Adelaide, who received it with a smile. With little more than a quick prayer of thanks, the two attacked the meat with relish, savoring each bite. Though it was unseasoned, after an entire day of light rations the steak was as welcome as a full course meal from the palace kitchens. Once he was done with his meal, Allard set about cooking the remaining cuts while Adelaide lay back next to the fire with a content sigh. "That was quite good, Al. I guess I can forgive you for waking up this early and making me wait around all morning."

Even though he knew she was teasing him, Allard was about to shoot back a retort when he was cut off by a sharp rustling from the grass surrounding their camp. He dashed to Adelaide's side just as a humanoid form shambled out from the long grass. Letting out a startled shriek, Adelaide grabbed Allard's hand hard enough to turn her knuckles white and pulled herself to her feet, watching the newcomer as it jerked its head this way and that. For a few moments, it didn't seem to notice the two, but eventually its gaze settled on them, staring with empty eye sockets set in a rotting face.

"Go that way!" Allard shouted. "I'll distract while you escape and catch up."

Adelaide started to protest, but stopped when two more forms tumbled out of the grass, both in a similar state of undeath to the first. But while one of the newcomers was just as decayed and rotted as its companion, merely another zombie, the second was nothing more than bones bound together in a human form by lines of a dimly glowing purple energy – a bonewalker.

Trusting Adelaide's better judgment would lead her to run, Allard let go of her hand and ran towards his pack where his bow rested. The undead snapped to attention, the first zombie crouching down over the ram's carcass and tearing into it while the other two turned their focus on Allard. Picking up his bow and stringing it, he started backing away from the camp, keeping an eye on the undead. Both seemed content to shuffle after him at a slow pace, little more than walking speed, but they were focused on him with a grim determination and he had little doubt they'd chase him long after he exhausted himself. Allard hesitantly nocked an arrow, remembering how little it had done against the vampire, and leveled it at the zombie. He loosed the arrow into its chest, but the zombie didn't even flinch and continued forward unphased. Shaking his head, Allard took another step back and nocked another arrow. Aiming at the bonewalker, he struck right where its chest would have been, watching in dismay as the arrow clattered off after hitting a rib. Remembering his experiments of the night before with renewed irritation, he clicked his tongue. *Flame enchanted arrows would be* very *helpful right about now.*

With no apparent way to damage them, he turned and ran for a few seconds before slowing to a jog. Checking once to make sure the two undead were still following, he paused and scanned the area. Spying Adelaide on a hilltop waving both arms over her head, he changed course. When he reached her, she waved at the plains below and said, "There are more of them in the grass."

Following the path her hand traced, Allard noted that several more patches of grass moving. Straining his eyes, he could make out the vague forms of human figures. Most still moved towards the campsite, but the two he had attempted to fight as well as three others whose attention he assumed Adelaide had drawn in passing made their way towards the hill.

"I think our only chance is to abandon our supplies. I can't fight these things. Regular arrows won't inflict lasting harm on zombies *or* bonewalkers."

Slowly spinning in a circle, Adelaide surveyed the plains around them and shook her head. "Begrudgingly, I must say running away is the most favorable approach presented to us. I see little alternative, but without the advantage of height we will not be able to see them coming, so we will be forced to be forced to proceed blindly will the undead are not similarly hindered."

Allard traced over the paths of the undead below, trying to find a clear path through them, but paused on seeing a sparkling pillar rising from the grass beyond the camp. He shook Adelaide's shoulder to get her attention and pointed. "What is that? How long has it been there?"

Shortly thereafter, another pillar rose several yards from the first, scattering clumps of dirt through the air. Narrowing his eyes, Allard noted that it had erupted from the ground close to where an undead had been. Adelaide met Allard's eyes and shrugged. "Magic?"

"I think our best bet is with whoever cast that. I'd wager they have little love for these things too."

Taking Adelaide's hand, Allard crept down the hillside with his friend in tow, searching for more signs of magic. As they grew closer to their campsite, Allard picked out the soft sound of singing on the wind. The song lacked words but as they drew near, Allard was struck with the unshakable image of a woman singing to an empty lake beneath a moonlit sky.

In the middle of the clearing where their campfire had been, a woman stood facing off against four of the undead – two zombies and two bonewalkers. Dressed in long black and silver robes that barely cleared the ground and a matching, crooked hat that rested atop long, white hair, Allard realized she was no ordinary mage, but a witch. As he watched, she raised her voice and sang a sequence of four high notes. An equal number of stone spikes swirled into existence over her shoulders in response. As the last note faded, the spikes launched themselves at the hapless undead, pinning them to the ground. The woman spun as she continued her song and lashed out with a small marble rod like a conductor's baton. A strand of black energy spun out from the baton, textured like gnarled wood with knots every few feet, and snaked through the air to spear each monster through the chest in turn. The undead lay transfixed for a moment, held perfectly still, before crumbling apart into black ash. Battle finished, the witch flicked the baton towards the sky, cracking the strand of energy as if it were a whip, and both energy and song faded out with one final note, leaving the plains silent once more.

The witch stood facing the empty camp for several seconds, idly tapping her baton against her leg, before letting out a sigh. Shaking her head, she said, "Are you children going to *come* out, or must I *force* you out?"

Adelaide yelped and stepped back, completely foiling any chance they had at remaining hidden. Not that it would have helped, if Allard's suspicions were true. Well aware of the reputation the woman standing before them had, he decided they were better off doing what she said rather than risk making her angry. Steeling himself, Allard tightened his grip on Adelaide's hand and swallowed his fear, stepping out into the campsite. He bowed towards the woman, as politely as he could manage. "Thank you for killing those monsters, ma'am. We were worried about how we'd escape when you showed up. Those monsters ambushed us out of nowhere right as we finished our lunch."

Taking a moment to survey the camp, the witch let out a scornful laugh when her gaze landed on the remains of the ram carcass. "Hardly surprising.

The blood of that beast you butchered attracted them. Why did *you* think they showed up?"

Though her accent was strange and placed emphasis on odd words, Allard was surprised by how straight-forward her speech was. There was something surreal about speaking to a nigh mythological figure like a neighbor on the road and he found himself stuttering as he replied, "R-really? I hadn't realized that all undead like blood. I thought only vampires drank blood."

The witch shook her head. "No, no, no. Now you've gotten two matters confused entirely. It *is* true for the most part that only vampires drink blood, though that in itself is *something* of a fallacy depending on your definition of 'undead' and 'vampire', but there's an important distinction to be made in the *premise* and the *conclusion*. Vampires and their ilk drink blood because it is the most *efficient* medium through which pneuma, ki, quintessence, whichever you prefer, is expressed. This latent energy exuded by all living is, however, the same force *unintelligent* undead such as these are drawn to and feed upon. And as I have previously stated, blood, especially freshly spilled blood, is the most efficient medium for such and therefore gives off the strongest aura. Honestly, you wouldn't last an hour in the Forest of the Dead." The witch paused, continuing only as an aside. "Though I *do* suppose it is odd to encounter undead beings such as these this far south."

Adelaide snapped out of her reverie and stepped forward, eyes wide. "Are you really a witch? That magic you used was incredible! You didn't even incant a spell. I thought all mages had to speak actual words when casting."

The witch looked blankly at Adelaide for a few seconds before settling on a bemused expression. Chuckling, she pointed her baton towards the sky and whistled. A thin pillar of stone grew from either end of the baton, forming a simple staff that she leaned on as she responded. "There are those who call me a witch, and I cannot say they are *entirely* inaccurate, but I've mostly put that in my past."

Adelaide rushed forward, inspecting the staff with joy in her eyes. She looked up at the witch, ready to ask another question, but it died on her lips when she noticed the pointed ears just peeking out from beneath the witch's hat. Putting one hand to her mouth to stifle a gasp, Adelaide didn't even bother trying to hide the awe in her voice when she spoke. "Are you one of the Folk? But you look too tall for Forest or Mountain and too, well, frail for Desert."

Rolling her eyes, the witch ruffled Adelaide's hair. "You're just as bad as Morry, constantly pestering me with questions. Calling me one of the Folk is *also* not entirely inaccurate, though I am certainly not any of the Folk as you recognize them. And I would point out that you left one of their kind out in the first place, two if you count the Void-folk, but I've never been able to prove their existence."

Adelaide started to reply, but Allard placed a hand on her shoulder and shushed her. As she turned back with a questioning, and somewhat irritated, glance, he shook his head. Bowing again, Allard spoke, a slight quiver in his voice. "I beg your pardon ma'am. My sister here doesn't mean to insult you. She has a naturally curious mind that tends to get her into more trouble than she can handle. I can honestly say that she did not know who you were, great Witch of the New Moon."

Turning to face Allard, the Witch's eyes narrowed. "Hmm. So you *do* know who I am, boy. I suppose there's no point in asking *how*. Infamy does this sort of thing to you. Now then. You seem to have a good head on your shoulders. So tell me, why are the two of you out here, by yourselves, in the middle of nowhere *?*"

Proving just how little she understood the danger they were in, Adelaide turned to face Allard with startled eyes, silently pleading with him not to tell the truth. Swallowing once to steady his nerves, Allard brought his gaze up to meet the Witch's golden eyes. "Well, my sister and I were out camping. She doesn't get to see the countryside as often as I do, you see. But then we ended up getting lost after our boat drifted too far downstream and so we've been trying to find our way back to civilization since then. Anywhere we might be able to find our way home really."

The Witch stared at Allard in silence for nearly a minute, an inscrutable expression on her face. Finally, she raised her staff and pointed north-east. "There's a town in that direction, Zephyr's Blessing. If you continue to travel at a *reasonable* pace, you'll reach there tomorrow, shortly before noon. Now, on to *my* concerns." She raised her hand and spoke a word in Mystic under her breath. A thin disk of nearly transparent crystal coalesced from the air and swirled above her palm. She whispered another short passage, causing a thin line of golden fire to appear on the disc's surface, tracing a rune upon it in a language unknown to Allard. "This is a simple charm. If you set it in your campfire tonight, it will prevent you from being detected by any undead creatures until morning. I am *willing* to give it to you if you would answer me a few questions." She waited until Allard nodded. "Very well. The two of you said you are from around this area, yes? Well what do you know of the River Sage?"

"The River Sage? You mean the Ember King's companion, Seras?" Coughing uncomfortably, Allard continued. "Well, we're actually from up the Summerblood, a small village called Regina's Bounty. We have a legend that Seras settled there and her grave is marked by the Weeping Tree, a short distance from town in the woods."

The Witch growled in irritation. "I *thought* I was done with you fools. Even when I leave the village, I still hear that idiocy. While your 'Weeping Tree' is certainly a fascinating object, constructed from a naturally synthesized lattice-stone hybrid of waterstone and starstone that even, to my observation, grows as stone should not, it means nothing. At least not to *my* goals. I already checked and *it* was not there."

Adelaide furrowed her brow. "It? Are you talking about the grave or something else?"

"*That* is neither here nor there. I will tell you I am searching for something left with her and that is *all* you need to know. Now continue."

Feeling a little insulted that his village's legend, a mark of some pride, had been so casually dismissed, Allard paused to think before replying, "Well, that's the first thing that comes to mind. If you're looking for legends of the River Sage, maybe you should try looking in the town of Chancewind? It's said that Seras founded the monastery around which the town was built."

Snatching the charm out of the air, the Witch took a step forward and pointed at Allard, fury in her eyes. "Of *course* I tried looking in Chancewind! Where do you think I looked first? Now do you have any other inane suggestions or is that it?" Allard shook his head, but much to his surprise, the Witch held out her hand containing the charm. "Very well. A promise *is* a promise. Take the charm. I suppose I might as well check Chancewind again. Magic has the stubborn habit of making *inconsequential* meetings such as these relevant in hindsight, and I may have missed something. I would *hate* to spend years looking for something right under my nose just because I ignored you on the principles of coincidence." Allard took the charm from her hand and she stepped back, raising her staff. "I'll be there for a week if you can remember anything else."

Striking the ground with her staff, she muttered a sentence of Mystic and vanished, leaving behind only the sound of rushing wind. Allard stumbled back in surprise, hearing Adelaide gasp behind him. Pocketing the charm, he crouched down to inspect the ground where the Witch had been, but could find nothing but ash and dirt. "By Seras's stars, what was that? Did she just use a spell to take her to Chancewind? Can magic *do* that?"

Adelaide didn't respond and he turned to see her standing with fists balled at her sides. "Who said you could say I was your sister? We don't even look anything like each other!"

There was truth to her complaint since they shared neither hair nor eye color and Adelaide had generally sharper features all around, but her lack of awareness throughout the entire conversation grated on Allard's nerves. Glaring at her, he replied, "Well I had to give some excuse, didn't I? I couldn't tell her you were the heir to the throne, and why would the two of us be together if we weren't related?"

"Right. Because the Witch of the New Moon, one of the most powerful mages of the world, would fall for such an obvious lie. I'm sure she doesn't suspect a thing. And neither you nor her had any right to call me out on my behavior. I was behaving perfectly civilly."

Allard chuckled, ruffling Adelaide's hair like the Witch had. "Yeah, yeah. I believe you. But if you're asking me, I think she liked you. She looked more amused by you than anything else and she didn't get angry until I failed to provide useful information."

"Honestly, that surprised me," Adelaide said, beginning to pack up their things. "After hearing all of the ghost stories about the Witch of the New Moon, I thought she was supposed to be evil and menacing, you know? That she would capture us and imprison us in her lost tower so she could do magical experiments on us. Or at least put some sort of curse on us before she left. She seemed more temperamental than anything else." Adelaide whirled around to face Allard, puzzled expression across her face. "How did you know who she was anyways?"

"I told you earlier that I'd heard she'd been around Regina's Bounty in the last letter I got from home. And even though I know next to nothing about magic, it was clear that she wasn't just some half-baked practitioner. Those two together made it seem a reasonable guess. The witch-white hair clinched it."

Adelaide frowned, obviously unsatisfied with the answer, but said nothing further. Allard sighed and threw the pot at his feet her way, receiving a surprised squawked in reply. "Now get back to packing. We can't afford to waste daylight if we want to reach Zephyr's Blessing tomorrow."

Chapter 15

Moonday: 4th of Hernus, Year 1980 R.S.

Erica drew to a stop before the sitting room door. With all that was going on, she found herself dreading the confrontation awaiting her in the room beyond. She'd first agreed to speak with Thanasis out of courtesy, and some genuine desire for discussion with another apprentice mage that wasn't associated with the insular Tycortua Mages' Guild, but now that the time had come, it felt ill-suited to the current events. Putting aside the recent attacks and missing Adelaide, the latter of which Thansis shouldn't know about if the palace staff were keeping quiet like Estelle had ordered, there was her brief encounter with Duke Gerald the day before. She still wasn't sure what to make of him, or what he'd said, but it left her disconcerted and unprepared to face another Perloran.

Steeling herself, she shook her head as if that could dislodge her uncertain thoughts and knocked twice, opening the door without waiting for a response. The sitting room beyond was, unsurprisingly, furnished in the same style as many of the rooms Erica had encountered in her years at the palace. To her left, a pair of couches faced each other before a hearth with a built-in firestone and, to her right, two ladder-backed chairs sat on either side of a matching tea table, set for a meal. The dividing line between these two sections of the room, lounge area and dining area, was made clear by the arched window opposite the door, standing from floor to ceiling and filling the room with enough sunlight to give the room an airy feel, almost as though it were a garden patio instead of a sitting room. As Erica entered, Thanasis rose from one of the couches, setting aside a book he had been reading. Bowing once with, to Erica's eye, a bit too much flourish, he held his hand out towards the table. "Miss Erica, a pleasure to see you on this fine day. Shall we?"

Erica returned the bow, albeit in a simpler manner, and took a seat. "I'd be glad to. I don't know about you, but I'm famished. After oversleeping, I hardly had any time for breakfast." Erica could smell the aroma of freshly baked bread mingling with that of cooked meat sneaking from underneath the covered plates. "What have you brought from the kitchens this afternoon?"

Thanasis drew the cover off his plate, unleashing a cloud of steam. "While I can say little for the bread, as I simply asked the cooks to provide whatever they prepared normally, the heart of the meal I think will prove to be something the likes of which you've never seen before. I thought to challenge your Tycortuan chefs a little, to see if they could handle true culinary artistry. This is something of a staple dish in Perlora – a pan fried cut of meat served with slices of a starchy fruit indigenous to my country. Simple to describe, but difficult to execute if you can't manage the spices in the sauce correctly."

More than a little skeptical, Erica raised the cover to her own plate. The dull, red sauce slathered across a bit of meat sandwiched in between two long pieces of fruit hardly looked appetizing and did little to convince her of Perlora's supposed 'true culinary artistry'. Particularly when it wasn't like Tycortua was known for having bad food, not like the Naktikans who thought boiling everything was a viable cooking strategy. Erica picked up her fork and gestured towards her plate. "Well, as much as I enjoy talking up the food before we eat it, why don't we move on to the entrée of the conversation?" Thanasis' face remained unchanged. The joke, while amusing in Erica's head, seemed to fall flat when spoken out loud. Clearing her throat, she continud. "Anyway, from our introduction the other day, it sounded like you aren't associated with any mages' guilds. But if that's the case, where did you learn magic? I imagine either a guild or the Perloran court mages would have picked you up if you attended an academy. But to me, it seems as if you're still free."

"'Free' is an... *interesting* choice of word, though I suppose not incorrect. And you're right on the mark about my education. I haven't attended any academy, at least not for magic. If I could, I would like to go to High Worldheart, but... As much as magic interests me, it's little more than a hobby, a passing interest. Somewhere along the line, my family picked up a few old tomes to decorate the shelves of an office. I found them when I was young and took an interest in them, so my father agreed to supply me with a few more and I taught myself from them."

Teaching oneself magic from a book was a fairly difficult task, as Erica knew from personal experience, and seemed to indicate something of a talent for the art. "But that still doesn't explain why it's 'only a passing interest' or why you haven't pursued it any further. It sounds like you're good at it, so why not get better?"

Thanasis frowned. "It would be different for you. From what I can tell, *all* you are is an apprentice. For me, I'm still the heir to my family, even before being a mage. A Perloran viscount's seat on the Council of Twelve may not be hereditary, but there are still duties for me to attend to and I can't let myself be distracted, especially once I do inherit my father's role."

With that, Erica remembered just who it was she was talking to. It was easy to forget just how out ranked she was by most of the people who came through the palace on a daily basis since Adelaide rarely acted like a princess except when it was convenient for her. Pausing to take a moment to compose herself, Erica took a bite of her meal to mask her unease, finding herself surprised by the pleasantly peppery flavor of the meat. As Thanasis smirked at her appreciative nod, she let out a thoughtful hum and replied, "You are right that I don't really know what your circumstances are like. The only thing I can relate to is being self-taught."

Thanasis leaned forward. "Yes, I figured you were in a similar boat in that regard. I haven't seen many who could teach you here. Not to offend, but your court mages seem as insular as Perlora's guilds. And as for what you're learning, you mentioned that your name was Greenmaiden 'after the position you seek'. What do you mean by that? What's a greenmaiden?"

Erica laughed and shook her head. "Oh come on, you know." On seeing Thanasis' confused expression, she reeled back slightly. "You mean you don't know? I thought that they had greenmaidens and greenmasters everywhere. It's honestly not that exciting really. I suppose the best thing to call it would be a village doctor. Healing minor ailments and injuries and providing blessings for appropriate occasions."

"So then am I correct in assuming you're not actually from Riverluck, but somewhere in the countryside? By the Flowering Court, how did you end up an apprentice mage in the palace then?"

Remembering that trek through Thicket Forest, Erica set down her silver-ware with a wry laugh. "That is a story for another time. Suffice it to say, Princess Adelaide bears a commanding presence to say the least. But yes, my friend Allard – he was the one next to me the other day – and I come from a small village next to Thicket Forest on the other side of the Summerblood. It's called Regina's Bounty."

Thanasis shook his head, astonished, and reached underneath the table. Bringing forth a dark, glass bottle, he poured himself a glass of wine and raised it in the air before him. "Well then, cheers to you. I thought I'd done a good job teaching myself. But you couldn't have had more than one book on the subject, if that. I imagine such things are hard to come by anywhere smaller than a large town."

Erica shrugged, feeling less impressive than Thanasis seemed to think her. He gestured to her glass, but she shook her head. "I'll stick to water, thanks. And I did only have a collection of notes from my predecessors, but it wasn't so bad really. I honestly didn't even think that much about how many things I couldn't learn until I got here. I was able to learn everything I needed to know at the time from those notes."

Thanasis began to attack his food once more. "And was that the magic you used two nights ago?"

"Some. The healing spell, yes. But the cleansing ritual is something I learned here. It was a bit of an expansion upon a basic rite that I already knew to banish misfortune from a house at the New Year, but a bit more heavy duty."

Thanasis raised an eyebrow at this. "I'll say. There's quite the difference between casting a good luck charm and eradicating a high class undead, even if it was young and weak." He paused. Though she couldn't be sure, Erica was fairly certain he was looking more through his magical senses than his eyes. "Well, I suppose that's only to be expected of Tycortua."

Unsure what to make of that, Erica frowned. "What's that supposed to mean? Tycortua's hardly known for its magical practice, not like Maripphi or the academics on the Teacher's Eye. I mean, classical wizardry aside, our regional Inceptions are fairly unimpressive. Gamblers, Truthspeakers, and Dreamspinners can only really manage one note tricks when compared to the likes of Maripphi Worldweavers or even Austallan Mirror Mages."

Scorn colored Thanasis's voice as he replied, "It's not so much that you excel at magic as it is that you can find anything in Tycortua. While, as you said, you don't have a specialty in magic, or anything else for that matter, your kingdom is capable of existing on its own. A self-sufficient unit. You don't need to rely on other nations for anything, save for if you desire to."

Well aware their conversation had ceased to concern magic and slipped into exactly what she didn't want to talk about, Erica's confusion turned to unease. Trying to gather her thoughts, she took a sip of water and considered just what

Thanasis was trying to imply. "Is this about the negotiations then? Do you think Tycortua doesn't have the interests of the Western Alliance at heart?"

Thanasis stared flatly at Erica. "That is another discussion entirely and one better suited to our elders, conversing in official channels. What truly irritates me is how the shadow of the Sunfire Empire has fallen upon the world. Every country that was once a part of it has stagnated for the past thousand years. Only Tycortua and the two on the Threefold Eye were spared this fate. I bear neither your country nor theirs ill will, but you can't understand the struggles we've had."

It didn't take much thought to know what he was talking about since it was common history. After the Ember King slew the Dusk Tyrant and reclaimed his throne, the leaderless remnants of the other nations had flocked to him and the common people's admiration of such a great hero had led to the Sunfire Empire consuming most of the continent. By all accounts, it wasn't even intentional on his part and had simply happened as a natural result of his campaign to free those same countries. Nypheos and Lugherion aside, since they had their own circumstances, Tycoruta escaped that fate since the kingdom had been Zephyros' land and the Ember King had been content to leave his friend and companion to his own devices and rule over what was his. But even knowing this, Erica couldn't understand just what Thanasis was getting at. Everything she'd learned about history taught that Tycortua had always lived on a dagger's edge, only remaining united for so long because no one dared show weakness to the kingdom's larger neighbors. Erica frowned, unable to keep a thread of sarcasm from her response. "'The shadow of the Sunfire Empire'? If by 'shadow' you mean a millennium of prosperity which left its lands relatively stable even when the empire itself fractured. If anything, I'd say it was Tycortua that's stagnating, isolated in a world united under one flag."

Shaking his head, Thanasis laughed. "Oh, I'm sure it seems that way to you. Looking at it objectively, compartmentalizing a nation like that is incredibly *efficient*. The Sunfire Empire thrived because of it. When the fertile lands east of the Summerblood took care of agriculture and our people could train with experts in academics, magic, and combat in the likes of the Teacher's Eye, Maripphi, and Naktikos, it made sense for Perlora to turn all of its efforts to managing economy. We didn't need to worry about anything else, we were part of a greater whole. But when the Empire fractured? All we were left with was wealth and commodities. No means of production, no means of education, and no means of protection. We only lasted as long as we did because the Summerblood protected us to the south and Tycortua stood as a buffer to the east. If you don't believe me, then consider the Auris Empire. They were only a small theocracy when the Sunfire Empire fell, but they swept through the east all the way to the Golden Hills simply because they were the first to assemble an army and all their enemies were farmers holding sticks."

Though she knew the broad strokes of the history he was talking about, something about it didn't sit right with Erica. More than anything else, it felt like he was blatantly ignoring how much things had changed. It was all well and good to say the Sunfire states stagnated until they were forced to change for their own survival, but Tycortua hadn't spent all that time pushing further and further ahead. She'd said it before, but Tycortua being the sole nation on the mainland that wasn't part of the Empire, it languished in obscurity for that first millennium, unable to contribute to the Empire and too small to overcome its influence. And now that the shattered states leapt ahead in their ambitions, they'd caught up to Tycortua, nullifying its sole advantage. Ligbhtly setting down her silverware, Erica replaced the cover on her own plate and set about tidying up the table. "Even so, Tycortua's the smallest nation of the south, in population if not area. To your point of protection, sheer population size means you could field a larger army than we could ever hope to. Or to our initial point, you must have more mages simply by virtue of the statistical average distribution of people born with talent for it. There must be more teachers and a better knowledge base just from the amount of experience."

Thanasis fixed her with an exasperated stare. "Of course you'd bring that up, it's the natural counter. But it fails to grasp the heart of the matter. Yes, we're a larger country and therefore have more potential candidates for any given role. But we don't have that all important resource you do: tradition. Your Tycortuan Regulars have two millennia of military tradition and training behind them and that means every one of their number is better than most of ours. And it's not just that. It's everything in the country, all those systems and traditions you've built up that let people focus solely upon their vocation. You say we have more mage's simply by statistical probability? Well remember that even your soldiers and workers can use magic, even if it's only a petty talent. You have village mages dedicated to the craft who learn by tradition and instinct. Without that same backing, that base for all of us to build on, all Perlora can do is desperately grasp at whatever crosses our path. Greedily snatch up fallen bits of knowledge and lore that drift to us over the ocean. Learn from whatever old books we get our hands on, even if the spells within don't match our Conviction."

"And so you're frustrated that you aren't strong enough to either pursue your dream or ensure the security of your country."

"My personal ambitions have nothing to do with this matter!" Pausing to take a breath, Thanasis looked down, embarrassed by his outburst. "Well, I suppose that isn't entirely true. I *am* disappointed that my studies of magic progress slowly because of mere geographical limitations. I *do* wish I could find some spell, some miracle, that would give Perlora prosperity. But that's just it. It's all about Perlora. I would gladly live the rest of my life without a single lick of magic if it meant knowing Perlora could thrive."

Erica raised an eyebrow, surprised by the wistful longing that filled his voice. The passion and anger seemed appropriate for the hot-blooded, confident image he presented. Quiet desire, less so. Yet despite her curiosity, she kept her expression neutral as she responded. "Oh yeah? That's pretty different from the impression I got earlier. I thought you were irritated by how much your duties kept you from furthering your studies and truly pursuing what you wished."

Raking a hand through his hair, Thanasis sighed. "It's... Well, I can't really say. I don't entirely understand my feelings myself. At the end of the day, Perlora is my home. I can't imagine living without the sea breeze against my face as I look out over Springstone from the family manor's terrace. Or the sunsets against the sea in winter. I love where I live and I want it to be safe. But I also enjoy studying magic, so I wish it was someone else's problem."

Feeling a sudden chill, Erica crossed the room and tapped the magestone set in the wall. A small spark of glowing light flickering in its depths for a moment before disappearing, the firestone built into the nearby hearth lighting up a second later with a soft hum. A pleasant warmth began to suffuse the room, but it did little to dispel the apprehension she felt, a feeling that only strengthened as she mulled over Thanasis' words. Frowning, she shook her head. "I'm sorry, but that's something I can't understand. I understand that lack of certainty, and for as much as I like Tycortua I'd never call myself a patriot, but magic's all about meaning and intention, right? So how can it help anyone if you're always pushing things off as 'someone else's problem'? Even when being a greenmaiden back home felt tedious, I knew it was important because other people's problems were my own and I could fix them. Coming to the palace feels meaningless at times, especially when Al and I get swept along by Addy's whims, but it's important because I can be there for my friends when they need me. Learning magic without any of that feels like it would jut be empty. Like learning medicine with no intention of treating anyone."

"Empty, hmm? Perhaps it is empty at that, but I prefer that to the alternative. You criticized me for trying to push it off to someone else, but you know just as well as I do that magic isn't an invincible art. I would simply say I have a better grasp of my limits. I'm not willing to approach a problem until I know I can overcome it. Until then, it *has* to be somebody else's problem."

His words still didn't sit right with her, but at the same time, Erica didn't exactly know how to answer without coming across as rude. If it were just her she might be making a fool of, that was one thing, but when she was talking to the son of another nation's representative, someone who had at least some influence on the diplomatic proceedings, she couldn't risk him holding a grudge just because she was too proud and petty to let him hold to his beliefs. Shrugging, she forced a smile, trying to keep her tone light. "Well that's enough of that. I already told you the kind of magic I've been learning, but what about you? I think I remember you using fire and wind spells, so am I right in assuming you're an elementalist?"

Thanasis returned to his previous seat on the couch and picked up one of the books scattered near it. Setting it on the table, he began flipping through it as he responded. "Yes, unfortunately. The native Perloran traditions are beyond me, so I've stuck with classical wizardry and beyond the basic cantrips anyone learns, those kind of simple spells are all I can manage. Not strong enough to destroy anything worth destroying and not good for anything else besides that." He paused, finding the page he was looking for and pushing the book across to Erica. "This is what I'm working on currently. What do you think?"

As she picked up the book, Erica noted how old it was, the leather cover so soft it felt like it would fall apart at the slightest touch and the title, *Communication With the Land: the Mage of Emptiness' Pride*, not one she knew. Taking a look at the indicated passage with a skeptical eye, she frowned the further she read. "Summoning elemental spirits to bargain for power? That seems dangerous."

Thanasis shook his head. "No, no, no. You're missing the bigger picture. It's all about opening a line of communication, you see. You know just as well as I that there's fully formed civilizations in other-worlds, like those of the sidhe or Herne's Folk. Or even the titans descended from the false deities of Nypheos.

If I could find a way to talk to one of them without forcibly ripping them from their world, then it would open up the opportunity for further alliances. Additional trade routes that are yet untapped."

Erica had to bite her tongue so as not to shoot back that it was a very Perloran idea. And, more distressingly, that he was conveniently ignoring some of the other less savory things that might answer if a 'line of communication' were opened. Something like a fiend of Upper Abbadon. In any case, the idea was flawed by nature. Frowning, she pointed to the accompanying diagram, a complex magic circle with various stabilizing runes aligned through the center. "Wouldn't work. You're talking about a true gate between worlds, like the stories say the Ancient-folk of Lanturia made. Something that can let an indeterminate number of people through, both ways, over an indeterminate length of time. A summoning circle only opens instantaneously and can only transport a single target."

Now that they'd moved on to magical theory, much of Thanasis' earlier irritation seemed to vanish. Picking up another book, this one on geometric constructs, he held up a hand to forestall her. "Wait, wait, wait. But it doesn't have to be a gate or doorway. For communication, all we need is something like a window. Something where we can see the other side and speak."

Since the spell in question dealt with the notoriously difficult subject of spatial transmission, it felt more like a thought experiment, the kind of unsolvable problem that Adelaide liked, but right then, that suited Erica just fine. "Should you be basing this on summoning in the first place then? The circular structure is limited in operation, so maybe it would be best to start looking at it from a communication standpoint and worry about crossing worlds later."

The conversation continued as Thanasis frantically defended his theory while Erica ruthlessly poked holes in it. But all the while, a thread of uncertainty lingered with her all the while. No matter how hard she tried to put it out of mind, her dissatisfaction with Thanasis' attitude refused to leave. Even when he realized it was time for him to check in with his father and the rest of the Perloran delegation, Erica found her complaints sticking where the discussion would not. As she left the sitting room and headed back to Adelaide's study, intent on getting a bit of her own research done, one thought echoed through her head. *But where does it end? If you put off problems like that, wait till you have enough strength then take them on, doesn't that mean you're making every problem in the world your own in time?*

Chapter 16

Ashday: 5th of Hernus, Year 1980 R.S.

Allard and Adelaide stood on the roadside just outside Zephyr's Blessing, watching other travelers drift in and out of the town's gates. They had made good time that morning and arrived a few hours before noon, so traffic remained light. Most of the other travelers they watched looked to be locals, or at least people who lived close enough to be considered as such, and the guards leaning casually against the gates only further proved this assessment, calling out a name with a wave every so often. The town itself looked mostly uninteresting from the outside, at least when compared to Riverluck. It was several times larger than Regina's Bounty, but after years living in the capital of Tycortua, Allard couldn't see the small town as anything other than sleepy, little more than a hub connecting the nearby farming villages. Content that Zephyr's Blessing was large enough for the two of them to avoid any untoward attention, yet small enough that no one was likely to recognize the princess, Allard turned to Adelaide and gestured up the road. "Well then, shall we be off?"

Not bothering to reply, Adelaide simply nodded and started slowly down the road. Allard shook his head as he followed, surprised by her lack of energy. *Usually, she'd be dashing into the town, yelling at me to keep up.* As if she could sense him watching, Adelaide stifled a yawn behind her hand and slowed just enough for him to catch up. *I know she's bad in the mornings, but it usually isn't this bad. Maybe it'd be best if we rested here for a few days, lie low until things die down a bit and I can get a letter to the capital.*

One of the guards at the gate wished them a good day as they passed and Allard raised a hand to return the greeting. On first glance, the town proved to be much as he'd expected from outside, the street they were currently on running all the way to the center of town before coming to a stop in a central plaza. As the main street, it bustled with life as the town's inhabitants went about their day, enough people out and about to fill the street with traffic. Many of these people were merely chatting as they ambled along their way, but it was enough proof that unimportant or not, Zephyr's Blessing was large enough to be mostly self sufficient. Most of the buildings lining the street were houses made of whitewashed wood that wouldn't have looked out of place in the lower city of Riverluck, but there were enough shops in sight to provide most everything the town's residents could need, their signs hanging out over the road and proclaiming their wares in painted letters that would have been bold and bright at one point, but had faded to a comfortable tone. There were even a few specialty shops for things like lattice engineering supplies and honed weapons. All of these things gave Allard the strong impression that this town was a lived in place. From the houses that looked as if they had stood for generations to the townsfolk greeting their neighbors as they passed, he felt almost at home and could tell the townsfolk had set their pace centuries ago.

Most of this went over Adelaide's head of course. She stood at his side gawking, eyes wide with excitement and previous exhaustion vanished. It was almost enough to make him regret having worried about her, if all it took for her to forget her problems was a single reminder of her desires. "Well, Al? What's our plan from here?" She started inching slowly up on her toes to peer over the crowd towards the main square. "I think we start our search in the center of town. We should easily find what we need from there."

Following her gaze, Allard caught sight of a piece of red cloth fluttering near the corner of the road. On the other side of the street, a similar piece of blue cloth could just be seen. An image flashed through Allard's mind of the market stalls which lined Riverluck's streets every Loamday. "Oh? And what exactly are we going to search for? I don't remember us looking for anything in the first place. Are you sure you're not just interested in whatever they're selling down there?"

Fixing him with a steady glare, Adelaide crossed her arms and replied, "That is entirely preposterous. I was willing to defer to your judgment out in the countryside, since we were in your domain, but now that we are back in civilization, my expertise is strong enough to warrant no guidance."

All of that to mean 'Quiet, I'll do what I want.' She turned back to the square and started down the street in a huff. Allard chuckled as he followed, muttering to himself. "One step into a town and she's back to normal. And here I'd started getting used to being relied on." He carefully stepped around a pair of men hoisting barrels onto a wagon, nodding his head in greeting as he passed, then raised his voice to address Adelaide. "Look, I think the first thing we should do is to find a place to stay. We should be able to lay low here while I send a message back to Riverluck for someone to pick us up."

Ignoring him, Adelaide scampered forward several feet, bringing herself next to a group of women who greeted her. She curtsied once before turning back to Allard, smile quickly turning to a scowl as they continued on their way. "That is entirely preposterous. Now that our situation is stable, we should make the most of our time out of Riverluck. Though finding a place to stay is not a bad idea. Sleeping in a real bed sounds like what I need. And a real bath. I will admit I had not thought about how difficult it would be to stay clean with just everfull bottles."

Remembering just how much time out of each day the latter had taken, a grim retort came to Allard's lips, but he bit it back before they entered the main sqaure. The moment he stepped foot into the plaza, the feeling of ease he felt on entering such a peaceful town vanished, replaced by something like an itch between his shoulder blades, as if someone was staring at him. He glanced over his shoulder, checking the street behind him, but saw nothing out of the ordinary. Chalking it up to a reminder of why they were there in the first place, he shook his head and turned to face Adelaide. "I can understand that you wouldn't want to just sit in a room at an inn for who knows how long, and I'm not recommending we do that, but we should at least stay in Zephyr's Blessing. And make sure to be inside by nightfall. We still don't know if that vampire decided to chase us out of Riverluck."

Adelaide sighed, alighting on the edge of the fountain that sat in the middle of the plaza. Carved from a simple gray stone, the fountain was shaped like a pair of birds, a swan and a crow, rising around an elaborate urn, each of the birds holding a waterstone in their beaks. The crow stood just beyond Adelaide, facing her with water spouting from its beak into the basin behind her. She idly ran her hand back and forth through the flow as she spoke. "Well of course leaving town is out of the question. I could hardly be expected to see everything here there is to see in only a day or two. You need to have a bit more of a sense of fun, Allard."

Allard scowled at this. His mood was further soured by a worsening of the sensation that had come over him, now a feeling of crawling dread. He gave another quick scan of the square, but could see nothing out of place, only several brightly colored stalls, each tended to by smiling merchants conversing with their customers. Even a ragged beggar woman sitting near the steps of the town hall, the only sign of any unhappiness he'd seen, maintained the friendly mood of the city, contentedly munching on a chunk of bread someone had been kind enough to donate to her. Trying to ignore the feeling, Allard held a hand out, helping Adelaide back to her feet. "Well I think you need to have a bit more of a sense of danger. Just because we're in a town doesn't mean you can throw all of our cares to the wind, Adelaide. We were in a more heavily populated, and more heavily guarded, area the last time the vampire came after us and that didn't help. What makes you think he would stop if he found us here?"

This earned him another unimpressed sigh. "Look, Allard, it should be a simple enough task to resolve. The fact of the matter is, we either have a solution that can stop the vampire or we do not. If the vampire lost our trail or stayed in Riverluck, then we are safe. If he does find us and whatever solution we come up with fails, there is little we can do to stop him. So we might as well let things be and have a little fun. There is little use worrying about it right now. Now shall we see what these people are selling?"

Throwing up his hands in exasperation, Allard stalked after her. "And what exactly would you suggest for our solution? Even if you're fine letting things be, I'd rather have a plan in mind, just in case. And it doesn't look like this town has much in the way of monster slaying services, so I'm open to your ideas on the matter."

Drawing to a stop a few steps before the stall, Adelaide turned to face Allard with hands on her hips. "You yourself mentioned that legends say vampires have little love for holy objects, yes? Well, why not seek sanctuary at holy ground. I am quite sure a town this big will have Teacher's Hall, correct? It is likely the safest place we will find with the blessings and wards the clergy place upon them, not to mention the easiest place to gain shelter with what little money we have."

"Fine. I'll accept that as a solution for now." Looking past Adelaide at the market stands, he sighed. "In any case, why do we have to look through all of these shops? You just said we have very little money. Shouldn't we save it for things like food?"

"Just let me have this, Al! You can see stuff like this whenever you want, but this is the one time I'll get to explore without Levi and the palace guard looking over my shoulder. If you really want to keep moving, then remember this next time you and Erica are having fun at a festival while I'm trapped at a boring dinner with a bunch of foreign dignitaries I don't even know."

Allard followed after her, his own annoyance fading. *Right. I should have thought of that in the first place. I take it for granted that she's normal since I'm her friend, but it's easy to forget Erica and I are her* only *friends. Duty aside, her dad won't let her leave the palace unattended. This is one of the only breaks she'll get, bad timing or not.*

As they moved from stall to stall, Adelaide gazing at their wares with wide eyes, Allard peered over his shoulder from time to time. The pressure on his back had grown, settling into something akin to a sense of paranoia. It was like there was someone hovering just behind him, staring at his back and keeping track of every move he made. There was no one behind him, of course, but the feeling refused to disappear and he was apparently the only one bothered by it. None of the townsfolk seemed to particularly care about two young travelers. The beggar woman might have looked their way once or twice, but the dirty blindfold wrapped around her eyes and tied back behind her dull, gray hair meant it couldn't be her. Allard tried to shake off the sensation and made to follow Adelaide to the next stall when a voice arrested his progress. "Excuse me, sir! Please wait!"

Allard spun around with his arms raised and fists clenched, only to be greeted by the sight of a strange man standing a few stalls back, one hand raised above his head in greeting and the other held before his chest, closed around a small object. The man was dressed much in the manner of an ordinary traveler and looked generally friendly by his expression, but something about him seemed simply off to Allard. His vaguely tan skin, light blond hair, and narrow face each might have been ordinary on their own, but together seemed eerily out of place. Indeed, as the man drew closer to Allard, he found his suspicions deepening. The color of his skin somehow managed to have both the cast of one who did not see the sun and a rich glow of health. His hair managed to look even, despite irregularities in both length and color. And his face was proportioned just slightly wrong, the eyes a bit too high and wide, the mouth a bit too long and narrow. Allard couldn't stop the sharp intake of breath that came on seeing the rusty-red irises of the man's eyes, circling slitted pupils akin to a cat's. Forcing a smile, Allard replied, "May I help you?"

The man held his hand before Allard, opening it to reveal what was clasped within – a small bronze medallion with a simple sunburst design raised slightly from its surface. Allard's eyes widened as he reached down to check his pocket and the man smiled pleasantly, responding in a courteous voice. "I believe you dropped this."

Allard nodded as he felt through first one pocket, then the other. "Thank you, sir. That is mine. I don't know how it fell out, but I'm lucky you found it before I got too far."

He started to reach towards the medallion, but the man drew his hand back, letting it rest against his leg. Allard glared up at him, but the words of anger died in his mouth and confusion spread across his face as he met the man's eyes. Nothing of malice showed there, only an odd blend of curiosity and mischief. The man smiled in a measured and calculating manner. "I would be happy to return it to you, in truth, but only if you would answer a few questions for me in exchange."

By this time, Adelaide had realized Allard was no longer behind her and ran to stand at his side. Looking at the man with an indignant expression, she pointed accusatorily. "Now what do you think you're doing? You admitted yourself that it belongs to my friend. Do you think you can just go around taking people's things and taunting them over it afterwards? I'll have you know that is an irreplaceable family heirloom. If you don't give it back now—"

The man raised an eyebrow and smiled, chuckling as he cut Adelaide off. "Oh really, hmm? A family heirloom? Honest? It seems the Golden Lady truly does smile upon me on this day." He started walking towards one of the streets leading out of the plaza, gesturing for the two to follow. "Come along now. I think you'll find I'm willing to be most accommodating on this matter. We'll be going to a café just beyond the square, so you don't need to worry about leaving the public eye. And you'll be getting a free meal out of this too. Quite a good deal for a few questions, hmm?"

Adelaide opened her mouth to reply, then closed it with a slight growl, stomping after the man. Allard raised a hand to stop her, not exactly willing to follow someone he'd just me, but she was gone before he could do anything but follow. All told, he was more mystified by the exchange that had taken place than suspicious. Particularly when this was the second time in as many days a stranger had come to them with questions. But the man was true to his word, entering a fairly busy café close to the plaza. After giving the whole room a cursory glance, Allard saw Adelaide standing before a round table, opposite the man who was seated and leaning back slightly in his chair. Allard approached and took a seat between the two. "Who exactly are you?"

Letting his chair fall back down with a soft clack, the man leaned forward and laughed as he met Allard's gaze. "Oh? I wanted to ask you questions and you think to ask of me first?" Adelaide started to speak, but he raised a hand to forestall her. "Now, now. I never said I wouldn't tell you. It's a valid concern in truth. I am Xavier Stormtide, proud son of House Grian and vassal to the Summer Queen."

Xavier looked at the two of them expectantly. Allard looked to Adelaide, hoping she might recognize something of foreign nobility, but she looked just as lost as he was, shaking her head in reply to the silent question. Allard turned back to Xavier. "I'm sorry, but neither of us have heard of House Grian or the Summer Queen. We've got Summer nobles of course, but our monarchy is separate from that system. Where was it you were from again?"

Xavier shook his head as a look of disbelief spread over his face. "Lies! It cannot be! Have the Steel-folk truly forgotten so much in so little time? Has the glorious might of the finest of the Golden Lady's Realms faded from their memory already? Perhaps they are too far gone already. Perhaps my mission was doomed from the start."

Exchanging a glance with Allard, Adelaide leaned across the table, a look of concern growing across her face. "Are you alright, Mr. Stormtide? We didn't mean to insult you or anything."

A grin spread across his face as he replied. "I'm only kidding. Spring's mercy, but it's to be expected, honestly. No one of note from Morningstar has visited this particular part of the Realm for the past two-thousand years. Yes, no one of *note.*" His face settled into a grave expression and he set the medallion on the table. Looking at each of the two in turn, he continued. "Now on to brass tacks. Allow me to ask, you two are familiar with the one people here call the Ember King, yes?"

"Of course we have," Adelaide said. "I don't think you'd be able to find anyone in the world that hasn't heard of him. He did end up saving it after all. What does that have to do with anything in the slightest?"

Xavier spun the medallion, staring at it until it clattered back down against the table's surface. He raised his eyes to meet Adelaide's gaze, almost as though he were looking into the depths of her soul. "What does it have to do with anything? In truth: it has everything to do with everything. That is why I am here after all." He pointed at Allard. "But that is not enough for me. You said that you know of him, but what do you know? That is the crux of it. Go, young man, and tell me his tale."

Allard shrugged, still on edge as he replied, "Alright then. The Ember King's tale? Well, without going too much into detail, the world was in danger of being conquered by the evil Dusk Tyrant. Ignatius Valeria, the Ember King, rallied the forces of humanity against his dark armies and fought back. Along the way, he gathered three companions; the River Sage Seras, the Storm Warlord Zephyros, and the Crystal Queen Regina. The four were able to face the Dusk Tyrant himself and defeat him, restoring peace to the land. Ignatius founded the Sunfire Empire and Zephyros founded Tycortua. Seras retired to the countryside and Regina apparently returned to her homeland. Some people say that when the Sunfire Empire fell one thousand years later, it was because the Dusk Tyrant had been resurrected and by the time the hero called the Scalebound defeated him, the royal family had been wiped out and the Empire shattered."

Xavier nodded. "Hmm, hmm. Yes, I didn't know about that last part, but you do know your side of the story well enough. You see, while what happened with the Ember King was primarily a concern of Earth, in truth the people of Morningstar are not entirely unrelated to this matter."

"You do realize we still don't know where or what Morningstar is, right?" Adelaide asked.

Pausing, Xavier flagged down the café's owner and ordered three sandwiches with coffee. Returning his attention to the table, he smiled. "Very well. Let me talk of home. As I have said, I am from Morningstar, the second of the Realms created by the Golden Lady and second again from the Golden Realm. Summer's glory, but it is a truly wonderful place. While some might complain of unstable magic forming the fabric of its reality and storms in the aether-chaos, or the beasts and monsters beyond normal reckoning that wander the wilds, it is home and there is no other place like it in all the Realms. It is rough and harsh, but beautiful in a way only the truly untamable can be. And honestly, the cities are safe enough anyway since the Monarchs developed the second skies. All told, that is what Morningstar is, the place I believe you humans call the Demon Realm."

Adelaide gasped with eyes wide. She opened her mouth to reply, but couldn't manage to form the words. Unconvinced, Allard shook his head and inspected Xavier more closely. As strange as the man looked, especially his eyes, he couldn't quite believe he was any less Human than the likes of the Folk. "The Demon Realm? I guess I've heard stories of it before, of terrible beasts that come to Earth from the darkness between the stars and ravage the land, but you hardly look the type. Are you really a demon?"

"Yes and no, I suppose. Am I really a demon, like the fiends of old? No. I'm not what would commonly be ascribed to the name, a malicious spirit from beyond the physical domain. But I am certainly not human as you are and my people are commonly called demons by those who see us. So in a certain sense, yes. Technically, you should call my people the Quatrainians, but without context that word means nothing, so there isn't really a good name for what I am. Demon-folk is as good a term as any, though some others call us the Fair-folk and we tend to prefer that."

Adelaide leaned closer to Xavier, a quizzical expression on her face. "Even so, you don't look like a terrible beast and hardly seem capable of ravaging the land."

Chuckling darkly, Xavier replied in a conspiratorial whisper. "In truth, there are actually three races of people native to Morningstar. The first are the Commoners, everyday people little different from you except for slightly greater strength in both body and magic. They even look mostly like you except for a minor thing like horns or wings or a tail. The second are the Knights, and those are the ones you are thinking of. They aren't beasts, terrible or otherwise, but they certainly look the part. No matter how many arms or claws or teeth they have, they are still people. And then there are the last, those like me." Xavier paused for a moment, looking Adelaide dead in the eye. As he did, the room seemed to darken around him and his nails seemed to start elongating. His eyes started to glow slightly as the irises expanded to fill the whites, pupils narrowing further. Allard thought he saw the shape of a colossal arm start to form in the shadows behind him, before everything snapped back to normal. "We are the Nobles, the families that rule over Morningstar. Most of the time we look relatively human, but if we ever need to exercise our full power, well, we can be a force to be reckoned with."

Adelaide shook as she nodded, eyes wide with fear. Allard couldn't blame her either. An overwhelming sense of dread accompanied the brief transformation, the type of primal fear that comes from facing something one knows is beyond them. Allard swallowed, mouth dry, before saying, "Alright, I'm willing to accept that you are what you say you are. But what do your people have to do with the Ember King and the Dusk Tyrant? And if you're from another 'Realm', as you said, how did you get here? And when are you going to give me back my medallion?"

Xavier sighed. "Ah youth. All in good time, my dear Steel-folk friend. We must start at the beginning after all. You see, this is a tale of long ago. In those times, Morningstar was ruled by the Four Monarchs, each setting eighteen great houses beneath them to govern various provinces. One such being my own, House Grian. However, not all were content with the way of things. Several of the families broke off from the rest and started a civil war. It raged on for a time and was eventually quelled under the might of the Monarchs, but one man was still not satisfied. When the lord of House Morata heard his comrades were seeking peace, he grew enraged. When the rest of his house urged him to accept as well, he slaughtered them all. In the remains of his house, he called out to a dark thing and made a pact with it, granting himself power beyond what any had known.

"When he arrived at the peace table, he was alone, yet the full might of the seventy-one other lords and the Monarchs was not enough to hold him back. A war more terrible than the first broke out, ravaging the whole of Morningstar and bringing my people to their knees. With great sacrifice, we were able to corner him, but he fled rather than surrender and face imprisonment. My people were not able to stop his flight and he found himself on Earth, in a land unprepared for his arrival. The finest Knights and Nobles of Morningstar threw away their futures to follow him. But when they arrived, they were astounded to find that a human hero, one of the weak Steel-folk, had already vanquished him, sealing him away at the cost of the hero's life.

"Much of that story is legend, and the details have faded with time, but one thing is certain: the lord of House Morata still lives today and rages against his bonds. House Grian swore in the aftermath of his first rise that we would watch the seal upon him. And so the Stormtides were born, my family who have sworn among all our house to watch for the rising tide of calamity. When the one you call the Dusk Tyrant began to gain power, drawing upon the dark forces Lord Morata offered, one of my predecessors felt Lord Morata's seal weakening and sent himself to Earth to bring an end to whatever might come. He was the one that you called Storm Warlord, Zephyros."

At this, Adelaide practically leapt forward in her seat. "What?! Zephyros was one of you Fair-folk? Are you serious? Does that mean that I'm descended from a demon?"

Xavier's eyes widened. "Oho. I suppose I know why the Golden Lady led me to you then. I don't know anything about your past, but if you truly are descended from Zephyros, then yes, you are part demon, insofar as my kind are demons. Though I wouldn't worry too much about it, in truth. Enough time has passed that your blood will not change your humanity unless you seek that change out."

Adelaide fell back into her chair, silent. She looked out the window, a far off look on her face. Allard sighed as he imagined the childish daydreams she was surely having. "So if Zephyros was sent to check on Lord Morata's seal when it weakened," Allard said, "is that why you came here? And more importantly, if the full might of your people couldn't kill him, then how was the Ember King able to defeat the Dusk Tyrant?"

Their food arrived and Xavier took a sip of coffee before he continued. "You assume correctly. I am here to ensure that Lord Morata does not escape his bonds. As for the second point, the Dusk Tyrant and Lord Morata were not the same person. As far as I can tell, the Dusk Tyrant was merely a man seeking power, a man who wished to conquer. Lord Morata did not escape his prison and the seal remained unbroken, but he was able to grant the Dusk Tyrant some of his own power so it might be accomplished. And that is why your Ember King could succeed. He faced only a fraction of Lord Morata's power, in nothing more than a human vessel."

Disturbed by the implication that there was something worse than the Dusk Tyrant waiting, Allard took a bite of his sandwich and tried to rally his thoughts. "If that's all true, then why are you talking to us about it? Shouldn't you go to the king or something? Anything we can tell you is something that anyone could tell you. And you keep saying something about 'the Golden Lady leading you to us'. What do you mean by that?"

"Ah, of course. In truth I *was* headed to Riverluck to speak with its king. As he rules the land of my predecessor, it was reasonable to believe he could grant mes ome measure of assistance. But that changed when I met you. You see, after defeating the Dusk Tyrant, Zephyros couldn't return to Morningstar. It's part of how the walls around our Realm work. But he did manage to send back a message detailing his story. Included in that story was a description of his friend, Ignatius. Your Ember King was noted to keep a bronze medallion on him as a lucky charm." He held up Allard's medallion. "A bronze medallion with a sunburst design. Now I'm not saying this is the same medallion, but it has the same design. And I just happened to find it on the ground and just happened to be able to return it to you. It all seems to be a rather happy coincidence, no? To me, it feels more reasonable to believe the divine providence of the Golden Lady is guiding my path and I was supposed to meet you."

While Allard did agree that it seemed a little *too* convenient to be coincidence, he found himself more suspicious of the circumstances than thankful. He knew his pockets were secure and there should have been no way his medallion had simply fallen from them. But at the same time, he didn't have a good explanation for how it had happened, especially since he'd been on guard since entering the plaza and felt confident he'd have noticed if someone picked his pocket. But before he could consider further, Adelaide turned back from the window, eyes gleaming and a wide smile across her face. "Of course! We'll gladly help. Once we return to Riverluck, I can let you speak with my father. While he begins making preparations and letting the other countries know of what's to come, we can go to the Order of the Eagle on the Threefold Eye to ask for their aid."

Allard sighed. "So much for subtlety then. I'm sorry, Mr. Stormtide, my friend is getting ahead of herself. We would gladly provide what help we can, if it means stopping another Dusk Tyrant, but we're currently in a bit of trouble ourselves."

Xavier raised an eyebrow. "Summer's glory, this is truly a good day. Not only have I found those who can help me, but they have been caught in the machinations of fate already. Tell me about your problem then. What seems to be the issue?"

"I hardly think this is related to your Lord Morata, but a vampire murdered a noble in Tycortua. A few nights later, we ended up chased out of the city by that same vampire. We're not sure if he's still following us, but we'd rather not meet him again either way."

Xavier nodded. "I see, I see. Truly, it may not be directly related, but this is surely the first step on our path to saving the world. These things all must happen for a reason, as the Golden Lady dictates. A challenge has been placed in front of you, to prepare you for what is to come."

Adelaide nodded along enthusiastically. "Yeah, he's right, Al. The fact that you had a medallion like the Ember King's must mean you're the next great hero. And I can be your Zephyros and Erica can be your Seras. Though I guess that makes Levi your Regina."

Setting his coffee cup on his empty plate with a soft clack, Allard shook his head. "There are several things wrong with that idea, Adelaide. Not least of which is that we should leave this to the professionals." Turning to address Xavier, he continued, "To that point, we aren't prepared to fight such a monster, Mr. Stormtide. The last time we saw him, all we could do was run. Frankly, our plan for now was to hide in this town's Teacher's Hall, hoping its wards would protect us."

Xavier placed a few coins on the table before responding. "Now, now, Al, you can just call me Xavier. And you can have this back." He slid the medallion across the table, placing it in front of Allard. "It would be best to spend the night in this Teacher's Hall as you said, just in case. You two head there and get things settled. I'll start asking around town to see if there are any rumors about this vampire."

Allard frowned as he picked up the medallion. Deciding the Quatrainian shared too much of Adelaide's obstinance for any protest to matter, he let it go and started to place the medallion back in his pocket. Then, thinking better of it since he'd almost lost the medallion once that way, he threw it in his pack. "You talk like you're coming with us. Don't you have places to go and things to be about?"

Adelaide rapped his shoulder with her fist. "You're being rude to our new friend, Al. Of course Xavi is coming with us from now on. It's like he said, these things happen for a reason, and he was meant to find us."

Allard sighed. "Fine. There's no use trying to convince both of you. Let's get going then."

Chapter 17

Ashday: 5th of Hernus, Year 1980 R.S.

Erica idly strolled down the hallway, Viola chattering at her side. In a pleasant reversal of the previous few nights, she had slept rather well, leaving her in a good mood this morning. Content to merely enjoy the day, she smiled to herself as Viola continued on, only half listening. "I was already excited about the festival, but to have a duel too? This year is twice as exciting as any in the past five. What do you think, Erica? Will Levi be able to beat Neriah?"

Shaken from her daydreams, Erica stumbled, clearing her throat to recompose herself before responding. "Ah, well, I don't really know that much about swordplay, so I can hardly put together a guess. I guess you'd expect them to be roughly evenly matched, since they both wear Ancient's Armor. Maybe Neriah might be at the advantage since he's seen more recent active combat?"

Viola laughed. "Oh come on! That's not what it's about for people like us. Let the experts and connoisseurs worry about the details like skill and experience. We're here to support our friend. So let me hear you shout it out at the top of your lungs."

Erica chuckled. "Alright, then I guess Levi will win."

Viola sprinted ahead of Erica, turning to face her as she continued walking backwards. "That's not enough by half. Let's hear you really say it!"

Erica started to reply, lifting her arms in a grand gesture, but stopped on seeing Estelle standing at the next corner. The castellan stood with arms crossed and foot tapping, as though waiting for something. Figuring she was in a less than amicable mood, Erica gave a polite bow as she greeted her, hoping to slide by quickly. "Good morning, madam. Vi and I were on our way to watch the duel. Was there something you needed before we go?"

Viola curtsied to Estelle. "I brought her as you requested, Miss Estelle. Is there anything else you require of me?"

Erica's mouth dropped open in disbelief as she looked back and forth between the two. Estelle nodded. "You may go, Viola. I shall handle things from here." Viola curtsied again, turning briefly to Erica with an apologetic look before running off down the hallway. Erica had a few things in mind to shout after her friend, but Estelle raised a hand and gestured for Erica to follow her before she could get a word out. "If you would come with me, Miss Greenmaiden. King Thierry has asked that you join him in watching the duel."

Letting out a disappointed sigh, Erica set off after Estelle, resigning herself to whatever Viola had dragged her into. "I assume he has something he wishes to speak with me about?"

Estelle let out an amused breath that could only generously be described as a laugh. "Right you are. Mister Crownguard would be joining you as well, but for obvious reasons, cannot."

As they exited the palace onto a garden terrace and descended into the grounds, Erica could see the arena for the morning's duel in the distance, just outside the palace walls. It had been hastily constructed and was not meant to be a permanent fixture, but looked just as good as the famed arenas of Nypheos to Erica's eyes. The circular design and open roof, as well as the terraced seating around the main battleground, was a testament to the inspiration behind the architecture – a duel between two bearers of Ancient's Armor all but equated in importance to the Nyphean Tournaments of the Council.

Yet for all of the excited atmosphere surrounding the arena, much of it was lost on Erica. As she silently followed Estelle through the delicately groomed topiaries of the palace gardens, their leaves and needles still glistening with morning dew, she was struck by how truly wonderful the morning was and couldn't help but sigh with contentment. On any other day, she would have liked nothing more than to wander amidst the white roses and blue irises planted to grow in patterns reminiscent of the wind. *But today I have work to be about.*

She closed her eyes and focused on the world around her, sensing the gardens in a blaze of color and life. Taking it all in, she attempted to store every bit in her memory. The warmth and light of the sun; the gentle cool breeze; the mild scent of the wet grass and blooming flowers. All of it combined to make a day like no other, a day that would never come again in all her life. She felt slight bits slipping from her mind as she concentrated, distracted thoughts eroding the memory in the process of its making, but at the end of a few moments the memory settled in her heart, warm as an ember. *And so this morning will be a part of me evermore.* She smiled with satisfaction. *I'd been worried I was getting lazy with my meditations, but it looks like I'm fine.*

After another minute or two, Estelle cleared her throat, placing a hand on Erica's shoulder to stop her. "Not to interrupt, Miss Greenmaiden, but we've arrived." Erica opened her eyes and looked up at the palace walls before her. A small box draped in sky blue cloth had been constructed on the walk above so the members of the royal family could watch the duel without leaving the safety of the palace grounds. Two more boxes had been constructed on either side of it, one draped in pale green cloth and the other in golden cloth, for the Perloran and Auran embassies, respectively. Estelle gestured to a set of stairs built into the wall. "If you would? His Majesty is waiting for you up there."

Shortly after Erica started to ascend the steps, she realized Estelle had no moved. She turned back, confused. "Aren't you coming too?"

Estelle laughed. "Unfortunately, no. While I would enjoy watching what Mister Crownguard and that Auran fool call dueling, I'm afraid I still have work to attend to within the palace. It's as they say, 'Riverluck never rests.'"

Erica paled. "I'm going to be talking to King Thierry by myself? But what if I do something stupid? What if I accidentally insult him?"

Just like that, all humor vanished from Estelle's face. Shaking her head, she said, "I will not be required at this meeting. I have already been apprised of everything that shall be discussed. And to the second point, you don't have to worry about offending the king. You're his daughter's dear friend. He knows you mean well."

With that, Estelle waved and started back to the palace. Unconvinced by the castellan's assurances, Erica stood frozen for a moment, keeping one hand against the wall to steady herself. Then, figuring there was nothing to be gained by just standing around, she steeled herself and headed up the stairs. On reaching the top, she looked down over the city as she crossed the walk. Though she had seen Riverluck from the palace windows before, there was something a bit different about seeing it from the top of the walls. It looked both so much closer and so much smaller. She could see the whole city, not counting the garrison on the other side of the palace, spreading out down the gentle slope of Riverluck's hill, all the way to the Summerblood below. And looking into the arena, she was reminded of just how big the city was. More people than she would have thought possible filled the stands, milling about and chatting with each other while they waited for the duel to start. Very few of them actually paid any attention to the combatants as they went through their warmups, Levi striding back and forth on one side of the arena floor while Neriah stood with a wooden practice blade in hand, slowly going through a set of parries and slashes on the other. Aware that she was only distracting herself, Erica clapped her hands to snap herself out of her reverie. *Alright. Time to stop putting it off.* Thinking as much, she strode towards the viewing box before she could lose focus again. Stopping just outside the sky blue curtain that served as a door, she knocked on the wood of the box, calling, "Excuse me, sir, you summoned me?"

"Of course, of course. Come in," the king replied.

Erica drew aside the curtain and took a step forward, bowing as she did. Thierry laughed with a shake of his head. "There's no need for that, Miss Greenmaiden. As I've said before, there is no need for such formalities with me. You do more for me than you could know, simply by being my daughter's friend. And in any case, I should probably be bowing to you with what I'm going to ask."

Erica straightened, brow furrowed in confusion, but the king said nothing more on the matter, merely gesturing towards the cushioned chair next to his seat. While it was nowhere as fine as the throne on which he sat, it was certainly nicer than any chair she had been allowed to sit on before and left her more uncomfortable for it. Sitting with her back as straight as possible, she turned to face the king, trying as hard as she could to imitate Estelle's stoicism. Thierry looked back at her with a bemused expression, shoulders shaking with silent laughter. "Oh, just relax. Even if I have things to discuss with you, we are here to enjoy a bit of sport. And I have royal duties to attend to first, so avail yourself of the refreshments."

Rising to his feet, the king walked forward to the edge of the viewing box, parting a nearly transparent curtain Erica hadn't noticed before. Noting that he had begun the duel's opening ceremony, Erica was more interested in the faint shimmer of magic she saw around the edges of the curtain, likely an enchantment to ensure that the private boxes were kept private. Content that she was free to do as she please without fear of anyone seeing her, Erica began wandering about the box as the king continued to address the crowds below. There was little furnishing, all things considered, with only a small a side table between the two chairs, a half full cup of coffee resting on Thierry's side next to a plate filled with crumbs, and a long table at the back, filled with a wide variety of snacks. For all the viewing box lacked in extravagance in its furniture, the food made up for in its variety. The table bore foods from all over the continent – from a plate of daggerfish prepared in the Austallan fashion and served with an odd green sauce to what looked like a bowl of genuine Desert-folk sandlobster soup on the other. Deciding it was safer to stick to the fruit, Erica set herself a plate of Skahian frost cherries and a glass of water and sat back down to wait for King Thierry to finish.

After a few minutes, Thierry slumped down into his throne with a sigh. Erica set down her glass and looked towards him with an inquisitive expression. "So how much can people see from the outside then?"

Shooting her an appreciative glance, the king smiled. "Well spotted. I should have figured you would have noticed the illusion spell. The crowds see me sitting with all of the dignity and rapt attention befitting a king watching his champion, not a tired old man who'd rather the challenger leave without a fight." Erica frowned. As far as she knew, the king was somewhere in his mid-forties; far from young, but nowhere near what she'd call old. "And more importantly, it makes you appear as though you are no more than a server to accompany the food. It would be somewhat counterproductive if people realized that this secret meeting is in fact a secret meeting."

"What do you mean, a 'secret meeting'? What exactly did you want to speak with me about?"

Thierry raised a hand to forestall her and nodded to the arena below where the two knights had donned their armor. Seeing them both standing opposite each other, roughly one hundred feet apart with swords held in a salute, Erica was amazed by how different they looked despite the similarities of their Ancient's Armor. Where the Crownguard armor possessed a kind of delicate elegance befitting the wind, the edges of the various plates curving at the end so there was hardly a straight line in all of the armor, the plate of light had a straightforward, stark design to it, all angles and flat surfaces. The comparison even extended to their swords which, though forged separately from the armor, managed to match almost perfectly to the individual styles. Where Levi's Whisperwind had a light, slightly curved blade meant more for slashing than stabbing, Neriah's Dawnsong was an exceptionally orthodox arming sword, the blade heavy and to the point.

After holding the salute for a few seconds, the two exploded into action, Levi raising Whisperwind into a defensive stance as Neriah lunged forward, crossing the space between them in a literal flash, golden light shining from his pauldrons like a pair of wings pushing him forward. Levi parried this initial assault, deflecting Dawnsong and letting Neriah's momentum carry him past, drawing a thunderous applause from the crowd.

In the midst of the tumult, Thierry leaned across to Erica. "There are two things, actually. The first largely pertains to what this duel could represent if my fears are realized, but we will get to that in good time. The second I believe to be more pertinent to you. I wished to discuss matters of my daughter." Erica felt a chill run through her at this, imagining what might have been discovered about Adelaide, and started to reply with face aghast, but the king continued before she could get a word out. "Oh, don't worry. It's nothing so grim. For that matter, we are aware that she is at the very least alive thanks to Archmage Dwyer's efforts. His scrying spell informed us she is currently somewhere west of Riverluck now, though it couldn't give a more concrete location. Something about an unknown source of chaotic resonance interfering with the spell."

Though relieved to hear her friend was well, Erica only felt more uncertain on hearing the king's description and furrowed her brow. *'Unknown source of chaotic resonance'? What does that even mean?* Below, the clang of metal upon metal continued to echo through the air as Neriah renewed his assault, using the speed of his armor to drive Levi backwards step by step with a flurry of passing strikes from Dawnsong, retreating before Levi could counter. The noise of it snapped Erica back to attention. "Well if you know where she is, then why do you need me? Can't you send a contingent of guards to pick her up?"

Thierry nodded with satisfaction as Levi caught on to Neriah's pattern, ducking beneath the next strike and sweeping his leg into Neriah's knees as he passed. But much to Erica's surprise, instead of falling flat on his face, Neriah twisted in midair as he fell and brought his own leg around into Levi's side with enough force to send him careening into the wall of the arena. Wincing as though he'd felt the blow himself, the king shook his head, tone distracted as he replied, "I already ordered Captain Jareth to take a squad and head to the closest town. He should get there within the next two days and will continue to search from there. However, we cannot sit idly by in the meantime. You see, when we were conversing over lunch yesterday, Chancellor Lukas noted

Adelaide's absence and began asking after her. Rather than admit any potential weakness, I told him she was busy researching the aftermath of the two attacks, trying to figure out what that strange cursed energy you discovered in Lord Reinhardt's manor is."

Though Levi picked himself up and charged Neriah, his first major offensive in the duel, Erica couldn't get excited, a feeling of horror growing in the pit of her stomach. The clang of metal on metal faded from her mind along with the cheers of the crowd as her suspicions over where the conversation was headed rose. Face growing pale, she stared blankly at the king. "So you want me to solve the mysteries around this high vampire all by myself then? Since as far as the foreigners know I'm Addy's 'assistant' and helping her with this research?"

Thierry turned his attention from the duel, gentle smile on his face. "Quite so, though I must point out I have no need for you to do it 'all by yourself'. All that matters is that you look into it enough to inform the others of Adelaide's progress, should they ask." Relief flowed through Erica and she leaned back in her chair, color returning to her face as the king continued. "But I would ask that you take this seriously. Estelle informed me the inquisitors have started stalking the streets of the Nobles' District after nightfall, so the Aurans will get answers whether we find them or not. And more importantly, if the palace guard does find my daughter, she will be returning to the capital soon and I would rather this business with the undead be concluded when she does."

Erica shot forward in her seat. "Wait, what do you mean by 'concluded'? I can research it, but if you really want this finished, you should be talking to Archmage Dwyer or Bishop Henri. I'm just an apprentice, I can't take responsibility for the whole capital."

Waving aside her worry, Thierry turned his focus back to the arena. The sound of clashing swords had faded as Levi and Neriah both disengaged, each carefully circling the other and waiting for the right moment to strike. "Nonsense," the king eventually said. "Apprentice or not, you have my daughter's trust and Sir Crownguard's faith in your abilities. That gives me reason enough to ask you. And as for responsibility, I have asked Estelle to suspend all other tasks assigned to you for the moment so you may spend all of your time on this problem. And when a solution has been found, Sir Crownguard and the city garrison will be called upon to execute it, so you need not worry about your ability to fight."

Erica slumped over, head in her hands. She felt as though she were in the middle of the two circling knights, standing at the tenuous point between disaster and calamity. Despite Thierry's reassurances, it felt as though he *was* expecting her to fix the problem with the undead and the slightest misstep would lead to the city's destruction, the negotiations' failure, and outright war among all the southern nations. "Very well. But aren't you just asking me about the how? Aren't the who and the why more important?"

Enraptured as Levi launched another assault, each heavy swing of Whisperwind crackling with the lightning that ran down its blade, Thierry leaned forward in his seat, voice downright apathetic as he responded. "Perhaps, but I find both of those less concerning in the moment. There's something I'm missing with undead and negotiations both, and the who and the why, as you said, must lie at the heart of it." He reached down to the side of his chair, pulled a thick book from a stack of texts, and held it out to Erica. "Take this, for example."

Erica turned the book over in her hands for a few moments. Its cracked leather cover and yellowed pages spoke to its age, echoed in the faded gilt in which its title – *Embers Extinguished* – was inscribed. And true to the title's word, flipping through the first few pages proved it to be a historical text on the fall of the Sunfire Empire. Erica frowned, idly skimming the text as she responded. "What about it? I don't see anything anyone didn't already know here."

"In this case, it is not what the book says that interests me, but who it was from. Before much of this started, the king of Montiamon sent me that book along with a letter asking me, among the pleasantries and assurances, to 'consider the words unwritten and the lesson they bear carefully.'"

Running through the events of the last days of the Sunfire Empire, Erica found herself at a loss for what the supposed lesson could be, especially with how it pertained to modern times. The Empire had fallen to a surprise attack the royal family was unprepared for thanks to their decadent lifestyles. All told, neither seemed especially pertinent to countries prepared for war at a moment's notice. Frowning, she snapped the book shut. "Is he trying to warn us about something? If so, what? Unless he's trying to blame his war with the Auris Empire on the Dusk Tyrant and the Witch of the New Moon, I don't see how it's relevant."

As if to punctuate her point, Dawnsong burst alight with golden fire just as Neriah caught one of Levi's blows, each strike of his subsequent counterattack burning hot enough to turn the sand of the arena floor to glass. Watching this, Thierry tapped his chin in thought. "I wouldn't be so sure. I admit that I don't know whether or not to trust Montiamon, particularly since it would be in their best interests to sow distrust for the Aurans, but the fact that their king only offered a vague warning instead of a request to take his side... Like I said, there's something I'm missing. I think the warning is that there is more than politics motivating the Aurans' expansion."

A memory of the oddly sharp cast to Chancellor Lukas' eyes, only breaking his otherwise lazy facade when it was clear he'd caught something that was supposed to remain hidden, flashed through Erica's mind. Neriah had seemed simple enough to evaluate, his devotion to the Empire and his faith straight-forward and unvarnished, but she was certain there was more to the chancellor than he let on. "So what, the Aurans are working for the Dusk Tyrant then? If that's the case, why would they assassinate their own general?"

Thierry shrugged. "Again, I wouldn't be so sure it's that. But I do think there's something hidden at the heart of their Empire. They were a small nation for centuries after the fall of Sunfire. Then all at once they took nearly the whole of the south-east. Where did that kind of military power come from? And, more pressing, why has no nation heard from their emperor? It's only chancellors and generals that answer our diplomatic overtures." As he finished speaking, the king turned to look at Erica, a carefully measured and emotionless expression overtaking his face. "As for the second, of course Tycoruta does not deal in assassins, but if we had experts on that matter, I'm sure they would say General Cyrus' death was a sign that he had come close to uncovering a truth those in power wanted to remain hidden. Perhaps the zealots like Neriah are being fooled. Or maybe they're the ones fooling the more moderate faithful."

Turning her attention back to the duel, Erica sighed. Neriah overextended on a strike and Levi took advantage of the opportunity to make a quick slash at his exposed chest, but Neriah, moving faster than Erica would have thought possible, dropped his sword and caught Levi's arm as it descended. Then, using Levi's own momentum and the enhanced strength of his Ancient's Armor, Neriah twisted and threw Levi over his shoulder, the Tycortuan knight falling flat on his back. Erica shuddered. "So you have no choice but to trust the Auris

Empire is exactly what it says it is or trust that Montiamon is an innocent victim with our best interests at heart?"

Thierry took the book back, considering it as he responded. "A simplification of matters, but perhaps. I would argue that everyone always has a choice. I could, for instance, elect to trust neither of them and ostracize both nations, perhaps leading them to unite against the common enemy Tycortua would provide. All I can do is try to use my knowledge and the wisdom of those around me to make whatever choice is best for my people. You say the warning Montiamon has given leaves us in the dark, but that is no worse than we were at the start of all of this. My instinct says to step lightly and *that* is what I will listen to."

As Erica considered her options, it occurred to her that every time she complained about her weakness, it had just been an excuse to avoid responsibility. All she could do was her best and trust those who were stronger and wiser than her to do what she could not. Nodding, she settled back into her seat, feeling at least resolved if not relaxed. "Alright. So then what do you want me to do about the who and the why?"

On the arena floor below, Levi had brought Neriah down with him and the two wrestled to gain the advantage. Thierry shook his head, returning *Embers Extinguished* to its stack and taking a bundle of papers from an adjacent pile. "I never said that. I would ask you to focus on the how if only one thing can be accomplished, but these might give you a good start for the others should you have the time. It's what information I have on all involved parties. Maybe you can find a motive in there that matches with your discoveries on the method. You can give them a quick read while a servant brings the resources you'll need for your research to my daughter's study."

Taking the papers, Erica quickly flipped through them. True to the king's word, each was a short summary of the members of the negotiations, including the absent Rugegans, with a description of the figure on one side and an analysis on the other. And the latter half of the packet detailed those not attending the negotiations, including the likes of the king of Montiamon and the remaining Councilors of the Twelve. But rather than focus on the documents, the king's last words stuck out to Erica. "So I'll be using Addy's rooms then?"

Thierry nodded, a frown growing on his face as the duel descended into a brawl, both knights abandoning all finesse in favor of brute force and laying into each other with punches strong enough to crack metal. "Quite so. And I'd ask that you spend your nights there as well, to keep an eye out in case anyone decides to investigate what my daughter's really up to and why she won't show her face. I won't have you take her bed or clothes of course. I'll have a spare cot brought into the sitting room along with your belongings before this evening."

Erica shook her head, amazed at the palace staff's alacrity. With the conversation fading, she pointed at the arena floor. "Do these things always end like this?"

Somewhere in the chaos, Neriah had managed to pick up Dawnsong and pin Levi to the ground, striking his helmeted face with the pommel of his sword over and over again. After a few seconds, he let go and Levi slumped over, unconscious. Thierry sighed, a sorrowful look appearing in his eyes as the crow roared in approval despite the brutality, and despite the fact that their champion had lost. "More often than you'd think, that's for sure." He idly looked to edge of the viewing box, then suddenly snapped back around, pointing to the refreshments table. "Go pour me a fresh cup of coffee, Miss Greenmaiden."

More confused than anything else, Erica hesitantly took to her feet. "I beg your pardon sir?"

"Go. Now."

Still shaken by his sudden change in tone, Erica rushed to comply. But she only just managed to reach the refreshments table and pick up the carafe of coffee when she heard the box's curtain being pulled aside. Looking back, she saw that Lukas had entered with Edan trailing just behind him. Erica felt a brief moment of panic when the chancellor took her seat, but then relaxed on realizing she'd been too surprised to set down Thierry's notes and they were still safely in hand and away from Auran eyes. Inspecting the chair closely, Lukas addressed Thierry, a strange note twisting his voice. "Oh? Were you expecting me, Thierry, or am I intruding upon other company?"

Chuckling, Thierry shook his head as he took Lukas' proffered hand. "I had hoped to get my daughter out of her room, this viewing box is easily enough guarded you see, but she had no desire to come, claiming she'd rather spend her time on something useful instead of a silly sword fight."

Erica had to hold back laughter at the king's blatantly false characterization of Adelaide, but Lukas seemed content with his explanation. "Ah, I'll bet you're glad she isn't here now though. I imagine it would have chilled her heart like the winds of winter to see her knight in shining armor defeated."

Thierry sighed. "I suppose that's true enough. Your champion did beat my own and, though it pains me to admit, I'm not entirely surprised. Neriah does have more experience in true battle, so for as much of a godsend as Sir Crownguard is, it's only natural he'd be less adept at dueling. Not only is he more focused as a monster hunter, but much of his early training was more aimed towards scholarly pursuits."

Raising an eyebrow, Lukas replied, "Oh? A scholar? You don't say." His eyes narrowed as he smiled in a downright devilish manner. "You know, Thierry, if Neriah were here, he'd accuse you of being a sore loser."

Thierry raised a hand in concession. "You may be right. But I can't be faulted for wanting victory for my own, can I?" He paused to wave Erica back to the chairs, taking the cup of coffee when she arrived. Turning back to Lukas, he gestured back towards the refreshments table. "Would you care for anything, chancellor?"

Lukas looked Erica up and down with a gaze of intense scrutiny. "Hmm. I'm fine, thank you. But in truth, I am curious about you, young miss. You were present at our arrival, yes? It seems that you're not just an ordinary servant, now are you? What's your story?"

Erica turned back to Thierry with a questioning glance. He nodded, an expression of assurance in his eyes, so she turned back to Lukas and bowed, trying to keep her tone as neutral as possible. "Perhaps. I'm something like Princess Adelaide's personal assistant. I've been serving under her for close to three years now. King Thierry brought me here today as part of his plan to lure Addy from her room."

Apparently satisfied, Lukas nodded. "Hmm, hmm. That will do for now. If you wouldn't mind, could you keep my Edan company while I speak with your king? She isn't that good at getting along with other people and I'm trying to help her with that."

Erica nodded warily, unsure of what to make of the request. Glancing over at Edan proved to be no help either, for though she had not brought her scutum and lance, she still wore her armor and the accompanying mask obscuring the top half of her face disguised any reaction she might have had. Without any good excuse, Erica resigned herself to it, replying, "At your command, sir, I will oblige."

Laughing, Lukas waved the two away without a word, turning back to the king as they left. The next few minutes found them standing at opposite ends of the refreshments table, watching Thierry and Lukas chat about the duel. Wanting to break the silence, but not especially knowing how, Erica shuffled back and forth on her feet, silently cursing the chancellor. *What in Seras's name does Lukas expect me to do? How am I supposed to know what to talk to her about?* Glancing at Edan, she considered the situation from the Aurans' perspective. *Or is this a trap, trying to draw information from me?*

All the while, Edan stood still, apparently content to say nothing. In the arena ahead, the audience slowly began to drain from the stands, Levi and Neriah having withdrawn to the arming room, and took their chatter with them, leaving the viewing box nearly silent. After another minute of that silence, Erica rolled her eyes, tired of doing nothing, and approached Edan. "Well there's no point in just standing around, is there?"

Edan turned to face Erica, saying nothing for several seconds. It may merely have been an effect of her mask's steady expression, but Erica could almost feel a level gaze fixed upon her, caught somewhere between confused and annoyed. When the praetor finally spoke, it was short and to the point, as if she wanted to end the conversation as quickly as possible. "Agreed. It keeps me from doing my duty. But I have been ordered to do so and therefore must."

Erica shook her head, leaning back against the table next to her, unwilling to relent. "But do you have to focus on your duty all the time? What do you do with your free time? Don't you have hobbies?"

Edan said nothing for several seconds, a slight tilt to her head the only sign she had heard anything at all. When she finally did respond, her tone was as disinterested as before. "What need do I have for hobbies? I am a praetor, an elite guard of the Auris Empire, blessed by the Endless Flame. I have a duty I have sworn to fill. Should I set that aside for idle tasks?"

Erica felt a familiar worry growing in her, like a voice quietly but insistently telling her not to let this go. "But you *are* more than a praetor, aren't you? You're Edan too, aren't you?"

Letting out a sigh, Edan shook her head. "Edan is weak and pathetic. Edan cannot fulfill her duty and protect that which must be protected. Edan cannot slay the demon plaguing both your kingdom and mine and see vengeance done."

"Demon? Do you mean the high vampire? Why do you call him a demon?"

Edan responded in a voice that shook with rage, hand tightening around a lance that was not there. "Because it *is* a demon. You call it a 'high vampire', but those are just pretty words. You ask questions about 'him', but that only serves to humanize it. You project yourself onto it because you wish it to be human and wish to see yourself in it. To find a way to reason with it and reconcile its evil with your own morals. But make no mistake, all it brings is desolation and death and naught but hatred resides in its foul heart." Erica opened her mouth to speak, but Edan swept her arm down in dismissal, continuing unabated. "And it is *nothing* like those weak things that attacked the other night. Yes, those were young and lacked power, but that is like comparing the reach of a dagger and a sword when your enemy holds a crossbow."

Erica stood taken aback, surprised by her outburst. "I'm sorry. I didn't mean to bring up such a thorny subject."

Waving off her apology, Edan turned to the table behind her to peruse its selection. "No, it is alright. It was inevitable, really. And you do not need to apologize for my hatred. Even if you do not find it justified, I am sure you could understand it if I say Cyrus was a mentor to me."

Struggling to remember the name, Erica eventually placed it as the Auran general whose death had sparked the war with Montiamon and nodded in understanding. "I see. Like you said, I do understand your anger. But even if I understand it, I can't agree with it. Not if it will lead you to to your death. How do you expect to kill this..." Erica paused for a moment, stumbling over the next word. "'Demon', yourself? He's taken down entire groups of trained soldiers."

Edan simply shrugged, keeping her eyes on a delicate pitcher of light golden porcelain, condensation beading along the icestones set in its base. Pouring two glasses of a liquid caught somewhere between orange and pink – Auran peach juice – she responded, "I cannot say. I do not believe myself so skilled as to succeed where my mentor could not. But if I want to see justice done to this foul creature, then how could I do anything but try? The Endless Flame will guide my lance, whether to victory or defeat, so should I fail it is only the will of the eternal."

Taking one glass in hand, she held the other out to Erica, who accepted it with a nod. Erica took a sip of the juice, not especially thirsty but neither wishing to insult Edan, and found its flavor sickly sweet. "And what then? What will you do once he's dead? With your vengeance done, will you be able to live your own life, or will you still be chained to your duty as you are now?"

Drinking deeply from her glass, Edan nodded in satisfaction. A content smile spread beneath the edge of her mask as she responded, eerie with her eyes still obscured by its emotionless bronze. "Who can say? I will do as ordered by the emperor, may the Endless Flame bless his reign, through his agents General Neriah and Chancellor Lukas. Should they command me to retire and live simply, it will be as such. I think I would prefer for things to continue as simply as they have before, however. But either way, it is impossible to tell with Chancellor Lukas. When that man is struck by one of his whims, he will stop at virtually nothing to achieve his satisfaction. So only the Endless Flame can tell what the future holds."

Almost as if he had overheard, Lukas called for Edan from his seat across the viewing box. Erica set down her glass, bowing farewell to Edan. "I guess you'll be going then."

Edan nodded, finishing her juice. "Indeed. I thank you for the conversation, Erica. I do not often have opportunity to speak with others and I would not mind doing so again."

With that, she turned to walk to the box's edge, holding the curtain open for Lukas. The chancellor paused on the threshold, however, turning back with a finger to his chin. "Ah. I almost forgot, but there is one more thing, Thierry. I've heard rumors of the Witch of the New Moon strolling around the Tycortuan countryside. Do you know anything about that?"

Remembering what Allard said days ago about his letter from Carlin, Erica froze. The king, however, merely frowned. "No, I can't say I do. Is this an official concern of the Auris Empire that is expected to be addressed at our next meeting?"

Lukas laughed, waving the question off. "Winter winds, it's hardly so pressing. Nothing more than idle curiosity. A good afternoon to you, heritor of the storm."

With that, he swept out of the box, Edan following behind without a word. When they were gone, Erica retrieved her sheaf of papers from the refreshments table where she had left them and returned to Thierry's side. He sat staring into the arena floor beyond, a troubled expression clouding his face. "Is all well, sir?"

The king nodded, waving a hand in dismissal as he stood up. "Yes, yes. Lukas merely wished to make conversation and gloat over his victory. That is not what worries me." He turned to face the direction the Aurans had gone, as though watching them make their way across the wall walk through the curtain. "You may go, Miss Greenmaiden. And what follows is not an order, but a request.

The chancellor briefly brought up the subject of the high vampire, after Edan's rather loud outburst. It is my belief and, I suspect from his comments, Lukas's as well, that one of the participants in the negotiations is giving it orders. Keep that in mind as you proceed in your search."

Giving one last bow, Erica left the viewing box and returned to the gardens below the palace walls. Though the morning's weather had not shifted, and was just as warm as before, a chill ran through her. She couldn't tell whether the cause was the king's last words or Edan's fatalistic attitude, but she was haunted by it all the same.

Chapter 18

Anemoday: 6th of Hernus, Year 1980 R.S.

Once again, Allard found himself in the blank expanse; chalky, gray dust beneath his feet and a soiled white sky above him. Though the woman from his previous dream was nowhere in sight, he was standing in the same place as before, the great hole in the world, like a piece of the night sky torn from the heavens, filling the horizon in front of him. As he watched, the stars in the void slowly spun and shifted. He unconsciously took a step closer forward. It looked unfathomably far away, but he still he felt as though he could reach out and touch its surface. As he lifted his hand up, something deep within the void changed and Allard was assailed by the sensation of something rushing upwards toward him. Barely a second later the hole's depths began to bleed an oily ink. As the liquid slowly filled the space, like dye being poured into water, Allard knew he should move away, but found himself transfixed with a sense of morbid awe. Though the void had been dark before, this was a different kind of darkness; a fluid black with a faint sheen. This inky liquid spread throughout the hole, swallowing up the stars and surging against glowing blue borders that Allard had not been able to see until now.

After an indeterminable amount of time, which paradoxically felt like only an instant, cracks spider-webbed their way across the boundary until it shattered in a great flood of ink. The liquid rushed across the dusty waste, churning its surface into a sickening mud from which plants began to sprout, all made of the same iridescent ink made solid. Before it reached Allard, the woman appeared in front of him, hands outstretched. The flood broke against her in a furious splash, leaving Allard unscathed save for a misting along one of his arms. The woman turned to him, the two safe in a circle of dust amidst a sea of ink. She shook her head, mouthing soundless words, though if her apologetic expression were anything to go by, Allard knew what she was saying. He placed a hand on her shoulder, meeting her gaze. To his surprise, his hand stayed where it was, not passing through her seemingly ethereal body. "It's alright. You didn't do anything wrong. I'll be fine."

He didn't know where the words came from, but the woman closed her eyes with apparent relief. At the same time, however, she continued to shake her head, showing she found his words to be of little solace. Allard felt himself fading, the world around him growing not so much dark, as simply empty. In this state of confused nothingness, he heard a familiar voice ring out. "But he never sleeps in this late. He's always up by dawn."

A man's voice, one he recognized as Xavier's, responded a moment later as Allard groggily opened his eyes. "I'm sure he's fine. Spring's mercy, you two have been traveling somewhat hard for a few days. It's probably just catching up with him now."

Allard swung himself out of the cot he lay in, bare feet sounding heavily against the hardwood floor. "I *am* fine. And I'm up. Is it really that late already?"

Xavier laughed from his seat on an identical cot in the corner of the room across from Allard. The rooms they had been given in the Teacher's Hall were rather comfortable, but small and lacking for furniture. Beyond the two cots, they had only been given a small table to set an old sunstone lamp on. Adelaide's room across the hall was similarly outfitted. After giving Allard a few seconds to wake up and rub the sleep from his eyes, Xavier shook his head. "Hardly, Al. I would say the morning isn't even half over yet. Adelaide is just overreacting. Honestly, she hadn't been up for more than ten minutes before you. She was just so consumed with worry for her dear, dear friend that she couldn't think straight. I imagine she didn't like the idea of touring the country without your sparkling presence."

Growling from her seat on the floor between the cots, Adelaide scowled across at Xavier. "Would you be quiet, Xavi? You know the point that I'm trying to get across. And I can handle myself just fine, thank you very much." Allard had a thing or two to say about that, but Adelaide continued before he could get a word in. "Regardless, he's your problem now Al, I'm going to start getting ready to go. You two get things settled here."

With that, she leapt to her feet, dusted herself off, and bounded out of the room. Allard looked after her for a moment before turning to Xavier with a raised eyebrow. "Did I miss something? What was that about?"

Xavier chuckled. "Oh, nothing. I was just having a bit of fun. Lies, but Adelaide doesn't handle teasing well, does she? That being said, there are important matters I wish to discuss with you before we plan our next move."

"Is this about what you learned in town yesterday? You refused to say anything last night. What changed this morning?" Xavier nodded, pointing towards the window. Allard pulled aside the curtain and was greeted with the sight of a ruined garden. When they arrived last night, the Teacher's Hall had been surrounded by a series of well-trimmed shrubs and several small patches of dirt where the priests grew their own vegetables. This morning, the vegetables had been torn from the ground and scattered about, the shrubs cut to pieces. Shuddering, he took a step back, eyes scanning the courtyard beyond for any threats. "What happened out there?"

Xavier crossed the room and stared out the window with an impassive expression. "If I had to hazard a guess, I would say we have confirmation that our vampire friend cannot enter holy ground." Allard's eyes widened with surprise and he opened his mouth to respond, but Xavier cut him off with a raised hand. "When I was scouring the town for rumors, I did hear that beggars and vagrants have been disappearing from their usual hangouts over the past few days. I didn't want to say anything without more evidence, until I knew I spoke truth, since any number of things could be the cause. This, however, seems to be a clear enough sign."

Allard stepped away from the window, considering the possibilities. "Is it though? If any number of things could be abducting vagrants, couldn't any number of things have torn up the garden? And why would anything, vampire or otherwise, do this in the first place?"

"Oh, but you see, all of the evidence points towards the vampire as the culprit. If we consider the situation, then the assumption can be made that he was in fact chasing you and Adelaide. If we follow that assumption, it is reasonable to assume he is the abductor, having need of sustenance as he waited to catch you on your return to Riverluck. And finally, the seemingly petty act of ruining the priests' garden makes sense if you consider that he did so out of rage upon finally catching sight of you, but immediately finding himself incapable of reaching you."

Allard began searching through his bag for the day's essentials. Though Xavier spoke as if his conclusion were a given, Allard still found himself unconvinced. "If you say so. It still seems awfully coincidental that he just happened to find us on our first night here. And even if he can't enter holy ground, couldn't he have tried throwing things through the windows? He's proven itself adept enough at throwing knives in my experience."

Picking up the edge of the curtain, Xavier let it run through his fingers before dropping it again. "I would imagine we have these to thank for that. He couldn't know which rooms we were staying in with all of them covered as such. And either way, I find it doubtful that a vampire can inflict any harm towards holy ground. Otherwise, why didn't he just burn the Hall down?"

Shuddering again, Allard realized just how fortunate they were that their gamble in seeking sanctuary had paid off. "So then what's our next move? You seem like you have an idea or two."

Xavier started towards the door. "Hmm, hmm. Truth be told, that I do. But breakfast first. We shouldn't get started without Adelaide. Now get changed and get ready. We have much to be about."

He closed the door behind him and Allard shook his head in exasperation, continuing with his morning preparations. He paused briefly on withdrawing his family's medallion. *I thought you were supposed to bring good luck? Couldn't you have sent the vampire one town over?*

Tossing it back in his bag with a sigh, he pulled out his spare shirt, the combat manual falling out with it. Allard considered the book with a scowl as he changed, picking it up when he was finished and idly flipping through it. This time he stopped on what seemed like a simpler spell, one merely intended to enchant the caster's body and increase their natural strength. Taking a deep breath, he spoke a word in Mystic Script and tried to focus on his arms and legs. As he tensed his muscles, nothing seemed to happen for several seconds. But then he thought he felt something like a light tugging in his chest. This was almost immediately followed by a sharp, burning pain on the back of his hand and he broke his concentration with a curse. "Crows!" Shaking his head, he shoved the book back into his pack and started for the door. *Ha. It looks like that spell's useless. I'll probably pull a muscle if I keep trying to cast it.*

After a light breakfast, the morning found the three meandering through town, following after Xavier as he searched for the shops he needed. The people of the town were as bright and cheery as the day before, bustling about their business or chatting with each other, and their attitude proved to form a disconcerting contrast to the morning's events for Allard. The thought that a monster could be haunting an otherwise normal town come nightfall was enough to make him shudder. As they drew to a halt before another general store, he approached Xavier, tapping his shoulder to get his attention. "I know you said that you like having a flair for the dramatic, but could you please tell us what your plan is for dealing with the vampire? This will be the third store we've completely cleared of lamp oil."

Turning to face him with a sigh, Xavier shook his head, a forlorn look on his face. "Oh Allard, must you be so terribly dull? Lies, your hair will go gray early if you keep worrying like this. But if you insist, I suppose I must tell you." He twirled and pointed to the sun above him, a wide smile spreading across his face. "If we cannot bring our vampire into the sun's light, then we shall bring its light to him. He shall burn beneath the fury of our lamp oil."

It was a reasonable enough plan, since few things survived incineration, but hardly answered Allard's question. "Yes, I had gathered as much from our previous purchases. But how exactly do you plan on getting the oil on the vampire and then igniting it? That's what I'm more worried about. I don't think he'll agree to stand still and let us dump gallons of flammable material on it just because we asked nicely."

Xavier chuckled darkly. "Well in that case, we'll just have to trap him, now won't we? If we can get him stuck in one place long enough, it should be easy enough to let everything fall into place. And that's where the next items on our list come in. Industrial grade waterstones should do the trick nicely."

"Does artificially running water work the same for exploiting a vampire's weakness?" Adelaide asked. "And what about the distinction between magically artificial like lattice-stones and spells and physically artificial like an aqueduct?"

Xavier nodded. "A good question, in truth. At the end of the day what's important is that it *is* running water, not *how* the water came to be running. It's a magically binding thing you see, not a matter of physical harm. And I can verify that this is a true fact. I actually had to deal with a little spitfire of a Gaean vampire a few years back. Different from a true vampire, and honestly much more pleasant, but the weakness to running water carries across."

While he wasn't sure what exactly a 'Gaean vampire' was, hearing mention of it was enough to make Allard frown in irritation. "If you've dealt with vampires before, then why do we have to go through all of this trouble? And didn't you say you were a Demon-folk Noble? Shouldn't you be powerful enough to handle this on your own?"

Eyes narrowing, Xavier scowled. "I told you the most I could manage was a few menacing shadows and a frightening cast to my features and I stand by that truth. Perhaps a minor illusion or cantrip for use in daily life, but nothing for fighting monsters."

"Yes, but why? You haven't really explained why you don't have all the fabulous power to be expected with your kind. And I'd rather understand why before I get myself into trouble trying to deal with something I already know is beyond my abilities."

Dropping any pretenses, Xavier met Allard's eyes with an expression of true sincerity, words filled with a deeper gravity than any he'd previously spoken. "Look. I mean no insult, but in truth, you won't understand my explanation since you know nothing of the Eleven Realms or transmission magic. It's because of the precise nature of transrealm travel that was used. I told you before that it is very difficult for my kind to return from the Physical Realm. Lies, it's difficult for us to *leave* Morningstar, but we at least have enough mages of great enough power that we can accomplish it. So in this case, instead of simply sending me here in my entirety and consigning me to this land for the rest of my life, we opted for a kind of quasi astral projection in the form of psionic refraction. Which is to say that while I am here in spirit, the body I possess is nothing more than a magically formed construct and thus possesses none of my power."

Allard shook his head in disgust. "So you're telling me that not only are you no more help than a regular person, but your life isn't even at stake here?"

"Do not doubt my commitment to my duty, Mr. Fortunata. As for the first, three of the Golden Lady's Keys were sent with me from Morningstar. But it turns out that possessing the Golden Lady's Authority is less useful on Earth than would be expected, since few things here are bound by it. As for the second, the psychic backlash resulting from the destruction of this body would be less than pleasant to say the least. It might kill me. It might leave me in a deep coma. It might just give me a splitting headache for several months. I cannot say in truth what would happen, but there would be repercussions."

"Setting aside transmission magic for the moment," Adelaide said, "could you explain to me what the Golden Lady's Authority is?"

Grabbing a hold of her shoulder, Allard pulled her aside. "Look Adelaide, save the scholarship for later. I think we should let Xavier handle this round of shopping by himself. We have some things to discuss out here."

Adelaide looked up at Allard in confused disappointment, opening her mouth to respond, but Xavier interjected before she could get a word out. "He speaks truth, Adelaide. I think we could use some time to cool off. Both of us."

Allard led Adelaide away. Glancing back, he saw Xavier stand still for a moment before shaking his head and walking into the store. Allard sighed and leaned back against the building behind him, watching the townsfolk pass by as they went about their business. He scowled, still irritated by his conversation with Xavier, and irritated all the more by the world's refusal to match his mood. The cheery atmosphere of Zephyr's Blessing grated on his nerves and he found himself thinking back to the morning's dream. At his side, Adelaide tapped his shoulder, speaking in a hushed tone. "Are you alright there Al?"

"Am I alright? Not really, no. After everything that's gone on, I'm afraid. His attitude is something like the last straw."

"Really? But isn't this the kind of thing that you'd dreamed of? Adventure and heroism? I remember what you said when you left your home. About how you felt there was something more in the world that you had to find."

Shaking his head, he laughed dryly. Fishing through his pocket, he pulled out his medallion and looked at the faded design on its surface. "Well, dreams are one thing and reality another. Sure, I've always wished for adventure, I've always wanted to be a heroic knight like those I read about in stories, but not like this. Not with the threat of death looming over myself and those I care about. Not with destiny and the fate of the world like you and Xavier were talking about."

"But that's how all the stories are. They're all like this. There's always danger and the hero is always facing death. That's what makes them stories that stick with us and inspire us. Because they were about good facing off against evil and winning despite that same danger."

Pushing himself off the wall, Allard started walking down the street, trying not to feel like he was running away from his problems. As Adelaide rushed to follow him, he replied, "I know that. Believe me, I know there's danger involved if you want to be a knight. That's why I said there's a difference between dreams and reality." He gestured towards the passersby. "But it's just that I can't accept something like *this* for myself. There has to be something more than just living a normal life in a normal town. My life can't have no meaning. I couldn't bear it if it did."

Adelaide pulled him to a stop, looking into his eyes with a maturity beyond her years. "Does your life require a meaning like that? Can it not just have whatever meaning you ascribe to it? And would it be so wrong to simply live happily with Levi, Erica, and me? I can promise that your life will never be boring in Riverluck's palace."

Unable to deny her and yet still feeling like she was wrong, Allard dodged the question. "We've drifted off topic, though you do bring me back to my initial point. I'm worried about you getting hurt. Why should we bother trying to kill something way out of our league? I can only see this ending with one of us getting hurt. It would be better for us to find a way back to Riverluck so that we can get someone who can actually handle this, like Levi."

Adelaide pointed at a pair of women, talking on the other side of the street. "Look at them Allard. Those are my people. All of them are. Do you honestly expect me to just leave a vampire to its own devices in my kingdom? To have its way with my people? What kind of a queen will I make if I abandon them now for my own convenience?" Allard started to respond, but she cut him off, jabbing a finger into his chest. "This is about more than the two of us. Xavi said that people have already started to go missing. What if they become vampires too? The problem will just spread. We have to stop this now, Al. For them and everyone like them with their 'meaningless' lives."

Allard froze, mouth open slightly in awe. For the three years that he'd known Adelaide, he had never felt her to be more regal than in that moment. As her friend, it was easy to forget that she really was the heir to the throne. The tailored gowns and finely wrought jewelry did little to make her look her role when she acted so casually and carefree. He nodded slowly, scowl easing from his face as he spoke. "You're right. I don't like it, but you're right. We have to try to do something to stop the high vampire. But I still think that we're being far too cavalier about this whole thing and I won't concede that point."

The passion vanished from Adelaide's face just as quickly as it appeared, replaced by her normal expression of blithe contentedness. "Well what exactly would you have us do? Zephyr's Blessing isn't exactly stationed with the likes of the Mage Corp or the Royal Griffon Corp. And if I remember what I overheard you saying correctly, the high vampire singlehandedly faced off against the entirety of Lord Reinhardt's house guard. I imagine the town guard here wouldn't fare any better."

Looking up at the sky above him, Allard watched a small wisp of a cloud drift its way towards a gathering of gray storm clouds on the horizon. With the sun on his face, warmth tempered by a gentle breeze, he found what remained of his irritation drifting away. The weather reminded him far too much of the summers back home for him to be upset. "Well, I guess we'd best head back to Xavier. He's probably close to finished in that store by now, don't you think?"

Adelaide chuckled. "It's only natural that you'd agree with me. The only thing that can match my overwhelming intellect is my charm and charisma after all."

"I don't want to hear about your 'overwhelming intellect' until it can figure out why everything you've done over the past few days was a bad idea. And just because I think we should listen to Xavier doesn't mean I'm going to apologize to him, so don't bother asking."

Adelaide nodded noncommittally, a mischievous glimmer growing in her eyes. "Right, right. But you'll never make friends if you're this grumpy all the time. In order to prove your amicable nature, I think you should buy me a snack."

Allard rolled his eyes and continued towards the general store. As they approached, the door opened and Xavier exited, dragging a large sack behind him. With hardly more than a nod of greeting, they rejoined him and started off towards the next store on Xavier's list.

Chapter 19

Anemoday: 6th of Hernus, Year 1980 R.S.

Erica set down her pen with a sigh. Adelaide's grand desk, at which she sat, was cluttered with a mess of notes and maps, its corners obscured by heavy books she had set aside for the moment. Looking out the window, she saw the horizon darkening to a muted purple as dusk approached. *Where did the time go today?* She regarded the untouched plate of cheese and bread she'd set on the windowsill. *It seems like hardly an hour's passed since Vi brought me lunch.*

With a wistful sigh, she stood and stretched her arms over her head before grabbing a slice of bread. She ate without much appetite as she circled the desk, looking over a map detailing the expansion of the Auris Empire, showing each subsequent conquest in different colored outlines. With a shake of her head, she removed one of the books from the desk and started towards her familiar arm chair in the corner. Snapping her fingers, she muttered word of Mystic and a small orb of golden light materialized just over the chair's backrest with a soft hum, illuminating *Quintessence After Death: The Soul's Permanence* in a homely glow. Scanning the page before her, she found her eyes glazing over as she was assaulted by descriptions of how necromancy twisted the natural lingering echoes of life into undeath. It came as an immense relief when a soft knock at the door interrupted her reading. Tossing the book to the floor, perhaps more roughly than it deserved, she stood and dusted off her skirt. "Come in, the door's unlocked."

The door opened to reveal Levi standing in the hall with a steaming mug in hand, its twin sitting on the floor next to him. Picking up the second mug, he slid into the room and pushed the door closed behind him all in one fluid motion, the hall visible for scarcely more than the span of a breath. Walking towards Erica, he brandished a mug towards her with a disapproving frown. "You should not be so carefree with your admittance. You are here to *keep* people from discovering Lady Adelaide's absence, not facilitate their efforts.

And furthermore, others might find exercising your paltry authority as a mere apprentice mage in your own lady's chambers a bit untoward."

Shooting him a level stare, Erica accepted the mug with a murmured thanks. Taking a sip, she was pleased to find its contents a slightly spicy tea whose warmth worked its way through her chest. Setting the mug down, she glanced over at where she had left *Quintessence After Death*. "Maybe, but I think I would prefer a brief jaunt to prison for impropriety over more of this mess. Even putting aside necromancy, which I think I understand as little as you do, I have no idea how I'm supposed to figure out who might have a motive. All the information I can find on current politics is stuff like how Rugego raised the prices on luxury wine labels in response to Perlora's windstorm crisis three years ago. I have no clue how I'm supposed to grasp the significance of that when Perlora isn't even known for their wine."

"Well I imagine you would have little luck puzzling out the situation that way. Everyone knows that Perlora's windstorm crisis caused their fishing industry to stagnate and therefore had the end result of stagnating the trade of seafood for grains with the Eastern provinces. Wine had nothing to do with that."

Erica lightly smacked Levi's shoulder on her way back to her chair. "Oh shut up. I get enough of that from the books, I'm not taking it from you too. And I swear that you just made that up anyways."

Shrugging, Levi strolled over to the desk to look at the map Erica had set out. Setting down his coffee, he pulled another map out of his pocket and unrolled it, comparing the two. Without looking up, he continued, "I doubt any of that matters anyway. Rarely do the politically or economically motivated resort to undead and curses. Too easy to end up on the wrong side of an inquisition. I would reckon whoever is behind this has more esoteric desires, so I would recommend focusing your efforts on matters and objects arcane." He paused for a moment, tapping the second map with his finger. Picking up one of the many pens scattered across the desk, he marked down several places before he spoke again. "I hazard there is little need for me to ask how your research is going then? Your tone seems to say it all."

Erica picked up *Quintessence After Death,* dusting it off and replacing it on one of the bookshelves along the wall. She found her gaze lingering on the other volumes surrounding it, text after text detailing the likes of modern astrology, the mysticism of herbology, and the foreign common sense of the other-worlds. She shook her head, amazed by it all. "I don't know how Addy can keep up with this stuff and more. Every day she has to study these kind of things and I don't want to spend even one evening on it. I don't think I could stand devoting my life to even one of these subjects."

"You mean the same Adelaide that abandoned her duties and went haring off into the wilderness while you cover for her?" Erica barely covered up a snort of laughter before Levi continued. "That being said, she does take her studies seriously. She tries her hardest to be a good leader. Or at least someone who will be a good leader in the future."

"And so she takes things less seriously now while she can? Yes, please tell me more about one of my closest friends who I spend virtually every day with." Erica slumped down into her chair with an exaggerated sigh. "Do you think you could give me a hand with this? Any scandalous news about the nefarious schemes of foreign nations? A monster hunter's insight on the habits of the undead?"

Levi chuckled softly, still puzzling over his map. A frown crept across his face as he continued his search, apparently dissatisfied with what he found. Stifling a yawn, he went to the window and took in the view of the northern end of the city. Past the palace complex, Riverluck's hill descended in an untamed tangle, none daring to build beyond the king's residence. Only the city walls and the northern garrison with its griffon aeries stood in his sight. "I would be happy to offer what aid I could in your studies, but my visit pertains to matters more pressuring than helpful. After hearing of the king's request to you at the duel, I wished to ask your opinion on matters."

Suddenly reminded of yesterday's duel, Erica looked over at Levi. "That's right! Are you alright? You aren't hurt or anything, are you? I know you had your armor on, but enchantments or not, that last brawl looked vicious."

Glancing back at her over his shoulder, Levi shot her a level stare. "While I would have preferred victory, one as weak as I could never hope to beat a true master swordsman. And for as much as being knocked out hurts, I am in fine condition. I find myself wanting more for sleep than time to recover."

"Well anyway, if I'm being perfectly honest, I haven't the slightest clue what the curse is intended to accomplish. Seras's stars, I can't even figure out potential motives for assassinations and undead and it feels like it's swiftly becoming clear I won't be able to figure out how this curse is supposed to work unless I know what it's supposed to do, leading us back to why."

Levi nodded. "That is quite alright. I had almost expected as much, all things considered. Meaning and intention, yes? I know little of magical theory, but recognize those are needed to understand anything. Now..." He gestured towards the desk before continuing. "Would you take a look at the map there?"

She rose and returned to the desk, looking at the map Levi had left there. It took her a moment to recognize it, but from what she could tell the map showed a rough sketch of Riverluck. A loose crescent of x's had been drawn in and around the area representing the Nobles' District, with a circle around the palace itself and another location. She looked up at Levi with a skeptical expression, uncertainty filling her voice as she spoke. "I can see this is Riverluck, but what are the marks you made?"

Levi returned to the desk and tapped each mark in turn, responding with a military precision as though offering a report to his superior. "These are the locations of undead forces sighted in the city, starting with the assault on Lord Reinhardt's manor. The circles are the two confirmed targets of Lord Reinhardt's manor and the palace. As for the others, they are a scattered collection of incidents as reported by the guards over the past few days." He tapped a spot to the south-west of the palace. "This was another manor raided, Lady Ellis if you are interested. Another Summer noble, curiously enough, but there were no casualties and few major injuries, the lady herself away to oversee the training of new members of the Royal Griffon Corp the night of the attack. Every other force found was caught moving through the city and dealt with before anything untoward could happen."

Erica raised an eyebrow. "No casualties? Then I can assume the high vampire was not present?"

"Indeed. Moreover, the roving bands consisted solely of zombies and bonewalkers. It would seem the high vampire is no longer present in Riverluck and with him, I hope at the very least, the enemy's capability to produce more lesser vampires."

Erica felt her stomach drop. "Doesn't that mean..."

"Tycortua is a large place. I am sure the two of them are fine and wherever the high vampire is, he cannot have caught their trail."

Even as he said it, Erica could tell it was mostly wishful thinking. To be sure, it made sense that the kingdom was large enough for Allard and Adelaide to have gone a different way from the high vampire, but it couldn't be coincidence it disappeared on the same night. "And this Lady Ellis wasn't at home when her manor was attacked? Does this mean Lord Reinhardt's death was more a matter of convenience than necessity?"

"A fair assumption. Comparing the two, Lady Ellis is an active commander and heavily involved with the Griffon Corp. Her death might actually impact our military structure, yet she lives while Lord Reinhardt does not. Perhaps the enemy felt a trained knight would fare too well against what lowly undead they possess, but not even an attempt was made."

All of which only served to muddy the waters further, leaving Erica more or less where she'd started. Sighing, she looked back down at the map. "Well either way, I still don't know what you expect me to see here. If someone was planning to attack us, the palace would be the natural first target, right?"

Levi nodded. "Be that as it may, why did they neglect to attack the palace again? Did they think they possessed too little power to effect an assault with no vampires in their army? Or do they have some sort of other plan in the city? But I can find no visible pattern and I see little point to why they attacked where they did. So do you have any idea whatsoever? Is there some sort of mystical significance behind the locations struck?"

Erica took another look at the map, this time with an eye for the arcane. Her mind naturally leapt first to geometry, a set pattern of magical loci inscribing the vertices of a regular polygon around a target area one of the basic principles of thaumaturgical numerology with the number of vertices dictating the general intention of the spell, but as Levi had said, there was no obvious pattern, no clear shape among the marks. So lacking any leads on that front, her mind settled on the memory of dark magic within Lord Reinhardt's manor, the chilling pulse that ran through an otherwise normal swirl of magic and the root of her research. Frowning, she looked back up at Levi. "Has the Mages' Guild investigated Lady Ellis' manor? Is there a similar magic pattern in her house as there was in Lord Reinhardt's?"Snapping his fingers, Levi pointed at Erica with a satisfied nod. "And that is why we continue to provide your pay. No formal investigation has occurred since there were no casualties. Which naturally means there might be something we missed, especially if it is magical in nature. Which leads to the next question: if this magic is present, what would it accomplish?"

Based on what Erica had seen at Lord Reinhardt's manor and throughout her first day of study, there didn't seem to be much practical application to that magic. Her first thought had been that it was just a curse laid upon the manor, since the way the dark energy had intertwined itself into the environment seemed to indicate it began and ended within the manor's grounds. There was nothing to indicate it was meant to actively do anything. Similarly, there was nothing to show that it was storing or building up energy for later use or that it was meant to interact with something outside the manor. But if this same curse had been laid upon Lady Ellis' manor, it seemed like it had to be used for something. Why would the undead forces go to the effort of placing the curse otherwise? And it couldn't be mere coincidence since Lady Ellis' manor had not seen the same kind of violence that might naturally give rise to a lingering miasma of dark magic. She looked back down at the map, trying to find some connection between the two manors. They did form a neat triangle with the palace, the length between the palace and both manors equal, but that only served to leave her even more dissatisfied. According to the geometric principles of magic, those three points would be set to affect the center of the triangle which looked to be nothing more than a simple street in the Nobles' District. She threw up her hands. "I've got nothing. Simply knowing the energy exists isn't enough to tell me what it does, even with two instances of it."

"It cannot be helped, I suppose. Do you wish to inspect Lady Ellis' house? Haste may serve us in this venture, if we wish to investigate before the Auran inquisitors."

Giving a one last look back at the desk, Erica considered the stacks of tomes and yellowed, old documents she'd avoided reading all night. Though the sheer amount of them spoke to how much work she had left undone, she desperately wanted to do anything other than continue studying for tonight and Levi himself had given her an alternative. Well aware she'd already made her decision and was just agonizing over it for her own sense of guilt, she ran back to her chair by the bookshelf, slinging her bag over her shoulder when she got there and rifling through it as she responded, "Please. Just give me a minute to find a few things that might help. Since I have a good idea of what I'm looking for, it should be easier than Lord Reinhardt's manor."

With that, she headed over to the set of drawers built into the corner of the bookshelves that held Adelaide's personal stash of odds and ends; a stash Erica had supplemented with a few of her own things over the years. Slipping a set of divining sticks into her bag, as well as a curse-breaking rod and a dampening spike, she nodded to herself. Giving the drawer one final pass, her hand brushed against Adelaide's magic detection bracelet, the leather device threaded with bronze wiring around a clear magestone. It was a simple device Adelaide had built as a science project and not something Erica should need since she could already sense mana flows on her own, but figuring it might provide some further insight or pick up something she'd missed, she tossed it into her bag.

Fully outfitted, she looked back up to Levi, but found him half-asleep already. Chuckling to herself, she reached back into the drawer to retrieve a packet of tea leaves she'd been saving since her first birthday in Riverluck. It was a blend grown in the Austall heights with a few herbs grown by the Forest-folk which supposedly aided in mental celerity. Rising to her feet, she snuck up to Levi and tapped him on his shoulder. Jerking awake, he looked about the room in a brief moment of confusion before meeting her eyes with an embarrassed grimace. She patted her bag once as he reoriented himself. "I'm all set, but can we stop by the kitchen first?"

"Lead on."

As they approached the kitchen, Erica could hear disgruntled conversation floating out from behind the closed door. On hearing it, and recognizing the speaker's voice, Levi groaned, gently massaging his temples. "With all due respect, I'll wait out here."

Erica suppressed a laugh and left him leaning against the wall with closed eyes. Inside the kitchen, Viola stood just before the ovens between two of the cooks, half directing them and half complaining about being kept at work this late. Continuing towards the cupboards where the cooking utensils were kept, Erica raised a hand in greeting, calling out to the maid over her noise, "Hey, Vi. What's got you so riled up?"

Leaving the cooks with one final order about the plating of the scones, Viola stomped over to the her. "Oh, you know how it is with this kind of thing. We get guests and they start running around like they own the place." Growling, she shook her head, continuing in a sullen half-whisper. "Not even that. They wouldn't be so annoying at their own home."

Finding the flamestone plate and a kettle, Erica took them in hand and set them on the counter. "You do realize that cleared nothing up, right? And why are you even taking care of this? Kitchen work hardly seems to fit your job. Especially since you can't make more than steamed potatoes."

"Hey. I'll have you know that steamed potatoes are a diverse culinary tool, serving as the blank canvas for an artist's touch of spicing. And I could cook more if I wanted to, but why should I if the palace cooks take care of servants' meals? And anyway, when Estelle heard that Duke Gerald had asked for snacks for an after dinner tea with his fellow Perlorans, she insisted that I be the one to attend to them."

Learning that it was the ambassadors, Erica nodded. It was precisely the kind of thing that Estelle would force on Viola under the pretenses of training. She'd probably called it something like 'memorization practice' too. After filling the kettle and putting it on the plate to boil, she turned back to face Viola, leaning against the counter as she did. "Is there really anything that important that you might overhear if it's just the Perlorans? I thought we were supposed to be putting up a concerted front against the Auris Empire."

Viola groaned, throwing her hands up in frustration. "I don't know! None of this stuff matters to me. You're lucky, getting to go off with Levi and have all sorts of high adventure."

Erica raised an eyebrow. "I really think you're overestimating what my job entails. Most days it's just keeping an eye on Addy and making sure she actually does what she's supposed to do."

Ignoring Erica's complaints, Viola shook her head, eyes alight with fervor. "Not these days! You got to go investigate a murder. And way back when you came here you got to travel across the country, on the run from undead and assassins. Undead assassins, even! There's the *potential* for you to get to see more than just this boring palace, even if you don't do it now."

Remembering the trek of three years ago, Erica sighed. It had been less an adventure across the country and more an overblown camping trip with a thirteen year old who had no idea what she was doing. All told, she'd be happy if she never had to spend another night in Thicket Forest. "You're still exaggerating things. There weren't any assassins, just the threat of them, and the only undead we saw were roving ones on their way north to the Forest of the Dead and one zombified wolf. And this 'murder investigation' has just been me looking at the aftermath. We already know who the culprit is, you know."

Viola shook her head mournfully. "You just don't get the Romance of it all, Erica. The mystery itself makes the adventure exciting, regardless of what that mystery is."

The kettle began to whistle, the water boiling, so Erica took two mugs from the cupboards, shaking her head as she poured out the water for tea. "What about the mystery of what our neighboring countries are up to? Is the Romance in that not enough for you?" Taking the mugs in hand, Erica nodded towards the door. "Well anyway, it was nice chatting with you, but I have another boring house to look over."

Raising her hand in farewell, Viola immediately returned to berating the kitchen staff, her attitude shifting from friendly to commanding just like that. Erica shook her head in amazement, returning to the hallway where Levi leaned against the wall most assuredly not dozing off. Or at least that's what she was sure he'd claim if pressed on the matter. After nudging his shoulder, he started upright, looking around briefly before taking the tea with a murmured word of thanks. With tea in hand, they continued on their way to the palace gates, nothing to look forward to save another long night's work.

Chapter 20

Anemoday: 6th of Hernus, Year 1980 R.S.

The streets of Zephyr's Blessing were eerily quiet, the dull thud of Allard's boots upon the cobblestones the only sound. He'd been less than amused when Xavier told him their trap needed bait and even less when it became clear that Xavier wouldn't be volunteering himself. Sure, he didn't want Adelaide to be the one facing certain doom if something went wrong, and maybe even if everything went right, but it didn't make him feel any better about putting himself on a proverbial platter for the high vampire. *With things the way they are, I might as well stick an apple in my mouth and be done with it.*

Shaking his head to dispel his morbid thoughts, he sighed and continued on his circuit of one of the blocks bordering the main square. He thought pacing the same two streets for the past fifteen minutes looked way too much like a trap, but their trap would only work here after all, so it couldn't be helped. He slid his eyes towards the alleyway that would serve as their 'cage' as he passed, the signs marking it obvious to his eyes. The town's mayor had been hesitant to let them pry up the pavement and dig a small trench connecting the gutter on either side of the alleyway, but he'd been willing to consider once they'd told him of the threat and happy to oblige once Xavier had named a price. Those trenches were enough to make Allard think it was easy to spot and that was before considering the net filled with flasks of lamp oil hanging halfway down the street. Sure, *he* couldn't see it, but he was willing to hazard a guess that a vampire would have slightly better night vision.

When he turned the corner, he noticed a light fog beginning to roil around his feet, curling up around the edges of the buildings like climbing vines. As he watched, it continued to thicken, steadily rising to fill the streets and coil around his legs. He began fingering the arrows in his quiver – Silver tipped, salt tipped, skewered with garlic, and, of course, the critically important ignition arrows with a flamestone embedded in their heads. Selecting one of the garlic arrows, he nocked it and continued on his way, sincerely hoping the vampire would wait till he was back in the square to attack. One more piece of the plan Xavier had failed to clarify for him: how precisely he'd get away if the trap failed and he was on the square side with an entire row of buildings between him and the escape cart.

As he weighed his options in his mind, considering whether he should just turn back now or continue on, the fog seemed to start moving of its own will, forming shapes not quite like monstrous faces just at the edge of his vision. A chill, entirely unrelated to the weather, ran down his spine and he was struck with the overwhelming sense that he was being watched. Figuring there was no turning back, Allard quickened his pace and took out the second object he'd prepared for tonight's plan. According to Adelaide, grain was the traditional way to exploit a vampire's arithmomania, so they'd made sure to buy a small bag of oats which Allard now opened and began scattering behind him as he went. Somehow, the whole thing felt strangely comic to him in that moment. Him going as fast as he could without actually breaking into a sprint and the vampire surely following just beyond, only forestalled by the trail of oats.

After a tense minute, Allard reached the corner on the end of the block, fog thick enough that he couldn't see more than a foot in front of him. Dumping the rest of the oats into his hand, he threw them all away from the square and started sprinting in the opposite direction. The pounding of boots on stone filled Allard's head and he wasn't entirely sure it was only his steps he heard. A few painstaking seconds later, he stood on the other end of the street, just inside the square. Pivoting, he planted himself and fired his arrow back the way he'd come, relying on blind luck to see him through. He was rewarded with the sound of splintering wood and a shriek of anger, followed by a sharp whistling of air. Without giving it a second thought, he dove to the side, a dagger cutting through the space where his shoulder had been. Grunting in pain, the stones an unfriendly landing pad, he rolled to his feet and kept running. This time he was sure he could hear the vampire's footsteps behind him, close enough to reach him even when dulled by the fog around them. Figuring he'd be caught before he reached the trap if he didn't do anything, he fumbled another arrow from his quiver, this one salt-tipped. He aimed it towards the buildings and heard the tip shatter against a wall, scattering salt into the street behind him. The vampire made no sound, apparently unaffected by the salt, but its footsteps froze for a few moments and when Allard next heard the telltale whistle of a thrown dagger, it clattered harmlessly against the street nearly a foot behind him. Allard smiled slightly, thinking to himself, *Looks like I can get him to count at least for a few seconds with salt too.*

With that, he set himself into a rhythm, counting off five seconds of running between each shot. The daggers started flying swifter and swifter with each arrow he shot and pause he forced, making him wonder just how many the vampire had on it. But despite their speed, they couldn't find their mark and he escaped the barrage with only a small cut along his shoulder. By then, eight arrows in, he'd reached the alley and felt a modicum of relief growing in his chest. It wasn't over, but the end was in sight. Leaping the trench between the gutters, he nocked a silver arrow and spun, steadily backing towards where he knew the net of oil hung.

Then the vampire slid into sight, crouched at the end of the alleyway. All shrouded in its tattered cloak, the fog seemed to lift slightly, as though it wanted Allard to see his hunter. Allard's gaze met the blazing red eyes beneath the black hood, framed by wisps of silvery hair that almost melted into the fog. There was nothing in them but the cruel calculation of a predator, but somehow the lack of personal hatred struck him and he could almost imagine that there was the slightest bit of respect there. Like in that moment he'd met someone he was meant to strive and struggle against and though they were forever fated to be enemies, two hunters struggling with savagery matched against human wit, their duel itself was something worthy of remembrance. Everything Adelaide said started sliding into place in his mind. She was his Storm Warlord and he was the Ember King and this vampire was the Dusk Reaver that started them on their journey. Then he remembered what else she'd said and tore his eyes from the vampire's before it could hypnotize him, letting loose with his arrow as he did.

The vampire leapt towards him with daggers drawn and fangs bared. The arrow took it in the shoulder, not pushing it back even an inch despite the force of it, but it let out a hiss of pain, more affected by the silver than it had been by the honed bronze. It paused to dig the tip out of its flesh, giving Allard the opportunity to retreat. Over the hisses of pain, he could hear the sound of rushing water, the trenches filling as Xavier turned on the waterstones. Content that the trap was as sprung as it could ever be, Allard turned and ran, forcing his already tired legs to give just a little bit more. As he reached the edge of the trench, he crouched down and leapt, only vaguely aware of the sound of a dagger splitting the air behind him. It took him in the leg with a flash of pain, dropping him to the ground just on the other side of the water. Pulling one of the two firestone arrows from his quiver, Allard rolled onto his back. The vampire stood frozen on its tiptoes at the very edge of the water, teeth gnashing. Not wanting to give it the chance to throw another dagger, Allard let loose with the arrow, its tip bursting into flames on contact. The vampire stumbled backwards, silently swatting the flames out as it did. Then, when it had stumbled back far enough, the net fell, Adelaide cutting the rope holding it up from her perch on the rooftop. The vampire looked up, frozen in shock as the pots of oil burst on the ground around it. Allard stumbled to his feet as it happened, smirking in triumph. Once more, its eyes met his, understanding dawning in them as Allard drew his second firestone arrow. Letting the arrow fly, he allowed himself a moment of levity, shouting at the vampire, "It's bad for your health to burn the midnight oil!"

The smile died on his face, however, when the vampire snapped its arm up faster than he'd have thought possible. Tearing its cloak off its shoulders, it whipped the oil-soaked cloth forward and caught his arrow mid-flight. The cloak erupted into flames, but the vampire simply let it drift to the ground, taking a quick step backwards to escape the storm of fire it sparked. Then, as if that weren't enough to make Allard's mouth hang open in disbelief, it quirked its head to the side with fangs bared, as if to say 'Is that the best you've got'. Allard looked up to the rooftop, hoping that Adelaide had already moved on to the cart. *I won't be of much help to her either way, with things as they are right now.* He flinched, feeling the dull pain of the dagger in his leg as he considered this. *But at least the vampire's still caught in this alley for now.*

Allard ducked around the side of a building, unwilling to just sit there and let the vampire toss daggers at him and started limping his way towards where their cart had been stashed, but a crunching noise that echoed out from the alleyway gave him pause. Against his better judgment, he went back and peeked his head around the corner, not even surprised by what he saw when he did. Completely eschewing the ground, the vampire was steadily making its way up the side of the building, clawed fingers digging into the wall and feet somehow managing to cling to the surface. Seeing Allard, or perhaps smelling him given the blood leaking down his leg, it turned its head to him with a snarl, standing upright on the wall. As it reached for a knife, Allard fled, cursing himself for assuming walls were a firm enough barrier and wondering if he'd be able to make it in time and. He was only slowing down with each step, the pain hindering his progress.

Weighing his options, he shook his head, leaning himself against a wall and pulling out another silver arrow. *Xavier and Adelaide will have a better chance of getting away if I don't lead the vampire straight to them. And hey, maybe I'll get lucky and stick him straight through the heart. How hard can it be, huh?*

Before long, no more than ten seconds, he heard the thud of something falling and the fog split before him in a great rush, like it had been blown away by an unseen wind. The vampire crouched at the other end of a hallway formed from mist, staring him down with dispassionate hatred. The sheer apathy of it, like the vampire didn't care who Allard was and would have hated him no matter who stood in his place, struck Allard. As he realized this was a hatred that could never change, that its unchanging nature was what defined the monstrous nature of a vampire, he was surprised to find himself pitying the beast. Looking at it that way, it felt no more evil than a rabid hound. *It's just like with the sheep,* he thought as he brought his bow to bear. *Necessary to fight and put down, but ignoble nonetheless.*

Despite this pity, he still let loose once the vampire straightened up and exposed its chest. But even if his aim was true, it would have come to nothing. The vampire once more flicked its hand and snatched the arrow from the air. Allard realized that he probably had a better chance of killing it when it was armed and let out a grim laugh. *At least when his hands are busy with daggers I might stand a chance of hitting him.*

The vampire snapped the arrow in two and stalked across the street, deliberately taking its time. Allard tried to nock another arrow, but by the time he raised his bow, the vampire stood over him and simply batted his bow aside. Clamping one hand around his throat, it lifted him against the wall as though he weighed nothing. It crawled up over him until it crouched with its knees planted on either side of his chest. As its fangs began to descend, he raised a hand almost unconsciously, as though he could stop what came next.

The vampire froze. Looking at his hand, then at his face, it cocked its head to the side in confusion. Releasing its grip on his throat, it leapt away from the wall. Backing away, it continued to look him up and down, clearly taken aback, almost frightened even. Much to Allard's shock, it spoke, "Who are you? What are you? How are you?" Shaking its head, it began to pace back and forth in agitation. Virtually its entire body was shaking. It continued, counting off on its fingers as it muttered to itself. "One and two and three and four. King and

Master and Dragon and Demon. The Fairy makes five and the Knife makes six. But why is there seven?"

Allard sat frozen, far too shocked to even consider trying for his bow again. Though it made a certain amount of sense that a vampire could speak, and many of the stories featuring them gave them far more humanity than just that, he'd assumed this one could not. It never had before, even when chasing Adelaide and him through Riverluck, so he'd never seen it as anything more than a monster. Even when he thought of it as a hunter just like him, the fact that it was a monster never went away. But hearing it rant and rave, even if its voice did come out in a grating croak like it hadn't been used for years, reminded him of another thing he'd forgotten in seeing it as nothing more than a monster. *This thing can think. He's choosing its targets with purpose. He has a motive, even if he's simply to serve another's goals.*

Then, without warning, the moment snapped in a torrent of water, seemingly springing forth from the very air next to the vampire. Allard thought he saw something sparkling drop to the ground, as if a stone had been thrown at it. Turning to see what had happened to the vampire, he found it at the edge of a swiftly expanding pool of water, snarling in rage. Suddenly, Allard felt himself lifted to his feet, and a familiar, albeit irritatingly so, man's voice spoke in his ear. "Come on now Al, no time to be sitting around like that."

On his other side, Adelaide chimed in. "Yeah, can you imagine how upset Levi would be if he found out I died because you were dragging me down?"

Getting his feet under him, Allard started limping along, supported on either side by Xavier and Adelaide. "What... How did you... Water?"

"Xavi bought another waterstone that he failed to tell us about," Adelaide said. "But we can explain the rest later. Let's just get you to the cart and get out of here."

Allard simply nodded, focusing on putting one foot in front of the other. Eventually he ended up lying in the bed of the cart, though he couldn't re-member much of how he'd gotten there. He could feel himself drifting off to sleep and dimly wondered just how much blood he had lost. It was all he could do to listen to Adelaide and Xavier talking as the former busied herself with something in a pack near Allard and the latter drove the cart.

Flicking the reins, Xavier glanced back to Adelaide. "We should continue on through the night. In truth, I've never actually seen her go all out, but the gaean vampire I knew claimed to be able to outrun a horse so I suspect this lesser vampire may be able to as well. Do you have any ideas of where we should go?"

Nodding Adelaide pulled out a pouch and roll of bandages. "I have a bit of an idea. Start us towards Chancewind for now. Is this the one?"

"Yes, that poultice should at least help stop the bleeding and keep our dear friend back there from dying, assuming the wound is as bad as it looks. Spring's mercy, I wish we had someone who could cast healing spells with us, in all honesty, but that'll be the best we can manage in this situation."

Something cold pressed against Allard's leg, sending a bolt of pain up his body. He tried to shift out of the way, but Adelaide held him down. Once he settled down, she began wrapping the bandages around his leg, letting out a wry laugh. "I couldn't agree more. If only Erica were here, she'd be able to help Al and probably do something about the vampire too." She paused for a moment, looking at Allard with an impassive expression. "Hey Xavi, why didn't he kill Al back there? Why was he just pacing?"

Xavier was silent for several seconds, only the clattering of wheels and hooves against cobblestones filling the night. Finally, he shook his head, seemingly at a loss. "Truth be told, I have no idea. Perhaps he was trying to lure us back, but we won't know until Al can tell us himself."

As the two quieted down, Allard's view faded into a strange half-dream. Even though it felt as though he could still see the world around him, the cart and his companions and the trees in the fields outside of town, none of it seemed to change. As though they were traveling the same stretch of road over and over again. And more than that, though neither Adelaide nor Xavier seemed to notice, they were accompanied by a third companion. The woman from Allard's dreams sat at his side, humming a lullaby as she held his hand. It could have been a mere trick of the night since she no longer appeared formed out of a softly glowing blue light and was instead more like a sculpture painted over by the shimmering ink he had seen, blending in with the starry sky behind her. But all the same, hearing her song echo in his mind as the boundaries between dream and reality blurred, Allard felt a comforting warmth spreading throughout his chest, the pain in his leg fading away with his consciousness.

Interlude B

Anemoday: 6th of Hernus, Year 1980 R.S.

There is a seventh.

Knife stood frozen at the edge of the rapidly expanding pool of water left in the heiress' wake, waterstone sparkling in its center. They should set off in pursuit, as the mission demanded, but this was more important. Or if not important, then worth the delay consideration would bring. By all accounts, it should not be possible for there to be a seventh bearer of a third-born's favor. Before Knife had become Knife, they had known the state of the world. There *were* the likes of the royal Dragon-folk to the South and a family of House Gaoth on the Morningstar who heard her whispers, but that was not this. There had only been the Master then, and Knife shortly after. Now, with events spiraling towards a confluence of fate, more had been added to that number, but they were all known to the Master and therefore his Knife. He needed to keep track of his allies for when they became rivals, after all. And this one – this fragile, pitiful child – was *not* one of them.

The water almost reached the edge of Knife's boots, snapping them from their reverie and forcing them to flinch back, lest the old blessings of life and death bind them. Taking a moment to survey the town, the fog obediently parting in accordance with their will, Knife considered the destruction of the streets. Flooding aside, fire was licking up the walls lining the alleyway the seventh one had tried to trap them in. Two things the townsfolk would notice before too long. With that in mind, Knife turned to the edge of town and started in pursuit of the heiress, albeit at a pace more leisurely than anything that could truly be called 'pursuit'. Because for as much as the mission demanded they continue their hunt, it did not demand haste in word, merely spirit. *And though the facts speak otherwise, a seventh is impossible.*

Silence reigned for two hundred and forty steps, Knife counting the buildings they passed to order their thoughts (*thirty-two*). Then they suddenly stopped, as if something had occurred to them. In truth, every thought running through their head had been carefully analyzed over the trek and finished by the two hundredth step, the pose a mere affectation. And in any case, they couldn't have stopped earlier if they wanted to, not with the count-cycle incomplete, and had little desire to start a new cycle while there were still conclusions to be drawn. Making sure not to look up at the uncountable stars, they turned and began pacing back and forth, from one street corner to the next (*eight steps*) and back, speaking aloud as they did. One of the second-born might overhear, but with the Mage of the Blossoming Wind as flighty as he was, it mattered little and Knife could almost imagine their voice was the Master's response to their queries, a comforting thought. "A seventh is impossible and yet he showed the marks, the brand upon his soul. How?"

Knife turned. "The marks are present, but merely that. Marks like footprints through snow. It means nothing without Conviction. Cause without effect, request without reply.

"Yet Knife has no such Conviction."

Enraged, they spun around, throwing a dagger with enough force to crack the pavement into bits (*twelve*). "Knife *is* Conviction, the Master's favor anchoring that which cannot be anchored turning to Knife's favor from the third-born."

Holding their hands up in apology, they turned again, conceding their act as devil's advocate. "And the boy is Human, no bound soul or mystically constructed being. He must have Conviction to possess favor." They paused on reaching the corner. "But it would explain Knife's miscalculation. With a third-born's favor, it was no mere chance its dagger missed."

Knife shook their head as they turned. "No. The boy has no favor. He cannot. He is not a seventh."

Chiding themself for such petulance, Knife wagged a finger back and forth in time with their steps. "It would explain his survival."

Through gnashing teeth, they responded, "No. It is impossible. Else why would the Master have sent us on such a mission? There is no reason for the chosen of the third-born to struggle against each other." *Yet.*

More than a little pleased with their logic, Knife nodded slowly, egging themself on. "So? What then does it mean?"

There was of course, only one conclusion. "Not favor, but something else. Marked? Or merely influenced? 'Footprints in the snow.'"

Content with their thoughts, Knife silently completed their circuit, continuing on their way out of town when they did. It would not do to discount the boy outright, such a miscalculation had cost them once already and only good fortune had allowed them to recover, stumbling upon the heiress in this paltry town, but he could not be a seventh. It was such a ridiculous notion that only overwhelming empirical data could prove it correct. Empirical data which would, fortunately, only be gathered in pursuit of Knife's mission. *And in any case, he'll be dead soon enough.*

Once they reached the town gates, dashing up and over with little concern for the shoddy fortifications, the trail forward was clear. Taking haste over caution, hoof-prints and wheel-tracks were clear as day in the dirt road. Closing their eyes, Knife measured the time. It would be difficult to catch such a cart before daylight, so there was no need for them to make the same mistake. Keeping their eyes on the track, they fell into a brisk jog, relieved they could finally cease worrying over such things that were beyond them. It was not, after all, a knife's place to wonder at the schemes of the ancient ones. No, that was for the knowing ones, those who held power and will. Those who sought the Regalia. Such a blade as they would be far better suited to cutting where they had been directed.

Chapter 21

Loamday: 7th of Hernus, Year 1980 R.S.

Erica set the sheaf of papers on Adelaide's desk with an irritated sigh. Investigating Lady Ellis' manor had been just as unproductive as she'd expected, only serving to confirm what suspicions she'd already had. There *was* the same omnipresent dark energy suffusing the walls and air of the building as there had been in Lord Reinhardt's manor, but just as before, it seemed almost stagnant, simply waiting until... Well, until something. And if that weren't enough, she was still trying to figure out just what was going on with the Auris Empire. She'd been forced to go to a breakfast with the representatives this morning as Adelaide's proxy, and that had only served to further her uncertainty. The discussions themselves were one thing, mostly just the Perlorans explaining what assets they had in a bid to make their position of independence clear, but what truly bothered her was Chancellor Lukas. She'd found out after the meal that he'd been the one to insist on a progress report of Adelaide's progress, and thus was directly responsible for her attendance, and all throughout the meal she'd noticed him looking at her out of the corner of his eye. Something about it, and his usual relaxed nature belying just how shrewd he was, made her feel like he knew something she didn't. And given the subject was herself, that was more than a little disconcerting. All she could think of was that he somehow knew Adelaide was gone, but there was no way to confirm that, at least in her mind, without implying Adelaide was gone in the first place.

It was times like these that made her question just why she was allowed to work in the palace. Even if her official position was apprentice mage, her only real job was to be Adelaide's friend, meaning she was vastly unqualified for anything outside of daily life. Quite frankly, she was glad that she'd been excused from any other meetings today under the pretext of Adelaide needing to study more on the history of Montiamon's involvement in world politics since the death of King Sanborn forty-six years ago. That wasn't to say she was free from all work, but at the very least she'd be doing something more in line with her talents. She wasn't sure just what she was supposed to find in the city itself, but there must be something connecting the two loci of dark magic. Picking up the pack of magic tools she'd prepared last night and slipping Adelaide's magic detector bracelet on, she started off to the rear entrance of the palace where she'd agreed to meet Levi.

The knight stood waiting just outside the door, looking no better rested than he had the day before. Pushing himself off the wall, he waved to her in greeting. "Are you ready then, Miss Greenmaiden? We have quite the day ahead of us. I have high hopes we shall finally make some progress."

"I can't imagine why. It's not like I found anything at either of the manors and that's where the cursed energy seems to be focused."

Levi shot her a cheery smile at odds with his apparent fatigue. "I suppose if nothing else, we shall be rewarded with a nice walk. Now shall we?" As they headed through the palace gardens, Levi glanced at Erica before saying, "That being said, can you tell me more about what you expect from this spell? On a theoretical basis, I mean."

Frowning, Erica thought back on the chapters she'd studied on dark magic flows. Most of the texts she'd read before this week had been books on healing, wards, and holy magic and, astonishingly, none of them had much to say in regards to unholy magic. At most they talked about how to structure wards to block the flows of such magic. "I don't expect too much, but if we look along the route that connects the focal points we might be able to put a few things together, maybe even find another locus if we can track the flows. And..." She trailed off, shooting Levi a wary look before continuing. "I don't want to insult you, but how much magical theory have you studied?"

"Less than I should, all things considered. I know a true monster hunter should know holy magic for healing and striking down monsters, the basics of unholy magic to know what they face, and at the very least some personal enchantments to aid in combat. The path of a monster hunter is more than knowing how to wield a blade, more than possessing a magic sword and set of armor, but I unfortunately only studied the basic foundations of magical theory. In short, you do not need to explain Inception, Conception, and Conviction for me."

That did make things easier for her, since the three pillars were the base of all magic and everything from there operated more through instinct than actual knowledge. But that being said, there wasn't much for her to say. As best she could figure, they were dealing with some form of necromancy, but that was a conclusion biased by the presence of undead. Unwilling to fumble her way through that conversation, Erica decided to to change tack. "If you don't mind my asking, why didn't you study more magic? Does your Conviction not match up with your Inception? Or can you use magic and just decided not to look into it further?"

By this time, they had passed through the gates to the palace grounds and were walking along the streets of the Nobles' District. There weren't many people about with the threat of undead looming, but enough of the highborn folk persisted in their morning strolls and it was clear they were what Levi was watching as he considered his response. "I suppose it comes down to a matter of Conviction. I never felt I had the talent for magic and so I never bothered to try. By the time it became necessary, it was impossible for me. And I know that is not how magic truly works, that technically anyone can learn it through enough effort, but those are all things said by mages who have already overcome that wall."

As someone who had been born with the knack, who'd never needed to struggle with the Conviction to cast spells, Erica didn't know what to say to this. He was right that strictly speaking anyone could learn magic if they were able to put in the work and convince themselves within their heart of hearts that they were capable of it. But he was also right that she had no idea what that was like, no idea what it meant to change her beliefs through sheer force of will. "Have you considered looking into an alternative to magic then? There's those stories about the physical mystic arts practiced in Viemer or the Critical Will of the Demonblade of Austall. Could you try learning one of those?"

Levi let out a wry laugh. "As soon as I have a spare decade of leave I will consider training under the Ki masters of Viemer. And seeing as the Demonblade invented his so-called Critical Will and neglected to teach it to anyone else before the Saint of Swords drove him across the seas, I think I will pass. It matters little either way. I only have to make up for my weakness with hard work, as I always have." Looking up, Levi took in the street around them. "If I am not mistaken, we are in the middle of where a straight line between Lord Reinhardt's manor and the palace would be. Can you sense anything here?"

Erica closed her eyes and focused her senses. Immediately however, she noticed there was nothing out of the ordinary. The environment was as clear as the sky itself, nothing marring the natural flows of air and water twining with the light from the sun and warming the twin pools of dark and earth beneath her feet, fire resting far below and out of sight. And there was very little artificial interference beyond a few pinpricks of light from the sunstone street lamps lining the road. Narrowing her eyes, she drew back her sleeve and twisted the dial on the magic detecting bracelet. The magestone set in its center remained stubbornly translucent, only a tiny white light shining in its center. After a few seconds, she shook her head, turning the detector off and facing Levi. "Nothing here. We should continue on to the manors."

Erica's mind spun with the implications of the lack of magical connection between the palace and the manor. As they continued making their way through the Nobles' District, the sun continued to rise and the cool of early morning gave way to a pleasant spring warmth. With the day in full swing, the streets started to fill, mostly servants running about on errands for their masters and guards patrolling – a good deal more of the latter under the current situation – but a fair number of young and supposedly fashionable nobles had finally woken up and set out for their poetry societies or whatever was in style this year. And, more to Erica's interest, work had begun on preparations for the festival. While the majority of it was to be centered in the Low City, there would still be a fair amount of celebration in the streets of the Nobles' District if the stalls around were any indication. And even though the Rugegan envoys had yet to show up and the festival hadn't officially started, several of these stalls were open and the festive mood from that had already begun in the Low City could be felt even here.

Then with no warning, a strange creeping sensation began worming its way up Erica's back. She couldn't see anything out of the ordinary, but a quick check of the magic detector showed thin threads of purple spiraling towards the white light at the center, a clear enough indicator of unholy magic nearby. "Looks like I got something," she said, turning to Levi. "Is this the place?"

Taking a moment to scan the buildings around them, Levi shrugged. "It's not the exact point between the two, but it's close enough." He nodded towards a nearby park. "Shall we relocate to somewhere other than the middle of the street?"

Like most of the parks in the Nobles' District, that one was far more orderly and structured than Erica was used to. In Regina's Bounty, the closest thing they had to a park was the central green with its old and gnarled oak tree growing in the center, little more than a common area for picnics and holiday feasts, among other things. And from what she'd seen of the parks in the Low City, they were of a similar bent with far less ornamentation and far more community within them. But between the neatly trimmed lawn and gravel paths crisscrossing it, the unspoken sentiment was clear: this park was meant to be looked at, nothing more. Taking a seat beside a fountain, water spouting out from the hands of a statue carved in the likeness of the River Sage, Erica began sorting through her things, preparing her foci for an identification ritual.

As she worked, Levi stood nearby, watching the young nobles go about their leisure while he waited. His face held an emotion somewhere between sorrow and longing. Setting down her divination sticks, Erica looked up with a frown. "What's up, Levi? Something wrong?"

He blinked several times before shaking his head. "No, not at all. There is nothing you need worry about."

Erica said nothing, merely fixing him with a steady gaze to make sure he knew she wasn't buying it.

Letting out a sigh, Levi raised his hands in a conciliatory gesture. "Very well. I understand. It is simply... The evidence of my inadequacies brought forth by the last few days reminded me of times long past."

Realizing this was a rare opportunity to learn something about Levi, someone she knew virtually nothing about personally despite three years of friendship, Erica felt her heart leap. "Oh yeah? Did you fail an important test or something?"

Levi frowned at her, eyes narrowed. "Do not think me ignorant to your machinations, Miss Greenmaiden. Simply concern yourself with completing whatever it is you are doing there." Wincing, Erica went back to her preparations, carefully chalking runes of Mystic script on the ledge of the fountain's basin. After a moment, Levi sighed. "Though I suppose if I have nothing to do but watch, there is little enough harm in you hearing it."

He sat down on the fountain a few feet from the runes. "It's as simple as this: I wasn't always the Crownguard. Most Crownguards train from the moment they can walk to take up the mantle and protect Tycortua. But for me it didn't start until I was fifteen. My older brother had it well in hand." As if he could sense what she was thinking, Levi simply shook his head, eyes sad. "And no, he didn't die from anything like you'd hear in a story. He just got sick one day and never recovered. It happens sometimes and everyone knows that to some extent, but it feels like when it happens to someone you know, it's too sudden."

Erica started muttering condolences, but stopped short. After that much time, it would only be a formality. And it wasn't what the conversation was really about either. "So that's why you never studied magic?"

He nodded. "Exactly. Aaron inherited the armor and the responsibility. I inherited the estates and the family's future." He shook his head as he looked up at the palace. "I always knew I was weak, that my brother would have done better. I know His Majesty would have you believe otherwise, but it's my fault Addy's been kept so close to the palace all these years. My fault that she was never allowed out to socialize with the other noble children. He couldn't trust an untrained child to protect his only daughter after all. He says it's his own paranoia after the old sidhe troubles, but I know better. I saw what my brother was like and I know that I can never hope to match up to what he was.

"My weakness never seemed to matter too much before, when nothing was wrong and I had it well in hand, but now I can't help but think that my brother would have done better. That he would have caught the high vampire earlier. That he would have been able to keep Addy from running off. That he would have found the one behind it all at this point. By Zephyros' banner, he probably would've beaten Neriah.

"Silly, isn't it? Wondering what I would've been if he were still here. I probably would've ended up a useless young lord idling his time away on bad art and philosophy everyone complimented just because of my name, huh?" Shaking his head one last time, he clapped his hands together, the noise of it invigorating him, and looked down over Erica's runes. "Well, have you completed your inscriptions yet?"

Any consolation Erica could have given would have only sounded empty. Saying he was doing well would be meaningless coming from someone who had no one to compare him to. She certainly thought there was nothing more that he could have done, in any of the cases given, but if that's what he was thinking, she wouldn't be able to convince him otherwise. She wasn't the one he needed to hear it from. And if he'd been hearing it for over a decade without believing it, hearing from her once right now wouldn't be any different. So she said nothing, merely nodding along in sympathy. Levi shrugged again, the gesture an idle and thoughtless thing.

Erica desperately wanted to ask what the 'old sidhe troubles' were. She'd known about Adelaide's considerably closed off lifestyle, her solitude the main reason she and Allard had been brought to the palace in the first place, but this was the first she'd ever heard of a reason why the isolation was so extreme. And in that same way, she wanted to offer some word of reassurance to Levi, to tell him he was doing as good a job as possible. But could sense this wasn't the time for either and simply nodded instead, picking up the divination sticks in one hand and placing the other on the edge of the circle of runes. "I was just waiting for you to finish. Are you ready?"

Shooting her a withering glare, he nodded. Taking a breath, Erica focused herself and began pushing magic into the circle, the chalk lighting up with a soft white glow. She tossed the sticks into the circle and they fell for only a moment before stopping and hovering in place, spinning slowly as they did. Levi looked over at her with a furrowed brow. "Should I understand the significance of that, Miss Greenmaiden?"

Frowning, Erica considered the results of her divination. The alignment of the sticks, spinning along an axis as though tracing out an invisible aqueduct, made it clear there was a directed flow of magic, presumably unholy given the context, and seemingly between the two manors. But that was all they told her. Nothing of the particular orientation spoke to the Conception of the spell or its caster's intentions. In fact, the lethargy of the flow seemed to indicate the magic was merely passive. Gathering the sticks up once more, she shook her head. "I'm not sure. There's definitely a connection present, but I'm not sure why. It doesn't seem to be doing anything."

"If this is a geometric spell as you hypothesized, could it be possible the caster has yet to complete the pattern? Two vertices hardly form a shape after all."

Erica nodded. "That's a good point. If the palace isn't connected to the other flows, the remaining vertices must be somewhere in the Low City. I don't know what they might target down there, but if we compare the distance between the two manors, we should be able to approximate where other focal points might be. But that doesn't solve the problem. Even incomplete, traces of the spell should be present in its construction. And it only raises the question of why the palace was attacked in the first place if it isn't included in the pattern."

Rising to his feet, Levi held out a hand to her and nodded towards the park's exit. "Well if that is the limit of what knowledge can be gleaned from here, we had best be on our way. I shall speak with Archmage Dwyer and request that he send guild mages to investigate further at the manors and the projected focal points once you have calculated them."

Erica shot Levi a steady glare. "Couldn't you have done that in the first place? Guild mages should be far more qualified than me."

The chuckle she got in response only served to make her more annoyed. Mainly because of how decidedly un-Levi it and the accompanying smile were, as if he weren't taking her complaints seriously. "No, for I would rather work with a friend. Professional mages are a nuisance in any case." He tapped his side as he walked. "You know... Whisperwind emits no magical residue while unsummoned and resting in Void-Space. Could whatever this spell is be waiting for an activation command before it takes shape and begins to look like anything?"

Erica sighed. "Unless this is an enchantment, where the spell is merely an empty vessel to hold magic, it shouldn't work the same way. The framework of the spell is present here in this world, so its 'magical residue', as you said, should show up too. But I'm still going to have to start looking into that, won't I?"

Levi's smile deepened. "Always one thing at a time, Miss Greenmaiden."

Chapter 22

Loamday: 7th of Hernus, Year 1980 R.S.

When Allard awoke, the sun was already well above the horizon, its light warm upon his face. At least as warm as it could be on a spring morning, but enough to rouse him nonetheless. Sitting up with a wince, the wound in his leg stinging with the sudden movement, he took the measure of his surroundings. Adelaide still lay asleep on the other side of the cart, some spare piece of clothing thrown over her eyes the only concession to the sunlight, while Xavier held the reins up at the driver's seat, drooping slightly with exhaustion. Looking to the roadside didn't tell him anything of particular use, the landscape still the rolling grasslands that stretched from the Summerblood to the coast, only broken by the occasional copse of trees. Gingerly shifting himself towards the front, he cleared his throat to get Xavier's attention. The man turned back and smiled tiredly. "Ah! It's good to see you awake, Al. How's your leg?"

Grimacing, Allard looked at his outstretched leg, the upper thigh still wrapped tightly with several bandages. "I'll be walking lightly for a little bit, but otherwise I'm okay. Whatever you had Adelaide put on it seems to have more or less closed the wound, though I imagine I'll need to keep it bound for a few more days regardless. What was that anyways?"

Xavier shook his head dismissively. "In truth, just something I'd taken with me from Morningstar in case I got hurt. I'm no medic, so I couldn't tell you what specifically is in it, but it's a concoction of various herbs bound together by alchemy. Binds wounds, kills infection, and neutralizes common poisons."

This piqued Allard's curiosity. "Was there something strange about the dagger? I don't think the vampire used poison before, so if something prompted a change in tactics..."

"I honestly doubt it. The wound was certainly bleeding a lot, but that was probably just the kind of wound it was. What about you? You couldn't kill the vampire, but did you notice anything strange or noteworthy about him?"

The vampire's crazed ranting echoed through Allard's head. Quite frankly, he had no idea what any of it was supposed to mean, despite the importance it placed on the titles and numbers. "Nothing comes to mind." He looked back over at Adelaide once more, still asleep. Finding no support there, he turned his gaze to the roadside. "If you don't mind my asking, what's our plan now?"

With the sun rising behind them, and a little to the left, they seemed to be going north-east, but that didn't mean they'd left the city that way. For his part, Xavier let out a thunderous yawn, leaning back in his seat slightly. "Ask the little lady Adelaide there. After she'd got you patched up she told me to head this way and then went to sleep without so much as a how you do."

Allard cast a wary eye on Adelaide, well aware of the hour. He looked back and forth between her and Xavier before he continued. "Right. Is there anything else you have to discuss with me right now?"

Xavier was silent for a few moments, staring at Allard. Yet for all his thought, he simply shrugged. "Unless you have anything in mind, no. I think you'd best start asking Addy so the two of us can actually know what we're doing."

"Sure, but are you absolutely positive there's nothing else we can be doing right now?"

Xavier chuckled. "There's no avoiding it, Al."

Sighing, Allard turned to consider the sleeping Adelaide. Resigning himself to his terrible duty, he reached over and shook Adelaide. "Wake up. It's halfway to noon already."

This earned him a coat to the face, Adelaide throwing her makeshift sleeping mask at him before turning over with only vague grumblings in response. Allard sighed in exasperation, looking to Xavier with a pleading expression on his face. The man just smiled encouragingly, turning back to the road and making a show of busying himself with the reins. Rolling his eyes, Allard shook Adelaide once more, putting a bit of force into his words as he spoke. "Come on, get up! It's daylight now, but that thing is sure to catch up to us before long. We need to come up with a plan."

She turned her head to fix him with a sullen glare. "I was up all night and I already have a plan. Ask Xavi." Xavier, for his part, remained unhelpfully quiet. Letting out a noise of disgust, Adelaide sat up, continuing with a heavy sigh. "I told him we were going to Chancewind. That should be enough, right?"

Glancing back over his shoulder, Xavier shrugged. "I honestly have no idea where that is or why it's relevant."

The glare Adelaide shot him looked sharp enough to cut wood, but he pretended not to notice and turned his back once more. "Fine," she said, glaring at Allard. "We can start from the beginning, but I'm eating while we do. What did we learn from last night?"

Allard shrugged and tossed a loaf to Adelaide as he responded. "Make sure the water surrounds vampires on all sides?"

"Hmm. That is a good first point to build upon. Expanded, it becomes 'Make sure we are thinking like a vampire does'. Their bodies don't work exactly like ours after all."

That seemed an understatement to Allard, having seen their pursuer openly defy gravity. Even thinking about it in the daylight sent shivers up his spine. "Yeah. And it's more than just magic. I've seen people move fast and strong, but he could do stuff that seemed like it shouldn't have been possible for anything but a spirit. I feel like my arm would break if I tried to move it that fast or at those angles."

With some food in her stomach, Adelaide's morning sullenness seemed to have vanished and she smiled at Allards words. "Exactly. I confess I could not see him as well as you could, as I was on the roof and trying to get away, but that ties into my next point. He possesses exceptional reflexes. Far better than any of ours. So how do we hit him?"

Allard remembered how the vampire could simply snatch his arrows out of the air. And how it didn't do the same to the waterstone Xavier had thrown. "I'd say if we can keep his hands busy, whether with daggers or something else, he'd compromise his own defenses. But I don't think I like that idea. At the risk of sounding plain, why don't we hit him with something he can't see coming?"

Adelaide smiled. "Right again. You're on fire, Al. If this is what being put in danger does to your tactical skills, we need to get you in the field more often." Allard frowned, some sort of retort coming to his lips, but she continued before he could say anything. "So it seems as though the biggest flaw of our trap was that it relied on you igniting the oil, hitting the vampire from where he could see you. But let us set that aside for now. We are discussing what we learned, not how to implement it."

Allard shrugged, thinking back to what had actually worked before the trap failed. "In terms of materials, it seems like silver does cause more pain than bronze, but isn't immediately fatal. Salt didn't seem to do anything beyond triggering its arithmomania."

Adelaide waited for him to continue, taking another bite of bread, but when it became clear that Allard wasn't going to say anything else, she sat up and cast a glance towards Xavier. "What about when he escaped? Was there anything you noticed about him from up close? Anything Xavi and I would have missed while we were getting the cart?"

The red eyes flashed through Allard's memory, filled with hatred. And the grating, ill-used voice. "Honestly... I'm not sure I can explain it. It might be something you had to actually see for yourself to understand, but the vampire was intelligent. He talked. But at the same time, that intelligence only seemed tangentially to hunting us. I don't think he actually care about hunting *us*, it's just something he has to do for some purpose. By Seras's stars, he only seemed to talk because he was confused, not because he wanted to say anything to me." He frowned, thinking of the stories of the Nyphean Talosians, metal soldiers that could only follow the orders they were given. "It's almost like he's closer to a tool than anything else."

At this, Xavier turned most of his attention back to the conversation, his head slightly tilted towards them to hear better. Across from Allard, Adelaide leaned forward, eyes narrowed. "What did he say?" She asked. "Could you make out anything meaningful from it?"

Allard shook his head. "It just sounded like rambling. He mentioned something about six people or things – a King, Master, Dragon, Demon, Fairy, and Knife – but I don't know what any of those are supposed to mean beyond the title itself."

Tapping a finger against her mouth, Adelaide thought for a moment. "Xavi. Do you think you could be the Demon?"

He shrugged. "'Could'? Perhaps. In truth, 'Demon' that could describe me in some context. But I don't know why this vampire would know about me or try to lump me in with the rest of the group."

She nodded. "And they are all generic enough to be impossible to apply to anyone in particular. But at the same time... If there's a 'Master' or 'King', then this vampire could just be a servant." She trailed off, considering for nearly a minute until she shook her head as though scattering the thoughts away. "A problem for another day. Is there anything else you can think of, Al?"

He shrugged. "Nothing comes to mind."

Silence filled the next minute, only the clatter of hooves and wheels on cobblestone beating a steady rhythm through the air, until finally Adelaide and

Xavier exchanged a glance and the Demon-folk let out an exaggerated sigh. "Lies, I'll ask it," he said. "I know this is a somewhat sensitive question, Al, but I'll put it to you straight. Why didn't the vampire kill you?"

Allard started to respond, indignant at what Xavier's suspicion implied, but his complaints died on his lips. Adelaide had told him about how vampiric magic could affect the mind. As close as he'd been, it wasn't a stretch to think the vampire made him into some kind of thrall. But he didn't have a better explanation to ease that suspicion. At a loss, he threw his hands up and replied, "I don't know. I really don't. It looked like something about me confused him or something. That's what set him ranting and raving like that. If you ask me, the only explanation is another lucky break for a member of the Fortunata family."

This did little to convince Xavier, his eyes narrowed and his shadow rising from the ground in the direct path of the sun, but Adelaide continued before he could say anything. "There's no use worrying about it then. There's definitely something strange going on here, but we won't be able to find the answers with what we know today, so if that's all we learned, we might as well move on."

"Yeah. I'd really like to get in on this plan of yours," Allard said. "Now we'd mentioned hitting the vampire with something he can't see coming, a plan Xavier's waterstone seems to support. The vampire's focus can only be in one place at a time, so if we have him looking at one person, someone else can hit him hard."

Adelaide nodded, waving her hand dismissively. "Yes, yes. That would work if we could get things set up right, but there's two problems with it. First, it means using someone as bait again. With how it turned out the first time, I'm not overly keen for a repeat performance. Second, we need something impactful enough to cause damage to him in order to 'hit him hard.'"

"Well that's all we can do, isn't it? Even if it is just little wounds each time, we can try chipping away at it till we win. And you said we were going to Chancewind, right? Maybe we can beg some holy water from Seras' monastery there and use that to do more damage."

Before he finished talking, Adelaide burst out in her best impression of a villainous laugh, flinging her arms out to the side. "Kahahahaha! You dream too small, Al! If there is an opponent you cannot beat, resort to trickery! And if trickery doesn't work, then fall back to overwhelming force!"

Suddenly understanding why she'd chosen Chancewind, Allard felt a sense of dread run down his spine. "No. We are *not* doing that."

"Yes, Al! If we're going to supplement our power in Chancewind, what better weapon than the great Witch of the New Moon herself?" She curled one hand into a fist and punched her other palm. "We trap the vampire, then bring the Witch and all her magical might down upon it like a hammer upon an anvil!"

Pinching his nose, Allard felt a sudden sympathy for Levi. He'd known Adelaide for three years, and been her friend for virtually the whole time, but never truly appreciated what it was like for her bodyguard to try and keep her under control. He imagined he could feel himself grow a new wrinkle on his forehead a he frowned. "Just because we met her once and she helped us doesn't mean she'll do it again. If you remember properly, she *did* start to get annoyed with us toward the end of the conversation and only seemed interested in pursuing her own goals. Asking her to deal with a vampire we can't kill ourselves is just asking for trouble."

Adelaide shrugged. "She seemed pretty nice to me. And we have something for her. She was interested in the Ember King's companions and Xavi here knows all about the Storm Warlord."

Remembering the stories Mal would tell about the Witch around the campfire when they were out on hunting trips back home, Allard felt a shiver go up his spine. Those stories always ended with something along the lines of 'and he was never seen again'. "Please tell her why this is a bad idea, Xavier."

The Demon-folk man didn't even bother turning around to reply. "Not from here. Don't know who this witch is or why she's so important."

Allard and Adelaide exchanged a glance. Even though they knew he was from an entirely different world, it rarely came up in conversation. Hearing he didn't know about something as simple as the Witch of the New Moon, a storied villain any child recognized, served as a grim reminder of just how little they knew about the man they'd put their trust in. Or at least Allard thought as much. As he watched Adelaide, he was frustrated to note she seemed more concerned with hearing him explain to Xavier, waving him on with an eager smile. Settling back against the walls of the cart with an inward sigh, he started in his best storytelling voice. "The Witch of the New Moon is, first and foremost, a mystery. No one knows who she truly is or where she came from, or even if there's only ever been one, but stories of the Witch have been told for over a thousand years. There are many stories, far too many to tell in this short a time, telling just how horrible she can be. A phantom in the night that appears from nowhere and disappears into nowhere, taking your happiness with her.

But to truly tell you of both her power and the devastation she is responsible for, there is only one tale to tell: the Tragedy of the Millennium Festival.

"It was a thousand years ago, a thousand years after the Ember King had slain the Dusk Tyrant and brought peace to the world, uniting all nations into the Sunfire Empire, save for those separated by sea and the kingdom given to his closest friend. The royal family, in their capital where World's Eye stands today, had been preparing a celebration all year, to recognize the thousand years of peace, but such things did not sit with the Witch of the New Moon. In her black tower of volcanic basalt, standing beyond the world's edge, the Witch looked down upon the people's joy and celebration with disdain. Their cheers grated upon her ears and the lights of their cities burned her eyes. Now no one can agree as to why she did what she did next, whether it was out of devotion to her fallen master or a desire to usurp his power for her own, but all know it was done out of hatred for the world that had found its way through the darkness. Climbing the mountain of Dusk's End, which stands over the Valleys of Death in the Stormwall Mountains, she entered Ash-star Tomb and cracked the seal upon the Dusk Tyrant, bringing his shadowy wraith back into the world once more.

"Down in the Empire, the people stood unprepared for the calamity that was sure to come. No one *could* know of it, for the Dusk Tyrant was long dead and they were sure of the might of their Emperor and his elite peers. But on the eve of the festival's beginning, an army of darkness poured into the capital, bringing devastation in its wake. Though the Emperor tried to fight back and stem the tide of destruction, the Dusk Tyrant's shade was too much for him and he was slain upon the steps of the palace, the rest of the royal family soon to follow. In that single night, the capital was brought to ruin, all of the heirs killed, and the Empire dealt a mortal blow, though it would take time yet to truly die. The survivors from the calamity spread to the far ends of the Empire, telling all of what had befallen them and their liege-lord. But even with this warning, there was little to be done. The army of darkness swept through the land, breaking all resistance they met. Indeed, the whole world would have been destroyed, by a mere fraction of the Dusk Tyrant's power, if it were not for a single hero who rose to restore order. No one knows for sure where the Scalebound came from, whether he was a Slayer knight from Naktikos or a member of the royal family who somehow escaped, but he fought back and eventually saved the world, though not the Empire. But that is another story entirely, for we are speaking of the Witch.

"During the whole conflict between the forces of light and dark, the Witch of the New Moon made no appearance. After loosing the Dusk Tyrant's shade upon the world, she simply vanished, escaping any punishment. The Order of the Eagle sent watchers from the City of the Scales to track her down, but no one found even a single trace of her, as if she'd vanished with the wind. Since then, stories tell of her appearing all across the continent. She shows up on moonless nights as a harbinger of death and destruction, always just before or just after terrible beasts set themselves upon a lone traveler or a secluded village. And still to this day, none know what she wants or why she chooses to bring calamity upon us. Just that to see her is to dance with death."

Xavier chuckled. "And that's who we're asking for help? Cheery."

Allard sighed, sensing he was at a two-to-one disadvantage in this argument. Ignoring the smug smile Adelaide presented him with, he turned to watch the terrain passing them by. But for as much as he thought seeking out the Witch was a bad idea, he couldn't deny the slightest bit of doubt that had slipped into his mind. *The stories all say she brings death and destruction, but she didn't kill Adelaide and me.* He frowned at this, finding it far easier to vilify a story than someone he'd met. *Just what is it she's after anyway?*

Chapter 23

Seaday: 8th of Hernus, Year 1980 R.S.

Slamming the book closed, Erica sighed and slid it off the desk she was steadily starting to thinking of as her own. It was somewhat distressing that she'd taken over Adelaide's workspace without a second thought, the princess' own books and lattice-stone devices neatly packed away in boxes on the floor to make room for her spell-books and charts of geometrically aligned magic flows, but with things as they were it couldn't be helped. At least that's how it felt to her. *And it's not like I've permanently taken it over, right?.*

But even as she thought as much, she knew she was only trying to distract herself from her frustrations. Since she'd gone out with Levi to check on patterns yesterday afternoon, Erica had been looking into the mechanics of inert enchantments. Rather predictably, none of the books she looked in were particularly helpful. Even with only a day's worth of research into the matter, it was exceedingly clear that such things could not be easily identified. More than one author said something to the effect of 'enchantments relying upon a trigger show no sign of their existence, for a spell's existence is equivalent to its effect. Therefore, if an enchantment is made to temporarily have no effect, then it can be considered to temporarily have no existence.' All of which was to say there was no way to know an inactive enchantment was present unless you already knew it was present. Picking the discarded tome up and putting it back in its proper place, with the care a book of its age should be given this time, Erica considered her geometric charts again, shifting her line of thinking. *But even if that's the case, the flows* are *present and visible, so to speak. So if it isn't an inactive enchantment waiting for a trigger, then what?*

All of these questions would be much easier to answer if she could figure out what the energy was actually supposed to do. But such a thing wouldn't be possible simply from analysis of the flows. Just like seeing a river from its banks doesn't tell you where it begins or where it empties, she'd need to be able to see the source of the magic in order to determine its purpose.

And despite spending a long afternoon trying out every one of the common geometric structures, she couldn't find any that made sense. Either the shape was centered on an irrelevant location or the number of vertices didn't make sense for a necromantic spell, each number possessing a particular meaning under common numerological theory. Even the most basic shape, a circle, wouldn't make sense since magic circles always represented either a barrier or a gateway. The former would have little offensive use and while the latter could be used to summon a fearsome monster from one of the other-worlds, a given summoning circle could only summon a single being at a time and there wasn't any monster Erica could think of that could threaten the combined might of the palace garrison by itself.

Muttering to herself, she looked down at the map one more time, then out the window behind her. All of this assumed the palace had no place in the design. She made that assumption since her own investigation had proven the palace to be unconnected to the magic flows, but if the palace were at the center of the pattern, then the two manors could neatly form the base of a shape. Most of the remaining vertices in this case would be placed in the hills beyond the palace, where only the barracks of the guard and aeries of the Griffin Corp lay. She'd discounted the northern half of the city thus far largely because of the garrison, assuming the town guard would have noticed if anything untoward had happened. But if someone were careful enough in their approach and avoided detection long enough to put down one of the enchantment's focal points, it was unlikely anyone would notice the focal point after the fact with so little out there. Erica took out several pieces of semitransparent paper and lay them over the map, sketching out the shapes with the palace at the center. Once she was done, she stood tapping the charcoal against her lip and wondered just what it was she was missing. *They certainly match up and the palace makes sense as a target for the center. But why is nothing showing up here and why isn't it connected to the flows?*

Her ponderings were interrupted by a quick rap at the door, which opened immediately after, Levi not bothering to wait for a response. He seemed un-characteristically rushed, clothing as wrinkled and rumpled as was becoming increasingly common these past few days, but Erica ignored his haste, intent on following through with her most recent idea. Only bothering to give a slight wave in acknowledgment of his arrival, Erica was largely unconcerned with whatever had brought him to her as she addressed him. "Morning, Levi. Do you know if there were any attacks or incursions around the aeries behind the palace?"

Levi stopped short, blinking in surprise. "Ah... Hmm? Nothing has been reported, but I can hardly say for certain. Is that truly relevant at the moment?"

Insistent, Erica tapped the stack of papers in front of her. "But take a look at this."

Levi fixed her with a flat stare, unamused, but took a seat on the other side of the desk and looked through her diagrams, comparing them to the map of the city himself. Finally, he sighed. "Very well. I can certainly check, but what would that mean for our investigation? Your own analysis of the magic flows aside, the palace mages have been extensive in ensuring the integrity of the palace wards after the last attack. Surely they would have noticed if something was out of place."

Erica nodded. "And even if there was, it's questionable how effective the spell would be if the palace is guarded by the combined efforts of several talented mages, including Archmage Dwyer."

"Indeed. And as much as I would like to discuss this further..." He stood and waved her towards the door. "I must insist you come with me. This is no time for idle conversation."

Erica rose and started to follow, but her thoughts immediately leapt to the worst thing she could think of and she felt a growing dread with every step. "What's wrong? Have there been more attacks? Or have you heard something about..."

Levi shook his head with a reassuring smile. "No, it is nothing about our friends. But it might be worse nonetheless. The Rugegan embassy has arrived."

As she stood waiting, Erica could only think about how different everything was from the last time they'd done this, when the Auran ambassador arrived. Sure, there were the superficial distinctions that anyone could see. For instance, they had elected to greet the Rugegans at the front of the palace instead of in the king's audience hall, the king standing on a raised terrace before the main entrance with a grand set of stairs sweeping down on either side, a member of the palace guard standing at attention on every other step. And neatly framing the terrace, Erica stood watching with a group of several advisors and courtiers she only knew in passing, all lined up along one side of the avenue leading from the palace gates with the Perlorans and Aurans similarly lined up opposite them, only their upper halves visible over the flowerbed median splitting the avenue in two. But the only difference that truly seemed to matter was the tension in the air. Last time, everyone present had been wary of those arriving, but there had been a kind of comforting unity to it. When it had been people from the Auris Empire, who the Western Alliance were all ostensibly aligned against, it was easy to split things into an 'us and them' kind of mentality. The Empire was a clear antagonist, if not villain, they all feared but could lend each other strength against. Here and now, the tension was not due to who was arriving, but the fact that they were arriving at all. Regardless of how they felt about the Rugegans themselves, everyone present knew their arrival was as good as a starting signal. With all of the players present, the idle politics and casual maneuverings would end and the conference would start in full. That alone would be enough cause to fill the air with a thick tension, like runners at the Nyphean Tournaments of the Council standing on the line and waiting for the race to begin. But with the added looming threat of undead attacks, there was another depth to the anticipation. The knowledge that now that everyone was in place, the culprit need not wait any longer to strike.

Silence filled the air as the Rugegan carriage rolled up the avenue, led by a dozen of their famed cataphracts and trailed by twice that number in halberdiers. Looking over the faces of those across the way, Erica was struck once more by the sheer strangeness to Chancellor Lukas. The Perlorans for their part had a near uniform gloom to them, the formality on both Viscount Myron's and Viscount Kasmy's faces doing little to mask their uncertainties. Even Duke Gerald, for all that she'd previously assumed him to be an exceedingly practical man, periodically ran his eyes along the guards overlooking the proceedings, these from the members of the Tycortua Regulars, as if they might attack or be attacked at any second. And while both of the chancellor's companions upheld their ever-present stoicism, particularly easy in Edan's case with her uniform's mask still obscuring any sign of unease, the very fact that their hands never left their weapons spoke to their feelings on the matter. But Lukas alone out of all the people there looked as if there were no place he'd rather be. He'd brought along a folding chair and lounged back in it as he waited, a lazy smile on his face and his eyes half closed. Erica couldn't help but shake her head as she saw him, taken aback by how little he seemed to care about everything going on.

But any further thoughts about the motives of the seemingly eternally relaxed man were cut short as the carriage rounded the large fountain at the end of the lane, centered upon a statue meant to portray the legendary clash between Zephyros and Ignatius, and King Thierry waved for both silence and attention. As he did, Archmage Dwyer stepped forward from his place beneath the portico and slammed his staff against the terrace once. The resulting boom, formed by a simple cantrip to enhance the sound, proved impossible to ignore. King Thierry waited patiently as the carriage opened and its occupants – two women and one man – carefully stepped out onto the pavement. When they had appropriately settled themselves, he nodded and spread his arms in greeting. "Welcome, our esteemed guests and friends Lady Sativus and Lady Tagetes. We are all happy to see you in good health, though we must wonder about your being the last to arrive. The good General Neriah, one of our guests from Auris to the east, spoke of troubles on the roads and we had grown concerned that the same might have befallen you."

One of the women – Erica assumed Lady Sativus for while both wore identical dresses in the traditional style of Rugego with the skirts cut in many layers of strips that had been enchanted to ripple like flickering flames, this one wore the crocus denoted by her family name emblazoned on her cloak – inclined her head slightly, waving the man forward with a few words whispered too quietly for anyone else to hear. From his own garb – a functional if somewhat extravagantly gilt cuirass and an extremely large sword at least five feet in length carried unsheathed and slung over one shoulder – Erica assumed he was a soldier of some sort, likely filling the same role as Neriah. He took a knee and struck a hand to his chest in a simple salute, his free hand easing his sword to the ground, and shouted up a response in the crispness of a report. "Captain Hirundo at your service, Your Majesty. Our travels were untroubled by threat of violence, our troop being too large for most monsters to bother. A larger than normal concentration of minor undead, largely bonewalkers and zombies, were noticed and my lieges assume this to be what you were referring to, Your Majesty, and what the esteemed General Neriah reported, but our Summer Guard made short work of them. Lady Sativus has recommended a survey of the area for search of an errant ghoststone cache once our business has been finished, but further discussion on that matter is beyond my authority. Our journey was lengthened by the destruction of the bridge from which Fortune's Bridge takes its name, forcing us to reroute back further along the Summerblood to the next crossing."

King Thierry paused, head tilted slightly in thought. A moment of silence followed as he considered the implications and Erica frowned, following a similar line of thought. The destruction of the bridge at Fortune's Bridge was no small action, cutting off the main thoroughfare between Rugego and Tycortua, and the rest of the continent beyond. Similarly, with the Summerblood as wide as it was, repairing it would be no small task. If it had been done merely to delay the Rugegan Embassy, then it was an action of incredible overkill. It left Rugego isolated and with no choice for travel or trade but across the Perloran border or through Perloran waters.

"Understood," the king eventually said. "In light of your news, we will be forced to increase patrols of the roads. And as for the bridge and survey, as you said, Lady Sativus, those are matters for discussion at a later date, for collaboration between our nations is necessary on both projects." Clapping his hands, he flicked an order to the guards on the stairs, all of whom snapped to attention and began to file back up into the palace. "Otherwise, it is good to see you have arrived safely. Now we can begin our negotiations in earnest. If you would follow us, our staff can see you settled into your rooms."

The Rugegans started up the stairs, their own soldiers following a few members of the palace guard to their temporary barracks, and the assembled audience relaxed somewhat, the formally neat lines breaking down as people began to scatter and go their own ways. Erica slipped back through the crowd, intent on returning to her research now that she was no longer needed, but someone grabbed her on the shoulder and pulled her into a lilac bush. She yelped in surprise, raising her hand and gathering up magic to defend herself, but stopped on seeing Viola, a finger raised to her lips. Relaxing, she glared at the maid. "What do you think you're doing, Vi?! Those branches really hurt, you know."

Viola continued to shush her, pulling her through the shrubbery and onto the path on the other side. Once they'd gotten far enough from the main avenue, she let go of Erica and turned back to face her. "Come on, follow me."

"That's it? Not even an apology for pulling me through a bush instead of just asking in the first place?"

Viola waved her on insistently. "Come on! Estelle wants to talk to you."

That alone was enough to make Erica take a second look at the path they were walking down. While, it wasn't terribly secluded, there was no one else in the immediate area and it was easy enough to see that this particular path would only continue to wind further into the gardens, losing the main path in twists and turns surrounded by flowering trees and flowing fountains. The intention of solitude was clear and set Erica wondered just what it could be that required such secrecy, especially as the old stories of Tycortua's rumored 'Quieting Star' began creeping their way into the back of her mind. More than a little disconcerted, Erica gave one last look over her shoulder before following, hurrying to catch up to Viola. "Wait, wait, wait. What's this about? She's not going to ask me to... You know, that kind of thing?"

This earned her a roll of the eyes. "The kingdom of Tycortua does not deal in such actions. She obviously wants to talk to you about how things will be starting."

Erica frowned, her earlier frustrations returning. "That may well be, but I don't know what she expects me to do. Doesn't she already know just how little I've been able to learn?"

"If things are starting, whether you know what will happen or not, then it's time to shift your priorities. If you can't prevent this spell from being cast, then figure out how to disrupt it. Now quit dawdling, Estelle will explain far– Eep!"

Viola leapt from the path with a yelp and slipped away through the plants with an uncanny speed, disappearing beneath a willow tree almost before Erica realized what was happening. Letting out a heavy sigh, she started looking around for whatever had set Viola off. A moment later, she heard footsteps crunching in the gravel behind her and Chancellor Lukas ambled around the corner, Edan keeping pace at his shoulder, with a bemused smile on his face. Seeing Erica, he raised a hand in greeting, mouth quirking up in a peculiar kind of smirk. "There you are, young assistant. Honestly, with these gardens as thick as they are, I'd almost believe you knew I was looking for you and were trying to lose me."

Erica gave a small curtsy before replying., trying not to think about how accurate his accusation was. "Begging your pardon, Chancellor. Is there anything I can help you with?"

"There's no need to be so formal, Miss Assistant. I'm not here for anything important. I just wanted to ask a favor of you."

Erica bit her tongue, forcing down her knee-jerk response to ask just how that was supposed to make her feel any better. Even if their countries weren't at war, the relationship between them was certainly strained and not in a position that friendly favors could just be tossed around back and forth willy-nilly. And when they were an ambassador and aide to the heir, it was far too easy to paint the scene as one nation's leader trying to tempt a rival's confidant to treason. "You'll have to forgive me, Chancellor, but I'm afraid that's not something I can so easily promise. Not without knowing your intentions. Now, if there's nothing else."

Lukas laughed. "Didn't I tell you to stop being so formal? That it wasn't anything too important? Winter winds, I just have a few things I wish to discuss with you."

Still unconvinced, Erica tried to subtly look around for Viola for support, but her friend remained hidden, assuming she was even still within earshot. "I can't imagine what you could possibly want me to tell you. My only specialty is in magic and I'm sure you have experts of your own who could answer whatever questions you have far better than I."

"Of course, of course. I had heard you knew a bit about magic, in truth. A most useful talent to be sure, and one that will become all the more useful in the coming days *I'm* sure. But I had other things in mind, if I'm being honest. Now that the Rugegans have arrived, the festival your own king has done us the extreme pleasure of hosting will start tonight. With that in mind, I wished to ask you to escort me and mine around. Having someone from the city to show us around would make the festival all the more exciting and I could get your perspective on a few matters."

Sure that nothing she said would dissuade Lukas, Erica decided it was time to resort to misdirection. "As much as I would like to help, I've already promised to attend tonight's festivities with a friend of mine and I'll be busy once we get back to business tomorrow."

Smiling triumphantly, Lukas leaned forward with his eyes glittering and sharp. "Excellent! Truth be told, the more the merrier! Is it Crownguard's squire? I understand you two know each other and saw you speaking together after our own arrival at the palace. I've been wondering about his unique position, but haven't been able to get a hold of him to ask. From what Neriah says, he's quite the intriguing young man." Something about the way the chancellor said all of these things set Erica on edge. On the one hand, it felt as though he knew she was lying and simply chose to lean into it. On the other hand, his sudden mention of Allard, while phrased innocuously, seemed a subtle hint that he knew what else the palace was lying about. Then the moment snapped, Lukas flashing a conspiratorial grin before spinning on his heel and waving over his shoulder. "Until later, then! I'll send someone to get you and your friend when it's time to meet."

With that, he was gone, just as suddenly as he appeared, leaving Erica at a loss for words. She stood frozen for several seconds before finally shaking her head with a sigh and starting back down the way she and Viola had been going before they were interrupted. Coming to a crossroads, she looked back and forth, trying to figure out which way to go now that she didn't have a guide. Folding her arms across her chest, she scowled at the whole situation, thinking out loud simply to break the silence. "And now I have to find someone to take with me or it'll be obvious I was lying."

"Hmm. Sounds like fun." Erica leapt back in surprise, more annoyed than anything else since she recognized Viola's voice. The maid had slipped back onto the path without her noticing, simply trailing behind her for the past several seconds without speaking up. Spinning around Erica, she planted herself in front of her and gestured towards the left pathway with an over-exaggerated bow. "This way if you please, my lady."

Erica's scowl deepened and she lightly smacked Viola in the shoulder as she passed. "Why didn't you help me out back there?"

Shrugging, a sly smile crept over Viola's face. "I'm supposed to be keeping myself discreet. I couldn't risk Lukas recognizing me. He's a sharp one after all. And you seemed to have things well in hand."

Feeling the inherent contradiction in Viola's statement if she planned on going with Erica to meet Lukas later that day wasn't worth pointing out, Erica contented herself with a resigned shake of her head. "Just take me to Estelle."

Chapter 24

Seaday: 8th of Hernus, Year 1980 R.S.

I t was late afternoon by the time their cart rolled into the gates at Chancewind, the sun shining down on the town almost like a celestial spotlight. Like all of the older towns and cities of Tycortua, built when peace was more of a hope and dream than a reality, it was built on a hillside to make it easier to defend in a siege. As they passed the walls and entered the town proper, Allard noticed that same sense of age permeated the entire town. The walls, while made of a sturdy stone which far surpassed the token defenses the wooden fences of smaller villages provided, were practically crumbling at their crenelations, a thick layer of vines both inside and out stretching to their tops as if pulling the walls down themselves. The streets, while smoother and more well-kept than the cobblestone roads found commonly even in Riverluck, were made of an irregular pattern of flagstones that almost seemed to have naturally fallen where they lay, moss coating the edges of the road and small tufts of grass poking through the cracks. The town was built with streams of water flowing alongside its roads and through its parks, in the same style still used in modern Riverluck, but they were far rougher and more natural than the fountains and ponds of the capital, like a natural spring opened at the hilltop and simply tumbled down between the houses. And that was all without considering the houses and shops themselves, the white, limestone buildings rising all across the hill. The ivy draped along many of their roofs and walls combined with their close proximity to each other gave the impression of a miniature forest of strange, stone trees. *It's like the stories of Austall's porcelain forest.*

Looking about the square just beyond the town gates, Allard shook his head with a mixture of awe and defeat. He'd known Chancewind was a larger town than Zephyr's Blessing, having centuries of history and an important monastery to establish its reputation, but he hadn't really thought about what that meant for finding the Witch of the New Moon. From where he stood, the town was almost like a scaled down version of Riverluck itself, the monastery standing where the palace would be. Turning back to his companions, he said, "Well? What's the plan from here? There's a lot of ground to cover, but I think the monastery is a good place to start since the Witch was looking for information on the River Sage."

Eyes sparkling with excitement as she took in the ancient town, Adelaide smiled. "Sounds good, Al. You start there and I'll investigate these streams. I think there's something vaguely mystical in their nature and I want to see if I can get any clues on that." As if completely unaware of the insanity of what she'd just said, she turned to Xavier. "What about you, Xavi? Where are you going to go?"

Before the serial supporter of Adelaide's absurdity could respond, Allard cut in. "No, no, no. We are not splitting up! Even if it's still daytime and the vampire isn't necessarily a threat, that doesn't mean there isn't any danger. And did you forget about finding the Witch? What do the magical properties of the town's water features have to do with anything?"

This brought a sullen frown to Adelaide's face, but did nothing to dull her enthusiasm. "But you said it yourself, Al, there's a lot of ground to cover. So what better way to make the search faster than splitting up? And if the streams are magic, that's just the sort of thing that might interest a witch. The monastery's a good place to start, but she said she'd been here before, so wouldn't she have already been there? We need to broaden our view if we're going to find her. And..." She began rummaging through her pockets for a moment before pulling out the vampire's dagger and brandishing it. "...if anyone tries to cause trouble, I have this dagger. We know it's sharp because I took it out of your leg."

Ignoring the fact that simply having a knife did not mean she was any better protected, Allard pressed his hands together as though praying, trying to calm his emotions and formulate a logical and well-reasoned response that even she couldn't reject. "Yes, we could search faster, but we have no way to contact each other. How would we let each other know where to meet up again? Or let each other know if one of us found the Witch? Or warn each other if one of us found the Witch and she tried to kill us? And in the first place, Xavier doesn't even know what she looks like."

"Truth be told," Xavier said, stepping between them, "I believe I can solve all of the problems presented. In, as you said, the first place, I know to look for white hair. We have witches on Morningstar too. As for safety, this town does look to be fairly well patrolled by guards, to say nothing of the monks from the monastery. I would imagine that so long as we keep to the main roads and don't do anything foolish, there is little threat of being attacked by rogues or robbers." Xavier pulled a piece of paper from his pocket. "And for communication, we can use this. If I tear it into three strips and put a little bit of blood on each, I can find an enchanter to establish a simple sympathetic link so we can write messages to each other. I shouldn't think such a mage would be too hard to find in a town with this kind of historical, and therefore mystical, significance."

Without waiting for a response, he folded the paper into equal segments and tore it along the creases. As Xavier held a scrap out in either hand, Allard took his with resignation. "Fine," he said, fixing Adelaide with a level stare. "But only if you promise to be careful. I'm supposed to be looking out for you and if anything happened to you, Levi, Estelle, your father, and Erica would kill me. In that order." Fishing around in his pocket, he pulled out his medallion and held it out to her. "At least take this. I can at least give you a bit of luck to go with you."

After snatching her scrap of paper triumphantly, Adelaide spun around and started up the road into town, only stopping long enough to slip the medallion from his palm to hers. "I knew you'd come around, Al! And I will be careful and not just because you gave me this stupid lucky charm."

Allard shot a glare after her, annoyed that she was still making fun of his family heirloom when she knew how much it meant to him. Xavier patted him on the back and walked back over to the cart, talking over his shoulder as he went. "Don't worry. Al. I'm sure the Golden Lady will watch over us and protect us from harm. And I swear by the Summer sun that I'll get the papers linked first thing after getting us a place to stay and keep our gear."

With a flick of the reins, Xavier left Allard in the square, cart clattering up the road. After standing there for a few minutes to let his annoyance fade, Allard set off himself, starting the hike up to the hilltop.

Just as Xavier said, the streets were strangely calm and quiet, even on major thoroughfares where he would have expected the hustle and bustle of daily life. That's not to say that the townsfolk weren't around or weren't going about their business, by all appearances they worked and sold and haggled just like every-one else did, they simply went about their business with a subdued attitude that almost seemed to approach solemnity. Even friends greeting each other and salespeople hawking their wares didn't dare to shout. In another place, this might have given the town an eerie air, but something about Chancewind defused any such sinister thoughts. Where elsewhere the guards posted on almost every street corner might have indicated iron-fisted control, here they managed to seem like nothing more than friendly watchers, waving to the townsfolk as they went by and pausing their patrols to help with things like moving goods and steadying ladders. All told, the town felt almost holy in the natural way that an undisturbed clearing deep in a forest did. If he didn't know any better, Allard might have thought he'd slipped into a fairy other-world, if not simply a dream.

And in thinking of holiness, it was impossible not to note the monastery's influence within the town, beyond even the confines of its walls. While most towns of Chancewind's size would have a few Teacher's Halls to accommodate the population, Allard passed six before he stopped counting them. In a similar way, it felt like just about one out of every ten people he passed wore clerical robes of some sort. To be sure, one of the Halls that he peeked into as he passed was being used more as a school than a church, but there was no denying that the Scholastic faith was ever-present even among the laypeople. Almost every house Allard passed had a Teacher's Shield hanging either above or next to the door, often accompanied by the strange looping design referred to as Seras' Knot. Even if the holy see of the Scholastic faith hadn't named the River Sage as a Saint, it was somewhat common to grant her the same devotion as a holy woman and that held true, perhaps unsurprisingly given her monastery, in Chancewind.

Thus it was much to Allard's surprise that when he did arrive at the monastery, he found it all but abandoned. The gates lay open, so there was no issue in entering, but there was no one on post in the gatehouse or anywhere in sight in the broad courtyard that stood on the other side. When he entered, his footsteps echoed around him as he walked across the slate floors, a testament to his solitude. Stepping into the cloister around the courtyard, Allard inspected the buildings around him, searching for signs of life. The large and blocky building to the immediate left of the gate, filling up the entire south side of the monastery, was by all appearances the clerics' living spaces, so he continued past it without entering, feeling it rude to intrude without invitation. This brought him to a set of stairs opposite the gates, rising further into the monastery.

At the stairs' summit, the pathway continued onward through well-kept gardens to a large chapel on the other end. He considered exploring the gardens, taking note that several streams bubbled up from the ground and ran out towards the monastery walls, apparently the source of the town's water, but something about the chapel drew him to it, like a light breeze was gently guiding him in that direction. From a distance, he saw something in front of the doors, blocking part of them from view, but he couldn't tell what exactly it was. As he came closer, he found it was a statue in the shape of a woman, presumably Seras herself, with water flowing from her outstretched hands. Immediately on seeing the statue, Allard was struck by the sense that he recognized Seras, as preposterous as it seemed. And the longer he considered the stone features, the more he came to realize just why that was. While he couldn't be sure, with the uncertainty of dreams being what it was, he could almost swear that the statue was an exact double for the woman from his dreams. As he contemplated the statue, and why he might be dreaming about one of the Champions of the Four Corners, he felt a strange pressure in his chest and a spreading coolness like he'd been particularly parched and taken a drink of what. Then a voice called out, snapping him from his reverie. "Can I help you, young man?"

Behind him, a man wearing clerical robes, albeit vestments appropriate to the current time of the liturgical year instead of the plain gray robes Allard had expected from monks, approached with a smile on his face. Allard's immediate impression was of suspicion, seeing a hidden plot behind the smile and something inhuman in the way the priest's long hair almost looked closer to a midnight blue than black in the afternoon sun, but he shook it off as nerves after so long a stretch of silence. His second thought was irritation about being called 'young man' by someone who couldn't have been that much older than him all things considered, but he swallowed his retort and gave the priest a respectful bow. "Yes, thank you. I came to the monastery looking to ask a few questions, but couldn't find anyone to talk to. If you don't mind my asking, where is everyone else?"

The priest gave a carefree laugh, waving aimlessly back the way he'd come from. "Oh, the monks tend to spend their days down in the town below, offering their services to the people. If you'd looked in the kitchen you probably would have found someone and I'm sure the prior is in the chapel's sacristy at this time of day." He started towards the chapel, arm raised to indicate Allard should follow. "Shall we retire to the sanctuary? We can talk there out of the sun."

But the statue still stuck in Allard's mind, even with everything else that was on his plate. Looking back up at it with a furrowed brow, he shot a question after the priest. "One thing first. Did Seras actually look like this?"

This elicited a thoughtful hum from the priest, who doubled back to stare at the statue with a curious expression in his eyes and a hand on his chin. After a moment of consideration, he shrugged. "Who can say? This monastery was supposed to have been founded by her and the statue's probably been her that long, so it certainly isn't impossible. But for anyone to truly know, they would have to measure their age in millennia instead of years." He fixed Allard with a piercing gaze as he continued. "And I would reckon that it doesn't matter either way. You would do well to not judge people merely by their appearance but by their actions, young man."

Allard couldn't help but sigh at the incredibly generic lesson the priest had managed to slip into the conversation. Shaking his head, he turned away from the statue and started towards the chapel. "I know, I know. I was just curious. That's not what I'm here about."

Quickly slipping past Allard, the priest opened the chapel doors and gestured within. "Of course. I can imagine anyone would be curious about so famous a figure. But tell me, what wisdom do you seek from the Monastery of Seras? You have the look of a traveler about you, so I'd guess it must be something your local Teacher's Hall could not help you with."

Nodding as he entered, Allard looked about the chapel before responding. All told, it seemed rather normal compared to the exterior, the same rows of pews standing before the altar that you'd find in any other Teacher's Hall. He did spy a pair of doors to either side of the altar, likely leading back to the sacristy the priest had mentioned, but otherwise it was comfortingly familiar. Even more so than the chapel in Riverluck's palace, this one reminding him of the Teacher's Hall back in Regina's Bounty. "It's a bit of a story, but the long short of it is that my friends and I came to town looking for..." He paused for a moment, figuring it probably wouldn't be the best idea to mention the Witch by her full name to someone without the full story. "For a traveling witch whose magic we have need of. We heard she was interested in the history of Seras and thought she might be around here."

The priest smiled. "Ah yes, the young lady with the white hair. She's been by a few times in the past week. She usually stops by in the morning to ask some of the monks questions before they go about their daily business and she hers, whatever that may be. But is your problem truly so great the clerics at the monastery cannot help?" He started walking down the aisle between pews and window, waving for Allard to follow. "Come. Walk and tell me what ails you."

Allard followed, taking in the stained glass windows as he gathered his thoughts. Much to his surprise, the images were more secular than he was used to, depicting the acts of the River Sage alongside the Ember King instead of tales from the Teacher's text and images of Saints, a fact that surprised him in how near it seemed to come to blasphemy. When he had come up with a suitable explanation he nodded to himself, trying to reply in as casual a manner as possible given the subject. "My friends and I ran into a bit of a vampire problem recently and it's proven to be rather difficult to subdue. We were going to ask the monastery if you had any holy water you could spare, but since we've seen this witch deal with other undead firsthand, we figured she'd be better at handling this sort of thing than monks who don't usually see combat."

"I see. That's entirely understandable given the circumstances. But you should be rejoicing, young man, for I can give you something better than just holy water. If you wish to fight this vampire, then you will need a place to fight her. And as I understand it would be difficult to force any undead creatures into hallowed ground, the monastery will not do. But the caverns in the hillside *below* the monastery should do nicely. Not only are they open spaces with nowhere for your quarry to hide and quite out of the public eye with no chance for townsfolk to get caught up in the fight, but the Chancewind springs flow through them. The caves themselves are not consecrated, but such running waters steeped in the blessings of Seras, if not holy themselves, should prove to be a great boon to you."

"That's actually really helpful," Allard said, frowning as he realized the priest had given him a plan far more detailed than even Xavier's. "Far more than you could imagine. Thank you so much. And you said that the witch we're looking for comes in the morning?" The priest simply nodded. "That's great. Thanks again, but I should probably let my friends know what you told me."

Raising a hand in a gesture of benediction, the priest nodded again. "Of course. I understand completely. But save your thanks, for it is my pleasure merely to serve."

Allard didn't even bother responding, just giving a brief wave to bid farewell as he ran out of the chapel. His mind was already running at a mile a minute, putting together the pieces of how they might be able to defeat the vampire. If the caverns met his expectations, they could conceivably end it all that night. Caught up in the sudden hope that they could overcome what had seemed to be insurmountable odds, he almost forgot about the paper Xavier had given him, folded up in his pocket. Drawing it out, he found two lines written on it, the second in handwriting he recognized to be Adelaide's and the first in what he assumed to be Xavier's.

Suitable lodgings found. Two rooms booked at the Spring's Cup Inn. Ask guards for directions, they'll probably know.

Al, help! I found something that could be useful, but I need you to come to the inn and explain the situation.

Even getting dragged around by Adelaide couldn't dampen his mood, his exasperated sigh coming from behind a genuinely amused smile. Fiddling around for a pen, he stopped at the monastery gates to use the walls as a writing surface, scribbling down a message of his own.

Yeah, yeah. I'm coming. We should all meet up anyway. Found interesting information. It might be time to start planning.

Chapter 25

Seaday: 8th of Hernus, Year 1980 R.S.

Erica grumbled to herself as she made her way through the familiar hallways towards one of the palace's side entrances, the setting sun casting an orange glow upon the marble floors. It was bad enough that she'd been roped into attending the festival when she had other things to do – the remaining half of a day she had since talking to Estelle not nearly enough time to prepare anything remotely resembling a counterspell for the necromantic enchantment – but the fact that Viola was coming with her only made things worse. To be sure, she was glad to have a friend with her and knew she could trust Viola to watch her back, but it was all about the attitude. She could tell from her friend's blithe humming, head slightly bouncing back and forth in time with her steps, that she was only there for her own amusement. She fully expected Erica to get wrapped up in some kind of troublesome situation and fully intended to watch her flounder. It was enough to draw a heavy sigh of exasperation.

This snapped Viola out of her daydreaming. "Don't be like that, Erica. It'll be fun! I already checked out the layout a few days ago, so I can show you where the good vendors are."

Well aware of just when Viola first surveyed the festival, Erica shot her a level stare. The maid ignored her, however, and continued chatting about this bit of food or that stage where a performance was scheduled for tonight, until they finally reached the side entrance. Chancellor Lukas was already waiting for them by the time they got there, Edan standing by as he chatted with, curiously enough, Thanasis. The three of them formed an odd trio of what seemed to be decreasing levels of formality; Edan still in her praetor's armor, Thanasis in a coat that while meant for day-to-day wear was still very finely made, and Lukas in a shirt and pants that were only slightly more acceptable for public wear than pajamas, clearly designed for comfort over practicality. As if he could hear the judgment in her thoughts, Lukas turned away from his conversation as Erica entered the room, lazily waving her over. "Excellent! So all the players have arrived. Now we can get on with the night's entertainment." He paused to look over Viola, taking stock of her in his strangely shrewd way. "And who might your friend be? In all honesty, I must confess I am disappointed to not speak with Crownguard's squire, but it seems you've brought interesting company nonetheless."

Giving a disarming smile, Viola waved aside his comments. "Oh not at all. I'm just another servant in the palace."

Lukas met this with a sharp smile of his own. "I'm sure. If you say so, it must be true."

Seeing an opportunity to cut in, and prevent the conversation from devolving into increasingly unsubtle accusations, Erica bowed slightly in acknowledgment first to Lukas, then to Thanasis. "Good evening, Chancellor. I see you've invited one of our friends from Perlora."

Thanasis bowed back crisply with one arm tucked behind his back. "Yes, the good chancellor here said he wanted my opinion on a matter of philosophical debate."

Lukas smiled, as if he were the only one in on a joke. "Yes, yes. I heard you and Thanasis were peers who already made some discussion on magical matters. I found myself curious to hear two different perspectives on my own questions." Shaking his head, he waved Edan forward. "But enough of that for now, by autumn's glory. Would you be so kind as to take the van with our friends, dear praetor?"

Snapping back a salute, Edan spun her spear up into a guard position and began marching out the door, forcing Erica to swallow a sigh at the sheer absurdity of it all. Shrugging, she turned to Thanasis. "I guess we should get going too, huh?"

The Perloran nodded back and followed the praetor, Viola close on his heels, but Lukas raised a hand to forestall Erica before she could take a step, whispering as he drew her aside. "There is one thing I wished to ask you alone before we attend to more important business. Truth be told, I hardly thought about your opinion at the time, but you were there when I asked your king about the Witch of the New Moon and I find sometimes the sparrow spots what the eagle misses, if you take my meaning. So have you heard any rumors or such?"

The image of Regina's Bounty swarmed with legionnaires and inquisitors flashed through Erica's mind and she shook her head. "Nothing more than ghost stories. Why do you want to know?"

Shooting her a sidelong glance and an inscrutable smile, Lukas replied, "Would you believe me if I said the emperor, may his foresight not outpace his wit, wishes to speak with her?" Before she could respond, he shook his head and started after their companions. "We'd best be off. Edan might worry if I stray too far out of sight."

His swift dismissal did little to ease Erica's suspicions. Her mind swam with conspiracies as to why the notoriously silent Emperor *Catellus Cyriacus Amadeus* I might want to speak with such an infamously evil witch. Whether it was a call for an execution or a sign of that same internal corruption the king of Montiamon seemed to warn King Thierry about. Then she remembered something Allard had mentioned offhand, when he fold her what Neriah said before they met the inquisitors in the barracks. *A general sent to Naktikos, war against Montiamon and Aingriya, and this search for the Witch of the New Moon. It's not just these talks. What's the Empire planning?*

Shaking her head, she hurried after Lukas and the others.

The ensuing walk through the gardens was short and, for the most part, silent, with no one quite sure what to talk about or willing to break the silence. And it was not lost on Erica that Viola slowly drifted back from the three in the front to join Lukas a few paces behind, like the maid knew he was only there to watch and fully intended to share his amusement. This silence persisted even when they left the palace grounds and entered into the city proper, but for an entirely different reason. With the streets as decorated as they were, and the various attractions set up at intersections, it was hard to not get caught up in the flow of things while taking in the sights, both Erica and Thanasis awestruck at the sight. Up in the heights of the Nobles' District, there was a kind of elegant extravagance to their surroundings, the wealth of the target audience clear in the detail given to the decoration. The trees in the parks were adorned with small sunstones set in colored glass cages and hung between their spring flowers as if the branches were blossoming twice over. Likewise, the fountains had directed lamps fixed near their spouts, so the water sparkled with multicolored light that scattered into a fine, glowing mist as it fell. And from their place on Riverluck's hillside, it was easy enough to see the rest of the city had elected to make up for their lack of delicate finery with volume, the normally white buildings painted in a patchwork rainbow of light that shone so brightly it was hard to remember night was falling. Even the Summerblood was brought into the festivities, illuminated barges gently floating about just outside the docks.

And all of this was without the stalls and stages themselves. As it was now, most of the attractions had a certain refinement to them – the stages set up as temporary theaters reminiscent of the old Nyphean style, vendors selling garments and trinkets whose gilt and glitter felt more suited to a court than a street, and the music filling the air carefully coordinated symphonic ensembles set just far enough from each other that they wouldn't overlap – but Erica knew that spoke nothing to what they'd find the further down they went. For instance, even the food lacked what she considered the proper touch to it, the air missing the traditional festival mélange of melting sugar and frying dough in favor of the near floral scents of delicate sweets made from a variety of exotic fruits. And there were few of the usual games of skill, but mostly chance, she was used to seeing, though she was reassured to see a small group of people gathered around a man dealing out cards with a marker board behind him set with the winning combinations. The fact that there were still people who would fall for the tricks of Gamblers, the fortune mages of Tycortua of which the host almost certainly was, even after all these years gave a kind of wry humor you could only experience if you grew up in Tycortua. Thinking better of it, she gave the group another look and thought she caught sight of a few Auran robes mixed in among the Tycortuan dresses and coats. That set her mind spinning and she turned to her companions with a thoughtful cast to her face. "Hey, Thanasis. Do you know if any Perlorans besides those in your group came to Riverluck for the talks?"

Snapping his attention away from a nearby play depicting the epic of the Desert-folk champion Dreith, a heroic tale currently fashionable among nobles for its exotic setting and propensity for fights that involve killing very large monsters with very small knives, he perused the crowd briefly before shrugging. "I think I see a few people who might be Perloran around. It doesn't surprise me. It's not as if you were keeping the festival that came with the talks a secret and so it would make a fun vacation for anyone who could afford to make the trip."

"Agreed," Edan said in a flat voice. "Tycortua maintains a spot on the list of approved nations. Citizens of the Auris Empire have the Emperor's blessing, may the Endless Flame bless his reign, to travel without fear of corruption by dark forces."

The fact that, in all likelihood, all four nations had citizens present in a not insignificant capacity sparked something in Erica's mind, and she started looking at the necromantic spell in a new light. She was so struck by this new detail that she almost missed out on Edan's rather interesting comment about Tycortua, deciding to file that away until the next time she could talk to Levi. But before she could consider much further beyond the idea that perhaps the spell might be meant to target all nations present equally, Lukas interrupted. "Enough of that kind of dull talk. Honestly, we're here to have fun, not talk about politics."

Edan saluted, nodding solemnly. "Acknowledged. I shall commence with having fun." She paused for a moment, head tilted in thought, before turning her gaze to Erica, much to the latter's horror. "Miss Greenmaiden, what activities can one perform for leisure while maintaining a proper situational awareness."

Erica had no idea what any one of the group members might like and had been more or less expecting the decision to be forced on her. Expectation, however, only served to make the moment worse when it came. Especially since she knew Lukas was planning something, or at least assumed as much, but didn't know how to avoid playing into his hands or even if that was something she should be trying to do. Trying to think as quickly as possible, she turned away, raising a hand to her mouth to cover her frown. *Come on, think. What would Mal have us do at festivals? Scratch that. What would Paula do?* As nothing continued to come to mind, her previous memories of festivals in Regina's Bounty seeming widely ill-suited to the occasion given the difference in scope; she decided the only path available, much to her chagrin, was to pass the buck. "Well what kind of things do you usually do for fun? What would you have us go to if we were in Dawnbreak?"

Drawing to a halt, Edan surveyed the city below them, then looked back up the hillside before pointing down at the Summerblood with her spear. "I surmise based upon my cursory survey that your city has no space for an amphitheater or circus. Do you usually host naval battles upon the river?"

Not even bothering to dignify that with a response, Erica simply continued down the line. "Thanasis?"

For some reason, he seemed reluctant to answer, eyes drifting to the side and response barely audible as he gave it through the corner of his mouth. "I mostly just study."

Throwing up her hands, she let out a sigh of exasperation and turned back to Viola. "Fine! You mentioned a place that sells profiteroles. Take us there and I'll think of something on the way." Viola nodded in response, giving a lazy salute of acknowledgment before dashing to the front of the group to lead. Erica shook her head as she continued, feeling unused to being the center of things. "But could we at least talk about something on the way?"

Thanasis nodded in agreement, looking back towards Lukas. "That is a good point. The chancellor did ask us here to discuss matters of magic, correct?" For his part, Lukas raised his hands in innocence, as if to tell the group to leave him out of it. Something which only made Erica more suspicious. "I believe you mentioned you've been studying a particular bit of magic recently, Miss Greenmaiden?"

Sparing a glance towards Edan to make sure they weren't excluding her by talking about things beyond her interests, Erica found the soldier intent nonetheless. "Yeah. I've been trying to help dismantle a curse laid down upon a certain manor." Even though she didn't identify Lord Reinhardt, she was fairly certain the others still knew which manor she was talking about by the way they nodded along. "It's been frustrating since I can't even figure out what it's supposed to do, much less how to stop it."

"And you can't simply eradicate the magic flows with a cleansing spell?" Thanasis asked.

"We still haven't found the exact source. It looks more like an ambient atmospheric alteration that's been placed over the household."

"Then burn the house to the ground," Edan suggested. "The dark energies will have no place to hide and any that escaped the cleansing flames would be incinerated with the morning sun."

While Erica wasn't entirely surprised to hear such a recommendation from one of the famously zealous Aurans, it still caught her off guard and she struggled to think of a good reason as to why they couldn't do that. It would certainly work as intended, it was just... Especially when the person recommending it considered the ends far more important than the means, assuming the stereotypes were right. The best she could manage was, "That certainly is *a* solution..."

She was saved from any further attempted justifications when Thanasis cut in. "Well hold on a moment. While certainly true that the curse is undesirable, as Miss Greenmaiden is attempting to remove it, can we be certain that the very energies and magics used in its construction are evil? You said dark energies, but a distinction must be made between dark magic, in reference to the elemental force complementing light, and unholy magic, that which is founded upon harm of others."

Edan, unimpressed, shook her head. "Darkness is darkness. It matters not what form they take, when the forces of evil impose themselves upon the innocent, they must be purged all the same."

Eager to forestall a budding idealogical argument before it gathered steam, Erica held up her hands in a conciliatory gesture and spoke in what she hoped was a diplomatic tone. "You both bring up good points. The fact of the matter is that elemental darkness is distinct from what could be called evil magic, being more of a facet of nature than anything else. As with most magic, it's the intention behind it, the Conception of a given spell, that shapes the outcome more than anything. And in either case, I'm sure this one is sourced in unholy magic, being mostly necromantic in substance."

Smiling triumphantly, Thanasis gestured towards Erica as if she'd just proven his point. "See? It's the intention that matters, not the source. Even with unholy magic, it can at least be taken apart delicately and studied so that a better understanding of the countermeasures can be made. Don't your clerics and medics study the very diseases they cure? It's the same thing."

All in a matter of moments, the air around the two shifted almost imperceptibly. Edan's hand tightened to near a fist on the haft of her spear, the point tilted forward just slightly, and a slight charge filled the air as magic began to gather around Thanasis, the spice of it, for lack of a better term, a clear sign of its incendiary intent. Desperate to avoid genuine conflict, Erica searched for something nearby to distract them, finally settling on a minstrel with a strangely large and bow-less fiddle, but Lukas interrupted them before she could, shooting Edan a chiding look. "Now, now. It seems we've rather gone off topic. Looking at it another way, you said you don't know what this curse does, yes, Miss Assistant? What do you mean?"

"It's just that there's no obvious target," Erica said, letting out a breath of relief. "If you think of the curse like a circle, the center of it's empty."

The anger drained from Thanasis as he started considering this with a furrowed brow. He turned himself away from the group, speaking his thoughts out loud. "Well it can't be summoning at that size, but containment perhaps...?"

Edan waited for Thanasis to make some response and provoke her further, but none was forthcoming as the Perloran continued muttering to himself. After a few seconds, Viola piped up for the first time, letting out a heavy sigh as she did. "This is all boring stuff. It's a celebration, so why are we still talking about work?" She gestured at a stall they passed where a vendor was grinding juice frozen by a icestone into a kind of sorbet. "I'm used to things like this. What are festivals like in the Empire? Are they as violent as Eddy made them out to be?"

Edan whirled around at being referred to so casually. Erica imagined her eyes were wide with anger, but Lukas waved her down with a slight smile. "You'll have to excuse the praetor. Truth be told, she's rather unused to, as you complained about, setting aside work for celebration."

This did little to soothe Edan's if the set of her shoulders were any indication, but she offered no challenge beyond a sullen mutter. "That's not true. I've participated in the Dawnbreak Spearman's Tournament every year since I was old enough to qualify."

Lukas raised a hand as if her words had proven his point. Feeling a sudden relief at not having to keep talking about her work, Erica picked up where the chancellor left off, feeling no need to try to keep the interest out of her voice. "So then what kinds of things do you usually have at your festivals in the Empire? I know the food's different, but what about the decorations? Do you make things this colorful too?"

Lukas glanced at a string of colored lanterns hung between two buildings, a common enough sight in streets festooned with the like until it gave the appearance of a spider's web wet with morning dew. "No, nothing quite this... Well, if I'm being honest, *gaudy*. Though it is somewhat refreshing to see a festival not in the monochrome red of the Endless Flame, may no insult be laid upon its wondrous consistency."

At this point they were near enough the boundary between the Nobles' District and the Low City, more and more of the less restrained festivity leaking through the closer they got. Yet for all the roughness of it, tables now set up in the streets where families and friends openly drank and games were being played that any other day would be called illegal for excessive gambling, Lukas smiled. "This is more what I'd expect, truth be told. For all of the Aurans' devotion to order and propriety, they have a tendency to cut a little too loose at their parties. I've never seen more alcohol than at a Dawnbreak carnival and never more buildings burned than in the wake of a bit of Empire revelry gone too far." He sighed, strangely wistful despite the destruction he was describing, before shaking his head and continuing. "But don't let that put you off. Perhaps I can convince the other officials in the emperor's court, may he never let the wine go to his head, to invite your king to a carnival of our own once this is done. As a sign of the friendship between our nations."

Though he spoke with the same casualness as always, the seeming sincerity of the words took Erica by surprise. For all of the Auris Empire's reputation for conquest and crusading, she'd never expected to hear talk of friendship from one of their diplomats. Especially when the current problems she was trying to solve would likely be grounds for invasion in the name of holy protection in any other circumstance. And she wasn't the only one. She could see Viola's brow furrowed in a confusion that matched her own. Unable to hold back her shock, bordering on disbelief, she replied, "Friendship? The Empire thinks of Tycortua as a friend?"

The Aurans exchanged a glance before turning back to Erica with quizzical expressions. "Of course," Lukas said. "Winter's winds, Edan did say Tycortua was an approved nation mere minutes ago. We've long held Tycortua as a sister nation to our own, in the same way that our founder Ignatius was like a brother to your first king Zephyros."

Mind reeling, Erica couldn't figure out where to start. Even putting aside the fact that the stories said the Ember King was from what had now become Pazyerra, World's Eye the capital of the empire he forged, the very idea that the Auris Empire never considered Tycortua a threat or even subject to suspicion seemed inconceivable. Before she could put together a response, Edan continued, "Didn't the gift we gave you make that much clear? We had it inscribed with the tale of the Storm Warlord's duel and subsequent banding together with the Ember King for that very reason."

Erica froze. Remembering the pale purple stone shot through with near glowing green striations, she could not believe it was as clear a message as the two made it out to be. If for no other reason than that the inscription was nearly illegible, the language unrecognizable. Feeling a chill run down her spine, Erica replied with a question meant more to confirm a sneaking suspicion than anything else. "What was the gift you gave us? What did you have this story inscribed in?"

Lukas shrugged. "A simple ruby, or at least as simple as a gem the size of your fist can be. The color represents the Endless Flame, may it's redness shine forever, just the same as the symbol on the opposite of the tale."

At that, the world snapped, everything sliding into place. As Erica started piecing together what had happened, how the other gem had gotten into the chancellor's hand and therefore into their vault, she felt the air grow cool, like the clammy cold of a crypt. And removing any doubt that it was just her mind playing tricks on her, Thanasis looked up from his mutterings, head snapping first back up the hill they'd come from, then down to her with concern on his face. He opened his mouth, the question clear enough even without being spoken, but before he could get the words out, a scream cut through the night.

Chapter 26

Seaday: 8th of Hernus, Year 1980 R.S.

The reason for Adelaide's message became clear the instant Allard caught sight of the inn. Even if he wasn't particularly well versed in the intricacies of armor design, he could tell the difference between the standard jack of plate worn by the town guards and the ornate, runed cuirasses worn by Riverluck's palace guard, two of whom were standing on either side of the inn's front door. Nodding to them as he entered, Allard found the common room entirely cleared of patrons, the innkeeper nervously fretting back and forth behind the serving counter as he overlooked the assembly which might as well have fallen from the sky for how foreign it was to him. Another two palace guards leaned against each wall, rounding out the ten for a standard squad, keeping an eye on the one occupied table in the room. Of the three seats taken, Adelaide sat across from the squad's captain, if the plume on his helmet were an indication, with Xavier between them. The room was silent as Allard entered, Adelaide and the captain simply staring each other down as they waited, but Adelaide leapt up as soon as the door opened, dashing across the room to grab Allard's arm and drag him towards the table, chattering as fast as she could manage as she did. "Thank the Teacher you're finally here, Al! I was just minding my own business, taking samples of the spring water when one of these guards took me and insisted I accompany them back to the capital immediately. I tried to explain why we need to stay in town to take care of the vampire, but they wouldn't hear any of it, saying something about my orders being superseded by my father's in this situation. They only let me come back to the inn because I told them you were here and we needed to wait for you to get back."

It seemed as though she had more to say, only pausing to take a breath before sitting down, but the captain didn't give her the chance, standing to extend a hand to Allard in greeting. "It's good to see you both safe, Mr. Fortunata. Though I'm sure you understand there will be repercussions for taking the princess from the capital unsupervised and unguarded."

Allard recognized the man as Captain Jareth, a fortunately familiar figure among the ranks of Riverluck's guards. He shook his hand with companionable vigor, letting out an exasperated sigh as he did. "Yeah… I'm well aware of how irresponsible my actions were and understand that I shouldn't have done them. And that I'm the only one responsible."

The two of them both looked at Adelaide, but she either didn't notice or refused to acknowledge their judgment, crossing her arms with a sullen frown. "Hey! Stop trying to take credit for my brilliant ideas!"

Allard and Jareth simply exchanged glances and nodded. All things being considered, it was fairly standard procedure among the palace staff to ignore most of what Adelaide said on the principal that she ignored most of what they said, electing to instead hare down her own path and leave them to pick up the pieces. Once he was sure Adelaide didn't have anything else to say Jareth nodded, motioning the rest of the squad towards the door. "Well then, there's no time to waste. Now that both of our wayward travelers are back we should get on the road before night falls."

Allard raised a hand to forestall them, bracing himself for an uncomfortable conversation. "Actually… I think we should stay the night in town to finish off the vampire."

The guards froze, keeping their eyes trained on their captain as they waited for his judgment. For his part, Jareth stood completely still, silently considering Allard for several moments. Allard squirmed under his gaze as it seemed to pierce through to his soul. "Look, Mr. Fortunata. I know that you've never particularly stood within the normal chain of command as Sir Crownguard's squire, but you *are* still a squire and now is not the time to force the issue of rank."

Taking a deep breath, Allard ignored the captain's rejection, almost an order in itself, and took his seat across from Xavier. He waved Jareth back to the table, decidedly ignoring the barely stifled chuckles coming from some of the guards as he replied. "I know, sir, but I don't mean to make this a matter of orders. I really think this will be the best chance we get to kill him. Could you tell him, Mr. Stormtide?"

Glad to finally offer his input, Xavier raced to Jareth's side and, throwing an arm over his shoulder, steered him back to the table. "Young Al speaks the truth, Jerry." Allard winced, feeling nicknames weren't a good start to the conversation if Jareth's unimpressed glower was anything to go by. "You see, my dear captain, it's clear from Riverluck to Zephyr's Blessing to here that this fiend is following our fine young friends. There's no reason why he wouldn't follow us on the road tonight. Now I understand how you feel about your princess. Lies, if my Summer Queen were in trouble I'd drop everything and burn whole cities to see her safe. But here we can fight back. Out of town, we're exposed and just waiting for an ambush to cut a swath through us."

Adelaide nodded enthusiastically. "It's just like I've been saying! If you really want to protect me, then start listening to me and get to work. It'll be much easier to get the trap set up with eight spare sets of hands."

Still grumbling under his breath, Jareth took his seat. Looking back and forth between Adelaide and Allard he shook his head. "So you're telling me that I should believe the words of two kids and a man I've never met?" Allard looked to Adelaide for help, but Jareth continued with a sigh, not bothering to wait for a response. "Regardless, how certain are you this vampire is truly a threat? The guards and I were able to handle ourselves well against its kind the night you ran away."

The fact that there was more than one vampire came as a shock to Allard, and judging by the way Adelaide started, her as well, but he just shook his head. If the palace guard had been able to fight against them with ease, at least enough that Jareth had no obvious injuries, then they couldn't be the same as the one that had followed them around the countryside. "I suspect he's a bit more powerful than the ones you fought. We tried to kill him last night and I barely escaped with my life. And I know you're a bit more suited to fighting monsters than I am, but he escaped the trap we set and made it look easy."

The captain raised an eyebrow at this. "So you're telling me that even though *it* almost killed you once already, in a trap that didn't work, you want to try to trap *it* again?"

Though the particular emphasis with which the captain referred to the vampire was not lost on Allard, he couldn't bring himself to respond in kind. Now that he'd heard the vampire speak to him, the feeling that it was a hunter not so different from him only grew stronger. That though it was a monster, though it hated him and humanity with all its might, it was not worth hatred in kind. Merely pity. *Crows, if I were cursed, I'd probably be just like him.* Pushing those thoughts aside, knowing they would fall flat with a professional soldier like Jareth, Allard replied, "But this time we know where we went wrong and how to fix those problems. And we won't even have to fight him ourselves. We know the Witch of the New Moon is in town and where she'll be, so we'll get her to kill him for us."

This news sent a ripple of unease through the entire room and the innkeeper dropped the plate he was washing with a gasp of horror. Jareth said nothing for a moment, finally taking his helmet off and setting it on the table before him so he could run a hand through his hair. "Crows! The Witch of the New Moon?! You're really selling me on this plan, Al! But *no*, you're right, I'm *sure* she'll just happily agree to help us and then go on her merry way with our souls intact." He shook his head, muttering a stream of curses beneath his breath as he tried to compose himself. "The blighted Witch of the New Moon... What next? The Demon Blade of Austall coming in for backup and the Golden Hills Raider waiting with horses for our retreat?"

Adelaide stepped forward, raising her hands in a placating gesture. "There's no need to concern yourself with such things, Captain. We know what the Witch wants and have easy access to the information. We've already dealt in good faith with her once before and are no worse for wear." She paused for a moment, a smug smile creeping across her face as she continued. "And she seemed to like me too. We have a nice rapport building."

Jareth rested his head in a hand and let out a resigned sigh. "Fine. I have no way to deal with this. Crownguard's supposed to be the one to deal with resurrected threats from antiquity, not the palace guard. Crows... Tell me your plan and if I think it sounds like it could work then we can go ahead with it." He looked up, shooting a look at Adelaide as he continued. "Go ahead with it while our princess stays here under close guard."

This, rather predictably, raised all manner of complaints from Adelaide, but Allard ignored her for the moment, aware of how little time they had to get things settled before nightfall. "I'll explain while we walk. If we're going to do it, we'll need to get started sooner rather than later." He stood and started towards the door, only stopping to turn back for a moment as he remembered a crucial part of the plan. "Oh. And make sure to bring some shovels. We'll need to do some digging."

Looking around the cavern one last time, Allard shook his head in amazement. Just as the priest said, the caves beneath the monastery provided a battleground perfectly suited to their needs. The one he stood in was an oblong space nearly forty feet in length and about half that at its widest, the floor remarkably smooth from centuries of erosion. Though there were stalactites scattered in a sparse pattern across the ceiling, many of them shining with moisture and dripping water onto the floor in an uneven pitter-patter, they were stubby things, easily fifteen feet up and well out of reach. Even assuming that the vampire could keep hold of one of them, slicked with water as they were, it'd be hard pressed to grab them at that height. And speaking of water, the natural springs did not disappoint. The whole cave was slanted slightly, the entrance where he stood downhill from the far end, and a crystal clear stream of water trickled merrily from one of the tunnels deeper in, pooling near the entrance before draining out through a small hole, presumably onto the hillside somewhere. He did find himself looking at the tunnels on the far end of the cave with some distrust, the twisting paths providing a way for the vampire to hide or escape should things take a turn for the worse, but eventually just shook his head and let it go. They'd done all they could in the time they had and it would just have to do. Checking over the circular trench they'd dug in the middle of the cave one more time, he nodded in satisfaction.

Content that things were as set as they'd ever be, he turned and stepped back over the threshold they'd made at the entrance, the first back up plan. It was a short walk up through the tunnel back to the surface, but even that was long enough for Allard to marvel at just how perfect it was for their purposes. The tunnel they chose seemed virtually designed for their use, a crevice that naturally opened up into the water-carved caverns below and was smoothed into an even passage by human hands over time. This meant, of course, that it was one of the few dry tunnels in the hillside, letting them lead the vampire inside in the first place. It made him wonder just how much of these caves, was natural and how much magical. Erica said magic was about mystery, about meaning and intention, and he was starting to see some of what that meant. It was undeniable these caves were magical, the priest himself said the water was blessed to a minor degree just by mere association with the monastery, but for them on this night, it was a more subtle thing. The caves were a perfect weapon against the vampire, almost like the earth was lending them a hand, and that little mystery in itself was like a small bit of magic.

Less than two minutes later he could see the starry sky through the tunnel mouth, sunstone light glowing from either side where guards stood watch. Seeing the cheery, golden light, a smile rose to his lips unbidden as he stepped over another threshold dug into the hillside, the second backup, and out into the night air. *I guess this is hope, isn't it? I have no reason to be so certain this trap will work any better, but somehow I just know things will turn out.*

He laughed at the absurdity of his unfounded confidence and nodded to the guards on watch. They returned the gesture in kind, but otherwise said nothing, leaving their posts to rejoin the bulk of their squad where they rested on the hillside. Allard was fine with that. He was only really on speaking terms with the guards he played cards with like Jareth and he found he wanted the time alone to think before things got started. *This vampire... Adelaide compared him to the Dusk Reaver, but what does that really mean?*

His thoughts ran back to his discussions with Erica about how magic worked its way through history. How it adored meaning and intention. The thought of just how much things would repeat tickled the back of his mind, the mere reflection of each repetition meaning enough, and all he could think of was how the Ember King felt when he faced his first enemy, when he first started his journey. If he felt like Allard did in that moment too. If, as Adelaide said, this vampire was Allard's Dusk Reaver, did that mean things had been as chaotic and frantic as they'd been to Allard for Ignatius too? *When you hear the stories about heroes, they never seem to be afraid or anxious. They win because of course they do.* He frowned as he thought this, hand tightening on his bow. Looking out over Chancewind, his eyes wandered through the dark streets cutting channels through the pools of light marking homes. *But was the Ember King this scared when he fought the Dusk Reaver? Was he this in over his head and only able to keep going because one of his friends kept dragging him along?*

Thoughts spinning in such gloomy circles, he was glad to see Jareth approaching. "Is everything prepared, Mr. Fortunata?" The captain asked.

"Yes. The trenches have been properly carved and the flood gates appear to be in perfect form."

Jareth glanced back to the rest of the guards with a frown. "Is there anything else you need us to do? Digging that much that fast has left my squad tired."

Allard shook his head. "No. You should be good. All that's left is waiting."

The captain nodded and took up a place beside Allard, his gaze wandering over the town's walls and gates. "How do you know the vampire will come after you? How will it find you?"

That touched upon a rather uncomfortable subject for Allard, since he wasn't quite sure himself. It was bad enough to consider how it had followed Adelaide and him from Riverluck. That in itself bothered him, since they'd hardly followed a simple path. But if it were that alone, he'd be willing to chalk it up to bad luck. It was the vampire's words that made him want to stop thinking about the whole thing. They were in large part why he'd started thinking about magic again tonight. Meaning and intention. He'd said something about there being seven where there should only be six and Allard was willing to read between the lines and assume he was the seventh. *But the seventh what?* He had a good idea that the vampire would hunt him down if for no other reason than that. *Though I can't say for sure if he would try to kill me or capture me.*

Aware the silence was starting to drag, he quickly shook his head. "He'll come. He's found us before and he'll find us again. He's come too far to just let us go now."

Jareth shrugged, unconvinced and unconcerned. Though Allard hadn't heard him say it, he knew if the vampire didn't come tonight, Jareth would drag them all back to Riverluck come morning. "I'll set Sir Rousseau and Dame Fortier on watch in the cave for now. The rest of us will head back to Her Highness to stand by."

Allard held up a hand in farewell as Jareth started down the hillside, shouting orders over to the guards. As Allard made his way back to the tunnel entrance, intent on finding a good place to sit and wait, two soldiers came up behind him, one clapping him on the shoulder without a word and continuing down into the caves. The other, Lina he presumed based on the long hair streaming down her back, stopped beside him and gave him a smile. "Don't worry. We'll be on guard. Elroy," She nodded towards her companion with shockingly red hair, "Might be a bit unreliable, but I'll keep him in line. Bring the monster down and I'll cover you till he throws the switch."

"Thanks. It means a lot that you believe me."

With that, she followed after her friend, leaving Allard alone. With nothing to do but wait, he tried to set back into his old hunting habits. All in all though, it only really made him laugh with how things seemed to come back around. He'd left his village seeking adventure and the adventure he got found him, for all intents and purposes in a hunting blind, waiting to lure prey into a snare. Sure, the town at night was nothing like the forest, putting aside the buildings and lights below him; the silence after everyone had gone to bed was almost disconcerting when compared to the rustling of leaves and animals in the underbrush. But either way, it felt the same. He let out a small laugh, amused at how despite traveling to Riverluck and serving as a squire, he found the adventure he'd left home seeking as a hunter stalking prey. *Meaning and intention, hmm? What's the meaning of adventure if it's the same either way? Or is this just magic's way of telling me here's no point in a hunter trying to be a knight?*

Time slipped by in a blur and before he knew it, he noticed a light fog creeping up the hillside. He immediately tensed up for action and nocked an arrow. Waiting only until the fog was thick enough to block out the buildings below, he edged his way over to the entrance to the caves. There, he stood with one foot in the grass and the other precariously perched on the water-smoothed stone.

A whistling split the air. The moment he heard it, Allard slid down the tunnel mouth. He heard the ring of metal on stone behind him, but didn't bother looking back and tossed aside his bow as he righted himself and broke into a run. He scattered oats behind him with every other step, receiving a furious hiss in response after a few seconds. The noise filled the tunnel behind him as he went, steadily increasing in volume the longer he continued to foil the vampire's approach. He could hardly believe it when the tunnel opened up into the chosen chamber, his flight taking less than half the time it took him to climb the same route mere hours before. With the end in sight, he tore the bag of oats from his belt and threw it aside to start sprinting unhindered. The hissing stopped soon after, but he was already most of the way to the trench at that point and any fear he might've had was banished when he saw the guard Lina leaning out from behind one of the few remaining stalagmites, sending a minute ball of fire flying over his shoulder with a shouted warning.

Seconds later, Allard passed the midpoint of the carved circle, Lina warding back the unseen vampire with another three fireballs. A glance to the side showed her partner, Elroy, crouched next to the edge of the stream running along the cave's side. Elroy nodded, knocking aside the makeshift dam they'd set between trench and stream. By the time Allard reached the other end of the circle, the trench was filled with a gently flowing trickle of water, rising even as he stepped over it.

Allard stopped when he reached Lina and turned around, finding the trench filled to the brim and the vampire crouched at the edge and looking for all the world like someone stopped just before running off a cliff, torso wavering slightly with arms held to either side for balance. At his side, Lina let out a whoop. "Looks like we got it! Give me a second and I'll have it burning before you can say 'This is the end.'"

She took a step forward, outstretched hand coming alight with magical fire, but Allard didn't let her get any closer and, taking her other arm, and dragged her back. "Not a good idea! Let's get out of here. Follow us, Elroy!"

The guard opened her mouth to complain, but hardly got out the first syllable before a knife flew towards them, missing by mere inches. They met up with Elroy just before the mouth of the tunnel, only stopping for a moment to flood the first fail-safe trench that blocked off the exit back to the hillside. Yet for as calm as their trip back outside was, Allard couldn't help but feel somewhat disconcerted. It felt like things had gone far too smoothly, despite the trouble the vampire offered last time. *Not a thing went wrong with the whole plan.* He thought as he picked up his bow. *Were we that much better prepared this time? Or am I just missing something?*

This sense of worry followed him all the way up to the entrance, until he stood back outside with Elroy, waiting as Lina set up wards around the second failsafe. With everything else done, there was nothing for him to do but return to the inn, but something felt wrong about just leaving without a word. Finally, he decided on stating the obvious. "So your partner's a mage, huh?"

Elroy nodded. "Yeah. A surprising amount of the military are, though it's limited to one or two things they're really good at. Don't let Lina know I told you, but she can't really do anything besides a few fire spells and simple healing prayers." He paused to look back towards her. "Hey... Thanks for saving her back there. We fought some of the lesser vampires back at the palace and thought you were just blowing smoke about how much of a threat this one was. If you weren't there, we would have tried to take it on ourselves and we'd both be dead."

Allard just shrugged, feeling it, was only natural and hardly worth talking about. "And I wouldn't have been able to trap him without you. Or you wouldn't have been in danger in the first place if I weren't here. Don't worry about it. It's just how things are." He paused for a moment, then nodded towards town. "I'm heading back to the inn. Are you guys coming?"

Elroy shook his head. "We'll keep an eye out here until the captain sends a change. Go on ahead and report for us if you don't mind."

Allard nodded back, giving a small wave as he cut over to the monastery's road. He was glad to be done of it all, feeling almost like a bad dream that would be gone when he woke up in the morning, but even still... It felt silly to be so worried after the fact when he was so hopeful beforehand, when his hopes had been rewarded, but all the same he couldn't shake the feeling. After all, as if to justify his paranoia, the fog still hadn't cleared yet.

Chapter 27

Seaday: 8th of Hernus, Year 1980 R.S.

Mere moments after the first scream, it was joined by a chorus of answering cries, ranging from shouts of terror to the inarticulate bellows of a struggle. The music and other sounds of festivity did not so much as cut off as they were drowned out by the rising cacophony of conflict within the streets of the city. The Aurans and Viola began looking about, their heads whipping back and forth with each new sound as they tried to catch sight of the cause, but Thanasis didn't bother, simply meeting Erica's eyes with a knowing nod. The noises seemed to be approaching, but it hardly mattered to Erica. Even if she hadn't put everything together yet, she knew the direction they needed to go was away. Shouting to get the group's attention, she hurriedly waved them back the way they'd come. "We need to get back to the palace now. Hurry!"

Chancellor Lukas met her eyes with a piercing gaze and opened his mouth to argue, but then thinking better of it, bowed his head in acquiescence. Snapping his fingers once, he gestured Edan forward, signing something to the praetor with his other hand as she passed. Looking back over her shoulder, she fixed Erica with the inscrutable gaze of her bronze mask. "Tell me, mage of Tycortua, what do I face on this night?"

Erica began to respond, but was cut off before she could get more than two words out, a humanoid shape hurtling out of the night towards the group. She instinctively threw her hands up, shouting the Mystic for a simple shield spell, and the creature bounced off the glowing wall of feathered light that appeared before her, showing itself to be a human skeleton stripped of flesh but bound together by lines of shimmering purple smoke, minuscule points of green light where its eyes would be. Thanasis cursed, starting a spell of his own, and Edan whirled around to come to their aid, but another three came out from the sides, taking their attention away from the front.

The ensuing fight could hardly be called as much, with how quickly it was over. Three lines of fire streaked from Thanasis's outstretched hand and slammed into the bonewalker on his side, its rib-cage crumbling in a burst of flames and the rest of it falling after. Behind Erica, Edan dispatched her two assailants with contemptuous ease, both falling to the ground in a clatter of bones as she spun her spear through them in a single, fluid movement. But Erica was left cursing her general lack of combat spells as the final bonewalker wound up for another attack. She had the cleansing ritual, but not only would casting it take longer than it would take Edan to swing around and dispatch it, such a complex spell would be dramatic overkill for such a relatively weak foe. The fact of the matter was that even though it was weak, so weak that it didn't even bear the threat of breaking through her shield, Erica was utterly useless in bringing it down. Moments after its bony fist sparked off the shield, Thanasis quite literally blew away the bonewalker; a simple wind spell enough to knock it to the ground and scatter the bones.

With that, it was over. Turning back to the group, Erica found Lukas standing with a hand on Viola's arm, a glint of metal in her hand. "Let's let the professionals handle it, hmm?" He said with a knowing wink. Then, turning to the group, he continued with a severe frown. "And I think you speak true, Miss Assistant. It would be best to get back to the palace. Perhaps you can tell us what you know and what it has to do with our gift to the king as we go."

Erica nodded and began to follow, but Viola stopped her before she could get more than two steps in. "Hold it. Erica. What about the people? Don't tell me you don't hear that."

The sounds of combat and strife were near continuous at this point, individual voices indistinct as they all blended together in a dull roar. A part of Erica screamed that her friend was right, that they couldn't just ignore what was happening around them. Couldn't just leave the unprepared townsfolk to their fate when they had the power to help. But, bitter as it felt, she shook her head. "I know, but we're best off if we get to someone that can actually do something about all of this. If we get to the palace, then Levi or Archmage Dwyer can do something."

Viola hardly seemed satisfied, but let her pass, saying nothing more as she slipped to the back of the group. Thanasis took up a place at Erica's side in her wake, leaning in to speak just above a whisper. "This spell. What do you know about it? Is it only animating bonewalkers, or can we expect more powerful undead to appear? And where did they get all of the bodies?"

Erica looked up to check their progress before responding. The roads had already started to clear, so they had little trouble trekking back up through the Nobles' District. Moreover, having Edan at the front of the group served well to encourage any remaining on the streets to get out of their way, to say nothing of dealing with any stray bonewalkers. Content that things were, at least for the moment, stable, she turned to answer Thanasis. "Like I said earlier, it seemed like the spell had a hole in the center, right? Well I realized I was looking at it all backwards. I assumed the structure was indicative of a geometric spell simply based on the flows I could trace. So the hole made no sense. Geometric spells are intended to be centered upon something. Unless the flows are meant to inscribe a circle."

"But wait. Magic circles have three uses. Warding, binding, and summoning. The first two make no sense given what's going on. And if the dead lord's manor is one of its anchoring points, it must be far too large to actually work. No mage dead or alive could summon something that would need a circle half the size of a city."

All of which is exactly why Erica had discounted it in the first place. A circle made no sense if you were trying to attack a city. The only offensive application, as Thanasis had said, was to summon a creature and any given summoning circle could only be used to summon one creature at a time. Assuming it was opening a gateway to an other-world. Shaking her head with a grim smile, she couldn't help but feel a kind of begrudging respect for how the enemy mage had wriggled around the rules. "That's true. If you're summoning in the normal way. But if the spell is meant to call things already present to a location instead of transporting them though space, well then it's nothing more than a high powered beacon, like a smaller version of the Forest of the Dead up north."

"So, Miss Greenmaiden, if they're being drawn to a beacon, and this beacon is marked by a boundary circle, then where are all of the undead going?"

"Well they'd be going to the..."

She trailed off as she realized what he was saying, just in time for Edan to pull up short at the front of the group. Looking past her, Erica could see the entire road blocked by a roiling mass of dead things. More than simple bonewalkers, though they certainly formed the majority of the assembly, she could spot shambling corpses in various states of decay and tattered robes floating through the air with ethereal claws and ribs showing through the tears.

The zombies were little more of a threat than bonewalkers, possessing only a greater toughness, but the ire-wraiths were undead creatures of far greater power and all of them were present in numbers far greater than they could handle. Erica started to suggest that they retreat, or at least find another way around, but the back lines of the horde turned as they approached, scores of eyes burning with cold light boring into them. Edan simply set herself into a guard stance. "I doubt I can handle the ire-wraiths while dealing with the others. Can you burn them out of the sky, Perloran? And simply try to shield us from getting flanked, Miss Greenmaiden."

The matter of fact way in which she spoke belied the inevitability of what was coming. As Erica began reciting her shield spell, the undead surged forward, not even half their number turning back to overtake them, but that more than enough to overwhelm the small group of four, Erica only then realizing that Viola had slipped away. Thin arrows of fire streamed into their ranks, Thanasis casting spells as fast as he could speak, but for every one he took down, they advanced another ten feet, the gap steadily closing. Finishing off her own incantation, Erica cast twin shields on either side of the street, slanted to funnel the charging horde towards Edan, but that could only buy them a bit of time. The fact of the matter was, they could not weather the swarm and they would get overrun.

But then everything changed in a moment, a storm piercing through the heart of the horde. Glowing with blazing blue light, Levi appeared as if from nowhere, scattering the undead like leaves in the wind. Erica had known how powerful Ancient's Armor was supposed to be from the stories, and she'd seen Levi fight before, but it wasn't until that moment that she understood just how powerful Ancient's Armor truly was and what it meant for its bearer to unleash its full power and go to war. Beyond the simple physical enhancements, each set of plate had been forged with a fragment of one of the elements within it, wind for the Crownguard plate. And so as Levi laid about himself with Whisperwind, a tempest of raging winds swirled outward from his armor, blowing aside anything that got too close to him. And with each swing of Whisperwind, lightning crackled from the enchanted blade, arcing through the winds to incinerate bonewalkers by the handful. Levi by himself was no match for an army of the undead, but with that kind of magic in his armor, an army couldn't reach him. Even the skies were no refuge for the ire-wraiths, Erica watching stunned as Levi leapt as though stepping upon the wind itself to cut through two that seemed ready to run, the spirits burning away in a flash of lightning.

In hardly more than a minute, the whole assembly was broken, loose robes and charred bones littering the street. With no enemies left to face, Levi turned to the group with Whisperwind resting on his shoulder, the winds dying down as he brought the Crownguard plate back to bear and sent its helmet back to Void-Space so they could see his face. Scanning the group, he fixed his sight on Erica and strode over to her, addressing her firmly enough to remind her that he was a soldier, even if she hardly ever saw it. "There you are, Miss Greenmaiden. Report."

Still flabbergasted by their sudden salvation, and somewhat stunned to be called to task like a member of the guard, Erica floundered, looking to the others for support. But they seemed content to let things between the Ty-cortuans remain that way, Edan taking up a lookout nearby while Thanasis and Lukas stood aside in opposite poses, the former politely listening while the latter pointedly ignored the conversation. Setting aside her nerves for the moment, Erica asked, "How did you find us Levi? Shouldn't you be at the palace protecting the king?"

"The palace is secure for the moment. Archmage Dwyer called in the arch-bishop to place a ward around the grounds and the palace guard are holding fast. As for the former, I was on my way to Lord Reinhardt's manor, figuring I might be able to stop this if I could break the spell there. I saw the fire from your friend's spell and came to investigate." His eyes hardened in between words, tone making it clear that he was demanding, not asking as he continued. "Now report. What is going on and how do we stop it?"

Taking a deep breath, finally allowing herself to relax for a moment now that death was not imminent, Erica nodded. "Of course. The spell I was investigating is beckoning these undead to the palace. The Auris Empire's gift was replaced, the gem in the vault probably some kind of targeting rune for the spell."

Levi immediately turned back the way he came, clearly expecting her to follow. "Right. And destroying it will break the spell?"

Erica rushed after him, dimly aware the others were also following. "Yes. Well, no. Kind of? If we do that, the undead will stop coming towards the palace, but it won't stop the spell from acting as a beacon. They'll still come, they'll just be aimless and less aggressive."

Frowning, Levi tapped his sword up and down a few times on his shoulder, humming in nervous thought. "And I suppose breaking the spell will do nothing to banish the undead already here, now will it?"

Hearing him say as much sent another flash of guilt through Erica, reminding her of Viola's complaint. "But disrupting the spell is the only option left available to us. Destroying the anchoring points should cause the spell to dissipate. We know where two are, and mages can lead teams to follow the flows towards the others. I imagine they form a regular polygon around which a circle could be inscribed in any case."

At this, Lukas let out a heavy sigh. He drew a small stone out of his pocket as he approached, Erica starting on her shield spell in panic until she realized it was only a messaging rune. "I suppose it's time for our inquisitors to earn their keep. They'll be disappointed to miss that vampire they're hunting, but I suppose it can't be helped. That murdered lord's house is one of the spots, right? I'll call Neriah and we can handle it if you two will start tackling things in the other direction."

Levi paused for a moment's thought, briefly meeting Erica's eyes with a question in his own. Thinking about how Lukas and Edan had acted tonight and what they'd said, she decided they could trust them, at least in stopping the spell. It was hardly a simple decision, even an admission of trust as straightforward as that a concession, but she nodded. Content, Levi nodded up towards the left side of the street. "Continue up that street to reach Lord Reinhardt's manor. The damaged windows have not been replaced as of yet, so you should be able to recognize which house it is."

Neither Lukas nor Edan said anything, the former merely giving a slight nod back in response and placing his thumb in the center of the messaging rune as he walked away while the latter sprinted ahead of him before slowing to a steady stalk, spear forward and mask swiveling to either side as she regularly surveyed their surroundings. With only one member of the group left unaccounted for, Thanasis looked back and forth between the Tycortuans and the Aurans. Finally, he let out a heavy sigh, shaking his head as he spoke. "I don't find myself much wanting to, but I'll go with the chancellor. They could use a mage to guide them."

There was a lot he wasn't saying and Erica could tell that putting his trust in the Empire represented a far greater risk for him since while they had made their amiability towards Tycortua clear, their attitude towards Perlora remained conspicuously unspoken, but he left it at that, not even waiting for them to agree. Giving one last nod of acknowledgment, he ran off into the night after the two, a conjured flame in his hands lighting his way. Levi watched him for a moment as he went before shaking his head and starting in the opposite direction. "We had best be off then. It will take longer for us to reach Lady Ellis' manor, but I imagine we will have an easier go of it. Stay close and I can take care of any undead we come across."

"What? That's it? But what about the other points? What about the city? Are you really just going to leave it like that? I saw ire-wraiths back there and you do know how they form, right? Anger at an unjust death. Which death by ire-wraith tends to provide plenty of. If we leave this alone, half the city could be newly formed undead. You're the Crownguard, there must be some way for you to repel these undead, right?"

Levi snorted. "Come now, Miss Greenmaiden. Do you really think the Aurans are the only ones with messaging runes? Or that King Thierry would let his general run off into the night with no way to report back on the situation?" He reached down to his side, a section of his armor dissolving into the wind for a moment so he could reach through and pull a pouch off his belt. "The Regulars we have stationed in Riverluck were already mustering when I left. Now all I need to do is tell them where to go. It is a shame the streets are too narrow for the Griffon Corp to help, but..."

He trailed off with a sigh, shaking his head. For her part, Erica was surprised by how simple of a solution it was. It seemed, as morbid as it was to say so in the situation, underwhelming. After all of the build up, the days of investigating, the enemy's grand stroke would be undone in a single night with only a fraction of Tycortua's military force. She couldn't help but frown, wondering why this was their enemy's scheme if it could be so easily undone. "Is this really it then?"

Levi shrugged. "Well that is simply how it ends up sometimes. I am sorry you will have little to do this time around, especially with how much work you put into this, but you *are* the one who figured out how to stop the spell. With it out of the way, everything should get wrapped up rather neatly."

This did little to ease her dissatisfaction. Sure, she wasn't the hero of the hour, but that was more Allard's dream anyways. What bothered her was that even if things got 'wrapped up neatly', as Levi said, there was still one fairly large question left unanswered. "Yeah, but what about the culprit? Are we just going to let them get away scot-free? And if this was their big plan, it feels like a pretty poorly thought out way to try and attack anyone attending the negotiations. Between you and Neriah, the ranking officials would be able to easily escape through undead this weak."

By the frown that crept across Levi's face, her comments struck a chord. "Perhaps. It does gall me that we cannot uncover the culprit's identity, but we simply do not have the requisite information at this juncture. And as you said, I can find no way to justify laying responsibility at the hands of any of the nations. For the Rugegans and Perlorans, this plan could only ostracize us as their ally or galvanize the Aurans to invade them. For the Aurans, it is a calamity of too small a scale to use as justification for a holy crusade and will certainly do little to draw us into their conflict with Montiamon. And as for that mountain kingdom, I fail to see how such an ineffectual attack could accomplish anything beyond drawing more ire than they have already received. With things as they are now, it simply makes no sense."

All of a sudden, something sparked in Erica's head and she remembered what Levi had told her back at the beginning of all of this. Hearing the nation's motives laid out so clearly, and seeing the apparent incompetence of the attack firsthand, she could only come to one conclusion. "Unless it's not about politics."

"Hmm? What was that?"

Feeling the pieces start sliding into place again, Erica felt herself growing more and more excited the more certain she grew that she'd figured it out. "It's not about politics! We've been looking at it wrong the whole time. The culprit doesn't actually care about the Aurans' war or the Western Alliance. There's something else they're after. Think about it, the night of the attack on the palace, there was one group of vampires that had no clear target: the ones heading towards the treasure vault. Why would they be going there, especially if the targeting rune was already in place and they'd only be jeopardizing its discovery?"

"So they are seeking something in the vault after all? I could grant you that all of this does make for a fair distraction, but why? We saw nothing that looked worth stealing when we checked, remember?"

"Maybe, but we have an edge now. We can't just let the culprit get away. Not when we have a chance to catch them."

Levi turned on her with a stony glare. "A chance, do we? What chance is that? And what would you have us do? Let the city stay under this spell until we figure it out? Let the people continue to suffer just so we can catch one villain? And here you criticized me about leaving the same less than five minutes ago."

It stung. More than anything, because Erica knew how right Levi was. Even if she hadn't said as much, she implied that they should leave the spell up for a little longer, because it was clear enough to both of them that the culprit would run back to ground the instant their spell failed. If they were willing to go to such lengths to make a distraction and take attention away from themselves, then they wouldn't dare move out in the open. Her face burned with embarrassment as she struggled to find a justification. But then, realizing that they didn't necessarily need to abandon either cause, she smiled. "Well then that just means we'll need to work fast. You'd better get that message to the king. And make sure to have them send someone on to Lady Ellis' manor, because I have a plan."

Chapter 28

Seaday: 8th of Hernus, Year 1980 R.S.

Erica couldn't help but feel nervous as she walked up to the palace entrance, walking down the same avenue the Rugegans had come down just that same morning. Even after so little time, it felt different enough to give her chills, the night casting the previously beautiful decorations in a morbid light, particularly when considering the scattered bones and other assorted parts sticking out of the bushes. She knew the grounds were safe at this point, the palace guard having established a secure perimeter, but there was still that looming dread in the air, the feeling that something would jump out at her at any moment. And yet most of her nerves were for an entirely different reason. Through it all, she could still feel the tenuous threads of the necromantic ritual spinning through the air, like the brief snatches of the Summerblood she could see from the windows in the palace on a clear day. Spinning, but less powerfully than before, the flows having already frayed once and then twice as anchoring points were eliminated. Closing her eyes for a moment, a single thought ran through her head, almost like a prayer. *I hope I can pull this off before they hit the last one.*

When she opened her eyes, she could see a small group assembling on the terrace, where King Thierry had stood that morning. Taking a deep breath, she settled herself into the role she'd decided to play, reminding herself of what she was supposed to be saying and, more importantly, what she wasn't supposed to be saying. By the time she reached the courtyard before the terrace, noting the coach that was waiting nearby with two soldiers – Regulars, not palace guard – sitting in the driver's seat, the group had already descended the stairs to meet her, Estelle leading the guards as they carried a large, cloth-wrapped package. Erica looked past the castellan to inspect the package more closely. It was perhaps three feet long and half as many wide, thick enough to have held any number of items. And judging by the way the guards carried it, not too heavy, the two of them merely required to ensure whatever was within did not break. She nodded, content that it was roughly the size she'd been expecting. "So this is it then?"

After waving the guards over to the coach, Estelle turned back to Erica with a quizzical look on her face, responding with more uncertainty than Erica was used to hearing from a woman she'd always felt knew everything. "I suppose it is. Though I can't imagine why you want us to move it. Especially now of all times. Are you certain you'll be safe with only two guards? With the city as it is?"

She was far from certain, forcing herself to resist the urge to look up to the sky and check to see if anything was waiting up there, but knew there was no way around it. The fact of the matter was they couldn't bait the culprit out if she was surrounded by an army. She'd have to have faith that her trap would spring before they could get away or she got killed. And in the meantime, the only thing she could do was act confident. "Of course. Now's the *best* time to move it. With things as chaotic as they are, nobody will be able to pay attention to such a plain coach heading down to the docks."

Estelle hardly seemed convinced, but she contented herself with a shrug. Erica turned to the coach herself, intent on getting started before another anchoring point vanished and their odds of success decreased that much more, but Estelle leaned forward, stopping her with a hand to the shoulder. Sparing a brief glance around the grounds, eyes far sharper than most watchmen's, she whispered to her conspiratorially, "But how did you figure out what they're after?"

Erica simply shook her head. "If you think about it for a bit, you'll figure it out too."

Estelle let her go with nothing more than a raised eyebrow and the clear expectation of an explanation once things were settled. Erica hopped into the coach, sitting opposite the package, and rapped on the roof. With that, the soldiers flicked the reins and the coach lurched into motion. As the wheels rattled over the cobblestone paths winding through the gardens, Erica tried to keep track of their progress through noise alone, not daring to pull aside the curtains hiding her from view. Before long, she heard the sounds of combat, the shouted orders of captains to the guards lining the grounds cutting through the clamor of metal upon bone, the moaning and chattering of monsters, and the dull thumps of spells impacting. As the noise grew closer, there was another round of orders followed by a thunderous explosion and she imagined the lines of undead besieging this section of the palace crumpling as scores of them disappeared into a fireball wrought by several mages working in concert. The stamping of boots that followed matched the marching of guards in her mind as they formed a small lane for the coach to pass through. And then, after only a few seconds, they were past the fighting and racing through the streets of the Nobles' District.

Erica settled into making her own preparations, closing her eyes and reciting the same prayer over and over again to hold the spell at the ready. In the midst of that repetition, she was only dimly aware of how much time passed, feeling as though each second stretched into minutes. She almost missed feeling another tremor run through the ritual sensed at the edge of her awareness; a sign that Estelle had returned to the palace vault and destroyed the targeting rune. Her nerves threatened to make her stumble over every word as she tensed up, expecting the attack to come at any second.

When the attack finally did come, it was far more subdued than she had been expecting, only a sharp whistling sound and a jostling of the coach as one of the soldiers shouted a warning. The coach lurched to a halt and a whinny rose up from the horses as the reins were drawn short, followed by more thumping as the soldiers leapt from the seat. One of them rapped on the door as he passed. "It's time for us to get out of here, Miss! We can't handle this many!"

But Erica remained where she was, knowing the soldiers would abandon her when she didn't follow and fully hoping they did so. She simply sat waiting, continuing her incantation as shuffling sounds drew closer and closer to the coach. She waited as long as she dared, feeling that whatever was coming was almost right outside the door, imaging a rotted hand stretching out for the handle, before clapping her hands together in prayer and speaking the final word of her spell. "Cleanse."

Holy silver light shone out from the carriage, nearly blinding her, and filled the streets beyond. She could hear the shrieking of monstrous voices before they faded into gasps of almost relief and a distinctly human voice cursing in the center of it all. Erica grabbed the package and slipped out the other door, grunting with surprise under the weight of it. She had expected the package to weigh little more than the box that held it, but it seemed like Estelle had gone the distance to ensure appearances were kept. Taking to the streets, she could hardly manage more than a steady jog as she tried to find a good way to carry the deceptively cumbersome package, especially as she was forced to pick her way through the smoldering remains of what had been undead creatures moments before lest she trip. After a moment, the same voice from before cried out and Erica knew she'd been spotted, turning around just in time to bring her hand up and cast a shield spell as a stony gray cloud of magic streaked towards her, breaking against the shield and scattering a noxious smoke before her.

A figure swept through the smoke, a man she guessed from the voice, wearing an all encompassing black robe with a mask in the shape of a wolf's face. His hand swept out to the side, already tracing shapes with a wand in preparation for another spell. "You didn't think that I wouldn't notice you escape, did you? Or did you think that two mere soldiers who flee at the first sign of trouble would be enough to overcome the might that has been granted me?"

He punctuated his questions with a harsh word of Mystic, flicking the wand down and sending a pair of shadowy blades shrieking through the air. They broke against the shield in a burst of dark energy, but it shattered in response, slivers of light falling to the ground like broken glass before vanishing. Weighing her options for a moment, well aware she was close to exhausting her reserves of mana after the night's trouble, Erica shook her head and dropped the package, stumbling backwards as it fell to the ground and feeling her breathing grow ragged with fear – at least she hoped that's how it appeared. The man crept forward, keeping his wand trained on her, but otherwise doing nothing to prevent her slow and steady retreat. For a moment, she found herself wondering if he'd let her go, feeling a genuine spark of fear, but he stopped on reaching the discarded package, turning his attention away from her and crouching down over it. He began laughing as he unwrapped it, shoulders shaking. He spared a look up at Erica, triumph in his voice. "And now I have one of the Regalia in my hands and have assured myself a seat at the side of the victors. Though I admire your audacity, a gambit this incompetent could not possibly hope to fool me and your kingdom can die knowing it failed to protect your founder's last legacy."

Feeling that was far from a good sign as her continued health went, Erica let her eyes widen, hoping that it came across as awed. "You're right. But once we knew that you were after it, we couldn't simply let you take it. We had to hope you would continue to act as you had and take our chances."

The man turned back to the now unwrapped box, placing his hands reverently upon it. "Yes. I cannot blame you for following your convictions, but you simply could not see through my subterfuge nor prepare for my true might and intellect when I brought it to bear." As he spoke, Erica flicked a hand up towards the sky, sending a tiny pinprick of light flying. She worried that he might see her do it, but as preoccupied as he was, he didn't seem to notice and continued unphased. "And now, let this mark the moment of rebirth as I claim the cloak for my own and with it dominion over the darkness of the Garden of Serpents!"

Throwing back the box's lid in a single motion, sending it clattering across the street to Erica's side, he knelt frozen for a moment, hands held above his head. The inside of the box was lined with a fine red velvet to match the deeply stained wood of the exterior and filled entirely with simple stones from the garden. After a second, he began laughing, and slowly took his feet. Turning to face Erica, he addressed her with a disconcerting lack of anger. "What's the meaning of this? You wouldn't have dared to leave it back in the vault while my army assaulted the palace. Is it in the coach? Or did you realize what you held and claim its power for yourself?"

The spark of fear in Erica began to grow as she realized that things were about to swiftly come to a head, but then she heard the soft sound of rushing wind from overhead. Smiling confidently, she held up her hands in acquiescence. "It's just like I said. We had to hope you would continue to act as you had: incompetent."

Like that was a signal, the night was filled with the sound of displaced air, followed by twin impacts as two men in armor landed on the ground to either side of the culprit. Erica glanced up, briefly catching sight of the griffons they'd ridden before they began soaring back towards the aeries near the palace. As she lowered her head once more, she turned to the nearer of the two knights, fixing him with a withering glare. "It took you long enough. I was running out of time and might have been forced to resort to drastic measures."

Levi shrugged as he dusted himself off, nodding over towards Neriah. "I thought it would be best to pick up some reinforcements on the way, just in case." Satisfied that everything was in order, he pulled Whisperwind from thin air, lightning crackling around his hands as it formed, and pointed it blade first at the culprit. "And I figured we might need a witness to confirm that we truly have the right man."

Even with the odds clearly flipped against him, the culprit continued to shake with what may have been fury, but looked more like insanity to Erica, as he blatantly ignored the changing situation and kept his gaze fixed on her. "Incompetent? Me? With the power I've been granted? Fine. If you need proof of the futility of your actions, I'll slaughter you all and bring you back to tell me where the cloak is!"

A writhing mass of bladed shadows launched itself from his wand, but it was an empty threat. Before it could even make it half the distance to Erica, Neriah interposed himself before it, Dawnsong cutting through the spell in a blaze of golden light. The Auran general shook his head, setting himself at the ready to match Levi. "Accept your fate, foul mage! For I wield the coming dawn in my hands, to banish the darkness of your vile night!"

What happened next could hardly be called a fight. The close quarters, and Erica at the fringes, did prevent the two knights from using the full power of their Ancient's Armor, but even handicapped in that way they were still two of the greatest soldiers on the continent and the culprit merely one mage. He threw himself back as Neriah charged, waving his arms quickly as though gathering the shadows to him and sculpting them into armor. When this spell finished, he stood at twice their height, his lower body encased in ink-black darkness, and he swung his arms downward, summoning a rough hammer of magic to smash the knights. But Levi and Neriah dashed out of the way with a casual ease, hardly needing more than a moment's notice to set themselves again and launch into a counterattack. From there, the culprit never got another chance to attack, as he found himself constantly pushed back by an endless barrage of blows coming from alternating directions. The street was filled with flashes of light and sparks of energy as shield after shield was raised to deflect the magic swords, yet Erica could tell clearly that the only reason he gave them as much trouble as he did was because Levi and Neriah were trying not to kill him, only incapacitate him. The struggle took no more than two minutes before the culprit finally slipped, raising his arm too slowly and letting Whisperwind slip through.

The force of the blow threw him from his summoned armor, slamming him against one of the buildings lining the street as sparks of lightning danced across his chest. But before either knight could apprehend him, the mage drew a vial from his robes and laughed as he unstoppered it. "I can't believe you pushed me this far. Perish in the dusk!"

A liquid darkness poured out of the vial, far more than such a small container could fit. As it fell onto the street, it clung together instead of flowing as it should. Levi and Neriah exchanged a glance and backed away from the growing mass, uncertain what they faced. After a few seconds, a rough sphere the size of a person hovered over the road's cobbletones, its surface constantly shifting with an inky iridescence. Then it popped like a bubble and a strangely familiar, gangly figure landed on the ground in a predatory crouch. Content that it was a monster and not a spell, Levi lunged at it, Whisperwind booming as it arced towards one of the creature's arms. But the monster was faster than it looked and slid out of the way, batting Levi aside with enough force to crack even Ancient's Armor. Then the monster stood at its full height, head and shoulders above even the tallest person Erica had ever seen, and Erica realized where she recognized it from. With arms long enough to touch the ground, tipped with claws nearly a foot long, and a face that was little more than two eyes burning like cold white stars and a mouth filled with viciously sharp teeth, it was undeniably similar to the illustration of the Dusk Reaver from Adelaide's book about the Ember King.

The Dusk Reaver looked back and forth between the two knights, Neriah standing his ground with Dawnsong raised in a guard position and Levi staggering to his feet, then fixed its eyes on Erica. Before it could move, Neriah interposed himself between it and her and said, "Stay back, Tycortuan mage, and do not look directly at me. The Endless Flame's light shall banish this monster's darkness."

As Erica took cover behind the carriage, she could feel a blistering heat on her back, light filling the alleyway. When she peeked back around the driver's seat, she saw Neriah shrouded in blazing sunlight, no more than a silhouette visible through the halo his Ancient's Armor cast. He dashed at the Dusk Reaver faster than Erica could track, the light leaving spots in her vision, but it matched him and flowed out of the way. Neriah made three more passes in as many seconds and Erica realized he'd never hit it. Whatever speed his armor gave him, he could only travel in straight lines and the Dusk Reaver dodged in curves, body compressing and expanding as it flowed beneath and around his charge. It couldn't manage a counterattack, but it was slowly leading him away from the culprit who was already taking his feet.

Then Levi rejoined the fight, sweeping Whisperwind at the back of the Dusk Reaver's head with a crash of thunder. It turned at the noise and caught blade on its forearm, even the mystic sword cutting little more than a flesh wound, but the battle turned nonetheless. Neriah started his next charge before it could regain its posture and it barely managed to dodge out of the way, skin steaming with the heat of the Ancient's Armor. And with it thrown off guard,

Levi earned another cut across its chest. It lashed a hand at him in response, but he was prepared this time and caught it on Whisperwind, deflecting the arm up and over his head. Neriah's next charge took the arm off at the elbow, Dawnsong's enchanted light cutting through whatever protections it had like paper. As Levi saw this, he nodded to himself and flung himself at the Dusk Reaver, wrapping his arms around its neck and trying to bear it down to the ground. Its teeth gnashed at his vambraces, cracking the metal, but it was an empty threat. Distracted as it was, it couldn't avoid Neriah's next strike and Dawnsong took it through the chest. Light filled the Dusk Reaver for a second. Then it vanished, like a shadow in the sunlight.

Seeing his last resort fail, the culprit turned and ran. He barely made it ten feet before, the two knights caught up and cornered him, one on either side. He tensed himself up briefly, as though he were going to try to resist one last time, but then he collapsed to the ground, shaking his head with a sigh. He looked back towards Erica in her hiding spot behind the carriage and she could hear the resignation in his voice as he spoke. "Where is it? At least tell me that much. How did you manage to get the cloak out of the palace without my knowing? How did you find out about the Regalia without the Immortal Mage's guidance? He told me I was the only one."

Erica shot him a smirk. "We never had it. We've never even heard of this 'Regalia' of yours. We just needed you to think we did."

The culprit let out a pained groan, realizing how he'd been played, but it was cut off before it could escalate to a wail, Neriah rapping him on the head with the hilt of his sword. Shaking his head, he picked up the mage and flung him over his shoulder. "What a fool. A fool once for relying upon the powers of evil to grant him victory and twice for being deceived so easily." After scanning the area once to check for any straggling enemies, he jerked his head back towards the palace. "I'll be taking this one back to face judgment. As Crownguard here said, justice can only be guaranteed if all concerned bear witness to this villain's unmasking."

And just like that, everything was over. The culprit was caught, and Erica could feel his ritual just barely hanging on, two more of the anchoring points having been destroyed during his capture. As Levi approached, Whisperwind dismissed and Ancient's Armor evaporating into mist, she felt a strange kind of relief, a peace as everything came crashing down at once – the happiness at their success, the fear she had been keeping suppressed when it looked like she might not get any backup, and the satisfaction at no longer having to research that infuriating spell. But there was just the slightest hint of something else at the middle of it all, something eating at her mind.

As he approached Levi gave her a nod of acknowledgment, a slight smile adorning his face. "Congratulations, Miss Greenmaiden. Your plan went off without a hitch. If this is anyone's victory, it is yours." Pausing, Levi noticed her expression and his brow furrowed. "Are you alright? Were you injured or is there something still amiss?"

She shook her head. "I'm not sure. Everything should be wrapped up now that we caught that mage and broke the spell. But there's still something... I guess it feels like this only raised more questions than it answered."

"What he said about the cloak and this Immortal Mage, hmm? It certainly does warrant investigating, if we can even find out which cloak he meant with only the title of 'Regalia' as clue, but I do not think we need to worry about that for now. All of the south will stand alert now, even if this so-called Immortal Mage sees fit to send another minion."

"Well there is that, but it's more that something about this just feels weird. I guess it's about motivation. I can't figure out what he would have to gain through all of this and I don't know that it matters who he was. It seems like nobody would gain anything, no matter what this cloak is. He said it would give him some kind of power and standing with 'the victors', but could any amount of power be worth making four nations your enemy?"

Levi narrowed his eyes. "Hmm. I see what you mean, but I have no answer. I cannot imagine a power to contest even the army of Tycortua alone. But if there is such a power..." He trailed off. Though she had no way to know for certain, Erica felt sure he was thinking back to his conversation with the king in the chapel, several days prior. "I think the only thing we can do right now is find out who he is and go from there."

With that, they headed back to the palace. The trip back was entirely un-troubled, not even a single monster crossing their path as they went. The final anchoring point had vanished, and the spell's flows with it. With the streets abandoned and the night finally still, Erica felt a quiet kind of contentment, like she and Levi were the only ones in the world in that moment, and he hardly there. It was like that moment was her reward, a time completely free of concerns given to her by the world for completing her task.

When they did return to the palace, they were immediately led into a conference room where representatives from all the concerned parties waited. Neriah and Lukas stood near where King Thierry sat, somewhat conspicuously she thought, given the help they'd offered tonight, while Duke Gerald and Lady Tagetes sat opposite each other somewhat in front of him. And in the middle of the room, the culprit knelt with his hands bound behind his back and two members of the palace guard overlooking him. Levi went to stand opposite the Aurans, nodding Erica towards a corner of the room where she could watch with Thanasis and Edan, the two having followed Lukas here. Neither of them said anything as she approached, only offering nods of acknowledgment, but they both looked somewhat worse for wear – Edan's armor scratched all along its length and Thanasis' clothing singed along the edges and smelling of smoke.

Once Levi was in place, King Thierry ran his gaze over the room, meeting each representative's eyes briefly. "We would have the mage who dared to attack the assembly of our four nations and, more personally, commit the unforgivable sin of injuring my people, unmasked. Do any of you disagree with this course of action?" The air hung heavy with silence, no one saying a word. Nodding once, the king raised a hand and gestured to one of the guards. "Make it so."

The guard bent over to pull the wolf mask off of the mage, his partner keeping his spear pressed against the man's back just in case he tried anything. In one fluid motion, the mask came off and a sharp gasp pierced the silence, coming from next to Erica. She didn't even have to turn to know who had done so or why, seeing Viscount Myron's face revealed. Before any of the representatives could react, Thanasis surged forward, eyes wide with disbelief. "Father? Why?"

Viscount Myron ignored his son, staring dead ahead. No one spoke, all eyes turning to Duke Gerald, until King Thierry broke the silence. "Duke. Explain this and know that if the actions of your councilor represent the attitude of your nation, there will be a price to be paid."

Any doubts in Duke Gerald's own motives were dispelled the instant he spoke, the cool anger in his voice a pale shadow of the sheer rage that shone in his eyes. "I am just as surprised as you are, I assure you, Your Majesty. I would hear an explanation for this treachery myself."

Harsh laughter tore through the room in response, Myron shaking with the same unstable energy Erica had seen back in the streets. He shook his head with a broad grin across his face, as though he were the only one in on a joke. "Treachery? I am doing what needs to be done. For centuries, Perlora has languished for lack of power, but I would have made it the strongest nation in the world. With but one piece of the Regalia we would stand above even the might of Ancient's Armor. I would have used its power to ruin any other claimants, the likes of the Immortal Mage and his Knife, but you have chosen to let them roam free. The only treachery here is yours, and that of everyone else in this room, for choosing to let humanity die."

The king shook his head sadly. "So it's insanity then? We won't have our judgment interrupted by your ravings again."

With that, the king gestured to the guard again and Myron was gagged once more, his laughter vanishing as the silencing spell upon the cloth took effect.

Neriah stepped forward with his arms crossed, gaze firmly fixed on Gerald and heavy with suspicion. "Even if you say that, claim surprise at this madness, how can we trust the words of one who may be corrupted with darkness? The Auris Empire cannot be satisfied until your nation has been assured pure through the investigation of inquisitors blessed by the Emperor, may the Endless Flame bless his reign, and the villain's evils have been burned from this world upon the Endless Flame's pyre."

Gerald shook his head. "I'm afraid that's something I can't allow." Neriah started to respond, face set in outrage and hand half stretched towards Dawnsong's hilt, but Gerald raised a hand to forestall him. "Oh, by all means, you can send inquisitors along. As long as they're willing to follow my own questioners' lead. And you can have Myron once we're done with him, but I... have a few questions I'd like to ask first."

Neriah glanced down at Lukas who shrugged apathetically. "That may be an acceptable compromise. Shall we retire to discuss details?"

This last was accompanied by a token glance to Thierry, who raised his hand in acceptance. "You are dismissed. We will have Myron escorted to an appropriate prison, pending transfer and punishment."

The duke stood and the two of them started towards the door, Lukas idly following behind Neriah, before Gerald stopped suddenly, as though remembering something. Turning back to Thanasis, who was currently collapsed on the floor and staring blankly ahead, he addressed the young man sharply, though without any ire. "You had best come with us, Viscount Thanasis. These matters concern you too and I'll have to help you settle into your new position."

Though he nodded in response, he made no motions to get up and Edan bent down to pick him up, setting him back on his feet and steering him towards the door. She paused briefly to turn back to Erica, nodding slightly. "Don't worry, I'll keep an eye on him. We can discuss the rest later."

This left Erica largely confused, since she wasn't exactly sure why Edan felt she would be concerned about Thanasis nor why they would have to discuss anything, but she simply nodded back in response. Shortly after the Perlorans and Aurans left, the king waved the guards away. They picked Myron up, one on either arm, and dragged him from the room, another four guards joining them as they continued out of sight and on to the prison, a structure Erica had never actually realized Riverluck had. With only Lady Tagetes remaining, aside from the Tycortuans, the Rugegan representative stood and bowed her head to Thierry. "It seems that things are settled for the night. My only remaining concern is with what this means for the Western Alliance, but I feel that is a discussion best saved for when we are better rested."

Eyes narrowing, Thierry tilted his head to the side. "We beg your pardon? Should the actions of Myron have any effect on our current agreements? Perlora seems innocent in all of this."

Lady Tagetes smiled, a harsh and humorless smile. "Even so. Good night."

With that she started towards the door, only pausing once her hand was on the knob to wait for the king's dismissal. After she'd left and the door clicked closed once more, Thierry slumped down in his chair, letting out a heavy sigh and massaging his forehead with one hand. "I don't much like the way I see things going."

Levi grunted in agreement. For her part, Erica still wasn't precisely sure what it was the king was talking about, merely aware it was something about politics she still wasn't able to see. She stepped across the room, speaking with brow furrowed. "Your Majesty? Is all well?"

"Nothing you need concern yourself with, Miss Greenmaiden. It seems you have completed my task for you admirably. I will think of a proper reward in time, but for now I have nothing else for you to do. You may retire to bed and report to Estelle in the morning as usual."

It felt as though there was still something that she should be doing, that if Myron's actions could have a lasting impact in the nations she should continue looking for something to do about it since it might lead to that missing thread she still felt gnawing at her, but Erica merely bowed back in response and slipped out of the room with a nod of farewell to Levi. But as she left, that uncertainty only grew within her as Myron's words echoed in her head. *He said 'Regalia', but whose? Zephyros's? The Dusk Tyrant's?* She paused to look back at the room she'd left with a frown. *And this 'Immortal Mage' he mentioned. That sounds like a lead on another enemy, but why was Addy's dad so quick to dismiss everything as insanity?*

Stifling a yawn, she shook her head and headed for her quarters. Those thoughts were beyond her after such a long night. But just as quickly as they were gone, another memory came to mind, one that she could no so quickly dismiss. As she thought back over the night, she found every memory steeped in that same the feeling of uselessness she'd felt every time they'd come upon an enemy. The awareness that no matter how much she said she studied magic to help people, she could only rely on others. *I think I know what I'll be studying in my free time now.* She thought, idly clenching and unclenching one hand into a fist. *I said I came along to Riverluck all those years ago to look after Addy and Al, but how can I do that if I can't even fight the lowest form of undead?*

Chapter 29

Magiaday: 9th of Hernus, Year 1980 R.S.

" And I just don't see why we couldn't have flooded the caves once it was
• • • trapped. Wouldn't that do the job just as well?"

Allard sat on a bench in the monastery's courtyard, listening as Jareth tried to make a last ditch ploy to change their plan. The closer sunrise came, and the Witch almost certainly with it, the more frantic he seemed to come up with an alternative, though he tried very hard not to look it. *He's doing a good job of keeping his voice cool.* Allard thought with a sigh dangerously close to a yawn. He followed this up with a glare over at Adelaide, who was entirely too energetic for the morning hour. *Well of course, she got a full night's sleep after all.*

As if to prove his point, her eyes lit up as she replied, an infuriatingly smug smile on her face. "While the theory is sound, that would merely neutralize the vampire, paralyzing him for as long as it remained submerged. We want to destroy him outright." She slammed a fist against the palm of her other hand to punctuate her point. "And what if he ended up getting washed out somewhere else? Then we'd be back at square one. Trust me when I say relying upon the Witch is the optimal solution."

And for as much as he'd blame his sour mood on a lack of sleep, that was what frustrated Allard the most. While he certainly agreed that relying on the Witch of the New Moon *was* the optimal choice, it still galled him that he couldn't do a thing. The whole trip through the countryside, he'd been dragged along at another's behest. First merely reacting to the situation, then essentially a pawn in another's plan. Even now, his own plan relied upon him not doing anything to help. It made him feel just as powerless, just as incapable of being anything more than a village hunter, as he'd always been. That if nothing had changed since he'd left Regina's Bounty, it was because he hadn't changed, not the world around him. *Three years, and my life's path is just as set as it was when I was destined to become another farmer.*

He clenched his fist as he thought this, as if he could pool all of his frustrations there and let it go when he opened his fingers. As if by focusing hard enough, then the world would just snap and his hand would come alight with some grand power only he could wield. As if he could match Erica's years of training and study with one morning's sullenness. He could almost imagine he felt a slight tugging in his chest, but his hand was empty when he opened it, as to be expected. *If I'm supposed to be this generation's hero, then I'm not doing a good job of acting like it.*

His moping was interrupted as the first bit of sunlight finally crept into the courtyard, lighting up the gateway they were watching. At the other end, the chapel was backlit by the sun, just peeking over the horizon, giving it a striking, almost holy appearance. Adelaide waved them forward as she headed towards the gate as though that would speed up the Witch's arrival. Xavier followed close behind, the interested smile on his face showing what he thought about the meeting, while Jareth tarried slightly, shaking his head and muttering under his breath. Allard stayed where he was, figuring the three of them would have it well in hand, and leaned back against the wall behind him, closing his eyes with the intention of dozing while they got things sorted. This lasted all of five seconds, his rest interrupted when a resonant voice spoke out from beside him. "Well, boy? *What* do you want?"

Yelling in surprise, Allard flung himself from the bench, turning to find the Witch of the New Moon standing in plain sight next to where he'd been sitting. Though she carried herself with an almost arrogant air of nonchalance, the challenge burning in her golden eyes was impossible to miss. Swallowing once to gather himself, he stood up and dusted himself off before replying, "How did you know we were here?"

"That *didn't* answer my question. And did you *honestly* think I wouldn't notice people waiting in *plain* sight somewhere I'd been visiting for several days? And you've seen me teleport in front of you." She paused for a moment, some of the irritation draining from her gaze. "Though I suppose it is not a conversation without merit. The better question is how did *you* know *I* would be here?"

Still wary, Allard nodded towards the chapel. "The priest up there told me you'd been coming every morning."

The Witch's eyes narrowed at this, mouth thinning to a straight line. "Priest? Not monk?"

Allard flinched back, disconcerted. He'd noticed the vestments were different, but hadn't considered the distinction until she pointed it out. "He certainly seemed more like a priest than a monk to me. The robes looked far too fine for the ascetics here. Does it matter?"

For her part, the Witch simply lifted a hand to her chin, letting out a single hum of thought. She stood there unperturbed for nearly a minute, only snapping out of it when Adelaide pulled to a stop in front of her. "Hey, Miss New Moon! It's us again!"

Allard winced in exasperation, feeling every bit the same horror Jareth wore plain on his face. The Witch blinked back slowly, taken off guard by Adelaide's. Finally, she shook her head with a light smile. "*Miss*, hmm? I'm sure Isaheidar's boy would have *something* to say about that, but it's no matter. I'd rather not dangle you from your ankles for calling me an old hag. And I can see that it's *you*, people who never introduced yourselves. You're multiplying even." She gestured towards Jareth and Xavier, the latter waving back cheerfully. "Will you actually tell me what you *want*, or do I need to defer to your adult supervisor?"

Jareth's hand slid down to the hilt of his sword at this, but Adelaide didn't seem to notice. "Of course that won't be necessary. We came here for your help after all, so it would be rude of me not to tell." She paused for a moment, squaring herself up straighter and clearing her throat before continuing in a clear and formal voice. "Witch of the New Moon, my companions and I humbly request your aid in slaying a vampire we have confined."

The Witch's gaze lingered on Jareth for a time before flitting back to Adelaide with a raised eyebrow. "Oh? A *vampire* you say? And you can't handle it yourself with a squad of Riverluck guards at your back? Or did the captain here come alone?" She smirked, idly drawing her marble wand from its sheath at her hip and spinning it between her fingers. "If it's too strong for a handful of elites, then what makes you think *I* could handle it?"

Adelaide glanced over to Allard. Sighing, he shook his head. "Look, ma'am. From what we know of this vampire, he's stronger than the normal ones. Captain Jareth told us the palace guard took out several average vampires, but this one wiped out an entire manor's guard. He *is* too strong for us. But we've seen you take care of undead monsters before and heard the stories. He's not beyond you."

At this, the Witch cocked her head to the side, the slight smile on her lips showing what she thought about their assessment of her magic. "Oh? And why should I? You quote the stories about my powers, but forget what *else* they say about me."

Xavier stepped forward and gave a slight bow, characteristic smile upon his face. "Truth be told, I believe I can make it worth your while, my esteemed witch. As this generation's representative of the Stormtide family, I may be able to enlighten you on matters pertaining to my predecessor's actions as the so-called Storm Warlord here on Earth."

For a moment, the Witch said nothing, peering at Xavier's face with a curious expression. Then she nodded with a noise of understanding. "Right. Weird face. Insistence on honesty. Morningstar. That makes sense." She turned back to Adelaide and Allard with a mocking chuckle. "Seriously? Even with a *Noble* you can't destroy this pest? Either it's *far* more of a problem than you let on or your Fair-folk friend here is more pathetic than I'd have thought."

Xavier nodded, raising his hands in concession. "While, in truth, I appreciate your usage of the kinder title for my people, you must understand I'm not currently representing my full power. Would a mage of your caliber understand if I said transrealm astral refraction?"

Once more, the Witch let out a noise of understanding, nodding as if that explained everything. Twirling her wand about as though it were a conductor's baton, she started towards the monastery gate, walking with the utmost of confidence. "Well if a *Stormtide's* been sent, I suppose I *should* help you. Come. Lead me to the cornered rat and I'll show it I'm no cat to be trifled with."

The walk to the tunnel was short and oddly light to Allard's mind. For what they were about to do, slaying a monster and closing the book on what may well have been assassinations across two nations, everyone else seemed awfully laid back. The Witch and Adelaide chatted back and forth like old friends, with Xavier occasionally chiming in. The only other person who seemed to be taking things seriously was Jareth and even then, he seemed to rate the Witch as the greater threat if the way he stared at her back while keeping a hand on his sword meant anything. All told, it felt more like a pleasant stroll than a monster hunt. Allard shook his head in exasperation, just glad that the sunlight had seemingly burnt away the fog that followed the vampire around.

In a matter of minutes, they'd reached their destination, two guards still flanking the tunnel entrance. The guards snapped to attention as the group approached, admirably stifling any fear they might have had at seeing the Witch of the New Moon. "No movement, sir. The second checkpoint has held and unless there's another exit our survey missed, we can guarantee the monster is still down there."

Jareth nodded in thanks, dismissing them with a wave. "Well let's get on with it then," he said, turning to the group. "Your Highness, Mr. Stormtide, you two stay up here with Sir Lilyfield and Sir Proulx. I'd rather you return to the inn, but I doubt it will take that long. Mr. Fortunata, if you would help me accompany the Witch here down to the cavern?"

"What do you mean I'm staying out here?!" Adelaide snapped. "You expect me to simply sit idly by while this threat to my kingdom is brought low?"

Without missing a beat, Jareth nodded and moved past her to enter the tunnel. "Yes. And I think you'll find that everyone here agrees that there is no reason to potentially endanger the life of the heir to the throne just so she can watch a monster be put down. This is one thing I won't bend on, Highness. Even if you command me otherwise, my duty to your father overrides your own desires."

She stared back at him for a moment, but finally decided there wasn't any way she could talk her way into coming. Grumbling under her breath, she took a seat next to the entrance, making sure to shoot Allard a sullen look of over-exaggerated betrayal as she went. Once she was settled, Xavier moved to follow, stopping briefly to lay a hand on Allard's shoulder, whispering to him as he did. "I'll keep an eye on her in truth, Al. You go do what needs doing, young hero."

Well aware of just how little he was actually going to do, that served more as a blow to Allard's confidence than anything else, though he didn't let it show on his face. Waving the Witch over, he gestured towards the tunnel, letting her take the lead. Then, for what he hoped was the last time, he started down into the caves beneath the monastery.

By the time they reached the bottom of the passage, Allard felt fairly certain the Witch would be able to end it all with a single spell, but that changed the instant she stepped over the final threshold. Stopping suddenly, she inhaled sharply and flicked her wand down to the side, grip shifting so she was holding it like the hilt of a sword. Assuming an almost predatory crouch, she slowly stalked into the cave, hissing back to Allard, "*Something* is very wrong here."

Looking past the Witch's shoulder, Allard could see that the cave stood empty. Behind him, he heard Jareth's sword hissing out of its sheath. "Crows! How did it get out, Fortunata?"

Allard rushed past the Witch. As he approached the trench, he found it dry. Looking around the cave, he couldn't see the vampire out in the open, but knowing it was there sent a chill up his spine. "Stay on guard," he said, turning back to the Witch. "He stopped the running water keeping him in place and got out."

"How? Running water is an absolute bane to vampires. It should not have been able to circumvent this."

Carefully creeping forward, Allard inspected the juncture with the natural spring, noting a slender obstruction damming it. Pulling it out, he flinched back in horror, dropping it as he realized what it was. "Seras's stars! He cut off his own arm!"

It was a ghastly thing, with monochrome ashen skin and nails grown a half an inch past the fingers, coming to a sinister point. And it was surprisingly delicate, thin enough that Allard couldn't see how it had possessed enough strength to lift him. If he hadn't known where it came from, he wouldn't have thought it was real. Yet for as eerily flawless as the rest of the limb was, a ragged tear showed where it had been torn from the body, cracked bone jutting from the wound.

"It cut off its *own* arm?" The Witch said, approaching with a furrowed brow. "No undead save a *lich* should have the presence of mind to think so laterally, even if such a thing would--"

"Behind you!" Allard shouted, cutting her off as he saw a blur of movement in the darkness towards her back. Faster than he would have expected, the Witch spun, bringing her wand up in a smooth arc with a harsh whistle. White light shone from the end of the wand, solidifying into a length of crystal that cut the incoming knife out of the air with a dissonantly pure chime. Setting herself at the ready, the Witch faced the vampire with her wand raised in a practiced fencer's stance, the crystal growing from it smoothing to form a slender blade and delicate crossguard, the perfect image of an espada ropera were it not for the too-thin hilt the marble wand made. She dashed forward, starting into a wordless, lilting song as she did. Even to Allard's senses, the sheer weight of magic in the air was palpable, the air over the Witch's shoulders spiraling and solidifying into a set of four crystal thorns. As her song rose in volume, the Witch flung her offhand forward, sending the spikes forward at the vampire.

The vampire dodged and leapt past the summoned spikes, flinging another dagger as it landed. The Witch easily flicked it aside, bringing her sword down on the rebound, but the vampire effortlessly ducked under it. The way it shifted its other shoulder forward seemed to indicate it meant to stab at the Witch, but the vampire had evidently forgotten that it was missing an arm. Recovering from its misstep, it retreated several feet before spinning back to face its opponent.

The vampire set itself for another pass, another dagger dropping into its hands from the folds of its ragged cloak with a simple flick of the wrist, but then it paused, glancing back at Allard. He fumbled with his bow, trying to nock an arrow, but before the vampire could close on him, another few notes of the Witch's song heralded another spell. The vampire was barely able to dodge out of the way as a cluster of lights burning like miniature stars crashed into the ground where it'd been standing, exploding into nebulae of pale blue and violet plasma like tiny clouds of stardust. Without waiting to see if the vampire survived, the Witch spun into her next spell.

From there, the fight continued spinning onward in an almost inevitable dance as the Witch slung spell after spell at the vampire, refusing to give it a moment's respite now that she'd regained her composure. She stepped closer and closer every second, one hand directing her magic and the other cutting knives out of the air. For its part, the vampire managed to settle into a steady rhythm, its focus now entirely on the Witch after its brief moment of hesitation. No matter how many spikes of stone or shining stars she sent its way, the vampire ducked and weaved around them, always finding a way to fling another of its seemingly endless knives with unerring accuracy. But the equilibrium they'd found themselves in was clearly an unequal one, the Witch advancing where the vampire could only desperately counter.

The Witch entered lunging range and her song rose to a crescendo, taking on a triumphant tone. The ground rippled beneath the vampire, its feet slipping into the stone as if it were water. As it stumbled, the Witch struck, cutting off her song with a sharp whistle. The vampire tried to throw one last dagger, but the Witch's sword took it in the arm, batting it away to leave its chest exposed. The gnarled vine of dark energy she'd used to kill several of the zombies and bonewalkers a few days ago wound around the Witch's free hand, leaping forward like a snake to take the vampire through the heart.

The moment it happened, Allard could tell something wasn't right. When the Witch had used that same spell against the weaker undead, they died in an instant. But somehow, this vampire didn't seem to care. It took the spell full on without flinching. It leaned forward into the spell, bringing itself closer to the Witch and the vampire's bared fangs reminded Allard it had another weapon besides its knives. The Witch's lunge left her exposed and the vampire leapt for her neck with unnatural strength, the stone crumbled around his legs. The Witch drew in a sharp breath, eyes widening in disbelief. "What?! You're no ordinary—"

Time seemed to slow for Allard, though he knew it was only in his mind. He snapped into action without even thinking about it, but his mind belabored the point as it happened. He knew he wouldn't be able to help. He knew he could only watch events unfold, see the Witch fall and their plan crumble. But he couldn't bear to simply let it happen. He felt powerless. He felt like he'd only been drifting along with the current, letting others make his decisions and lead him along. But more than any of that, he felt like in this moment he had to at least try. Everything inside him screamed, begged, for any way to change what was happening. One thought drowned out everything else as he stretched a hand out towards the two of them. *Please, I don't care what it takes, just let me make it in time!*

A pointless sentiment. A worthless gesture. Even as he watched, he heard the Witch whistle again, a sparkling pink light forming between her and the vampire's body. But against all odds, he felt something... rush within him. There was a tugging, then a brilliant heat centered in his chest. His outstretched hand came alight with a burning glow, like someone had splattered hot oil on the back of his hand, and a torrent of inky darkness rushed towards the vampire, like a miniature cataract whose jagged edges reached like razor sharp claws. It crossed the cave in an instant, taking the vampire in the waist and tearing it in half, swallowing up its legs and flinging its upper body halfway across the cave.

Allard snapped back to his senses as the Witch's spell coalesced into a shield of rosy quartz in the shape of a crocus in bloom. As she saw the spell Allard cast, her eyes widened further, burning with an overwhelming fury. She whirled around to face him, looking only long enough to be sure that he was that source. Growling with rage, she shook her head and pointed her sword at the vampire, its blade crumbling as a black emptiness like a hole in the world took form at the wand's point. "To the *stars* with subtlety! If the cave falls around us, then so *be* it. Celestial Void!"

The last bled naturally into a piercing whistle, rising to a haunting melody. The emptiness collapsed into an orb roughly the size of a fist and shot from her wand. It seemed to bend the world around it, wind rushing towards it as it flew through the air. True to her word, the stone above and below crumbled and drew itself towards the darkness, vanishing in its depths, and the ground started shaking. The vampire tried to push itself out of the way, but now only a one-armed torso, it couldn't move fast enough and the spell dug itself into its stomach. With that, the vampire began to fall inwards, torso swiftly shrinking into the eerie emptiness. In a last ditch effort, the vampire ran its hand through its neck, severing its head through sheer brute strength before it could be swallowed up. The Witch just shook her head, closing her free hand with a tsk. "Giving up all pretenses then? As if I'd *let* you."

The spell collapsed in on itself, darkness vanishing as it erupted into a pillar of blazing light. Flicking her wand, it tilted sideways and flew towards the severed head, spearing it and burning it away in an instant.

With the vampire destroyed the pillar of light froze and the Witch stalked towards Allard. Before he could say anything, she grabbed him by the arm and started dragging him back towards the tunnel mouth. "*Where* is it?" She snarled.

All at once, Allard was reminded of just how alien she was. It was easy to forget when she acted normal, but her pointed ears and golden eyes were clear signs that while she might be Human, she was certainly not a human. Likewise, if she truly was one of the Folk, her relatively youthful appearance, apparently only a few years older than Levi, would not represent the weight of years she'd lived. For as much as he'd managed to ignore the stories about her this morning, their terror returned and he found he could hardly piece words together. "Uh... What? I don't..."

They passed by Jareth, who'd been standing guard the whole time, and she waved the captain forward without a word. Once they were all in the tunnel, she clicked her tongue once and jerked her head back towards the cave. A roar answered her as her spell detonated and Allard could feel a searing heat on his back, light blazing from the cavern so brightly he could see it even looking the other way. The Witch relaxed somewhat, grip easing on Allard's arm, but none of the harshness left her voice. "Don't *pretend* you don't know. Stony death, but I'm a fool! You lived near the grave so of course it makes sense that you'd have the medallion. Now *where is it?*"

Something told Allard that telling her where it was would be a bad idea. He wasn't certain the Witch would just let them go if she did get what she wanted. And knowing she, or at least one who bore her title, had revived the Dusk

Tyrant and the medallion was supposed to be connected to the Ember King, he was even less certain it would be good for the world if she did. "I don't have it anymore. I noticed it had fallen out of my pocket sometime after we got to Zephyr's Blessing."

Not exactly right, but certainly the truth. The Witch met his eyes, staring as she silently judged him. Finally, she broke contact with a curse. "Stony death. Of all things... I'm already behind and now *this*."

With that, she let him go and continued stalking her way out of the tunnel, apparently unconcerned with Allard now that he had nothing for her. Allard stood frozen for a moment, still unsure how to react. He only snapped out of it when Jareth caught up to him, nudging him in the shoulder. "What was that about, Mr. Fortunata? Is everything still alright or has the Witch turned on us?"

He noticed the captain still had his sword drawn. Even if the Witch of the New Moon had cast the two of them aside and felt content to ignore them, Xavier, and more importantly Adelaide, were waiting just outside the tunnel. And while he felt fairly confident the Witch had no particular reason or desire to hurt her now, Allard didn't want to find out what would happen if she found out Adelaide had the medallion she was looking for. Or what would happen if Adelaide thoughtlessly gave it to her. "I'll explain later, let's just get outside first."

As he emerged back into the sunlight, he found the Witch in the middle of gently, albeit somewhat rudely, shoving Xavier aside. "I don't *care* what you know about Zephyros," she shouted. "I was looking for information on *Seras*, not all four of the Champions, and I *already* found what I needed." Giving the Demon-folk a sideways glance as she passed, she let out a snort of derision. "And I would guess I know *far* more about your predecessor than you ever could."

Xavier's mouth snapped shut. He stepped back, stunned, as as he tried to puzzle out the implications of what she'd just said. Adelaide leapt up from where she was sitting, looking back and forth between the Witch and Allard before dashing in front of the Witch. "Wait! What's wrong? Did Al do something to annoy you? You were able to kill the vampire, right? So everything should be—"

The Witch cut her off with a sharp hiss and a baleful glare, a stark contrast to her previous attitude towards the girl. She took Adelaide by the shoulder and stared down into her eyes, ignoring the hiss of swords being drawn behind.

"*Listen*, girl. I am only interested in recovering something I lost many years ago. All the rest, and all of you here, might as well be sand on the shore for all I care. Your *friend*," The slight emphasis she placed on the word was not lost on Allard, "Lost the medallion, something which *irks* me to the core, but I desire a second perspective on matters. Tell me *when* it went missing."

To her credit, Adelaide managed to keep her composure, a brief glance at Allard the only concession to her growing confusion. "How should I know? I barely pay attention to the stupid thing and only packed it with Al's stuff because he likes it. All I know is that he first pointed out that it was missing two nights ago, back when we were in Zephyr's Blessing."

The Witch sighed, shaking her head as she released Adelaide. "What a pain. Now I have *another* town to try searching without inciting mobs. Lovely."

With that, she took a step to the side, vanishing in a swift rush of wind. For a moment, the hillside was silent, all present taken aback by the suddenness of her departure. Then the guards sprang into action, as if they had only just remembered what their jobs were, pulling Adelaide back into their midst and forming a perimeter around her. For his part, Jareth sheathed his sword, rubbing his brow with a sigh as he pushed Allard forward and gently steered him towards the group. "I believe I asked for an explanation, Mr. Fortunata?"

Adelaide chimed in, trying to slip out from behind the guards to no avail. "Yeah! What in the name of Zephyros' banner happened, Al? I was worried when the hill started shaking and it looked like the monastery was going to collapse. Then the Witch comes out here all angry and asking about your medallion. Why didn't you tell–"

Allard shushed her. "Let's not talk about it here. She might still be watching. Or listening. I think we should get back home so we can figure out what we should actually do about all of this."

The guards looked to Jareth as one. The captain, at a loss, gave a curt nod and left Allard to join them in starting back down the hillside, Adelaide shepherded along in their midst despite her attempts to drop back and join Allard. Allard moved to follow them, but stopped himself after a step, looking back towards Xavier. The man had been awfully quiet after being shut down by the Witch. "Everything alright there, Xavier?"

Xavier simply nodded, apparently not nearly as lost in his thoughts as he looked. Or at least just as aware despite being so contemplative. "Quite alright, Al. Just disconcerted to be honest. The Witch says she knows more about my predecessor than I. Startling to say the least, since that begs the question of how much more she knows about Lord Morata and the events of two thousand years ago, but I'd be lying if I said that's what concerned me." He shrugged, letting his hand drop from his chin as he started walking, as if the conversation had reminded him he should be moving. "Truth be told, what could it have been that Zephyros didn't want our family to know?"

Chapter 30

Sunday: 10th of Hernus, Year 1980 R.S.

Allard let out a heavy sigh as he fell back into the plush chair. He could only stand to pace for so long after all and two hours was enough. He wasn't exactly surprised that he'd been locked away in the small sitting room the instant he and Adelaide had returned, Jareth had told him as much would happen, but that didn't make it any less boring for him while he waited. Especially since he knew he was missing out on an explanation of what had happened in the capital while they'd been gone. The subdued tone to the crowds as they'd made their way through the city spoke volumes, as did the bonfires every few street corners and the slashes and claw marks on many of the buildings. He knew Erica would let him know once everything was settled, but that didn't mean he wasn't irritated in the interim.

Eventually the door finally opened and a member of the palace guard leaned inside, gesturing for him to follow. The walk through the palace halls was fairly short and mostly uneventful, but did offer him two particular bits of insight. As to the first, he found himself shocked to see how late it was once he finally passed a window, the sun already slipping past the trees of Thicket Forest across the Summerblood. The day had slipped away faster than he'd realized and it was hardly a reassuring sign when it meant they'd been discussing things for half a day. And as for the second, he was disconcerted at just how many Auran soldiers were walking about the palace, often casually chatting with palace guards and staff. Especially the inquisitors, who'd been eager to speak with him after hearing about both the high vampire's death and the witch who'd made it possible. Once more, he couldn't help but wonder just what had happened while he was gone.

When they reached the king's study, the guard knocked on the door once, waiting until permission came from within to open it, wordlessly nodding Allard on while he remained behind. Allard had been in the king's study a few times before, noting again the carving on his desk of the Judge Gidiar's famous hunt of the demon boar Taredson, but not often and only on occasions that had made him similarly uncomfortable. The king himself sat in his comfortable-looking stuffed chair behind the desk as he fixed Allard with a heavy stare. The other concerned parties sat in an arc around the desk as though he were facing trial; Adelaide, Levi, and Estelle on the king's right and Erica and Xavier on his left. Swallowing once, Allard bowed deeply, putting as much sincerity as he could muster into his voice. "I'm very, incredibly sorry, Your Majesty. I know that I shouldn't have taken Adelaide out——"

The king cut him off. "Oh please. Everyone here, except perhaps your new traveling companion, knows who's at fault and I can assure you that an appropriate punishment has already been determined and sentenced."

This last was accompanied by a pointed glance towards his daughter who, for her part, tried as hard as she could to look innocent.

"But, and I don't mean to insult you when I say this, is that really alright?" Allard asked. "Even if we all know that, most people won't see it that way. And if you aren't going to punish me, what were you discussing for so long?"

Estelle chuckled as she raised her hands from her letterboard. A shiver ran down Allard's spine. He'd heard that laugh enough times to know it never meant anything good. "That won't do at all, Mister Fortunata. While His Majesty knows you are not guilty of kidnapping his daughter, you are still responsible for shirking your duty as squire to the Crownguard and potentially endangering the heir, an action that runs directly opposed to your position's mandate. Sir Crownguard and I, as your direct supervisors, have determined an appropriate task for you to... seek atonement."

Allard felt his mouth dry and tried to muster up an appropriate response, but Levi broke the silence with a sigh, shaking his head. "Stop toying with him, Estelle. It really is nothing quite so bad, Sir Allard, and in fact pertains more to the changes in circumstance we have found thrust upon us. I think you will be happy to accommodate His Majesty's request when all is through."

"That is correct," the king said, picking up where Levi left off. "If what your companion has told us is true, then there is much to discuss. Now if you would take a seat, Mr. Fortunata?" Once Allard his way over to the room's remaining chair, he turned to Erica. "Now Miss Greenmaiden, if you would?"

Erica immediately rose with an immense amount of discomfort clear in her stance and face and tone. "Yes, of course, Your Majesty. But don't you think it would be better if Archmage Dwyer——" Her complaints were cut short by a chorus of dismissals from half of the room. Letting out a nearly inaudible sigh, she forced herself to stand a little straighter and continued. "Of course. As has become clear from Mr. Stormtide's words, it seems the Dusk Tyrant, or the power behind the Dusk Tyrant rather, is at work once more in the world. We'd expected something to happen, since this is the two thousandth year since his defeat and the last millennial anniversary ended with the destruction of the Sunfire Empire, but he as good as confirms it."

"Are you kidding?" Allard said. "What happened while I was gone that would make you believe this?"

Xavier smiled wanly. "Be honest with me, wouldn't you rather we take this seriously and have it be nothing than the other way around?"

Allard remained silent, realizing there was little he could say that they wouldn't have already discussed, and ceded the floor once more to Erica. She offered him a brief smile and nod of assurance, showing he wasn't the only one who felt uncertain about all of this, before she continued. "With this in mind, though *we* can take the attack on Riverluck and Mr. Stormtide's word as proof, it is unlikely the rest of the world will be able to. The best course of action we have found for us to take is to consult the experts on this."

Allard drew in a sharp breath, leaning forward with rapt attention once more. "Do you mean...?"

King Thierry nodded with a chuckle. Sliding forward a thin stack of sealed envelopes, he pulled the royal seal from one of the drawers behind him. "Indeed. Tycortua will be sending a delegation to escort Mr. Stormtide to the Order of the Eagle at the City of the Scales, so he may apprise the Watchers of Midnight of what is to come. Sir Crownguard, his squire, and Miss Green-maiden will be required to come along in order to attend to Tycortua's heir as she leads this delegation as a *furthering of her studies of diplomacy.*" This was accompanied by another pointed look at his daughter and Allard wondered just how many textbooks she'd be required to read through for *her* punishment. Clearing his throat, the king pulled forward another paper, this one filled with text Allard recognized as the hallmark of official proclamations and signed in royal blue ink, and after dipping his seal in wax, stamped it down at the bottom, flourishing the paper as he continued. "And with that, it is done. Your orders have been signed and sealed. You will set sail for the Threefold Eye from Port Dicefall next Sunday."

Not bothering to look up from her notes, Estelle chimed in almost the instant he was done speaking. "And you, Mister Fortunata, will be stopping at the Grand Cathedral of the Teacher on High Worldheart on the way back, to beg forgiveness for your breach of conduct and accept what penance they place upon you."

Allard silently cursed the fact that he wasn't going to get away with just accompanying the group on their trip. Especially when he thought about the enormity of confessing before the leader of his faith and how mortifying that would be. Thierry glanced towards Estelle out of the corner of his eyes as he handed both the order and stack of envelopes over to Levi. "Quite right. It'll be a nuisance for all involved, but it's the only way we'll keep people from hounding me about lax security." The king paused, clearing his throat before he continued. "Now. There is one last thing I wish to discuss. And to be clear, this cannot leave the present company. Understood?"

Uneasy, Allard exchanged a glance with Erica and found her just as lost as he was. After they nodded their assent, the king gestured to Estelle and the castellan withdrew a single paper and a thick tome from her bag. Handing the paper to Allard, she said, "This is the transcript of Viscount Myron's unmasking. As I am sure you are aware, Mister Fortunata, the Perloran fool had a few *interesting* things to say."

At Allard's side, Erica drew in a sharp breath. "Do you mean what he said about 'the Immortal Mage'?"

"Quite so. Regardless of the man's folly, we cannot ignore such a striking lead."

Erica furrowed her brow. "Really? With all due respect, I kind of thought we were, with how quickly Addy's dad brushed it aside."

The king let out a humorless laugh, accepting the tome from Estelle. "Not so. I wished to curtail discussion because I was reminded of this. A gift from the king of Montiamon, a historical text which describes how the corruption of the Sunfire nobility brought the Ember King's Empire down from within, reborn Dusk Tyrant or no."

Allard remembered the Auran soldiers he'd passed earlier. "Are you saying we can't trust the other members of the Western Alliance?"

"I'm saying we should step lightly. The Rugegans all but admitted they have little trust at the moment and I think we should meet them in kind. If this

Immortal Mage could sway a Perloran Councilor of the Twelve, there's no telling who he couldn't bring to his side."

Shaking his head, Levi rose and stood before the king. "And yet if Immortal Mage served as guide for Viscount Myron, we cannot afford to rest upon our laurels. There is still an enemy that threatens us." His face set itself in a fierce glower and he dropped to one knee before continuing. "No matter how old or powerful this necromancer may be, I swear I shall bring him down, Your Majesty. I doubt even this so called Regalia could stand up to Whisperwind's might. I would ask you to help me search through the archives for clues to his identity, Sir Allard."

Though he acknowledged the oath with a nod, the king waved off Levi's words. "You are borrowing problems from the future, Levi. Let us take these things one at a time. For all we know, the Watchers of Midnight have been tracking the Immortal Mage for months and need little more than our strength." He turned to the rest of the group as he continued. "Now go. You're all dismissed. Rest for tonight and start packing tomorrow."

All stood at the sudden dismissal, save for Estelle, and quickly bowed before exiting. Levi clapped Allard on the shoulder as he passed, offering him the first words of greeting since he'd come back with a sardonic smile. "Glad to see you return in good health, Sir Allard. I must say there have been times when even I wondered what the point of my having a squire was, but if it means I can shove the blame on you for situations like this, I shall consider it a fair bargain."

Without waiting for a reply, he set off down the hall at a purposeful clip, intent on having the last word. Xavier likewise bowed his way out of the conversation as Allard was trying to think of a comeback to shout after Levi, leaving the three youths to themselves. After a few seconds had passed and Allard realized the moment had slipped away, he settled for grumbling complaints to himself. Erica chuckled at that, softly rapping Allard on the shoulder to get his attention. "It *is* good to see you safe though, Al. I can't tell you how worried we were about you. Both of you," she added with a stern look down at Adelaide. "I hear you had quite the adventure, you vampire slayer you."

He shook his head, thinking about just what his 'adventure' entailed. "Hardly. I've had hunting trips with Mal and Kal that were more exciting but with less impending death. And as for the vampire, I didn't even kill him. Honestly, if he's the kind of thing we'll be going up against if the Dusk Tyrant does come back, I'm going to need a bit more than a bow and arrows."

Erica tilted her head to the side, mouth quirked up in an amused smile as she took in his words. "He, huh? Funny, I said the same thing. The praetor didn't like it, but..." The two of the shared a glance as she trailed off, Allard nodding in agreement to her unspoken question. Then the moment passed and Erica's expression became strangely grim as she continued at almost a whisper. "And I'm with you on the bow. I'm not nearly there either."

The mood thoroughly soured, the three of them walked in silence for a few moments before Adelaide piped up. "Argh! Why are you two being so dour about all of this? Come on, it's the first time we'll get to go to another country! Isn't that exciting?"

As she pointed it out, Allard realized she was right. For the first time in his life, he'd be well and truly leaving home. He'd see the sea and go somewhere he'd only dreamed about as a kid, experience new things and broaden his horizons. Despite it all, he couldn't help but be cheered by that a little, realizing that now he actually was taking one step closer to become the kind of traveler he thought he'd be by going to Riverluck. "Yeah, that's right. It's the first time either of us will get to go somewhere outside Tycortua. You too, huh?"

"Exactly! That's the spirit." Adelaide said, eyes taking on a dreamy cast. "Think of all the things we'll get to see. The Lanturian Gate at High Worldheart, the black citadel of the Watchers, the monument to Racleon and Achulian.... Oh! Do you think we'll get to stop into Lugherion for a bit? Or maybe Nypheos. I think they're supposed to be holding the Tournament of the Council this year. And––"

Erica shut Adelaide up by placing a hand on her head and gently squeezing, fixing her with a withering glare. "'And maybe this time I'll remember to pack my own clothes.' Is that what you were going to say, hmm your Royal Thieveriness?"

Blinking in surprise, Allard only then remembered that Adelaide was still wearing one of Erica's dresses, as she had been the entire trip. He chuckled as he watched her squirm under Erica's hand. "Ah stop! I promise I won't do it again. It was important this time and I was going to give them back."

"It's kind of strange though, isn't it?" Erica continued, ignoring the princess. "I wonder what the people back home would think. I bet Mal's eyes would fall out of his head if he knew we were going to travel so far."

Allard laughed, thinking of their friend and his tendency for theatrics. He still remembered how Mal had acted when he found out Allard and Erica were not just going to go to Riverluck, but do so in the company of the princess. Along that same course, his thoughts turned back to Carlin and particularly about what his brother's last letter had said. He turned back to Erica. "Talking about home does remind me: just how much of Adelaide's and my story did you hear?"

"I think we got the gist, though I'd still like to hear it from you. What's this got to do with home?"

"Well did any of your siblings tell you the Witch of the New Moon was looking around Regina's Bounty in the last round of letters you got?"

At this, Adelaide surged out of Erica's grip and swung around Allard, putting him between her and Erica. Rummaging about in her pockets, she pulled out Allard's medallion. "Speaking of, are you finally going to explain why you didn't want her to know I had this? You should have it back by the way."

As Allard took the medallion and stowed it in a pocket, Erica replied, "Right. I remember you telling me about Carlin's letter. I have some news on that front too. Seems like the Aurans are awfully interested in her too." She paused, brow furrowing with concern. "And there's another thing. Neither the king nor Levi mentioned it, but Viscount Myron summoned a creature when he was about to get caught. I can't say for sure what it was, but it looked just like pictures of the Dusk Reaver."

Allard frowned, looking back and forth between the two of them. "Really? The Dusk Reaver? That settles it then. Even though I was skeptical earlier, I do think we should be careful on this trip. Something's clearly going on and the Witch is part of it. We should sit down and talk about this before we go to sleep."

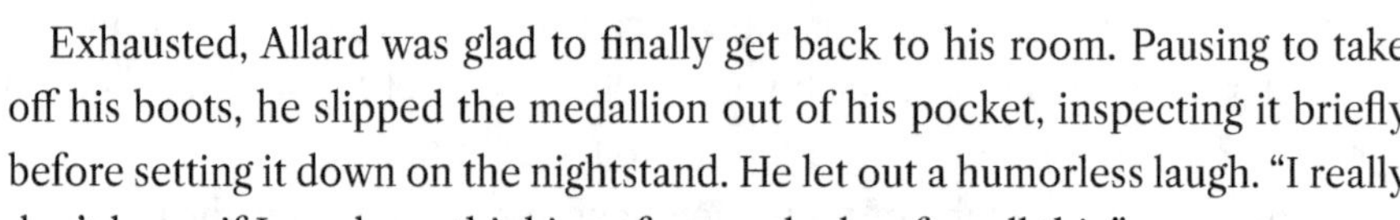

Exhausted, Allard was glad to finally get back to his room. Pausing to take off his boots, he slipped the medallion out of his pocket, inspecting it briefly before setting it down on the nightstand. He let out a humorless laugh. "I really don't know if I can keep thinking of you as lucky after all this."

The medallion, predictably, gave no response. Allard shook his head Even though he was still in his traveling clothes, he didn't care enough to change right then and, after shutting off his sunstone lamp, let himself fall onto his bed. In a matter of minutes, he was asleep.

Once more, Allard found himself dreaming of a strange place. He wasn't sure if he was in the same place as last time; the chalky dust he'd previously seen replaced by a loamy black soil and the dirty white sky nowhere to be seen, the heavens looking far more like a simple night sky, though perhaps with fewer stars than he was used to, no more than three hundred in total. Plants unlike any he'd ever seen, even in the depths of Thicket Forest where the underbrush tangled together until there was hardly any space underfoot and it began to climb the trees, rose around him in a thick verdure. Their broad, glossy leaves were longer and wider than an oaks, their vibrant flowers almost alien when compared to the likes of crocuses and lilies, and their fruits surrounded by a strong and sickly sweet scent a far cry from the mild aroma of apples and grapes. And all of it was colored strangely, almost monochrome. They all seemed to be made of the same black substance, the differences in the coloration almost a trick of the light in how the iridescence of their inky texture presented itself. That more than anything made Allard sure he was in the same place as last time.

More than a little disconcerted, Allard looked down at his arm where he remembered a faint misting of the dark torrent brushing against him. He found a design almost like a tattoo, spiraling like ocean waves down his lower arm until it ended in three irregular patches spotted across the back of his hand. Figuring there was nothing to be gained from staying in one place, he headed forward, pushing his way through the lush undergrowth. Already, he felt as though the dream had taken longer than the others, time passing almost normally instead of in the vague half-reality of dreams. Lacking any obvious destination, he had decided to approach one of the two enormous trees he could see at the edges of the garden. The one to what he had arbitrarily decided was the east looked strange, its ten primary branches far too precise and all of its limbs equidistant and grown at exact angles, so he decided to head towards the western tree, one that looked like a far more normal orchard tree, an indeterminable fruit heavy on its limbs. As he grew closer to the tree, Allard looked once more at the sky, trying to find any familiar constellations among the stars. But he felt himself being drawn into them, struck by a sense of invincible distance that he hadn't felt before and with it an overwhelming dread.

The feeling started to overwhelm him and he unconsciously stopped, falling to the ground as his knees gave out, but he kept his eyes locked on the stars above. Then it was all gone in an instant, someone picking him up and setting him on his feet once more. Turning around, Allard found the same woman from before, but now she looked far more solid and real. She no longer glowed with an ethereal blue light, its lines making up the edges of her body like a sketch, instead looking much like the plants did, made up entirely of the inky darkness that surrounded them, the liquid sculpted into flesh and cloth. She smiled gently at his inspection, head tilting to the side in an affectionate gesture and eyes wrinkling fondly. Then she spoke, and this time Allard could hear her words, her voice smooth as water and with a musical quality to it like a trickling stream. "It's going to be alright. I'm here to take care of you now."

Allard woke with a start, gasping with a sharp intake of breath. Looking about, he was reassured to find himself still in his quarters at the palace, the moonlight leaking in through the window proving it to still be the middle of the night. He searched the room, getting up to check under his bed and in the wardrobe and opening his door, looking either way down the hall, but he found nothing out of place. Even so, however, his dream left him filled with a certainty that there was something nearby, that he was not alone and something had its eyes on him. The woman's words echoing in his head, he returned to his bed and settled in once more, but sleep was hard to come by and when morning finally came, the pressure on his back, the feeling he was being watched, hadn't eased in the slightest.

Epilogue

Seaday: 15th of Hernus, Year 1980 R.S.

The figure stood still as a statue, looking out the window and giving no sign that they'd heard the door open behind them. Knife knew better. Even when they were in their best condition, the Master always knew when they approached. Now, with a half-shaped body still bending itself to their will, there was simply no way they hadn't made a sound. Knife gave it no mind. It was the Master's way of reminding them of their place, to show his back entirely open and vulnerable but give no impression of fear. After all, even if Knife took it to mind to attack him, the conclusion was foregone. Regardless, they took their position on the floor behind him, kneeling with head bowed to count the floorboards. *Eighty-four.*

The Master continued to stand silently, looking at things only he knew. Knife had checked the windows on the way in (*fifteen*) and thus knew this one only looked out over more houses, and none of them important. Finally, once he was sure the proper ceremony had been attended to, he spun around and glided across the room to settle into a plush chair set behind a desk, his staff resting against one of its arms. "You failed, my knife."

Knife made no response. None was expected of them. They merely used the pause to count the objects on the desktop (*twenty-seven*).

"The heiress escaped and the country remains stable, I still have no idea of the cloak's location, and you come back to me nearly a week later, shambling about in some drunkard's skin."

The body was a rough one, its bulk ill-fitting to Knife's own form, but acquired out of desperation. After spending so long digging their way out of the collapsed cave (*Seven thousand nine hundred and twenty minutes*), Knife had little strength left for anything but an easy target. And they preferred to spend as little time as possible as merely a limb. Knife was unconcerned, knowing the Master was more concerned with the damage's source than its results. It would be as it should be in little time in any case.

The Master shook his head, tapping a bony finger against the chair's arm. "The others will let me hear no end of this failure. And do you know who is to blame?"

Knife said nothing, counting the pictures of the prior owners of the house, hung upon the walls (*nine*).

"That accursed Perloran! I give him my finest tool and he can't even use it properly? You should have bathed the city in blood, my knife, and opened the vaults for me in a single night. But I suppose this is what I get for relying upon another's judgment. Come, attend to me."

Knife shot up, unfortunately unsteady in that accursed body. They had known choosing someone at least six inches taller would throw off their balance, but that didn't make it any less infuriating. Shuffling around to their master's side, Knife looked down at the indicated document. Even though the room was unlit, Knife could tell right away they were looking at a map of the continent; neither they nor the Master requiring light to see. The map had been marked heavily across the continent in several differently colored inks (*five*) but Knife ignored those as they had nothing to do with them. The Master tapped on the Threefold Eye, the island home to the twin nations of Nypheos and Lugherion and with them the Order of the Eagle. "You'll be going here, to Nypehos, next, my knife. And I tell you now that though you go there to aid one of my associates, you should ignore what he says and trust your own judgment. This lesson has taught me that even a knife better knows how it should cut than any of these foolish schemers."

Knife agreed. Viscount Myron had been a fool for sending them out of Riverluck. Even if the heiress was a target, killing the Crownguard would have done almost as much if not more in destabilizing the kingdom. With their champion dead and their defenses compromised, it would have taken little prodding to convince the Auris Empire to invade. And though they weren't sure they could kill the Crownguard, Knife had thought of several ways (*thirty-eight*) to get past his Ancient's Armor and found themself disappointed that they hadn't had the chance to try. Wasting a sharpened knife was insult to blade and whetstone both.

The Master began drumming his fingers, his free hand flicking back and forth through the air to direct documents into several stacks (*seven*). "Read through these before morning. The top page of each bears my commands pertaining to the given group and shall make the rest self-explanatory. Then head to the docks and seek out the trading vessel *Temelus*. I've chartered the ship to disembark for Seras's Aria tomorrow and intend for you to be onboard."

Falling to a knee once more, Knife bowed their head to accept the command. In an instant, all thoughts of Tycortua and the unused plans stored up were swept away. The mission ended, they no longer mattered. And beyond that, the next mission should be a simple one, with little need for Knife to think more than as a knife. Seven stacks of paper and Nypheos in the seventh year? It could only mean one thing: Tournaments of the Council. Straightening back up, Knife plucked the papers from the air, keeping them in their stacks, and shuffled out the door, to give the Master his privacy. As they walked through the house, searching for a convenient closet in which to stay out of the way and prepare, Knife was surprised to find two thoughts lingering still. *Why are there seven? What makes the Crownguard more than a Knife? Why are there seven? What makes the Crownguard more than a Knife?*

Book 1 End

Dictionary of Terms

Undead – A catchall term for creatures that have been magically animated through the particular school of magic known as necromancy. Most often, these creatures are raised specifically by a necromancer and are bound to follow that necromancer's commands, but the proper circumstances can result in undead naturally occurring, in which case they often possess little motivation or intelligence beyond the drive to consume life.

Bonewalker – One of the most common forms of undead, bonewalkers are magically reanimated skeletons, the bones cleaned by the necromantic energies and bound together by the same spell that animates them. They possess a form of sight, granted by the spell, but it is largely alien to conventional human sight, more along the lines of a sense of the varying levels of life within the surrounding environment. They are rather weak, since the spell animating them can be disrupted if the bones are separated or destroyed.

- ***WotL:*** *When did 'Bonewalker' become standard nomenclature and why?*

- ***TWS:*** *It's better than when they were just called skeletons and you know it.*

Zombie – A second of the more common forms of undead, zombies are little more than reanimated corpses, like bonewalkers but with flesh on the bones. This makes them somewhat tougher, since the spell is more difficult to disrupt, but they are still only about as strong as the average human. Similarly, the spell can only preserve the integrity of the corpse for so long, so if the body is damaged enough, it will 'die' again.

Ire-wraith – A mid tier undead, just threatening enough to be ranked above low tier like bonewalkers, zombies, and more relevantly, poltergeists. Ire-wraiths are semi-corporeal spirits formed by the lingering grudges of the unjustly slain. As in, literally composed of anger. That makes them problematic since most of the time someone dies from an Ire-wraith attack, they're unjustly slain. Tends to cascade into an infestation pretty quickly. Otherwise, not too difficult to kill as long as you have magic or honed weapons that can disrupt their phasing abilities.

Vampire – Unlike the other listed undead, vampires are something of a variable-tier creature. A newly raised vampire isn't much different from a zombie, just with enhanced physical capacity, the ability to walk on walls, and enhanced healing. The major difference comes from the demonic possession of the corpse that separates a vampire from a zombie. It's only when they've been around for a while and absorbed enough life force that the demonic spirit grows strong enough for stuff like transforming into pests, summoning fog, and hypnotizing with their eyes. Takes about a decade before they can fake human intelligence and a century before any kind of "high vampire", evil lord or lady in a gothic castle stuff can happen. Die to decapitation, incineration, and holy means. Staking and drowning paralyzes them, they can't cross running water, and garlic burns them. And of course, arithmomania. They *can* enter places uninvited and the sunlight only seals their power since they're nocturnal creatures, so don't count on those common stories. This is all, also, just for regular vampires. Gaean vampires are an entirely different beast and there is, admittedly, a vast array of 'bloodsucking monsters' which share similarities to vampires without adhering to the specific definition. For instance, Strigoi and Revenants share some features with vampires, including an undead nature, but, lacking a demonic, animating spirit, do not have the same suite of abilities. Similarly, Baobhan Sith, Kyuketsuki, and Empusae are all forms of bloodsuckers, but are starkly different from vampires in practice as each is a member of a different other-worldly ancestry.

- ***WotL:*** *What the hell kind of distinction are you making between a classical vampire and a 'Kyuketsuki'?*

- ***TWS:*** *A very subtle one. The latter is rooted in the same kind of origin as Oni and therefore not technically undead in the same way.*

- ***MotBW:*** *I mean, they do tend to be more stable than regular vampires.*

- ***WotL:*** *I'd keep arguing over your pedantry, but it turns out I don't care.*

Gaean Vampire – A catch all term for things that are 'like vampires, but a step beyond'. The only definition that can encapsulate the entire scope of what a Gaean Vampire's existence is 'a bloodsucker that came from the earth and shall return to it', thus providing the title of 'Gaean'. With that being said, it's mostly a poetic way to describe that they are beings with no progenitor in terms of vampirism; in short, what has been described before as a 'True Ancestor'. For example, the definition could be used to describe both a being whose latent nature was awakened through a dark ritual, like Erebus' Miss von Jormungandr, or a demonic spirit made physically manifest, like a certain lich's familiar. The former, however, was once human and forged into something else while the latter is a being whose spiritual nature was always vampiric. The only commonality uniting them all is that they must consume blood in some manner, though many find other sources of sustenance, such as religious devotion or hopes and dreams.

- ***WotL: Sigh**. Must you?*

- ***TWS:** Hey! If I didn't say it, someone would've.*

- ***WotL:** It's only the three of us. Who— Never mind.*

- ***MotBW:** Yeah. I totally would've.*

- ***TWS:** And what about the Warden of the Void? She chats with us sometimes. Or my Rounds of Winter?*

- ***WotL:** I hate you both.*

- ***Warden of the Void:** Tea on Tuesday?*

- ***TWS:** Of course.*

Griffon – One of the classic magical beasts, a flying creature with the front of an eagle and the back of a lion. Not especially interesting, as magical beasts go, but that's where their true value lies. Since they don't have anything like fire breath, the ability to teleport, or human intelligence, it makes them comparatively easy to domesticate. Originally native, at least on this continent, to the Golden Hills, the Tycortuan military has a long tradition in training them as war beasts for their enhanced strength and the aerial superiority they give as a flying steed. They are actually surprisingly loyal once a bond is formed.

Fae Wolf – Honestly, I don't know what you expect me to say here. It's pretty much exactly what it sounds like. A wolf from the other-worlds of the sidhe, effectively what our wolves would be like if they evolved in a world with magic and the common sense of fairyland. That being said, they are 'just wolves' with claws and fangs as sharp as honed swords, fur as tough as metal, and the kind of non-sentient intelligence common to a lot of magical predators. And they're often about the size of a pony.

Sandlobster – The Hell Sea's awful. Sandlobsters are, exactly what they sound like, lobsters that live in the dunes of the south-eastern desert. Just lobsters about twenty feet long with razor sharp pincers, a thirst for blood, and carapace harder than a lot of warded armor. And they don't even have the decency to taste good boiled. The meat's far too tough unless you cook it just right, in that Desert-folk way. They also have too many legs. Makes me glad the Forest-folk killed all of the web-spinners centuries ago.

True Dragon – The embodiment of destruction, terrors which make manifest Humanity's primal fear of fire, darkness, and serpents. They are exceptionally rare, rare enough that it's uncertain how they're born since they can't maintain a population themselves. Scholars theorize they're born from magic itself to serve as calamities that purge the world like a forest fire. They grow larger than the average dragons and are most famous for their magic-repelling scales. These scales actually function by accumulating naturally synthesized Nihil Iron in the body. As such, the older and more magic resistant a true dragon gets, the darker their scales turn. Green dragons are the youngest, eventually turning red until the oldest and most dreadful of them are left as black as cast iron. Black dragons are immune to all magic and told about in myth and legend as the kind of monster that heralds the world's end. True dragons have no more intelligence than that of a predatory animal, but they are born from malice and carry that same evil within them.

Snow-folk – A people that live in Skahios, in the foothills of the Stormwall Mountains. They possess an innate connection with ice and snow, actively surrounded in an aura of cold. Their exact classification is somewhat difficult to define, since they exist somewhere between human and sidhe. Though they are called by the appellation of 'Folk', they did not descend from the Ancient-folk as the rest of the Folk did, the appellation more descriptive of their shared Humanity than anything else. 'Snow Fairy' might be a more accurate term, since they do exist within the same taxonomic line as other sidhe races and originated from an other-world, the Crystalline Forest to be exact, but they are generally more Human than most other sidhe, so this has fallen by the wayside. They are a kind of elemental being raised into Humanity, standing at a crossroads between Human and fae. Danus Homo Sapiens Sapiens Brumus.

- **WotL:** *Oh. You're still trying to do that whole taxonomy thing.*

- **TWS:** *It's important! For clarity and recording knowledge for the future.*

- **MotBW:** *Gotta say, I'm with her on this one, pal.*

- **TWS:** *But it makes perfect sense: just include a Realm before the Kingdom to determine which mystical 'common sense' the species developed in and a sub-sub species to act as an identifier of 'spiritual DNA'.*

- **WotL:** *And the fact that genetics stopped making sense several calamity cycles ago?*

- **TWS:** *Let me dream.*

Sidhe – Fairies, put simply. More broadly, the term 'sidhe' refers to those of fairy-kind that possess a human-like intelligence. That being said, they cannot be described as having 'Humanity' in the same way as much of the Folk or humans, coming from different origins and possessing strange perspectives on life. There are those like the Aos Sí and Snow-folk that are somewhat human, and can generally interact with humans as equals despite their shared origin, but most of them are entirely foreign, having originated from other-worlds in which the common sense of reality is different.

Fey or Fae – The broadest descriptor of fairies. Generally, the term is only used as a name for the members of fairy-kind that possess no human-like intelligence, but it can be used as an adjectival descriptor of the likes of the sidhe. Worth note that there's a whole lot of varieties that get lumped together without consideration for the subtle differences between them. For instance, the Seelie and Unseelie of Tycortua, Tylwyth Teg of Skahios, Gloaming and Auroral courts of Lacalba, and Hyakki Sith of Austall are all considered the same except for nationality despite important differences in nature and rules.

- **WotL:** *'Hyakki Sith'?*

- **TWS:** *Look. It's the best I could come up with since they do contain* *attributes of both.*

- ***MotBW:*** *I would point out Sith, Sí, and Sidhe are all fundamentally the same word.*

- ***WotL:*** *And for that matter, wouldn't Sith Yagyou make more etymological sense?*

- ***MotBW:*** *And that is more indicative of the same concept of Trooping Fairies than a group classification.*

- ***TWS:*** *Kris, help! My friends are being mean!*

- ***'GA':*** *You dug this hole. Fill it yourself.*

Herne's Folk – The residents of the other-world known as the Primeval Forest, created by the leader of the Wild Hunt, the Ageless Hunter Herne. They, and their leader, hold Humanity in contempt for the constant struggle beyond civilization and the natural world. While Herne's Folk do not actively war against Humanity, they often cause problems and consider any travelers lost in the woods fair game. Their mischief ranges from malicious pranks to outright hunts, depending on their target's disposition. They can be easily identified by the antlers that grow from their heads and the white harts they ride. Also worth note that they, much like the Snow-folk, are a kind of elemental being raised into near-Humanity. Hernus Homo Sapiens Cervus.

- ***TWS:*** *I don't suppose--*

- ***MotBW:*** *Nope. The 'Ageless Hunter' is still being a stuck up jerk. Not a chance of help unless either of the sealed Primordials break out or the Celestial Wall falls.*

Forest-folk – The descendants of the Ancient-folk who took shelter in the Forest of the Dead when the great calamity of ten thousand years prior struck the world and destroyed the Ancient-folk Empire. The unstable magic within them adapted itself to the Forest, granting them a connection to the magics of Water and 'soft' Earth, in the form of plant matter. Likewise, their eyes are adapted to the fogs of the Forest and can see through fog, mist, and smoke. They are faster, but at the cost of a more fragile constitution from lighter bones. Terrus Homo Sapiens Arcanus Sylvannus.

- **TWS:** *How crazy is it that after so long Elves actually just naturally developed?*

- **WotL:** *They aren't Elfs. Elfs are fae creatures and the Forest Folk are too Human.*

- **TWS:** *Spade a spade.*

Desert-folk – The descendants of the Ancient-folk who took shelter in the Hell Sea when the great calamity of ten thousand years prior struck the world and destroyed the Ancient-folk Empire. The unstable magic within them adapted itself to the desert, granting them a connection to the magics of Wind and 'dry' Earth, in the form of sand. Likewise, their senses adapted to the conditions of the desert such that they can sense vibrations through their hands and feet, as well as send out pulses of kinetic energy through their hands to sense pockets of water beneath the surface. They are tougher and overall more nimble than humans, albeit not as agile as Forest-folk or dexterous as Mountain-folk, but not quite as strong as humans in a general sense, much of their musculature dedicated to endurance over raw power. Terrus Homo Sapiens Arcanus Solitus.

Mountain-folk – The descendants of the Ancient-folk who took shelter in the mountains of another land when the great calamity of ten thousand years prior struck the world and destroyed the Ancient-folk Empire. The unstable magic within them adapted itself to those mountains, granting them a connection to the magics of Fire and 'hard' Earth, in the form of stone and metal. Likewise, they have a greater sensitivity to changes in the air, resulting from a combination of more sensitive olfactory capabilities and pressure detection within the ears, allowing them to gauge the safety of deeper caverns, where danger may not be visible. They are stronger and more dexterous than humans, but not quite as swift, taking a more scholarly lifestyle. Terrus Homo Sapiens Arcanus Montis.

- **MotBW:** *Continuing the theme: Dwarves?*

- **WotL:** *Continuing the theme: Dwarfs are fae. These are not.*

- **TWS:** *I'd still say they're more like Elves anyway.*

- **WotL:** *Why do I even bother?*

Void-folk – A race descended from the Ancient-folk that have been hypothesized, but never discovered. Since there are descendant races tied to Water, Wind, Fire, Light, and Magic, with all sharing a connection to Earth, it stands to reason there should be one with a connection to Dark, but they have not interacted with the world at large. I wouldn't worry about them if I were you. Terrus Homo Sapiens Arcanus Nihilus.

Citadel-folk – Like with the Void-folk, another one of the peoples who descended from the Ancient-folk. They fled across the ocean and built themselves citadels in which they study wisdom and knowledge. As such, they do not exist on the Lataoccas super-continent. Not especially relevant to the discussion at hand save for the fact that they exist. Terrus Homo Sapiens Arcanus Prudentius

Ancient-folk – They've been mentioned enough that I might as well put in a brief note. They were the race from which the rest of the Folk are descended. As a young race, they had a natural affinity for magic. This made them powerful, but also unstable, so when they fled their cities after the great calamity of ten thousand years prior, the one that started the current calamity cycle, this unstable magic mutated them into the rest of the Folk. Only their capital city of Lanturia weathered the storm, its inhabitants becoming known as Ancient-folk by the humans of following generations even though they should properly be called Mystic-folk. All but extinct now, after Lanturia was destroyed a little more than two thousand years ago. Not, as you might think, the ones who forged Ancient's Armor. Terrus Homo Sapiens Arcanus. Terrus Homo Sapiens Arcanus Magus for the Lanturians after the fall of their empire.

Steel-folk – Not, precisely, another member of the Folk, but the common name given to humanity by other races. It is worth not that each clan, as it were, of the Folk calls themselves human. They simply allow humanity to take the name because they do not wish to draw their ire. To this point, the particular appellation of Steel-folk does not refer to humanity's use of forged tools, but their grim determination. Among the Folk, it's said "You may anger one Steel-folk, or even two, but if you drive them into a corner they will resolve themselves and hunt you down with hearts of iron and minds of steel." History has given some merit to this attitude, since more than one species which threatened humanity was hunted to extinction. Terrus Homo Sapiens Sapiens Ferrus.

 • ***TWS:*** *Ha. 'Human'. As if they're anything like our old people.*

- ***WotL:*** *'Our' is a strong word.*

- ***TWS:*** *Yes, yes. But you know what I mean. These guys naturally use magic without even thinking about it. I'd bet the average Steel-folk would win a fist fight against an old human ten times out of ten.*

- ***MotBW:*** *Outside perspective here. The difference is negligible in the grand scheme of things.*

Demon-folk, Fair-folk, Quatrainians – The native people of the Demon Realm Morningstar. Split into three different peoples of Nobles, Knights, and Commoners, all have the same origin despite their differences. All are Human in mind and spirit, but only the Nobles and Commoners can be considered as Human in a taxonomical sense, Knights possessing diverse, beastly forms. Nobles are a bridge between the two, possessing both a humanoid form and beastly 'Noble Form', more powerful even than the Knights. Their technical name is Quatrainian, but a longstanding connection with the Sidhe, all the way back to their origin, has left them more than a little Fey and given them the title of Fair-folk. As for the title of Demon-folk, part of that is a result of their forms instilling fear in other Human races, but there is a certain kernel of truth in it. Put simply, their originator should have thought a bit more about what she was doing when she decided to make them in seventy-two distinct Houses. Quatrainus Homo Sapiens Nobilitus, Quatrainus Infernatus Sapiens Sapiens, and Quatrainus Homo Sapiens Sapiens, respectively. Spiritual genetic identifier depends upon which cycle of Houses the individual belongs to, according to Monarch.

<u>Human</u> vs. <u>human</u> – A subtle but important distinction. The former refers to the innate dignity possessed by those with, depending on personal philosophy, a soul and or sapience. Put another way, it's the quality of possessing an understanding brought up in the common sense of human-kind. Which brings us to the latter. Spelled as such, specifically with a lower case 'h', human refers to the race once known as 'Homo Sapiens Sapiens'. Noteworthy in that while the Steel-folk have the current claim to the title of humanity, and are admittedly the closest in current nature to that particular species, just about all Human races except for the Quatrainians believe themselves to be *the* human race.

Witch-white Hair – While witches themselves are a complicated and nuanced discussion, namely in the distinction between what a witch's oath entails and more explicit 'soul selling' of downright evil mages, the topic of their hair is an easier conversation. Simply put, all witches have the same white hair from the moment they swear their oath. For mystically relevant reasons, it can't be avoided and serves as an undeniable identifier. With that being said, it's important to distinguish between witch-white hair and naturally white hair since the latter still happens, mostly through old age. Witch-white hair is actually a kind of permanent illusion cast over the witch – in this way it bypasses even dyes and other attempts to alter the color. As such, chemical structure of the hair remains unchanged. You can distinguish between witch-white and natural white by the way it's... shaded, so to speak. Witch-white hair reflects light at a standardized angle, no matter the directional velocity of oncoming light. This gives it a kind of flat, monochrome cast that looks wrong to human sight. Likewise, the binding affects, to the best of my knowledge, all of a witch's hair, including eyelashes, eyebrows, and facial hair.

- *WotL: Thank the Lord you stopped there.*

- *TWS: That's neither a question I wish to ask nor an answer I wish to receive. Quoth Sincerity: "Have you ever considered there might be some questions you shouldn't ask?"*

- *WotL: Sincerity?*

- *MotBW: **Sigh.** Another problem you're forcing into my lap, isn't it?*

- *TWS: Hey, hey, hey. I'll be putting top agents on the case. But yes.*

Inception – One of the three pillars of magic. Inception governs, most broadly speaking, the cultural definition of magic an individual experiences. Put another way, it's the means by which a person views magic as a whole, the ways in which they believe magic can be expressed. The various 'schools of Inception' are the magical traditions learned among Humanity, each with their own capabilities defined by rules and guidelines.

Conception – One of the three pillars of magic. Conception is perhaps the most difficult to define because it, broadly speaking, governs how an individual perceives an individual bit of magic. Practically speaking, it determines the effect magic has on or by an individual because of what they think that bit of magic should do. Mages speak of shaping the Conception of the spell, and that's what is meant: altering how one thinks of the intention behind a spell and the effect it should take. More broadly, Conception is the limitations one puts upon magic in terms of what they believe is or is not possible by magic, even within their school of Inception. For example, it's far easier to conceive of a small effect taken upon something right in front of you than a large effect something halfway across the world. Quite frankly, just about the only major impossibilities for magic are true resurrection and negative time travel. And there are exceptions to both of those rules, the former if it is fueled by a spiritual miracle and the latter if the success of the time travel was verified in the past and causality is kept stable.

Conviction – One of the three pillars of magic. Conviction effectively defines what magic means to an individual on an individual level. It determines the extent to which they can use magic themselves, the extent to which they believe they can use magic. It tends to be a difficult quantity to define because it is at once a binary 'yes or no' and a gradient. If someone believes themselves to be incapable of using magic, if they have no Conviction, they won't be able to. And it's very difficult to change Conviction in that regard because it more or less means reorienting the common sense by which you live, telling yourself that the impossible is not in fact. On the other hand, not every mage can cast to the same strength and that's Conviction as well. If you think your spell will be weak, it will. The opposite is not necessarily true, but it is a critical first step.

The Guidelines of Physics – The laws by which the world functions in the absence of magical interference. Gravity and thermodynamics, for instance. They tend to work as they should most of the time, but magic outright ignores them as it pleases. For example, magic outright creates both matter and energy on a regular basis, though destruction can only be effected on recent magical creations, and the macroscopic view of the cosmos shows them expanding in open defiance of gravity, thanks to the Unlimited World Phenomenon. Looking at it on a human level, trying to apply the Guidelines of Physics to magic only makes it harder to cast spells. Magic dislikes being forced to abide by rules which are not its own, so trying to use the Guidelines to ensure an effect which doesn't match with your Conception of a spell will backfire and result in the spell doing nothing.

- ***WotL:*** *You know you're the only one who still cares about these?*

- **TWS:** *Ha. I'm hardly a scientist. I barely have the average level of training in these kinds of things.*

- **WotL:** *And yet...*

The 'Unlimited World Phenomenon' – The unofficial (as in named by me) natural phenomenon by which the universe is constantly expanding. This extends on just about every cosmological level. For example: Earth grows at a rate proportional to its current size. In response, the balance between it, its moon, and the other planets and the sun of the Sol system is adjusted so that they do not experience any gravitational disturbance. This puts it further from the sun, so Sol grows. Similarly, because it's larger and its orbit is wider, it no longer experiences the same circadian or seasonal cycles, so its rotational and revolutionary speeds accelerate, the increase in pressure this would exert on the planet's surface ending up diffused by the field generated by the Gaea Core. It's uncanny how well things adjust to preserve a set balance. Over the some thirty-five calamity cycles I've been alive, Earth's size has just about doubled, not counting other-worldly interference, and it's still going strong.

- **MotBW:** *'Gaea Core'?*

- **WotL:** *I hate that I get what he means by that.*

- **TWS:** *Yeah! It's the locus of mystical energy sourced by the planet itself. Still trying to figure out if it's sentient.*

- **MotBW:** *Please try not to accidentally anthropomorphize this one.*

Mystic Script – The written language used by mages. The language itself isn't all that important, just the fact that it's been standardized across most magical traditions. So the magical significance behind it grew because everyone used it, not the other way around. It is a fully functional language, it's just not commonly spoken in the modern world since it was the language of the Mystic-folk and all but four of them are dead. It does serve as the root for all of the other Folks' language, so it isn't without merit to learn. The script itself is also in that frustrating, cursive, runic script the Folk still use today. Impossible to read if you have bad handwriting.

Hero-mage – One of the Nyphean schools of Inception it revolves around superimposing the deeds of a mythical figure upon yourself and using magic to replicate that deed. Put more simply, temporarily enchanting yourself with a shadow of an ancient hero's power. Often a very powerful school, given the figures it emulates, but somewhat less varied because in order for the spell to work, you have to be doing something similar to the hero's deed. For instance, if you're trying to emulate the way a sailor killed a quasi-leviathan with a harpoon, you'd need to use a spear-like implement and be fighting an aquatic creature. If you were on land or using a sword, it wouldn't work because you aren't emulating the deed. Kind of a pain.

Glyphmaster – Term for the practitioners of one of the Skahian schools of Inception. It revolves entirely around filtering magic through particular glyphs and runes to produce an effect defined by the word written. It tends to be a school with slow preparation time, since the word needs to be made physically manifest, but it is incredibly reliable and quick to cast once the glyphs and runes are formed. More experienced casters can chain magic, using simple cantrips to form runes of light to cast on the fly. The best Glyphmaster in modern times uses something called 'Empty Tome Self-suggestion' to induce a kind of synesthesia that allows her to see glyphs merely by perceiving magical flows and cast nigh-instantaneously, proverbially emptying the spellbook of her mind into the world around her, but that's a rare form of genius.

- ***WotL:*** *'Empty Tome Self-suggestion'?*

- ***TWS:*** *Her title, not mine. And who am I to argue with the Champion of Skahios?*

Honing – A generic term for enchantments place upon weapons and tools that improve their destructive capacity, more or less. It's a more narrowly scoped term than warding because it just about only refers to enchantments that reinforce the material of a tool.

Warding – A generic term for enchantments placed upon armor, clothes, and jewelry that protect the wearer in some fashion. Most often, this is used to refer to the enchantments smiths use to reinforce the strength of armor's material, allowing the likes of bronze to become stronger than steel. So-called 'Siegebreaker Charms' also fall under the umbrella of wardings. These are a set of enchantments meant to disrupt the flow of magic and protect the wearer from spells which are either loosely formed or do not directly target the user. Wards are considered separate from wardings, despite the similar verbiage, as defined by the intended object enchanted. Simply put, wards aren't worn, wardings are.

Ghost Vision – A spell which grants the caster vision into the past. It can render inanimate objects perfectly, but struggles with anything living or magical in nature. Likewise, the 'memory' of the past fades with time, accelerating the more people and magic moves through the space. In an undisturbed location, a caster might be able to see as far back as a year. In a busy place like a town plaza, it would be difficult to see more than a few minutes back. Similarly wards can be placed to disrupt the memory permanence of a location, preventing anyone from seeing what happened there for a given time.

Augury – A spell which allows the caster to consult with a higher power of some sort. This can be a deity, the source of a great deal of philosophical discussion, or simply powerful other-worldly beings. The accuracy of the consultation largely depends on who is being asked. They can only answer what they know, after all, and some will only answer according to their disposition.

Lattice-stone – Stones which consist of crystallized elemental energy. More to the point they are loci of the particular element they are aspected to and facilitate in either bringing it into the world or directing its flows. They naturally grow in areas suffused with their particular element and come in two types: active and passive. Active stones constantly generate their aspected element, regardless of external influence. The rate of emission is constant, though application of the same element or unaffiliated magical energy can temporarily accelerate it. Passive stones do not emit the element naturally and instead store it until triggered by unaffiliated magic. A worthy complaint might be that strictly speaking all crystals are 'lattice stones', but the title was given to these because the particular lattice structure they hold actually transmits magical energy like nerves in a human body transmit electricity. The network increases in strength the larger it grows, so bigger lattice-stones are not only more powerful in channeling their energy, but more difficult to break.

- *WotL: Aren't all crystals lattice stones by definition?*

- *TWS: Quiet you.*

Magestone – Magic aspected lattice-stones. They are, admittedly, irregular among lattice-stones and not so much producers of magic as facilitators of it. They excel in either anchoring or conducting enchantments and spells, depending on whether the stone is passive or active, respectively. This makes them very useful in the construction of lattice devices, as they can transmit an intended effect and store it. His then refines the effect into something that can be transmitted more discreetly as a factor in another spell. Likewise, unaffiliated stones make for exceptional switches, as anyone can trigger them and they only emit a small spark of neutral magic, which can jump-start most spells. On a less engineering focused side of things, they can also be used to store vast quantities of magic, which tends to be useful for mages who need to cast more spells in one sitting than they are capable of in. Grow at the boundaries between Earth and other-worlds.

Waterstone – Water aspected lattice-stones. They constantly drip water, like an ice-cube that never fully melts. More importantly, this water is always clean. This makes them useful sources of drinking water, especially for travelers, as well as the fundamental basis of all modern towns and cities sewage systems. Just about every house in modern times will have at least one lattice-shower for bathing and an Everfull Pitcher for drinking. Aqueducts studded with waterstones pass greater masses of water across fields to irrigate crops and cisterns with waterstones in the wall supply large populations during siege. Sewers themselves use waterstones to ensure steady drainage and swift removal of waste. Waterstones are fairly common as well, growing naturally at the bottom of natural water sources like rivers and lakes.

Windstone – Wind aspected lattice-stones. They emit a gentle breeze. On their own, windstones aren't considered especially useful, but provide interesting effects when synthesized with other elements. Particularly, fire and ice make for good regulators of internal temperature and force stabilizes the directionality of the wind while the wind smooths the output of the force, making the synthesized stone useful for either steady, even force over long periods of time or launching objects at rapid speed with high accuracy. Grow in high places, where the air is thin and wind blows strong.

Icestone – Ice aspected lattice-stones. They naturally emit cold, despite the apparent paradox in defintion, making them useful for temperature regulation and especially refrigeration. Naturally grow in esepcially cold places, with the Frozen North above Austall one of the greatest sources of icestones.

Firestone – Fire apsected lattice-stones. They naturally emit warmth, so they are prominently used as a safer replacement for open flames in the likes of cooking and internal heating. Naturally grow in especially hot places, with the Hell Sea one of the greatest sources of firestones.

Sunstone – Light aspected lattice-stones. They naturally emit light and as such are used for internal lighting. Fairly straightforward. Grow in places that get lots of sunlight.

Forcestone – Kinetically aspected lattice-stones. They do nothing until provoked, at which point they emit bursts of kinetic energy. This makes them useful for moving things, but they are limited in scope because of Teufel's propulsion problem. Simply put, regulation of a forcestone's output is irregular and they can only output evenly at speeds between zero and five miles per hour or speeds in excess of mach one. They are still useful for carrying heavy loads, providing some form of transport that will never tire, and launching objects in a destructive capacity, but that's about it. Grow irregularly, at points where naturally ecosystems shift, even in subtle manners.

Endurestone – Earth aspected lattice-stones. They emit little energy themselves, by the nature of what earth is, but are notably all but indestructible. This same property can be extended to other objects with the proper enchantments and inscriptions, making them prized material in just about every field of construction. They naturally occur in lattice-stone caches deep below the earth, making them rare and difficult to mine as well.

Synthesized Stone – Artificial lattice-stones made by combining two or more differently aspected stones into one. The process is notably finicky, and can result in the destruction of all involved stones in an explosion of raw elemental force, but it's necessary since the operation of some devices requires more than one force be applied. For example, synthesized wind-forcestones make for superior levitation enchantments as the wind element stabilizes the output of the force and prevents the enchanted object from swaying. Alternatively, fire-sunstones are prized by weapon-smiths for their ability to emit directed burning rays.

Base Configuration – A manner of applying lattice-stones to an object with minimal alteration. In this form, the extend their natural field of influence around the object, as if it were part of the lattice-stone itself, and imbue it with the properties of their elemental force. This allows simple but effective enchantments such as swords that ignite what they strike or armor that can absorb lighting, the intention of the enchanted object determining the 'polarity' of the elemental force, so to speak.

Galecaster – A lattice-stone device meant to overcome the capabilities of a standard crossbow. It used a synthesized force-windstone set at the base of a long barrel to propel bolts forward at incredible speeds. As in, about half the speed of sound, incredible speeds. Very useful weapons in terms of distance, penetrating power, and aiming capabilities. Though their most useful feature might be ease of loading, since all you have to do is drop a bolt down the barrel. But they're also, for the most part, prohibitively expensive. Synthesized stone aside, you need properly reinforced bolts and proper wardings on the barrel of the weapon itself in order to fire it, all of which requires a significant investment of time by expert lattince engineers. A cheaper alternative to lattice cannons, sure, but still expensive. They also, still have the crossbow's eponymous cross at the front, even though it isn't needed for the weapon to operate. Marksmen say it throws off aim if it isn't there, but it's just in their heads.

Autoquills and Letterboards – Lattice devices which operated based on an enchantment of sympathetic bonds. The letterboard is a simple, wooden board carved with the letters of the alphabet. The enchantment links the letters carved to the autoquill such that when a letter is touched, the quill will write the appropriate letter in the hand to which the quill was originally calibrated to. The back of the board, where the mechanics of the enchantment are implement, is a mess of bronze wiring and magestones. Each letter has its own magestone wired to a central hub. This hub stone is then sympathetically linked to one near the tip of the quill, relaying the signal of the letter. Distance causes interference in the bond and letterboards can't be used more than thirty feet from their autoquill.

Everfull Pitcher – Or bottle, jug, bowl, etc. Any sort of vessel that's been set with waterstones in an appropriate formation so that they continually produce fresh water. The systems have been all but perfected by now, so there's even models with icestones accompanying to keep the water chilled or firestones you can activate to easily boil it for tea and such. Most models have a runic line that senses when water touches them and deactivates the waterstone, so you never even need to worry about turning it off or on.

Defianium – An incredibly heavy and durable metal, made from an alloy of Hernesteel and tungsten that's been suffused with earth aligned magic, often as a result of nearby deposits of Endurestone. It's too heavy to use for anything particularly mobile, but works great for reinforcing buildings and stuff. It has a high melting point and is one of the most durable metals known, so anything reinforced with it will be very difficult to break.

Iron – The metal formed by the chemical element iron. Simple as that. But it is worth note that it's utterly magically inert. Can't be affected by magic, can't be changed by magic, absorbs the magic of those who intentionally hold it. Nothing else to it. Can't even be used as an anti-magic measure because it only disrupts pure magic, not the physical effects of it. As such, the people of the modern world have passed it over for metals which can achieve similar or better performance and easier forging with proper enchanting. To that point, even the forging process of steel has been forgotten because no one sees any point to experimenting with iron. Notably, iron from before the gates of the Realms and other-worlds were re-opened is exempt from this and evolved into something else entirely, called 'Cold Iron'. Similarly, there are incredibly specific magic nullification enchantments that can only be applied to iron as it's forged, transforming it into Nihil Iron. Both materials are incredibly rare and valuable.

Nihil Iron – Iron whose magical inertness has been reinforced by anti-magic enchantments. It no longer merely repels magic from itself, but consumes magic it comes into contact with. It's immune to all magic, and can cut through spells and shields, though it still struggles against the physical results of spells, like a shield of compressed air for example. Only occurs naturally in the scales of true dragons and only one family of Mountain-folk to the far west of Lacalba knows how to forge it.

Elemental Alloys – Just a side note, really, but it's more convenient to get it out of the way now. Metals that naturally grow with an affinity for a given element, all named after the respective member of the Seven Primordials. Sirisium for wind, Vivieryl for water, Sophinum for light, Lilithium for dark, Athanum for fire, Hernesteel for earth, and Adamuadria, of all things, for Magic. Don't worry too much about it. Also not alloys, but don't quibble too much.

- ***MotBW:*** *Didn't* you *name Adamuadria?*

- ***TWS:*** *I didn't think it would stick.*

Thousand-year Willow – Once more, exactly what it sounds like. Wood from a willow tree that's a thousand years old. Not especially exciting on its own, but the sheer magical significance behind anything living that long, especially since a willow tree *needs* magic to live that long, makes it a powerful catalyst for magical objects, especially those associated with the 'soft' earth element, or plant matter, and the water element. Good for staffs and wands.

Ancient's Armor – Not, in fact, armor that was made by the Ancient Folk. I reiterate. It's actually far, far older than the Ancient Folk and they were just as stumped as the humans when trying to replicate it. The best they could manage were the battle suits of their Stone Defender pilots, but I digress. Ancient's Armor refers to seven suits of full plate mail that are each imbued with a fragment of primordial elemental energy. This makes them just about the toughest armor on the planet and enhances the physical capabilities of the wearer, the particular focus depending on the element. Each also gives the wielder a limited control over the element of choice, making them a devastating weapon to face. The flame plate was worn by the Ember King, the wind plate by Zephyros, and the darkness plate by the Dusk Tyrant. The light plate was recently uncovered in Auran territory and the water and earth plates were lost a long time ago. Don't worry about the magic plate, it's probably fine. Also the largest contribution to the dearth of plate mail in modern times, since people have taken to the mistaken belief that so much armor needs Ancient's Armor enchantments to work or it'll be too heavy. The fact that they can't replicate Ancient's Armor has led to most smiths giving up on even trying for a lesser model of warded plate mail.

Whisperwind – The legendary blade of the Storm Warlord that has been passed down with his Ancient's Armor by the Crownguard family for generations. Its enchantments are powerful, giving it increased speed on top of the natural lightness the Sirisium its forged from gives and imbuing each of its strikes with electricity, but that's not where its true power lies. Though just about no Crownguard has used it properly since Zephyros, its true worth comes in acting as something like a tuning fork for Zephyros' personal magic 'Lightning Blood'. Actually a sylphid blade forged on West March, for what that's worth.

Dawnsong – A magical sword passed down by the generals of the Auris Empire. While it is a treasured blade noteworthy enough to be named, it should be noted that it isn't equal in power to Whisperwind and nowhere near the likes of true holy blades or weapons that have sublimated to mythic status. Its enchantments focus primarily upon destructive force, shrouding the blade in fire and light that burns targets. Forged from a bronze-Sophinum alloy.

Sunfire – The sword of the Ember King, Ignatius. It's actually kind of a ridiculous sword since it's not only a holy blade, but a true mythic weapon. Originally belonging to a dragon-slaying knight from a little over thirty-five calamity cycles ago, the holy enchantments on it give it increased effectiveness against undead monsters, demons, and, of course, dragons, allowing it to cut through the scales and hides of such monsters with ease as well as granting the wielder resistance to spells they might cast and draconic fire. Furthermore, the enchantments built up by sheer age and mythic quality surround it with an aura of holy fire that burns the unholy while leaving the innocent unscathed. Best described as an arming sword with a squared tip. Seems to have been forged of damascened steel, before iron's magical inertness was even a problem. Age metamorphosed it into something different, stronger, and magically capable. A truly unique metal that surpasses even Cold Iron.

- ***MotBW:*** *'Holy blade'? 'Mythic weapon'?*

- ***TWS:*** *Yeah. I classified mystic weapons according to power and source on a grid of three. Ranges between enchanted, mythic, and divine. Holy blades are of the sacred source and stronger than Blessed Weapons but weaker than the Empyreal Swords.*

- ***WotL:*** *And where do the Cutsteels fit into this?*

- ***TWS:*** *Same category as Empyreal, but elemental instead of holy. I call them 'Primordial Blades'.*

The Sunfire Empire – The empire founded by the Ember King, Ignatius Valeria, over the course of his campaign against the Dusk Tyrant. It eventually grew to cover the whole of Chevaladin except for Tycortua, which he allowed his friend Zephyros to maintain control of, and the Threefold Eye, separated from the mainland by the ocean. Its capital lay where World's Eye now stands, Pazyerra the last remnants of it after its fall in 980 R.S.

The Order of the Eagle, the Watchers at Midnight – An order of free-knights and free-mages founded on the Threefold Eye after the Dusk Tyrant was slain. As neither Nypheos nor Lugherion felt their ancient grudge was worth continuing if the world was at stake, they established the Order to preserve peace between the two of them and to keep watch for any other calamities that may come to pass like the Dusk Tyrant. In modern times, it is one of two great neutral powers, along with the Monarchy of Pazyerra, and is devoted to preserving the safety of Chevaladin. Though originally consisting only of Nypheans and Lugheri, they accept all who share their mission and are one of the most multicultural organizations on the continent. Based in the City of the Scales.

The Western Alliance – A political alliance between the nations of Tycortua, Perlora, and Rugego. Mostly meant to act as a countermeasure against the growing power of the Auris Empire, it also has policies included regulated things such as trade between the three nations and the allocation of military aid, should such an eventuality come to pass.

Wardens – The warrior caste of the Forest Folk, also known as 'Gray Ghosts' for the cloaks they wear, colored after the fog of the Forest of the Dead. Originally established as a force to wipe out the web-spinners indigenous to the forest that plagued the Folk, they are now the closest thing the Forest Folk have to an army. That being said, they are more hunters than soldiers, providing game for their villages and slaying monsters within the boundaries of the Forest. They are also the most commonly seen of the Forest Folk, venturing beyond the Forest to track down and slay monsters that have escaped. Tradition demands that Wardens face their trials at the age of one hundred, when the Forest Folk officially recognize themselves as having the proper mental maturity of an adult, and upon induction they are given a fog cloak and Warden blade, carved from wood and strengthened by many Druidic enchantments. Each Warden also receives a new name on rising to the position, often in reference to a predator of some kind.

Silver Moons – A silver coin, part of the standardized currency established by the Sunfire Empire. The exact coinage varies in modern times, depending on the nation, but the value is equivalent across borders, roughly five copper stars to one silver moon, four silver moons to a golden sun, and five golden suns to a platinum nebula. From there, crystal galaxies and diamond realms are too expensive for use as a common denomination. The same system of currency is actually used in the Realms, like Morningstar, too, since it came by way of Lanturia and Zephyros made sure to keep his kingdom's money consistent with his own.

- ***WotL:*** *It's all weight based anyway. As long as the coins are properly verified, nobody cares where it came from.*

Empire Common – The language spoken by the people of the Sunfire Empire. Though there are still native tongues scattered across the continent, just about everyone speaks Empire Common because of how far-spread the

Empire was. The alphabet it uses is, thankfully, the basic one standardized millennia ago by persons who will go thanklessly unnamed for all time. Truly a shame that people who worked so hard to make sure languages were readable will go unknown.

- ***WotL:*** *I don't know why you're so obsessed with that accursed script. It has no artistry.*

- ***TWS:*** *Yeah, but it's legible. I've dealt with too many mystic languages that think symbology means significance.*

Linguistic Addendum – It should be noted that in the preceding text, any words that are not rendered in my native tongue are *not* the actual words used, much like how I'm not actually writing in Empire Common. Generally speaking, any foreign word of that sort is meant to approximate the same sentiment as to what those currently living in Chevaladin would say. For example, Nyphean soldiers might be described as 'hoplites' and 'toxotai' both because those words do a good job of describing the equipment and strategy of such soldiers as well as adhering to the general flavor Nyphean culture, as it were. On the other hand, Rugegan 'cataphracts' and 'landsknecht' only really fulfill the former purpose, so this isn't always a perfect metric. Definition takes priority over culture, so case by case basis. The only notable exception to this is Old Sídhe or what the Quatrainians call 'High Royal'. That is rendered precisely as it is spoken.

- ***WotL:*** *Or you could, you know, actually* learn *the language.*

- ***TWS:*** *Come on! What's the point when they'll all be dead in one calamity cycle, tops.*

- ***MotBW:*** *You know this is why the rest of the world disliked your people.*

- ***WotL:*** *And what about that 'Babel Mending' enchantment of yours? Why haven't you distributed that to the populace?*

- ***TWS:*** *Well, some of my experiments aren't exactly... What's the word I'm looking for?*

- ***'GA':*** *Ethical?*

- ***TWS:*** *Yes. Thank you, Kris. I'm fine carving spells into my own flesh* *and bone, but I don't think that's something that should become wide-spread practice.*

The Realms' Calendar – For clarity's sake, the Realms, including Earth, follow a calendar of three hundred and sixty-five days in a year, spread across twelve months. The months are Lilius, Glacians, Viviaus, Hernus, Gaians, Aquans, Sophius, Athanasius, Inferns, Ventans, Adam, and Sirius. The new year starts with Lilius on the winter solstice and every three months marks the change of a season. Each season has ninety-one days, except for summer and every fourth winter, Glacians receiving an extra day known as the 'Lost Day'. The days of the week are Sunday, Moonday, Ashday, Anemoday, Loamday, Seaday, and Magiaday. The current year is listed as 1980 R.S., or Realms Standard. It should be noted that the year is marked as 2000 in Chevaladin, but Realms Standard tends to be a more useful metric.

- ***TWS:*** *And the current calamity cycle is the 36th, for those keeping track.*

- ***WotL:*** *Are you going to explain what a calamity cycle is?*

- ***TWS:*** *Come on! It's a super useful unit of time measuring fourteen millennia. I needed something in between millennia and eons.*

- ***MotBW:*** *What's wrong with eons? At least they aren't arbitrary.*

The Forest of the Dead – A massive, eternally foggy, forest to the north of the continent. It spreads from the northern foothills of the Stormwall Mountains to the Frozen North and extends all the way across the vast reaches of the Lataoccas super-continent until it thins out into the Silvamarca of Lacalba, subcontinent of the Silver Crescent League. It's notable for two things: A) Serving as home to the Forest Folk and B) Naturally drawing in untethered undead through unknown means. As a result of the latter, it's infested with a wide assortment of undead creatures and traveling through it is considered all but a death sentence for anyone not of the Forest Folk. It was also once home to the giant web-spinners, but the Forest Folk eradicated them after an extensive campaign.

- ***TWS:*** *Thank goodness. The web-spinners never should have existed.*

- ***WotL:*** *While I would point out spiders on principle serve an important role, I can't say I disagree.*

The Stormwall Mountains – A treacherous mountain range that splits the continent. Much as with the Forest of the Dead, it extends across the Lataoccas super-continent, but the range slides to the south as it continues east, eventually forming the south-western border of Lacalba. The mountains themselves are largely unexplored because they serve as the habitat for a wide variety of mystic beasts and experience a larger than average other-worldly influence. If you fail to adhere to the proper trails while traveling through them, you will almost certainly end up in some other-world or another, and few of the ones connected to the mountains are pleasant. The Mountain Folk make their home in some of the safer peaks and valleys of the range, with settlements like Solitude managing to claim notoriety outside of the Folk. Ash-Star Tomb also lies with the Stormwalls, atop Mount Sunrest in the Valleys of Death.

- ***MotBW:*** *Ah. 'Mount Sunrest'? Was it not Dusk's End?*

- ***TWS:*** *That's a poetic name given to the peak since it was the site of the Dusk Tyrant's end. And you know that. Why are you asking?*

- ***MotBW:*** *Just giving you grief. Wouldn't be the first time you forgot something.*

The Hell Sea – A vast desert to the south-east of the continent. Compared to the Forest of the Dead and the Stormwall Mountains, it's perhaps as large as the two of them put together and makes up a majority of the central region of the Lataoccas super-continent. It more than anything else is responsible for separating the three subcontinents of Chevaladin, Lacalba, and Marivento. It's separated from Lacalba and the Silver Crescent League by little more than a strip of the Stormwalls and acts as a secondary northern border of Marivento and Vallemor, the kingdom of the Dragon-folk, another hazard beyond their Exile Mountains. The desert itself lives up to the name and is infested with a wide variety of horrible creatures, a large majority of them vaguely insectoid. The Desert Folk make their home there and are one of the few people to have any sort of connection between the subcontinents, their caravans actually stretching from Chevaladin to Lacalba.

Realms – Worlds similar to Earth and yet different, tethered to it at appropriate physical anchoring points. There are eleven in total, including Earth which is not technically a Realm, numbering one for each Primordial Element, one each for the sun and moon, and Morningstar. To differentiate them from other-worlds, they're more like copies filtered to be of an appropriate element. To put it in metaphor, if a world is a single cell in the great tree of reality, then the Realms and Earth are all near-identical nuclei contained within the same, single cell wall. Another way to differentiate is the manner of connection. Other-worlds do not share a physical reality with Earth, but because their manner of connection thins the walls of reality, they can be physically accessed. Realms, though they share something of a physical reality with Earth, cannot be physically reached. Travel between them must be accomplished through mystical means, or short-cutting through other-worlds. The Silver Realm is an exception, but it is an exception among Realms too. Morningstar is noted for being incredibly difficult to travel from and more difficult to travel to.

- *MotBW: Another point of nuance would be that Realms can be constructed, but other-worlds cannot.*

- *TWS: Wait. Does this mean Brocéliande and the Isle of Apples are Realms too?*

- *WotL: It's complicated. Kind of a chicken and egg situation with their respective rulers.*

Morningstar, the Demon Realm – The second of the Realms created, after the Silver Realm of the Moon. As such, it was created without a proper understanding of the process and tethered to an unsuitable physical anchor. This makes it a treacherous world to live in, the fabric of reality itself tormented by regular storms in the aether-chaos. This makes it both a largely inhospitable place filled with mystic beasts more alien and dangerous than can be found in the other Realms and a Realm that requires particular safety measures to travel to and from. The native people are split into three different, though related, races: the Nobles, Knights, and Commoners, all referred to by the appellations of Demon-folk, Fair-folk, or Quatrainian. Other people have since immigrated to the Realm and there are several non-Quatrainian kingdoms, though they are not as prominent. The separation Morningstar has from the other Realms has insulated it somewhat from the calamities that regularly threaten the Realms which has the twin effects of leaving them somewhat more advanced and also capable of building more power on an individual level, making them more often than not the source of the larger problems that threaten the Realms.

Other-world – Spaces connected to Earth that are decidedly not Earth. A specific definition of them is difficult to truly pin down as a result of their variety. For example, both the Fey Demesnes and the domain of Nypheos' Hall of the Moon can be considered other-worlds, but they are not even remotely the same kind of world. Put simply, they're the kind of mystical land a traveler could find themselves slipping into if they walk through the wrong stretch of land. The most important feature in distinguishing an other-world is that they follow a different common sense than Earth's. To this point, though similar, they're different from Realms. Realms could be considered as something like a copy of Earth tethered to it through inhumanly complex magic. They share the same origin and followed (almost) the same path with only slight alterations according to the element of the Realm. Other-worlds, on the other hand, have a completely separate origin to Earth and only interact with it through a kind of magically induced super-positioning.

Void-Space – The space between the Realms, something like the connective tissue that binds them together. Decidedly not the void of space, between the planets and the stars, it's a strange place that's not quite other-world but not quite real-space either. Things work strangely there and distance becomes more of a guideline than a rule. It's hypothetically infinite, and for this reason many people use it as an extradimensional space to magically store objects in when they don't need them, but one with the proper ability to enter and traverse Void-Space could use it to literally walk between Realms. Likewise, there *are* things living within Void-Space, though all of them are considerably alien to Earth and the Realms.

Chephirah Camdyn, the Lioness of the North, the Galeforce Warden, the Unrivaled Blade, etc. - The greatest of the Forest Folk Wardens, a warrior bearing a rare epithet elemental affinity, that of 'Promised Victory'. She rose from obscurity near one hundred and fifty years ago, passing the trials to become a Warden at the young age of thirty. From there, she became an acclaimed figure and hero, attaining victory after victory and defeating villain after villain. But when she went against the Forest Folk elders' orders and killed Sanborn of Montiamon in the name of helping a friend, the elders declared that she had become intoxicated by her own self-righteousness and exiled her to the east, past the far reaches of their civilization. Though most agree they could do nothing to force her to follow their orders, she accepted, and has not been seen since.

Sanborn and Ivalyn – A story of nearly five decades ago and one that's proven to be somewhat contentious on the continent. Most people see it as a grand heroic tale, in which the great Chephirah Camdyn saved her friend Ivalyn from being forced into marrying the evil king of Montiamon. That the marriage was politically arranged and King Sanborn was largely regarded as a fair ruler before this instance are facts largely ignored. Either way, Chepirah Camdyn did duel King Sanborn and, predictably, killed him, 'freeing' Ivalyn. This of course led to her exile by the elders of the Forest Folk, since they'd expressly forbidden her from doing exactly that out of fear of war, but most humans of the continent still see her as a great hero, finding her punishment unfair.

Dreith, the Desert Folk Champion – A divisive figure and folk hero. A Desert Folk hunter, there are many stories of Dreith fighting monsters in the depths of the Hell Sea and protecting trade caravans traveling to Heartfire Bastion. Dreith and his stories are popular with many nobles of the lands near the Hell Sea, because of the thrilling fights described against such terrifying monsters and the Romance surrounding a figure cultivated as a dashing, exotic swashbuckler who defends the innocent, but members of the Folk have a notably sour view of him, seeing the stories as a deliberate ploy for fame and fortune, framing the simple actions of his job, things any hunter are supposed to do, as adventures of great heroism. According to them, he's as arrogant as the 'Desert Lion' was in his youth.

King Wilvan – A Pazyerran king of some five centuries ago. Having re-covered a set of Ancient's Armor from the remnants of the Sunfire Empire's treasury, he proclaimed himself the rightful emperor of the whole continent, the inheritor of the Sunfire Empire's legacy, and tried to use the Ancient's Armor's might to unify the land through conquest. He was stopped before much of his campaign could begin by the Gray Knight of Viemer. It's unclear which element of Ancient's Armor he wore, but scholars agree it makes the most sense for it to have been either the flame plate of Ignatius or the dark plate of the Dusk Tyrant. Storyteller's tend to favor the latter interpretation, for dramatic flair.

The Gray Knight of Viemer – A fabled figure that supposedly wears one of the seven sets of Ancient's Armor, though scholars can't agree on which element the plate represents. Stories about the Gray Knight have existed since even before the Ember King, leaving it unclear if the title has been passed down among the bearers or possessed by a single inhuman figure. The most famous tale of the Gray Knight is *The Uncrowning of King Wilvan* in which the Gray Knight confronted the Pazyerran king in the midst of his madness and demanded he step down or pay the price for his injustice. The crown still hanging on the Gray Knight's lance, embedded in the wall of the throne room, is proof of how that encounter went.

The Black Knight of Naktikos – A fabled figure much like the Gray Knight of Viemer who supposedly wears one of the seven sets of Ancient's Armor. Much of the Black Knight's profile is similar to the Gray Knight's, though stories about him have only been around for about one thousand years, his armor is usually believed to be the plate of darkness simply for its color, and regardless of whether or not it has been the same man the Black Knight has certainly always been male, simply based on the voice. Often roams the north of the continent, slaying dragons and the like.

Judge Gidiar and Taredson – An old Austallan ballad revolving around one of their old religious generals and his struggles against the Sidhe residing in the northern forests. It tells about how his home city was suffering under the rule of the fairy lord Ys Abdon, who demanded tribute of five young men and women each year to serve in his court. When Gidiar's betrothed was chosen for the next tribute, he traveled east to Naktikos and asked for help from his uncle, the lord of a nearby hold. With the help of his uncle's knights, he embarked on many adventures, fighting against Ys Abdon's fey. The specific story of this ballad is Taredson, a demon boar who served as one of Ys Abdon's generals. The story of the hunt is long, and Gidiar ends up fighting seven other boars before Taredson, but popular because of the wide array of characters and innocent tale of good and evil it presents.

The Demonblade of Austall – A figure from the tales of the Saint of Swords and one of her greatest rivals. In fact her brother, the Demonblade of Austall trained long and hard to become a better swordsman than her, even inventing a new system of Mystic Arts he called 'Critical Will', not sourced in Magic, Ki, or Aura. To prove himself better than his famed sister, he cut a bloody path across the north until she finally challenged and defeated him, forcing him to flee beyond the sea.

- *TWS: Can either of you explain how Critical Will works for me?*

- *MotBW: Not a clue.*

- ***WotL:*** *I thought this was your thing.*

- ***TWS:*** *I mean, I get why it works, but not how it works.*

The Saint of Swords – A famed Austallan hero, a genius swordsman who took up a position as a justiciar at the age of fifteen. Referred to as 'Saint' because of her role as a holy warrior of the Austallan faith, protecting the innocent and punishing the wicked. Famously defeated the Demonblade of Austall and repeatedly clashed with the Riptide Captain. In her youth, she ranged far and wide, seeking battles with a seemingly zealous fervor, but appears to have calmed down in modern days, retiring to her home in pursuit of philosophy and meditation when a mission does not require her presence.

The Riptide Captain – A folk hero mostly popular as a result of the pulp dramas written about her. Previously a pirate captain, she raided the southern coasts of the continent for years until her defeat at the hands of the Saint of Swords. Since then, she apparently had a change of heart and turned her strength to capturing her old comrades. In modern times, she is one of the preeminent explorers of the continent, venturing further out to sea than any other and facing monsters and sights none have seen. This, if nothing else, is what draws authors to her tale.

The Spell-blade of Maripphi – An old grand duelist of the Maripphi circuit. He was famous for the variety of enchantments he could lay upon his sword and the speed with which he could switch enchantments. This led him to three consecutive victories in the championships. He is more well-known, however, for his life after the Maripphi circuit. Growing disillusioned with the state of his homeland, where soldiers did little but fight for personal glory in duels and scholars locked themselves away from the world in their ivory towers the hopes of furthering magical discovery, he turned his efforts towards helping the commoners. The latter half of his life was spent protecting villages from monsters and defeating magi who believed any sacrifice was worth progress, even if it meant using other people as test subjects. He was beloved by the common folk for this, but the rulers of Maripphi did not like how close his campaign strayed to their research and declared him a traitor. Refusing to back down or flee, he was caught and hung from the gates of Rainhome. All in power at the time were deposed and killed in the ensuing riots, however.

The Golden Hills Raider – Not precisely a hero, per se, the Golden Hills Raider is a popular figure of folk lore in the south of the continent. In modern times, 'The Golden Hills Raider' is a title used as something of a bogeyman, a villain parents can use to frighten their children to behave, saying things like 'do your chores or the Raider will kidnap you'. Historically, the title is known to have been used by several bandit leaders in the Golden Hills, passed down from leader to leader.

The Flame-speaker – The first empress of the Auris Empire. Before her, Auris was only a small kingdom in the south of Chevaladin, notable for its devotion to the Endless Flame and the ideals of the Ember King. When the Flame-speaker was born, however, she possessed strange, platinum colored eyes and her parents brought her before the clerics of the Endless Flame once she was old enough to speak. Much to their surprise, she claimed to hear their deity's voice and prophesied to prove it. From then, she led the country according to the Endless Flame's words and, with the Knight of Gold-fire at her side, began its conquest of the nearby kingdoms. This conquest was justified with a prophecy about how the empire needed to 'grow strong for the day of eclipse, in which embers would be smothered, flame extinguished, and darkness would swallow the stars above'. After her, leadership of the Auris Empire was no longer dictated by blood, but whoever was born with platinum eyes after the previous ruler's death.

- ***WotL:*** *Platinum, eh?*

- ***MotBW:*** *I'm pretty sure it's just coincidence. I don't think my sister was ever there.*

- ***TWS:*** *Really?* ***Coincidence?*** *With one of your siblings involved?*

- ***MotBW: Sigh.*** *If she's willing to talk, I can ask.*

The Knight of Gold-fire – A wandering knight originally banished from his homeland. Little is known about his early life, but he somehow managed to find the plate of light and used it as he journeyed around Lacalba to test his strength against other knights. Eventually, his journey brought him to Dawnbreak and he found himself before the Flame-speaker. Something about her struck him and he swore his allegiance to her. In exchange, she gave him the sword Dawnsong and command over the Empire's armies. Notable in that he explicitly swore allegiance to the Flame-speaker, not the Endless Flame or the Empire itself. He was their strongest knight and pushed the Empire's borders with an unrivaled momentum until he fell in battle against the Gray Knight of Viemer

The Four Monarchs of Morningstar – Worth note since Xavier keeps mentioning the Summer Queen. The Quatrainian people have four nations on Morningstar, each ruled by one of the Four Monarchs. Calaze is ruled by the Fall Prince, Suanberg the Winter Queen, Fragnaheim by the Spring Prince, and Aeslios by the Summer Queen. The current Summer Queen, who Xavier and the Stormtide family directly serve, is one Elaine Valgrim, a sensible ruler who makes a study of the natural ebb and flow of magic and fertility of the land in the face of mystical calamity.

Teufel – An old Montian theoretical lattice engineer. He specialized in the study of propulsion and general force dynamics and was the first scholar to write extensively on the so-called Teufel's Propulsion Problem. Namely the fact that forcestones have inconsistent output that can't be regulated evenly. He tried a good many things, with the intention of building vehicles like the fabled Lanturian Stone Defenders, but could never manage to make anything worthwhile.

- ***WotL:*** *Why are you so obsessed with those things?*

- ***TWS:*** *Because they're **so cool**. Just look at the pilot armor.*

- ***WotL:*** *Yeah, well Misericorde's the only one who still has a suit, so I'll pass.*

The Champions of the Four Corners – The four heroes who led the resistance against the rule of the Dusk Tyrant, eventually defeating him at Ash-Star Tomb. The Ember King, Storm Warlord, River Sage, and Crystal Queen, they were named as such because they came from all lands and wielded the power of the four common elements. They were some of the greatest warriors and mages of their generation, the kind of rare geniuses that can change the course of history with just their power.

The Ember King – The hero who slew the Dusk Tyrant, the founder of the Sunfire Empire, leader of the Champions of the Four Corners, Ignatius Valeria. Originally the prince of a small nation to the south-east of the continent, after defeating the Dusk Reaver when it attacked his kingdom's capital, he rode forth on a holy campaign of justice (the tales' words, not mine) to defeat the Dusk Reaver's master, guided by the voice of the Endless Flame. The entire story's a whole thing, but in short, he united the nations under his banner and with his most trusted companions stormed Ash-Star Tomb, the temple topping Mount Sunrest and killed the Dusk Tyrant in a fight that's been described in suitably overblown terms by countless epics and ballads. From there, history agrees that he returned triumphant to the lands he'd united who more or less forcibly crowned him their emperor. His title comes from a combination of his sword, Sunfire, and his Ancient's Armor, which is agreed to have been the flame plate.

- ***MotBW:*** *Are we not going to talk about it?*

- ***TWS:*** *No.*

The Storm Warlord – Zephyros Stormtide, Quatrainian Noble of House Grian. Naturally, he was a pretty big deal. After coming to Earth from Morningstar, he decided he needed to rally humanity to fight against the heir of Lord Morata's power and decided to do that the only way he knew how: through conquest. He brought all of the land in modern Tycortua under his control before the Ember King took notice. Since neither of them were going to back down, they ended up dueling and somehow Ignatius won. Honestly, that more than anything should speak volumes to how talented a swordsman the Ember King was, since Whisperwind is nearly Sunfire's match, both wore Ancient's Armor, and Zephyros also had access to his Noble Form. Either way, his title comes from the enchantments upon Whisperwind, the wind plate he wore, and his magic known as 'Lightning Blood'. After the war, history states he returned to his kingdom and ruled until his death.

The River Sage – The Ember King's first companion, Seras is something of an anomaly in the Champions of the Four Corners as the only one of their number that was, more or less, just a normal person. Where Ignatius and Zephyros (arguably) were royalty and Regina a mysterious foreigner, Seras was just a village mage who joined the fight after Ignatius passed through her hometown. That being said, she was a village mage strong enough to completely defend her hometown from the Dusk Tyrant's army of monsters and fight on an equal level with knights wearing Ancient's Armor. As her title indicates, her magical abilities were focused largely around hydromancy and cryomancy, though it's generally agreed she used holy magic more often than either of those. The strangest thing about her is that while the stories agree she was originally from somewhere around Maripphi or Viemer, they also agree she ended up settling down somewhere in Zephyros' territory after the war, founding the likes of

Chancewind Monastery. No reasons for why she went there instead of home have been given.

The Crystal Queen – Perhaps the strangest of the Champions of the Four Corners, the Crystal Queen was a traveler from an unknown land who took up Ignatius' fight for her own inscrutable reasons. Her claim to fame lies in her magical ability, largely revolving around lithomancy which gave her the Earth inspired name. Some tales claim her homeland was devastated by the Dusk Tyrant as well, despite the fact that no known nation claims to be her home, and some scholars use this to claim she had a personal stake. Other scholars argue she was simply a woman with such a just heart that she could not ignore the Dusk Tyrant's villainy, and thus left her homeland to join the fight. Either way, it is agreed that after the Dusk Tyrant was killed and the continent saved, Regina Norn Silvercross left for her home once more, vanishing from history.

The Dusk Tyrant – The enemy the Champions of the Four Corners faced. Originally the general of a kingdom in the lands of modern day Viemer, he somehow managed to grasp the dark power of the Quatrainian Lord Morata. Using it, he swept through the unprepared lands and conquered them with an army of both human soldiers that rallied to his strength and dark creatures called forth using his own powers. After bringing much of the continent under his control, he marched on Ash-Star Tomb. Desperate to prevent him from achieving his goals, the Champions of the Four Corners set off in pursuit, defeating him at the brink of his victory. He was reanimated on the millennial anniversary of his defeat, but that was nothing more than a death knight, a hollow shell of the man that once existed, bound together by dark power. Wore the dark aligned Ancient's Armor and wielded a corrupted magic blade whose name has been forgotten.

- *TWS: Speaking of, how precisely did he get his hands on the Mortal Sequence?*

- *WotL: Why do you think I would know? I'm not responsible for all of my brother's weapons.*

- *TWS: Then why do you keep demanding I give you Rhonny?*

- *WotL: Because it **isn't yours**.*

The Dusk Reaver – A member of the Dusk Tyrant's army who would not even warrant a footnote in history were it not for the fact that it was the first enemy the Ember King faced in his campaign to save the continent. Information on it is scarce, and all anyone can agree upon is that it was some kind of monster former of darkness.

The Scalebound – The hero who defeated the Dusk Tyrant when he was resurrected during the first millennial festival. Much about the Scalebound has been lost to time, but there are two primary theories around his identity. The first claims that he was an illegitimate heir to the throne of the Sunfire Empire, explaining both how he survived the first attack that slaughtered the royal family and how he could carry on Ignatius' legacy. The second claims he was a Naktikan Slayer-knight, justifying his title as a reference to the dragon scales his armor might have born or his magic might have formed upon his skin. Either way, he was strong enough to defeat the resurrected Dusk Tyrant, but then vanished from history.

Saint Cornelius – A historical priest of the Path of the Teacher. He achieved fame after banishing a terrible face-changing demon known as the Nevertruth from High Worldheart, center of the Scholastic faith. According to the legend, the Nevertruth sought to use the Lanturian Gate in the holy see to open a portal to the underworld and draw forth the Witch of the New Moon's kin so that they might establish a kingdom of unholy magic. Saint Cornelius was granted divine wisdom and insight that allowed him to see through the Nevertruth's disguises and placed a seal on it so that it might never again come within sight of the sea.

- *WotL: Isn't the Nevertruth—?*

- *TWS: Yes, yes. All-fetch. You mind keeping an eye on that, Sirius?*

- *MotBW: Just because I can go just about anywhere doesn't mean I should always be forced into courier duty.*

The Endless Flame – The deity worshiped by the primary religion of the Auris Empire. Doctrine of the religion aside, the Endless Flame is, by common accounts, a large pillar of sentient fire enshrined deep within the palace complex of Dawnbreak. Descriptions seem to indicate the Endless Flame is an avatar of a being of deific power, like the gods worshiped on the Threefold Eye, but it tends to be mostly aloof to the affairs of the world, only occasionally speaking through its mouthpiece in the current emperor or empress, apparently the only person who can hear its voice.

The Golden Lady – The sole deity of Morningstar, worshiped by all of the Quatrainian people. She is supposedly the creator of the Demon Realm, and all the other Realms, and the religion worshiping her follows a strict code of honesty. Beyond the, quite frankly excessive, focus on the truth, the tenets are similar to most other religions, revolving around treating others well and behaving with righteousness. A... Kind of unmanifested deity with no avatar. She's a unique case among the world's deities and best left for later discussion.

- *MotBW: Thank you for putting that delicately.*

The Teacher – One of the three deities (kind of, trinitarian doctrine) worshiped by the Path of the Teacher, also known as the Scholastic faith, the Teacher is spoken of as a historical figure who was both a natural born human and one of the three persons of the one God of the religion. Accordingly, he taught humanity the core tenets of the religion and the meaning of righteousness, as well as performing many miracles. Thus he's generally seen as the founder of the religion. That being said, these stories seem to be exceedingly old and the current scholars of the religion can't agree on just how long ago this was supposed to have happened. The Path of the Teacher is known to be at least one calamity cycle old, mention of it recorded in some of the surviving Ancient-folk texts. An unmanifested deity with no avatar.

- *WotL: 'At least one calamity cycle old'. How very glib.*

- *TWS: Yes, well, can you blame them for forgetting just how old their world really is?*

The Maker – The second (technically first, but description of the Teacher was more important first for this document) of the three deities worshiped by the Path of the Teacher, the Maker is, as might be expected, the person who made the world. Most of the stories around the Maker are more foundational than those around the Teacher, explaining how things got the way they are instead the doctrinal focus given to the latter, but the Maker is not to be considered any less important. It is worth note that descriptions of the Maker and many of the early stories match closely with the deity worshiped in the Path of the Shepherd, Austall's chief religion. Scholars theorize the two religions have a common root, and some say the two deities are in fact the same. An unmanifested deity with no avatar.

The Counselor – The third (worth note that this is just description order, not rank) of the three deities worshiped by the Path of the Teacher. The Counselor is an interesting case among the three as a figure around whom almost no stories are established. The Counselor is mentioned as having existed in the stories of the Teacher, and doctrine is firm on Him and His purpose, but the Counselor seems to fill something more of contemporary role compared to the other two. He's the person that watches over and guides mankind in the present day, almost filling the role manifested avatars of other religions do, but without any such existence. Like the other two, the Counselor is still an unmanifested deity with no avatar.

Arcana of the White Angel – A magical text that deals primarily with healing magic. That being said, the manner in which it approaches the subject is notable esoteric, focusing on the soul instead of the body. The principles behind the magic the so-called White Angel pioneered involve a kind of quasi-manifestation of the soul, that by applying its perfected template to the injured body, any wounds can be reverted to their natural form.

Johannes' Fundamentals of Magic – It's... It's what it sounds like. It tells you about the fundamentals of magic. I don't know what you want me to say. Mostly just goes over Inception, Conception, and Conviction as well as the basics of elemental flows. The thing I find most interesting about it is that no one on this continent seems too concerned with the fact that Archmage Johannes was Magmellian. You'd think more people would start questioning where exactly that is, but oh well.

Alistair's Elemental Invocations – Nothing too exciting. It's a good primer on a lot of the basic spells any elementalist might use. As well as providing a discussion on the basics of the seven primary elements, it has details of several spells used in the Inception school of classical wizardry.

Rites of Land and Sky – Lame. Pass. More poetry and philosophical meditations on the nature of... well, nature, than an actual magical text. Sure, it's got spells in there and a lot of handy ones for stuff like hedge blessings, basic wards, and naturalization rites, but nothing exciting. Nothing listed in this book is new and you aren't going to end up doing stuff like creating your own other-world or channeling all of your magic through your circulatory system at once in a single accelerated burst with it.

An Adventurer's Guide to Monsters for the Scholarly Noble – Despite the name and cover, actually a really good source on the monsters of this continent. Written by a Desert-folk hunter by the name of Rion, 'the Desert Lion', it gives a thorough description of each entry followed by first hand experiences or anecdotes collecting from reliable, cited sources. Not as well known because it doesn't spice up the descriptions with stories and fables, but good if you actually want to know what magical beasts are capable of.

Communication With the Land: The Mage of Emptiness' Pride – A book as boring as the author. He wasn't an awful guy, of course, but just incredibly orthodox and straightforward. And the book reflects this. It's almost more a collection of methods for summoning and binding elemental spirits, as well as the foundational elemental channeling spells required to cast them, than anything original. It doesn't even mention the exciting elementals like Ink Demons or the Hellcat Valkyries of Athanasia.

- ***MotBW:*** *You have a strange definition of 'exciting'.*

- ***WotL:*** *'Hellcat Valkyries'?*

- ***TWS:*** *Hey. It's not like they have another name. And it fits: fire, cat, winged warriors.*

- ***WotL:*** *Yeah, but it's almost as inane as 'Rounds of Winter'.*

- ***TWS:*** *I asked one if it was okay to call them that and she just blinked.*

Embers Extinguished – Dull, dry, and derivative. It's a history text and not even one that has the amusing excuse of embellishment. It presents the historical events surrounding the fall of the Sunfire Empire, but with none of the fine details or hypotheses that make the subject fun to read about in the first place. Mostly glosses over the Dusk Tyrant's revival in favor of decrying the decadence of the court. Ironically, the stage plays are more useful since they at least have some truth slipped into the dramatizations.

Quintessence After Death: The Soul's Permanence – A... Questionable text on the manipulation of life force, particularly for the extension of one's own life or the reanimation of the dead. Honestly more of a cautionary guide, since just about every page has been retroactively annotated to explain how the methods detailed will corrode the mind and corrupt the target.

Guide to the Monarchy of Tycortua

History – Tycortua is one of the oldest nations on the continent – only Nypheos and Lugherion of the Threefold Eye predating it as they managed to escape the age of ruin brought about by the Dusk Tyrant intact – and thus it possesses one of the richest histories on the continent. A rich history only made all the richer by its unique status on the mainland as the only nation to exist outside the domain of the Sunfire Empire. That being said, much of this history was warped by the presence of Tycortua's founder, Zephyros. The lands of Tycortua were once home to other kingdoms and cultures, but much of the information surrounding them was quashed after they were conquered by the Storm Warlord and replaced by something of a fusion between the native culture and Aeslian culture from Morningstar. With all that being said, modern Tycortua came into being around two thousand years ago when Zepyhros came to Earth from Morningstar and conquered the lands it currently entails, eventually bringing their might under the Ember King's banner and helping him to defeat the Dusk Tyrant. Speaking of Zephyros, he was a Quatrainian – Demon-folk – Noble and that particular generation's head of the Stormtide family from House Grian. Much of the information surrounding Morningstar is irrelevant to Tycortua's history save for the point that the Stormtides were established to keep watch over one Lord Morata's seal, sending their greatest warriors to face him whenever they sensed his seal weakening as it did when the Dusk Tyrant drew upon his power. After the Dusk Tyrant was defeated, Tycortua was allowed to exist outside of the Sunfire Empire mostly out of respect for the Storm Warlord and the part he played in helping the Ember King. With the Empire ensuring peace and in control over much of the continent, Tycortua took a passive role in world affairs, mostly focusing in on itself and developing as a nation. This, of course, helped establish it as the world power it is today, since it was one of very few nations to remain stable after the fall of the Sunfire Empire. The next millennium was somewhat more tumultuous than the first, with war consuming the nearby lands as nobles jockeyed for power and sought to establish their own kingdoms from the wreckage of the Empire, but Tycortua stood strong throughout it all by virtue of their superior military might and the power of the Crownguard.

All of this being said, it is worth note that two thousand years is a very long time for a single nation to remain intact. An almost miraculous amount of time, all things considered. Much of this results from the same thing that led to its stability and developmental superiority: its isolation. For the first millennium of its existence, the kingdom was alone, surrounded by a single overwhelmingly strong empire. A promise had been made and the Crownguard's power was there to protect the borders, but those in power always worried about what that promise would amount to when Zephyros was nothing more than words in a history book. These worries only increased when the Empire shattered and the kingdom was now surrounded by power hungry nations looking for weak and divided lands to conquer. As such, it became common practice among the kingdom to present the heir of Zephyros as monarch no matter what, to present unity no matter what. Even when members of the nobility tried to band together and seize the throne, Crownguards thought to use Zephyros' arms to overthrow his weak heir, or younger princes or princesses coveted their sibling's birthright, they made sure to act as though nothing were out of the ordinary, for fear of showing weakness. Most of the time, they sought to keep the heir of Zephyros as 'monarch', nothing more than a figurehead to keep the country united behind while they ruled from behind the scenes. With this in mind, the royal family has been able to keep direct descent from the first king of Tycortua. This might seem to mean little after two thousand years, when a good percentage of Tycoruta – if not the whole south – can claim descent from Zephyros, but for matters of magical significance, inheritance matters. By that same token, even with a few rebellious Crownguards in their number, the Crownguard family can trace direct lineage back to the first of their number. The last coup occurred some hundred years ago, when a coalition of nobility banded together and usurped power from the throne. They regained power when King Thierry's great-grandfather, Turpin Martel Tycortua, and his Crownguard, Levi's grandfather named Maccabees Fierabras Crownguard, utilized a border conflict to reorganize military structure, intentionally placing themselves in easy victories that made them look like heroes while the nobility stayed behind in safe fortresses. As for how the monarchy regained power after these coups, it's curious, but each of the rebellious regimes ended up overthrown after no more than a generation, a better monarch than the one they overthrew taking their place. And all the conspirators conveniently disappeared, some would say into the darkness on a moonless night.

- ***WotL:*** *Quite the implication you're making there.*

- ***TWS:*** *Well, I don't know that it's true, but it seems a fair assumption given her history with Tycortua.*

- ***WotL:*** *I suppose we'll have to go to the scorekeeper then.*

- ***MotBW:*** *Why the hell would I know? You know I hate watching over individuals because it makes me feel like a stalker.*

Government – Quite frankly, the government of Tycortua is incredibly uninteresting as these things go. That is to say, it is a strict monarchy, ruled by a single king or queen. The position is hereditary – though not intrinsically patriarchal or matriarchical – and has been passed down, supposedly, in the line of the Storm Warlord Zephyros since the days of the Dusk Tyrant. The monarch holds absolute authority and is required to bow to no one, with no checks to their power. There isn't much else to say about this beyond anything you might usually find in a monarchy. One way or another, the monarchy has persisted for two thousand years without significant corruption or abuse of power, but there have been some unfortunate incidents over the centuries. Without going into it too much, *invested parties* made sure to remove monarchs inclined to corruption. Otherwise, there is a system of nobility in place to handle some of the finer details of governance, the country split into twelve separate districts each with six noble houses to overlook that particular section of the country. Of these houses both the royal family, known simply as House Tycortua, and the Crownguard family are considered among their number as families of the district surrounding the capital, though they have greater standing than the rest. The interesting thing about this, however, is that it shows signs of how the nation was founded in the principles of Morningstar, the seventy-two noble families mirroring the houses of the Demonfolk. As for the representation of the Four Monarchs, that is only really present as a formality in how the noble families have been divided. Strictly speaking, the noble houses are divided according to season, each season providing a general indication of what the family is traditionally responsible for in governing a district. Very loosely speaking, Summer families are responsible for military, Autumn for commerce, Winter for academics, and Spring for religion. There is a distinction between titled nobility, who hold these house positions, and hereditary nobility who do not necessarily. The title is inherited, but at the discretion of the previous owner. Similarly, if a lord or lady is deemed unworthy of the role, the governors beneath them are given the right to call for a hearing. If the noble is determined to be in dereliction of their duty, the current monarch will place a new family in the house role. With this in mind, each town or city has its own governor set under the jurisdiction of the local district's nearest lord or lady. Otherwise, the legal system is notably based according to the Morningstar code as opposed to the traditional Sunfire code formed by ancient Austallan Judges. This historically caused some conflicts over minor legal differences between neighboring nations, but accommodations have been made over the years. Quite frankly, the friction isn't as bad as it could have been since most of the crimes are fundamentally the same, save for some niche cases, meaning it's primarily a difference in punishment and rights.

- ***TWS:*** *Is it just me, or is it downright miraculous nothing's gone mystically wrong with the noble houses? Why, why, why do they keep insisting on sticking to seventy-two?*

- ***WotL:*** *Can't say I disagree. Especially since the 'Scholastic' faith is so prevalent. You'd think that would be an easy avenue for demonic influence.*

- ***MotBW:*** *Don't worry about it too much, either of you. The seal relevant to* those *powers is holding strong. It's just the jury-rigged seal on top of it that... slips.*

- ***TWS:*** *And whose fault is that?*

- ***MotBW:*** *Ah... I blame Sophia.*

Architecture and Climate – The climate of Tycortua is extremely mild. Summer's are pleasantly warm and winters cool without turning to bitter cold. Similarly, there is enough rainfall through spring and summer to ensure healthy growth of crops and a mild amount of snow in the fall and winter, to supplement aquifers and aid plants which require cold to trigger their growth in the spring. With all of that being said, Tycortua's architecture developed with little need for excessive environmental concerns. Buildings had to be closed off for the colder winter months, of course, but not insulated to the same degree as the likes of Naktikos and Skahios. In a similar way, building material was never much of a concern with plenty of lumber available in Thicket Forest and stone quarries scattered across the central plains and rich in the Golden Hills. In the broadest of terms, architecture was historically defined by the wealth of the settlement and what building materials they could afford. For countryside villages, houses and shops were built of wood in a half-timbered style; the frame is left visible on the exterior and filled between with planks coated in plaster. The roofs of such buildings are almost always a type of wooden shingle. In such villages, the only stone buildings tend to be fortifications, storehouses, and Teacher's Halls. Of those three, storehouses have no particular style, and are often sturdy, long buildings with cellars dug beneath and set with icestones for refrigeration, while the other two share a similar style with the rest of the nation. All Tycortuan fortifications are built of stone with high, crenelated walls regularly set with rounded towers meant as both watch posts and firing plat-forms for ballistae or lattice-cannons. Castles have a similar round tower design and are built on hills and surrounded by moats with a drawbridge and portcullis to prevent unwanted entry. Teacher's Halls and other religious or academic buildings, on the other hand, share a kind of Gothic style with a heavy focus on height. Interiors are designed with a multitude of arches, complementing the ribbed vaults used to hold up the buildings, while exteriors have a more pointed aesthetic, with tapering steeples and flying buttresses. All of this also aids in the construction of large, decorative windows, often filled with stained glass scenes. This style persists from the smallest villages to the great cities of Tycortua, but is best seen in the cathedrals of Riverluck, Teacher's Halls large enough to fit entire town squares in. More urban towns have a similar half-timbered construction for common houses, but with a brick infill instead of planks and slate shingle roofs. The wealthier residents build stone houses in a similar style, though out of aesthetic concerns rather than construction requirements. It's only in large cities like Plainsheart and Riverluck that nobility build their manors in a style similar to the Gothic used by the Teacher's Hall. They are further influenced, however, by the sprawling design of the Riverluck Palace. As such, most manors are vast complexes with a first floor that connects several taller outbuildings to a central keep. These outbuildings and keeps are in the Gothic style, while the lower floor focuses on using natural light to fill the corridors, lining them with near floor to ceiling windows only kept up by arches set in the walls. The greatest unifying trend among Tycortua's architecture is their odd instance on making their buildings white. This stems, to a certain extent, from the marble and limestone used by the wealthier households, but the white paint and whitewash used by commoners is more an attempt to keep the theme than a necessity. One of the suggested reasons behind this pattern is that it highlights the cleanliness of Tycortua's towns and cities, since these white walls are kept spotless. Another is that it provides a more interesting contrast to the gardens they grow within their cities, the green vines and vibrant flowers striking on a veritable blank canvas. There may be some credit to the latter theory, as most towns do have decorative public gardens in addition to the minor plots households grow for their own use, as well as fountains, streams, and ponds meant to complement the flowers and trees. Nowhere adheres to this theme quite as strongly as Riverluck, but it is present throughout the nation.

Language and Names – As with all nations in Chevaladin, the principal language spoken is Empire Common, the language of the old Sunfire Empire. The language itself is fairly straightforward, compared to some of the indigenous vernaculars, and continues to be used across the continent for that same simplicity. Put simply, it's a language closest in construction to a group of five similar languages from many calamity cycles ago. In terms of writing, Empire Common uses the old standard alphabet of twenty-six letters from 'a' to 'z'. The only slight divergence are accents upon the vowels, used to indicate the stress upon the syllables. Accented vowels indicate a stressed syllable. In the absence of an accented vowel, if the final letter of a word is a vowel, 's', 'l', 'n', or 'r', the second to last syllable is stressed. Otherwise the last syllable is stressed. Vowels themselves are pronounced according to the rules of the old five: 'ah', 'eh', 'e', 'o', and 'ooh'; respectively to 'a', 'e', 'i', 'o', and 'u'. There are enough rules to verbal conjugations across several tenses that the only thing worth saying is that there are six conjugations according to person: first person, second person, and third person in both singular and plural for each. All persons are neutral in both gender and honorific. Sentences are constructed in a style of Subject – Verb – Predicate. Empire Common is similar to Realms Common, as both share a root in the old Unified Earth Common spoken by the people of Lanturia, but different enough that speaking one cannot allow you to speak the other. The Quatrainians have an awareness of both languages, thanks to Zephyros' contact across the Realms and the Stormtide family's efforts, but Empire Common is considered a rarer language only used by scholars interested in the Lataoccas super-continent, both Lacalba and Marivento sharing usage of the language.

As for indigenous vernaculars, Tycortua has two somewhat prominent languages. The first was native Tycortuan, a language which was rendered all but extinct by Zephyros' conquest. In modern times, only scholars, historians, and theologians speak or write Tycortuan. The language is not worth discussing excessively for this reason. It used a written script more runic in nature than Empire Common's alphabet, with each letter paired to a particular symbological root that influences the pronunciation and meaning. For instance, the equivalent vowel 'a' would be pronounced 'a' with a wind root and indicate a meaning of freedom while it would be pronounced 'ah' with an earth root and indicate a meaning of steadfastness. This made it a bit of a pain, albeit a very poetic language, because a single word could have up to six conjugations depending on person and several different meanings according to symbological root, different ones applying in different situations. The other language is Morningstar's High Royal, brought to Chevaladin by Zephyros. The language is the same as the fae language known as Old Sidhe, virtually unchanged across calamity cycles. It's only really used by nobility and royalty in extremely formal situations. To an extent, it's considered the official language of Tycortuan scholarship and legalism, so it does have some influence in other nations as well.

The naming conventions of Tycortua are somewhat interesting when compared to some of the simpler forms from earlier calamity cycles. For a person's forename, the name chosen does not necessarily adhere to cultural standards, but follows a particular naming motif chosen for a given period. Each motif consists of a paired vowel and consonant, in either order, placed somewhere within the name. The period is traditionally four years, but often shifts when a member of nobility decides they want to. Each period must be at least a year long, with the major exception of the royal family who shift the naming motif at their leisure. This gives them a more diverse collection of forenames from a linguistic sense, but very similar names in terms of spelling. For example, Regina's Reckoners were born in a period of 'a' and 'l' and have the names Nalren, Mallory, Kalan, Paula, and Lalia. With that being said, naming motifs are no real indicator of age because, for instance, Viola could belong to the same naming motifs as Levi, Allard, or Phlox. Likewise, some families prefer to follow their own traditions, like the Rousseau noble family who always include the root 'el' in their names. As for surnames, villagers only give surnames for their own utility, little more than nicknames. They have their own methods of tracking family lineage and ensuring proper inheritance, so any given surname is only for the village's use. A given surname need not even be constant across a family. For example, Erica Greenmaiden's family is actually referred to as the Westhill family. Similarly, when outside of their given village, people tend to be referred to by village instead of surname. In towns and cities with higher population density, there are enough people that surnames actually matter and tend to be given according to occupation. The nobles use historical names for their families for their surname, out of tradition instead of anything else. Very few people in Tycortua use middle names. The major exceptions to this are the royal family and the Crownguard family. The royalty has no surname because they do not need one, so their second given name replaces the surname. The Crownguards also follow this tradition as they are royalty adjacent. Only a few rare members of nobility also give middle names, for personal reasons. For example, Lady Alice Iris Ellis was given a middle name in recognition of her parents' service to the royal family, who long used an iris as a secondary insignia.

Economics and Cuisine – Economically speaking, Tycortua is one of the wealthier nations in Chevaladin. But more importantly, it's easily the nation with the stablest degree of wealth, the likes of Perlora and Aingriya depending heavily upon the current market climate. This is as a result of Tycortua's strong degree of self-sufficiency. Since it needed to develop its own means of production for everything while the Sunfire Empire ruled, it now has far less need of any external goods when compared to the specialized ex-Sunfire states. So a majority of its imports are for commodity goods: the likes of dyes and fine fabrics, gems and jewelry, exotic spices and ingredients, and other nations' top of the line products. This in turn lets them use the ingredients they bring in to make better and better versions of their own goods for export. So while, for example, Tycortua's art style is not considered as technically good as Rugego's, the artists are capable of supplementing their modest talent with more vibrant paints and higher quality canvas. With that in mind, Tycortuan goods have a reputation for reliability over excellence. They are almost never the best in any category, but they manage to be consistently good enough that they are worth the price, especially since Tycortuan merchants know what price to set. In short: the price does not earn as much per unit, but tends to sell more units.

The economy is much the same on an interior, microcosmic level as well. Each individual town or village tends to be self-sufficient. Enough crops are grown to feed the village, local smiths can make what tools are needed, and hedge-doctors can treat all common ailments. The only settlements that do need to bring in outside food sources are the larger cities like Riverluck and Plainsheart, which can buy crops from local villages anyway. As such, each village tends to have an individual commodity they focus on as a community to sell externally. For example, Regina's Bounty, in addition to the personal farms, has a series of community vineyards in the nearby hills and an orchard. The fruit from these is used, when not necessary to supplement the town's food reserves in lean years, to make wines and brandies that are sold to other nearby towns. The profit from these sales largely goes to paying for community projects like construction of new irrigation aqueducts, repairs on the roads, and upkeep on the sewage system, but a certain amount of excess is allotted to everyone who contributed and worked in to covering the taxes to the royalty. Every village has a similar structure in place, the particular product produced depending on the village.

As for cuisine, Tycortua does have one of the most well developed culinary forms in Chevaladin. If anything could be considered the nation's specialty, it's cooking. Though admittedly other nations tend to argue for their own cuisine's supremacy. The mild nature of the Tycortuan plains allows them to grow a wide array of crops and raise most livestock, so there are few ingredients that cannot be locally sourced. Similarly, the fishing villages along the coast bring in enough fish of several varieties that they are capable of cooking seafood competently as well. Generally speaking, the limitation upon what is made depends more on seasonality of ingredients than anything else. And the seasoning of dishes is done with a kind of delicacy most other cuisines lack, Tycortua's practice of saucing dishes better than any other nation's and spice blends like the famous Herbs du Tycortua used all across Chevaladin. Any given dinner will have some form of protein cooked in a sauce accompanied by seasonal vegetables, wine or juice, and bread. To the matter of wine, it is something of a peculiarity of Tycortua, but they are one of the only nations to instate a legal drinking age, such matters far more common in Zephyros' Morningstar. To the matter of bread, the absolute pinnacle of Tycortuan cuisine is their baking tradition. Wheat is the most grown crop of the country and every family eats bread daily, most in country villages baking their own. More than that, however, the pastries they've developed are considered the best sweets in Chevaladin, with no other nation coming close. As a final note, Tycortuans often drink coffee in the mornings; the beans imported from the Sea Scar Archipelago and the brewed grounds pressed through cheesecloth. Princess Adelaide's fixation with tea is notably a personal preference and most of the nobility silently look down at her for it.

Fashion – The fashion of Tycortua is perhaps the least interesting thing about the nation, even more so than its very straightforward system of governance. Looking at it from a historical perspective, the best guess that can be figured is that as a result of the founder's complete lack of interest in clothing and great interest in warfare, the styles common to the region developed in two parts out of the local common garb and the uniforms of the military. Put another way, the commoners, generally speaking, continued to wear what they'd always worn while the nobles tried to adopt their king's style, or lack thereof, and gave themselves a more militaristic look. For most of the common folk, their clothing tends towards a certain simplicity, resulting from the mild climate and environment of Tycortua. Since the weather is never too hot in the summer nor too cold in the winter, they need not make special accommodations for them, and since the land is mostly rolling plains, there is no need for heavily protective garb. As such, commoners usually wear simple and comfortable workmen's clothes. This usually means sturdy pants and a simple pullover shirt for men and a dress for women, both cut in as plain and functional a style as possible. The differentiation based upon gender is not a hard and fast rule, and it is not rare to see women wearing pants and a shirt as well, if their occupation requires them to be able to move more easily or if they just prefer it, but that is the general trend. It seems to be a reflection of their trends in dress clothes, with it a far more firm rule, though not without exception, for men to wear slacks, a collared shirt with buttons down the front, and a vest on special occasions while women wear dresses with styles and cuts more focused on looking good than practicality. With regards to weather, the general concession given is the sleeve length and outerwear. In the warmer months, both genders wear shorter sleeves and in the colder months, both wear longer sleeves. During winter, both have similar styles of coats that they wear, Tycortua somewhat interesting in that they are one of the few nations to have developed coats specifically as cold weather wear, most nations still using cloaks for similar purposes and coats as more of a protective garb.

In terms of the fashion of nobility, it could perhaps best be described as stiff. To the point that everything about it has a tendency towards being carefully pressed or starched or held in place by various mechanisms to look proper and well put together. Men wear outfits that look similar to the uniforms of the officers in the Tycortuan army; pressed pants, shirts that button down the front, and light coats meant more for looks than protection or comfort. On the other end of the spectrum, women usually wear dresses with more superfluous cloth, the 'stiffness' of the style in how they almost sculpt the cloth after making it less pliable, forming it into shapes reminiscent of natural phenomenon. Usually wind, in keeping with the general theme kept out of respect for the Storm Warlord, but sometimes waves like water, ripples like flames, or jagged edges like rock features. The general exception to this, however, is the women of nobility that have more of a militaristic life themselves, either through personal vocation or house history. They tend to wear uniform-like suits similar to men, albeit cut differently to better fit their physiques. A more modern exception is in the current princess Adelaide, who could not be bothered to deal with fashion. While she enjoys looking good, she cares significantly more about ease of movement and, as such, had the palace tailors design a style of dress that ensured comfort and mobility for her, more like a simple tea gown. Both commoners and nobility wear boots for footwear though, the difference only in style. Commoners' boots are sturdy and simple, designed for lots of walking. Noble boots are more sleek and supple, having come from the design of riding boots. It is rare, only present in the highest of families, for anyone to wear the likes of slippers. Coloration of clothing varies wildly, among all walks of life. Since Tycortua has a steady economy and manages to keep a good trade system with all nations, they have access to a wide variety of dyes relatively cheap. At least cheap enough that commoners can have access to most colors in a general sense. As such, color almost always depends on personal preference, even on a daily basis. The colors of nobility are often more vibrant than those of commoners, but no more varied. The only exception to this is that commoners will often have their working clothes be done in more muted or natural colors, browns, tans, and blacks, so that they don't care if it gets dirty through work, saving their colored clothing for when they have the day off and the like.

Military – In regards to Tycortua's military, they possess one of the most balanced and advanced militaries of the continent, even when considering Naktikos was devoted to military training and development under the Sunfire empire. Generically speaking, this comes from a long history of development in quality over quantity. Tycortua is notably a nation of middling size when compared to the rest of the nations of the continent and therefore cannot compensate with massed numbers of conscripts when they were forced to do every job most nations had compartmentalized. For instance, the Tycortua standard armor is a kind of jack of plates, constructed in the form of a two layered leather coat with metal plates sewn on the inside. While not as effective in its base form, the fact that there are three separate layers to enchant – with two of them protected by the first – means they have a greater versatility in enchanted armor and generally have better warded soldiers. The enchantments tend to be a ward against piercing and slashing on the outer layer and a ward to diffuse blunt force on the interior, with the wards upon the plates depending upon the personal specifications of the wearer, though a siege-breaker charm is always included, as with most armor. In the absence of any requests, broadly scoped anti-magic wards are placed to diffuse the flow of wide-scoped spells. As for the specifics, it is difficult to talk about equipment outside of the confines of the specific military corp, Tycortua having diversified into several such divisions. They are the Tycortua Regulars, Shield Corp, Ranger Corp, Champion Corp, Mage Corp, Naval Corp, Guard Corp and its elite Palace Guard, and the Royal Griffon Corp.

The Regulars form the bulk of the military and are, putting it rather simply, swordsmen and swordswomen like you could find just about anywhere. Beyond the standard armor, they come equipped with an arming sword, enchanted with top of the line honings. Further equipment depends upon the individual, as the hallmark of the Regulars is their diversity in specialization, each individual having some sort of trick they make their own. For some this means the usage of a shield, for some a minor magical talent. It all depends on what the individual considers their best ability beyond swordsmanship. In the absence of preference, a shield is given, in the heater shield style. They distinguish themselves from the standard army of other nations through their diversity in abilities. While they are trained to fight as a group, relying on their swords and the people standing next to them, the lack of coherence among the group makes them hard to get a handle on when they use their specialization as an ace in the hole. This same lack of cohesion does not work against them because they are specifically trained to capitalize upon it. Individual squadrons train extensively to know what their comrades are capable of and the standard tactics given to all of the Regulars emphasize practicing ways to leverage one's individual techniques so they don't interfere with their allies. The Shield Corp is the primary defensive unit of the Tycortuan army and is both more heavily armored and equipped with heavy tower shields. Their armor is supplemented with a cuirass attached to the chest of their coat in addition to metal pauldrons, greaves, and vambraces. All of the metal pieces of armor possess lightening enchantments in addition to the strengthening wards to ensure they do not slow down the soldiers. For weapons, they are given long spears, as the Shield Corp's intended usage is to form a shield wall to break a charge. The Ranger Corp is Tycortua's contribution to the study of archery. Not much can be said about them since Tycortua hardly focuses on archery beyond the fact that they are intended to act as fire support for the Regulars and Shield Corp. They are somewhat more lightly armored, their coats having shorter tails and sleeves to make them lighter while compensating with bracers and gloves to protect the arms from the bowstring, though every group of about five will carry a pavise shield among them. Their bows are nothing special, not coming anywhere close to the longbows of Naktikos or the horse bows of Aingriya. The most that can be said in their praise is the wide range of arrows they use, almost acting as secondary mages with the amount of enchantments any given one has access to. The Champion Corp is Tycortua's cavalry, meant to break lines for the Regulars. The horses are armored in chain barding, itself heavily warded, but the riders still only wear the standard coat armor, the Tycortuans holding to the same mistaken belief all on this continent hold that metal armor would be too heavy for the horse on top of the barding. They are armed with a heater shield and a lance for the charge, swapping to an arming sword once they get into close combat, though the Champion Corp is rarely intended to stay in combat long, retreating to form up for another charge whenever possible. They like hit and run tactics. The Mage Corp uses the same wizardry taught common along the mainland and explained in further detail below, so there is little to note here. Simply put, they focus upon warding spells to protect the troops and evocations to act almost like magical siege engines. Similarly, there is little to say about the Naval Corp. Tycortua has a navy, but their focus is hardly upon the ocean, so the navy is more of a defensive structure to protect ports and merchant ships from pirates and hostile navies. The marines of the Naval Corp are little more than Regulars and Rangers that have trained to specialize in naval combat. Finally, the Royal Griffon Corp of Tycortua is known for, as one might guess, taming and riding griffons into battle in a way similar to the dragon-riders from Lugherion as well as the Realms of Erebus and Okeanos, though Tycortua has yet to develop their own form of drop-knights. The Royal Griffon Corp is made up of the elites of the Tycortuan army, drawing from each of the other divisions for their ranks. As such, there is no specific armament common to all of them, beyond something akin to the equipment they bore in their previous division. They are feared by other nations for their flight if not for their strength. As for the Guard Corp and the palace guard, they are simply Regulars who have been assigned to defensive positions in cities and towns, acting as a policing force as well. The Palace Guard – as one might guess – guard the Palace in Riverluck and the royal family and are considered to be the elites among the regulars. Those who place more of a focus on Tycortuan nationalism than efficiency prefer to call them the Paladin Corp. They differ in that they often carry pikes and are armored with a cuirass similar to the Shield Corp's. As a final note, one cannot speak of Tycortua's military without making note of the Crownguard. Even though there is only one Crownguard at any given time, a single soldier possessing Ancient's Armor is a force to be reckoned with, accounting for much of why Tycortua has not faced much war over the years. Simply by letting the Crownguard take the vanguard and crush an enemy's lines, they were often able to bring forth a swift rout of any force they faced. In terms of spycraft, Tyrcortua loudly and frequently claims that 'they do not deal in such actions'. Other nations, however, give little credit to those claims as the lurid tales of Tycortua's maids and footmen are extensive enough to make anyone wonder just what type of servant attends to them when they visit one of the Tycortuan nobility.

Geography – Tycortua's geography tends to be as mild as its climate. The lands north of the Summerblood are filled by rolling plains and thin forests. This provides them with excellent farmland, all the more because the soil of the plains is rarely broken by rocky ground and small streams lace the countryside. The plains are also mostly flat, even the few scattered hills suitable for things like terraced vineyards. Where the hills do grow thicker, there tends to be enough stone that mining is feasible. South of the Summerblood is a different story. Most of Tycortua's land south of the Summerblood is filled by Thicket Forest. Thicket Forest – unlike the woods to the north – is dark, overgrown, and filled with dangerous creatures. More than that, it's actually much larger than it appears on maps thanks to other-worldly influence. The borderlands of several fae other-worlds, the Enchanted Forest Brocéliande, and the Primeval Forest of Herne bleed through into Thicket Forest, making it easy to get lost and exceptionally dangerous to travel through without a guide. Likewise, the Golden Hills take up the south-eastern corner of Tycortua. While they are not as dangerous as Thicket Forest and have less other-worldly influence – though not none – they are much rougher terrain. The hills are steeper and rockier than those in the plains. This does, on the other hand, have the benefit of making them much better for mining and much of Tycortua's stone and metal ore comes from the Golden Hills.

It should also be noted that Tycortua experiences less other-worldly influence in general than the other nations of Chevaladin. For the most part, across the Realms nowhere can be considered truly safe unless it's within the confines of human habitation; a village, town, or city. Entering 'the wilds', even if that means an open plain where you can see for miles, means opening yourself up to the potential for mischief or worse from mystical beings. Tycortua, on the other hand, is mostly safe as long as you're in the northern plains. There are mystical beings that frequent the plains and it's certainly not without incident – seelie fae accounting for most of the former and things like dragons, stray undead, and werewolves accounting for much of the latter – but it's much less of a sure thing. A lone traveler can make it from one city to the next unbothered without being considered extremely lucky. There are a few minor reasons contributing to this such as the increased average ability of Tycortuans to defend themselves, but the most prominent reason is that the Unseelie and Seelie Courts of the Fae are the ones who fill the largest amount of the 'other-worldly influence sphere', as it were. Their particular nature among the fae makes them less inclined to seek trouble outside of their demesnes and they have something of a lingering affection for Tycortua sourced in the connection Zephyros had to them as one of the 'Fair Folk'. With a certain pact made ten years prior smoothing over any remaining animosity, even the unseelie fae are less trouble than other nations experience. Likewise, the rest of the 'other-worldly influence sphere' is dominated by the metaphysics of the Scholastic faith and the angels of Low Empyrean and the fiends of Upper Abbadon have their own particular rules of engagement.

- ***MotBW:*** *Oh. So you're leaving it at that then? Not explaining about angels and demons?*

- ***TWS:*** *I really don't want Fidesel yelling at me again.*

- ***WotL:*** *What did you do the first time and who's Fidesel?*

- ***TWS:*** *Uh... Certain matters of privacy and nonintervention. All I'll say is that she has my personal recommendation when the time comes.*

- ***WotL:*** *What. Personal recommendation? You don't mean she's on Morningstar do you? Is this another of your future sight 'Golden Marble' things?*

- ***'GA':*** *I should inform you my lord has left the room. And he neglected to mention that Fidesel and the others of her ilk were also... put out by his irresponsible forging of an artificial Holy Blade.*

- ***MotBW:*** *Makes sense. I think Arcalibur's cool, but it is a bit pretentious.*

Religion – The religion of Tycortua tends to be based in one that is more founded in the culture of the native peoples as opposed to the culture Zephyros brought with him from Morningstar. The main form of worship is found in the Path of the Teacher, a quasi-monotheistic religion that is fairly widespread throughout the continent and thus was the native religion of the ancient people of Tycortua. To this end, of the religion being widespread, the central cathedral of the Path of the Teacher is in fact located on the Eye of the Teacher, on the heights of the mountain High Worldheart is built upon. The Path of the Teacher is defined as being quasi-monotheistic as a result of the primary deity, the Threefold Divines, being three different figures that are simultaneously considered one deity yet three distinct persons. There are two principal tenets of the religion. The first revolves around the equivalent dignity of every Human and treating each other with love. The second revolves around the secondary name of the religion, the Scholastic faith. Knowledge and wisdom are critically important to the faith with ignorance considered one of Humanity's greatest evils, so the religion focuses to a heavy degree on the education of its adherents. To this end, the churches of the faith, Teacher's

Halls, double as school buildings and libraries. With this in mind, and the fact that every village has at least one Teacher's Hall, Tycortua is one of the better educated nations in Chevaladin, on average. Every faithful is supposed to dedicate at least half of their working hours to studying general knowledge for at least the first twenty or so years of their life. From there, they continue to learn and study, but only insofar as their faith does not interfere with their work. Tycortua's subsect of the Scholastic faith is slightly different from the mainline faith thanks to Zephyros' influence. In Tycortua more so than any other nation the River Sage, Seras, is viewed akin to a Saint and venerated as such. This is, technically, a heresy, but the holy see in High Worldheart tends to be willing to overlook it since it's not too far from accurate anyway. Likewise, the virtue of honesty is played up a bit more in Tycortua. There is even a small sect of the Tycortuan faith which, remembering bits of Zephyros' faith, tries to consolidate the Threefold Divines with the Golden Lady. That particular sect is less popular because it only avoids outright blasphemy thanks to the continuous efforts of its bishops to the alternative.

Magical Tradition – Tycortua's magical tradition is, while advanced in terms of its learning, rather lackluster in terms of creativity. This is to say that the bulk of its traditions are the same as the common standard throughout the continent. For instance, the most common tradition in both their scholarly and military magics is the wizardly tradition common to the continent. This tradition, as established as the norm by the scholars in High Worldheart, focuses upon the study of magic through an intellectual lens, treating it almost like a science. They each bear a spell-book in which they transcribe spells that they have studied. As previously noted, the military mages often focus on wards and evocations to study while the scholarly mages instead focus on various enchantments and spells to use in common life to supplement the advances brought about by lattice engineering. The spell-books themselves are not precisely required for casting a spell, as the magic comes from the casters themselves and is given form by the spell itself, not the book, but it is used as a memory aid for the ones a caster cannot or will not memorize and helps them to focus their magic. Similarly, this is where the common image of a wizard comes from, with most of them wearing enchanted robes for protection and comfort while carrying either a staff or wand, carved with the appropriate runes in both cases, to act as a further focus. Though for as much as this tradition is the same as traditions throughout the continent, it should be noted that the

Tycortuan wizards can rival those of High Worldheart, the academic center of the continent, with the universities of Tycortua holding almost as much esteem as it.

Moving on to clerical magic, it is likewise lackluster in form, being the generic faith-based magic that almost all clerical magics are derived from. They cannot really be called anything other than clerics, or devouts if they are not in fact ordained, and use their magic through sheer force of belief. It's simply one of those things that's common sense for magic users, that those who can use magic can use prayers interchangeably with spells, the spell being cast as something of an answer to their faith, if not an answer from their deity – though that is a far more nuanced discussion about metaphysics altogether. Tycortuan clerics and devouts only really focus on spells that heal, bless, and ward, only really being needed by the common people in most situations. It should be noted, bringing up their ability in the healing arts, that virtually all medical advances fall under the domain of such mages as well, medical sciences being considered virtually identical to healing magics in the same way wizardry is considered the same as engineering. As a result, medical advances in Tycortua, and throughout the world, have slipped somewhat due to their reliance upon magic. They excel at theory – understanding anatomy, biology, and virology – but are leagues behind what was common in the past in regards to devices and medicines. The only real combat spells these devouts possess are holy rites and exorcisms intended to deal with undead, fiends, and other such magical, unholy, and other-worldly beings. And like with the wizards, Tycortuan devouts make up for their lack of specialization in being very good at what they do. They are perhaps the greatest practictioners of faith based magic throughout the continent, Pazyerran Hierarchs the only ones that can really compete. They do not precisely require a focus, as their magic is based in faith and faith is usually independent of any symbols, but such symbols can help and devouts may use a talisman shaped after some symbol of their faith to aid in casting. And with both wizards and devouts, it should be pointed out that the strong tradition of magic within Tycortua permeates the citizenry in a way not experienced in other countries. While just about every village in the world will have a mage or two to perform wardings and honings on tools as well as minor healing spells, it is not to the extent as it is in Tycortua where it can be expected that every town will have mages beyond those, far more specialized. Hedge wizards and Greenmaidens or Greenmasters, as the case may be, are only found commonly in Tycortua, effectively everyday mages who make that their lifestyle without formally training at an academy.

Beyond those traditions, there are some magical traditions specific to Tycortua, though they are far rarer and in two of the three cases seem to be based upon the heritage of Tycortua's founder, the Storm Warlord Zephyros Stormtide. The first is the most complicated of the three, better described as a mystical tradition than magical one since its operations don't precisely follow the intellective structures of magic in redirecting the environmental magic into oneself to alter it in conjunction with one's internal magic before reemitting it the form of a spell. This tradition is referred to as Dreamspinning, and that tells you just about everything you need to know about it. Admittedly, the name isn't entirely accurate and seems to be a holdover from a basis upon the dreamwalkers of Morningstar who literally walk through the Sea of Dreams and are markedly different from Tycortua's dreamspinners. Tycortuan dreamspinners base their magic — for lack of a better term — upon the reading of dreams, both their own and others. This is used for a kind of minor future sight, allowing them to predict events based upon what they see or hear about dreams from others. By all accounts, it seems they possess some trained ability to see into the Sea of Dreams, but they cannot manipulate or traverse it as directly as Morningstar dreamwalkers. Likewise, they seem to able to call forth some sort of dream spirits to enact magic in the real world, something along the line of those spirits temporarily granting a part of the real world the logic of the Sea of Dreams to allow manipulation, but they do not seem to be bonded as familiars or representative of the caster in any way as a dreamwalker's Fetch is. Dreamspinners require no focus, everything they accomplish being done either while asleep or as an analysis of what was experienced while asleep. Even the summoning of spirits is something that is more completed in reality through the invocation of an agreement made while dreaming. The second tradition is far more straightforward, known as Truthspeaking. The fact that their entire modus operandi revolves around truths and negating falsehood makes it fairly clear that it must have originated from Zephyros' culture, the Fair and or Demon-folk of Morningstar prizing truth to the extent that it is integral to their very religion. As for truthspeakers, they are a kind of law mage almost, wielding binding spells that can seal contracts such that the participants cannot break them. That is only a generic statement of their abilities, but gives a good idea of what they are capable of. With this in mind, truthspeakers almost always carry around exhaustive references to the law to ensure that they will always speak the truth and what contracts they forge are made in truth. The final tradition unique to Tycortua is the rather infuriating tradition of the Gamblers. Quite frankly, it's a fairly minor magical talent that has no reliable use outside of a tavern. And it's this very reliability there and unreliability elsewhere that makes it absolutely enraging to deal with. Simply put, gamblers are able to magically influence the tides of fortune and chance. They can temporarily grant themselves bursts of good luck or others bursts of bad luck. The exact scope of what can be affected is linked to the strength and skill of the caster, but most can't affect more than the events of a few seconds in the immediate area. That being said, it is believed that some of the rather extraordinarily contrived events in history were caused by an incredibly powerful or foolish Gambler manipulating their craft. As might be expected, their focus is almost always something relating to chance, a favorite pair of dice or lucky coin. Though amusingly, it seems that loaded dice do not work for this purpose.

About Author

I have no interest in discussing myself. See: pen name. But I include this to discuss the pen name itself. Martlet di Rotstein is notably more of a title than name, carefully considered such that each part has personal meaning. The former part of the name 'Martlet' references the heraldic charge. In particular, its theorized significance in representing an unending quest for knowledge and learning; a symbol of my own desire to be a "wandering scholar", spoken in all seriousness and awareness of how silly that sounds. The latter part of the name 'di Rotstein' I won't go into too much detail with. Those familiar with the structure of surnames can puzzle out what it means and I will only note the differing linguistic sources are intentional in representing my own heritage. If you must know anything about me, I am a dyed-in-the-wool lover of fantasy and knights. That should suffice.

Acknowledgments

I would be remiss in coming this far without thanking those who aided me upon my way. Many thanks to all of my friends and family who were willing to read early drafts of this book. Simply that willingness was an immense amount of support. In particular I would offer thanks to my three college writing friends, two of whom shall remain unnamed for both our sakes. The first of whom I thank for seeing all this through from the very beginning and offering critiques on both this and other projects. The second of whom I thank for being a pillar of support throughout and believing in me far more than I've believed in myself. And the last of them I guess I have to thank. I *am* grateful that twisted jerk Michael agreed to take care of administrative matters pertaining to my being an author — and he's been a help for a long, long time — but he doesn't have to be so harsh and sarcastic about everything. I also thank my long-running TTRPG group who have been incredibly supportive throughout. Outside of those groups, I'd also like to thank two more friends in particular. The first is a friend in a gaming group whose given all sorts of good critiques and advice even at a late stage in the process. And the second is a friend that said he'd buy me lunch if I sent him a copy of this book when it was finished; a small silly thing, but even that means a lot.

In terms of professional aid, thank you to my editor, Jonathan Oliver. Your advice and criticism helped make this book what it is and I could not have come this far without you.

Finally, thank you to my parents, for putting up with this nonsense for so long.